MANY RAMAYANAS
MANY LESSONS

Praise for *Many Ramayanas, Many Lessons* podcast

'Everyone knows something about the Ramayana. In this brilliant narrative, the author summarizes the various Ramayanas ... The book tries to explain the differences between Valmiki Ramayana, those popular in south India, and those from the Bhakti-era in a very simple and realistic way. A must-listen audiobook for all.'

—**Vachan Hukkeri**

'Anand Neelakantan has done a thorough and meticulous job of collating the various versions of the epic ... He successfully highlights the important events in the life of Lord Rama and intersperses the text with profound philosophical lessons that we can draw from this divine epic.'

—**Rajeev**

'*Many Ramayanas...* should be on your list if you wish to know about Hindu mythology as it is. Anand Neelakantan has beautifully woven the incidents of the Ramayana in a chronological manner while highlighting its various versions. He focuses on how Valmiki's original was intended and how the story evolved through the medieval era, the Bhakti period and folklore.'

—**Meenakshi**

'Neelakantan's work is a valuable addition to the study of mythology and cultural narratives, offering readers a deep appreciation for the multifaceted nature of the Ramayana. Whether you are a scholar, a student of mythology, or a casual reader, this book provides insightful perspectives that will deepen your understanding of the timeless epic.'

—**Deepak Rustagi**

'It is nice to hear that even though the Ramayana is thousands of years old, new versions are created every few generations. This reflects the openness of Hinduism to change ... rather than being bound by dogma.'
—**Pramod**

'Brilliant! I never thought about the Ramayana beyond what was shown on TV. I learned so many nuances and discovered so many stories through this book.'
—**Chirag**

'The lessons are thought-provoking and provide valuable takeaways. I absolutely love this audiobook. I hope Anand Neelakantan creates a similar book on the Mahabharata.'
—**Arijit Dutta**

'It's a must-listen! If you have the privilege to listen to it together as a family, I recommend doing so.'
—**Harshada**

'A lot of lessons under one roof. It presents facts from various Ramayanas as they are ... without glorifying any character. Instead it highlights their actions and the resulting consequences.'
—**Dr Mahalakshmi**

'I'm grateful to Anand Neelakantan for this great storytelling of the epic, one that has been passed down through the ages, yet [one that] we know so little about. It was a great pleasure listening to the audiobook, as it didn't just touch my heart—it touched my entire life and brought peace within. The lessons taught in the book are truly life-changing, bringing peace to one's soul and satisfying the seeker within.'
—**Rohit**

MANY RAMAYANAS MANY LESSONS

ANAND NEELAKANTAN

HARPER
NON-FICTION

First published in India by Harper Non-Fiction 2025
An imprint of HarperCollins *Publishers*
4th Floor, Tower A, Building No. 10, DLF Cyber City,
DLF Phase II Gurugram – 122002
www.harpercollins.co.in

2 4 6 8 10 9 7 5 3 1

Copyright © Anand Neelakantan 2025

Based on an Audible Original, *Many Ramayanas, Many Lessons*

Inside illustrations by Subu Chowara

PISBN: 9789362139955
EISBN: 9789362131959

The views and opinions expressed in this book are the author's own and the facts are as reported by him, and the publishers are not in any way liable for the same.

The contents of this book include reference to various versions of the Ramayana, representing different time periods, regions and faith traditions. These interpretations are provided for educational and informational purposes only. The book does not intend to challenge, offend or disrespect any religious beliefs or traditions. The publishers and author disclaim any liability for any perceived offence caused by the discussion of these diverse narrations. Readers are advised to engage with the material in a spirit of scholarly inquiry, and bear in the mind the context in which it is written.

Anand Neelakantan asserts the moral right
to be identified as the author of this work.

All rights reserved. No part of this publication may be reproduced, stored in a retrieval system, or transmitted, in any form or by any means, electronic, mechanical, photocopying, recording or otherwise, without the prior permission of the publishers.

Typeset in 13.5/16.5 ArnhemFine at
HarperCollins *Publishers* India

Printed and bound at
Thomson Press (India) Ltd

This book is produced from independently certified FSC® paper
to ensure responsible forest management.

*To my parents, L. Neelakantan and D. Chellamal,
for introducing the Ramayana to me*

Contents

Author's Scribble		xi
Foreword		xiii
1.	The Beginning: Ratnakara Meets Narada	1
2.	The Poet Meets the Poem	7
3.	The Epic Begins to Unfold	12
4.	Dasaratha's Boons to Kaikeyi	19
5.	Shanta: Dasaratha's Eldest Child	23
6.	Rama: Dasaratha's Most Beloved Son	26
7.	Three Interpretations of Two Mantras: The Freedom to Choose	31
8.	Tackling Tadaka: A Life Lesson for Rama	37
9.	Rama Redeems Ahalya, and the Mahabharata's Story of Nalayani	41
10.	Janaka: A Saint among Kings and a King among Saints	48
11.	Sita's Swayamvara	55
12.	Manthara's Machinations and Rama's Exile	73
13.	Dasaratha's Deathbed	83
14.	Tales of Brotherly Ties in the Ramayana	88
15.	Surpanakha, Who Triggers the Final Battle	99
16.	The Kidnapping of Sita	109
17.	The Interjection of an Illusory 'Maya' Sita	123
18.	Jatayu's Funeral	127
19.	Rama's Karmic Debt and the Slaying of Kabanda	134
20.	Stories of Hanuman's Origins, Early Years and Youth	141
21.	Hanuman's Ties with Sugriva and His Meeting with Rama	152

22.	Bali and Sugriva: Their Origins and Rivalry	157
23.	The Day Narada Almost Got Married	166
24.	The Slaying of Bali	173
25.	Bali's Royal Funeral and Tara's Questions to Rama	181
26.	Hanuman Awakens to His Siddhis and Flies Over the Ocean	189
27.	Hanuman Tackles Lanka Lakshmi and Locates Mother Sita	198
28.	The Eighteen Curses That Destroyed Ravana	201
29.	Hanuman Meets Sita	210
30.	Ravana's Son Indrajit Defeats Hanuman	214
31.	Lanka Dahan: Hanuman in Ravana's Court	218
32.	The Defection of Vibhishana	228
33.	Drums of War and Tales of Espionage	234
34.	The War Begins	243
35.	Kumbhakarna Is Woken Up and Sent into Battle	251
36.	Kumbhakarna: Death of a Mighty Warrior	260
37.	The Death of Valiant Atikaya, and Kumbhakarna's Sons	265
38.	The Death of Indrajit	270
39.	The Legend of Ahiravana and Mahiravana	280
40.	The Fall of Ravana	286
41.	After the War, a New King in Lanka	294
42.	Sita's Trial by Fire	301
43.	Sita of the Adbhuta Ramayana	309
44.	Pattabhisheka: Rama's Coronation	314
45.	Valmiki's Ashram: Lava and Kusha	324
Afterword		*341*
Acknowledgements		*359*
Notes		*363*
Bibliography		*371*

Author's Scribble

This is the first in a series of books that I am writing about Rama, Krishna, Shiva, Shakti and other gods from the Indian Puranas. I am trying to compile various folk and oral versions and textual variations and narrate them as enjoyable stories. I have deliberately followed the tradition of oral storytelling in this written book, as this is how these tales have always been told in India. The story flows with the narrator taking detours to illustrate and emphasize a point, encouraging the listener or reader to pause and reflect. This book initially appeared in English and Hindi as an audiobook on Audible. For the printed version, I have added more stories, references and a bibliography.

Foreword

The Many Ramayanas

No other religious text or folk narrative has influenced Southeast Asia's heritage over the past three thousand years as the grand epic Ramayana has. The stories in this epic were originally carried to every region along the rim of the Indian Ocean and beyond, from Thailand and Myanmar to Bali, Java, Sumatra and Cambodia, by traders, sailors, soldiers, travellers, immigrants and even royal bloodlines. These epics and their stories became so deeply entrenched that we still see their influences and imprints today. For instance, Thai kings still bear the name 'Rama' to recognize his status as an incarnation of Vishnu, the Preserver of Life.

In medieval India, the caste system, originally a construct based on occupation, was hereditary. Each person was born into an unalterable social status that grew to be so rigid that most of the population lost their right to education and literacy. The Ramayana, however, remained a text accessible to all through the dramatic, oral, and the guru-shishya (i.e. teacher-student) traditions. The story was endlessly enacted and retold, and its lessons taught to be imbibed. To this day, particularly in rural India, the Ramayana continues to be considered a 'dharma shastra', a delineator of ideals, kingship and morals—a holy book for spiritual practice, a guide for value education, as well as an ever-popular source of entertainment. The Ramayana is all of this rolled into one.

This book is a humble attempt to share the little tidbits I picked up first from my father and then from the numerous storytellers of rural India, whom I have had the abundant pleasure of reading or listening to. The intention here is to open a window into the beautiful world of the many Ramayanas. Consider this book as a primer, a small but passionate attempt by one who was fortunate to grow up partaking of the waters of the vast oceans of the Ramayana and the Mahabharata, while also revelling in the wealth of folk tales of this magnificent civilization. As far as possible, I have tried to acknowledge all the written texts and scholarly works that I came across while writing this book. As I draw my inspiration more from oral tales, this book claims no scholarly authenticity and it should not be approached in an academic way. *The Rama Story: Origins and Growth* by Camille Bulcke,[1] *The Ramayana: Its Origin and Growth, a Statistical Study* by M.R. Yardi,[2] *Puranic Encyclopaedia* by Vettam Mani,[3] *Ramayana: A Comparative Study of Ramakathas* by A.A. Manavalan[4] and the critical essay *Three Hundred Ramayanas: Five Examples and Three Thoughts on Translation* by A.K. Ramanujan have served as my go-to materials. This is not a research book, but a mere collection of thoughts, tales and lores of a humble writer. For serious researchers on Ramayana, I have provided a list of books in the afterword that may guide them properly.

If this work helps you in some way to improve your life, do place your gratitude at the feet of the unknown masters from all corners of India and beyond, who have kept the tradition alive over thousands of years. If not, lay the blame at the door of a writer who failed to capture the enduring messages embedded in this epic. Whichever end of the spectrum you find yourself, I sincerely hope this book will prompt you to explore more of India's storytelling traditions. Once you are done with the Ramayana and the Mahabharata, try the five great Tamil epics—*Silapddikaram, Manimekhalai, Jivaka Chintamani, Valayapathi* and *Kundalakesi*—then the Northern Ballads of Kerala, and so on.

As mentioned above, there are multiple versions of the Ramayana. The epic differs from culture to culture, age to age, place to place. The Ramayanas of East Asia are markedly different from the versions that we are familiar with in India; also, folk versions contain significant variations from the traditional devotional versions. The Jaina, Buddhist and Muslim Ramayanas differ widely from Valmiki's narrative. Each era has produced its own retelling. The dynamism and adaptability of the text to different times and cultures makes it fascinating.

The Ramayana is still evolving today. There have been many versions written in recent years. Among many other authors, I too, wrote the Ramayana from the villain's perspective in my novel *Asura*,[5] from the perspective of the Vanaras in *Vanara*[6] and from the perspective of its female characters in *Valmiki's Women*.[7] My short stories are often written from the perspective of the women protagonists. For the television series *Siya Ke Ram* (2015–16), I approached the Ramayana from the point of view of Sita, and in *Sankatmochan Mahabali Hanuman* (2015–17) from the point of view of Hanuman. I wrote the story and screenplay of *Shrimad Ramayan* (2024) from the point of view of Rama.

This book thus attempts to bring the life lessons that oral storytellers of the Ramayana impart to rural audiences. Each bard has brought his own interpretation to various incidents in the epic. The version I present here is the one I grew up with in Kerala. My father, the late L. Neelakantan, was a storyteller par excellence, and he introduced me to the Ramayana. As Kerala has historically rarely been subjected to invasions, the narration has a more critical and confident tone than the Ramayanas of the Indian heartland (north India and the Gangetic plains). There, retellings in local languages and dialects evolved in reaction to Muslim subjugation and the increasing caste rigidity within Hindu culture. In the Malayalam oral tradition, artistes usually relate the story from multiple perspectives. For example, the eighteenth-century poet Kunchan Nambiar—often called the 'Shakespeare of Malayalam'—used his sharp wit in writing his renditions of the Ramayana and the Mahabharata.

It is also interesting to note that the folk versions are often sympathetic to all characters without clear-cut delineations of what is good or evil. Traditionally, the Ramayana was never considered a story of good versus evil. Along with its companion epic, the Mahabharata, it was about karma and karmaphala. There was no attempt to hide either Rama or Krishna's faults and shortcomings. Instead of villains, the 'pratinayakas' or anti-heroes possessed tragic flaws and their karma inevitably caught up with them. Karma spares none, not even gods and heroes. The cyclic nature of time or 'Kala' is another underlying theme in all these texts.

It was only in the Bhakti era, in medieval times, that the Ramayana became a 'good versus evil' story. In places where classical Hindu civilization still flourished without the dominating influence of Islamic rule, the more critical traditions and subaltern tellings continued. The Bengal Renaissance too discovered such retellings through classics such as Michael Madhusudan Dutta's *Meghanada Badha Kavya*.[8] With no clear-cut hero or villain, the advantage of such an approach is that one can learn life lessons from every character. Each one is human, layered, with flaws, ambitions, aspirations, dilemmas, joys and sorrows, all of which we can identify with. Each character evokes empathy. The greatness of the Ramayana and Mahabharata is that we can all identify with at least one character or incident as being relevant to our own lives. Every major incident throws up multiple questions and possibilities.

The purpose of a divine incarnation (an avatar) is to teach people how to live, rather than how to vanquish evil as is made out in later day texts. According to the Puranas, Ravana and Kumbhakarna were incarnations of Jaya and Vijaya, the doorkeepers of Vishnu in Vaikunta. The stories in these epics are part of a divine 'leela' or play by the gods. Both epics are about universal consciousness, where everyone is an aspect of the supreme consciousness. Every character is essential. Everyone acts according to their understanding of their dharma or what is right. Some succumb to their emotions, others overcome them.

Whether aware of it or not, we are continually doing karma. As per Indian thought, karma is supreme and Kala or time is the judge that dispenses the fruits of karma (karmaphala). By studying the Ramayana and Mahabharata, we can learn how to control our karma and make our karmaphala more palatable.

Whether we believe in the karma theory or not, such texts provide a sense of inner peace and harmony and a deeper understanding of life. Ironically, these epics also discuss the competing and contrarian ideology of 'niyati' or chance, which challenges the karma theory. Ultimately, we need to understand both theories to understand life. That life is a mix of karma and niyati is the conclusion we may perhaps arrive at while reading the multiple versions of these great epics.

In India,[9] it is not compulsory to believe in God, only in oneself—for belief in oneself is belief in God. These texts are not about acts by the divine, but about our divinity. We are parts of an infinite (anantham), unfathomable (ajnatham), indescribable (avarnaniyam) universe. Going a step further in self-realization, we know that we *are* the universe. Every act we do is a vibration (spandanam), and when our spandanam is in harmony with that of the universe, we obtain infinite joy (anandam). We become non-judgmental. We understand everything is a leela, a play. Life becomes bliss.

There are an infinite number of Ramayanas. If you remain unsatiated with these, you can create your own. For the innate worth of the texts (a genuinely spectacular human achievement) does not lie in the infallibility of the written word but in the deep layers of meaning within the stories, in the epic. The epic is not merely about events that happened long ago, but what is happening here and now, and will keep happening. We need only open our eyes to see the miracle of life unfolding before us.

1
The Beginning: Ratnakara Meets Narada

THE ROBBER STANDS BEFORE SAGE NARADA, NAKED SWORD IN HAND, THE fire of his bloodshot eyes fuelled by the pangs of hunger in his belly. He and his family have not eaten in days. The sage, dressed in simple clothing, appears poor. It has been a wretched week for Ratnakara. Perhaps the veena the sage carries will fetch some money.

'I can give you my veena, my son, but I do not know what you will do with it,' Narada says smiling. 'Why do you rob people?'

'Hunger,' the man growls. 'My family is starving. Why should the poor go hungry when there is so much wealth in the world?'

Narada listens quietly, then says, 'Oh, so you rob people to feed your family? But is that not adharma, a sin, my son?'

'How is feeding my family adharma, Swami? How can it be a sin? I am doing my duty as a husband and father. Now hand over whatever you have. Hurry!' Ratnakara is not prepared to accept that any of this is his fault. Any act, however heinous, is justified by claiming it to be one's duty.

'Does your family know you are a robber?' Narada's voice is devoid of malice.

'Of course they know!' Ratnakara retorts impatiently.

'You share the spoils with them?'

'Why are you asking so many questions? Are you playing some trick on me?' Ratnakara eyes the sage with suspicion.

Narada insists gently, 'Answer me.'

'Yes, I share the spoils with my family. I feed and clothe them. I provide for them. I am a good man!' declares the robber.

'Son,' says Narada, 'go home and ask your wife and children whether they are willing to also share in your sin. Whether they are ready to eat the fruits of your bad karma along with you.'

'Aha!' Ratnakara laughs. 'You take me for a fool. You will run away the moment my back is turned.'

It is a universal truth that we judge others by our own standards. Thus, Narada's reply surprises his assailant.

'I shall come with you. Take me to your home,' Narada says.

They soon reach Ratnakara's hut and his children run to greet him. His wife comes out, a smile on her face. But when she sees that Ratnakara has returned empty-handed, the smile vanishes, like sudden lightning in the summer. The children look at their father, disappointment clouding their young faces. Narada stands a short distance away, watching.

'I want to know one thing,' Ratnakara says. 'That swami says I am doing great sin by my actions, and I will suffer terrible consequences for my bad karma. But I did it for you, wife. I became a robber for you, my sons. Please tell me you will willingly share the fruits of my sin.'

His wife stares at him, her eyes wide with fear. The children cower behind their mother, their small faces peeping out like flowers from behind a rock. The woman reaches behind her and brings them forward, holding them tight, a faraway look in her eyes. 'Is it not the duty of the man to provide for his family? Why should my children eat the bitter fruits of their father's bad karma?'

Shocked at such callous betrayal, Ratnakara flings down the sword he carries and hurries away. Narada follows him. When they reach the forest, Ratnakara says in a trembling voice, 'I thought they loved me! I have wasted my life.'

Narada replies, 'Son, one must first love oneself before loving others.'

'But ... but ... isn't that selfish?'

'No, my son, by being compassionate to yourself you will be compassionate to the whole world. You will see the whole world as an extension of yourself.'

'I am a sinner,' says Ratnakara, his voice quivering. 'I have shed blood. I have neither been compassionate to myself nor to others.'

'It is never too late to change.'

'I am a sinner. I have blood on my hands,' moans Ratnakara.

'You are forgetting my first lesson—be compassionate to yourself. Forgive yourself.'

'My mind is agitated. My hands are shivering. I have wasted my life,' Ratnakara laments, shaking his head from side to side. 'I am a sinner.'

'Calm your mind, my son.'

'How?'

'Meditate. Do penance. Look deep into yourself.'

Ratnakara gazes at the sage, bewildered. 'But how? I am illiterate. I cannot read any holy books. I live in this forest. I am no one.'

'Chant this one word—Rama.'

'Raa ... I can't even pronounce it! I don't know what it means.'

'The meaning is what you must find, my son.'

'I cannot chant something I do not know,' Ratnakara protests.

'Alright. Can you pronounce "mara"—"to kill"?'

'Yes, but that is as in,' Ratnakara protests piously.

'Chant it. That which is darkness when seen from one side is light when seen from another.'

'I trust you, Swami,' Ratnakara finally says. 'I shall chant "mara mara mara".'

'Trust yourself. Don't worry about the meaning. Keep chanting "mara mara mara". The right meaning will find you at the right time.'

And so Ratnakara sits chanting 'mara mara mara' on the banks of the River Tamasa, the river of darkness. He sits looking into the darkness inside his mind. He does not know when his chant changes to 'Rama Rama Rama'.

Time passes. Ratnakara sits like a statue, his eyes closed, waiting for the spark to appear and dispel the darkness that lies coiled like a cobra in his conscience. The chanting slowly fills his mind with compassion. Compassion is sweet. It is fragrant. The fragrance catches the attention of the ants. They come to enquire. They find a man overflowing with sweetness. They know he loves himself and so loves every being, for he is learning to find himself in every atom of the Universe. They know he is them and they are him.

They carry soil on their little backs and build an anthill around him. They toil day and night. He is aware of their presence, so he sits still. This robber, who never blinked an eye while robbing others, who never thought twice about committing violence, now sits without moving so much as an eyelid for fear of hurting the little ants. Gradually, the anthill covers him. Millions of ants thrive in it. Ratnakara sits still, his chant of 'Rama Rama Rama' the only proof that he is alive. He goes hungry, so the ants will not be disturbed. He breathes slowly. The ants multiply.

The rains come ... then spring, summer, and winter ... many times over. Still, Ratnakara sits, covered in the anthill. Finally, the ants abandon their home and go in search of a new one. Just as he thinks of standing up and stretching his limbs, a cobra comes to live in a hole in the anthill. So Ratnakara sits still again, not because he fears the poisonous creature, but because his love encompasses the cobra. It nestles on his shoulders, crawls into his lap and lies coiled there, comfortable in the sweet fragrance of his compassion.

The River Tamasa flows on ceaselessly and merges with the River Sarayu, the meaning of which is 'that which flows quickly like Time'.

One day, when the cobra goes hunting, Ratnakara hears a familiar voice.

'Come out, my son. Break out of the valmikam (anthill). Come out into the light.' Sage Narada taps the anthill.

Ratnakara emerges, weeping. 'The cobra will find its home broken, Swami,' he cries.

Sage Narada smiles at the words of the robber-turned-saint. 'God knows how to protect all creatures. The cobra will find another hole. Never think you are so important. The world goes on with or without us. But it is time for you to go forth and spread the light.'

'But I did nothing! I just chanted "mara mara..."' Ratnakara pauses. 'I chanted "Rama Rama Rama..."' he cries in sudden realization.

Sage Narada smiles. 'Valmiki ... from today you will be known as Valmiki. I hope you have understood the meaning of Rama?'

'Yes, yes ... Rama is the light in our conscience. Rama is the light in the darkness. Rama is what is pleasing. Rama is the cause of joy in the world—jagadanandakaraka. But how do I spread this light in the world?'

'Write about Rama,' Sage Narada says and vanishes.

Valmiki walks along the banks of River Tamasa, wondering who or what Rama is. Of one thing he is sure, chanting Rama has changed him. Valmiki is now aware of himself. He can see the world with more clarity. Yet, deep in his mind, an inexplicable pain lingers. It is sweet and heavy at the same time. Had he been a woman, he would have understood it as akin to the pain of childbearing. The robber-turned-saint is brimming with the pain of creativity that longs to find expression. He does not know it yet but like the final stages of childbirth, he will soon go through shattering pain before creating something beautiful. He does not know it, but he is pregnant with a poem.

This version of Valmiki having once been a robber appears in medieval Ramayanas in various Indian languages, and in the *Skanda Purana* in Sanskrit. But the story has no place in Valmiki's own Ramayana, causing many experts to dispute his ever having been a robber.[10]

However, the journey into the world of the Ramayana is not about sticking to scriptural authenticity. The Ramayana is a story about discovering oneself, knowing one's passion, and changing for the better. It is about loving oneself and by extension, the whole world. There are countless Ramayanas, each valid and authentic. We are not searching for the right Ramayana but the right lessons useful to us in life. If one authentic Ramayana were enough, there would not have been countless others. Only a living entity evolves as the Ramayana has evolved through the centuries, mutating and growing through different languages and cultures.

The stories I will be using in this book are from various Ramayanas and not just from the Valmiki Ramayana.

2

The Poet Meets the Poem

KALIDASA, THE GREAT SANSKRIT POET, GIVES US A BEAUTIFUL DEFINITION of who can truly be called a kavi (poet). He says that only the 'rudithanusari kavi', the poet who is capable of empathizing with those who suffer, is a true poet. Valmiki's poetry also rose from deep anguish, yet his Ramayana is the poetry of compassion. Gandhiji, when asked what one could learn from the Ramayana, summarized it in one word: 'Don't'.

What did he mean? Perhaps the unfolding story of Valmiki will explain.

Having emerged from the anthill, Valmiki finds his mind is disturbed. There is the throbbing of creation in his subconscious. He wanders along the banks of the River Tamasa, trying to find the Rama inside him. Then on a day when the rain has receded and spring has sneaked in unnoticed, when love is in the air, Valmiki sees a vision that will change the course of mankind forever. He sees two birds in the act of love. He forgets himself, watching them with a bliss that can scarcely be expressed in mere words. Here is creation unfolding before him. He stands rooted, his eyes filled with inexplicable tears.

But the moment of creation is also the moment of death. A hunter, driven by hunger more powerful than love, shoots an arrow at the male bird and pierces his heart. The pain is felt intensely by the watching poet. The cries of the female bird for her lost mate fill the air. And from the agony of death, the first poetry of the human race is born. Ironically, the first words of this great poem are uttered as a curse. Valmiki cries: '*Maa nishada pratisthana tvamagamahsasvati samaa yat kraunchamithunamdekam vadhi kamamohitam*' (Don't, brute! You will never have peace, for you have killed one of the two birds while they were in the act of love.)

The hunter does not understand what the poet is telling him. The bird is merely food to him. He picks up the dead bird and walks away to cook it and eat it. Valmiki is gripped by extreme grief. When we become one with nature, everything affects us, even the death of a bird. Valmiki roams the forest, his heart heavy with sorrow. As he sinks deeper into depression, one day at dawn, he sees a vision. Brahma, the Creator, manifests before him. The endless universe stretches before and behind Brahma. Valmiki, a mere speck in the vast space of Time, a tiny drop in the ocean of Infinity, stands with his hands folded before the great Creator.

Brahma says to him, 'Valmiki, I put those curse words into your mouth for there is a rhythm to the curse. There is poetry hidden in it; there is a metre in the words, called anushtup. Write a poem about Rama. Tell the world a great story that shall endure till the end of time.'

'But who is Rama?' Valmiki cries.

'Your conscience,' Brahma replies, smiling enigmatically and vanishes.

Valmiki is even more troubled now. The curse plays in his mind, and more meanings emerge. There is something profound in the words. As he dwells on this, things begin to gradually clear and his grief slowly turns into a numbing ache. He understands that life and death are like day and night. There is a rhythm to life, a cycle. The hunter is no brute, he is just another creature, as important or as trivial as a grasshopper or an elephant. He cannot be blamed for killing the bird. But could he not have found a better way to fill his stomach?

Years before, as Ratnakara, Valmiki too had lived a life like that. Instead of birds he had hunted men, robbing and even killing them. But he had been lucky; he had been found by Narada, who showed him the path of light, the way of Rama. So is it not his duty to spread the light, to say 'Don't!'? Who better than he, who had faced the darkness and been shown the light? But the question arises yet again in his mind: Who or what was Rama?

When the writer is ready the story manifests itself, much in the same way that rain comes to a well-prepared field. And so the story comes to Valmiki. The Ramayana originates in the shoka (grief) of the poet. That which is born from suffering, from empathy, from shoka, is shloka. That is why most Sanskrit poetry is written in shlokas.

Valmiki asks Narada, 'Who in the universe is the perfect man?'

'Why do you want a perfect man?' Narada responds. 'What do you mean by perfect?'

Taking a deep breath, Valmiki says, 'The man who has the sixteen great qualities. One who is gunvaan (principled and has integrity), veerayavan (valour), dharmajna (follows dharma and righteousness), kritajna (grateful for every moment and experience), satyavaak (upholder of his word), drisha vrata (firm with his vows, deeds, decision and mind), charitravan (whose conduct is moral), sarva bhuteshu hitah (disposed towards the welfare of all beings), vidyavaan (knowledgeable), samarthah (competent), ek priya darshanah (delightful in appearance), aatmavan (courageous), jitakrodha (free of anger), dyutiman (splendid and brilliant), anasuyakh (free of envy), and jaata roshasya asya samuge devaah ca bibhyati (even gods cannot stand his valour in a war).'

Narada smiles, amused. 'But why do you need such a man?'

'I believe that is what Rama is, the perfect man, and I want to write his story,' Valmiki replies.

'Hah! The perfect man is an oxymoron,' Narada scoffs. 'However perfect a man, even if he is an avatar of Lord Vishnu, he will have flaws because he is human.'

Valmiki shakes his head impatiently. 'But does such a man exist? A man as I have described, possessed of all sixteen qualities?'

'Yes indeed,' replies Narada, 'and I shall tell you his story. I am no poet, just a humble minstrel cursed to roam till I find the edge of the universe. And, as you know, there is no edge to the universe, which wraps into itself. Thus I must roam forever, unto infinity, and it is the story of Rama that keeps me going. I shall tell it to you. But before I do, I must tell you what brought it all about—the cause.'

> Many believe that Valmiki Ramayana is the original and authentic Ramayana. However, there were and are many Valmiki Ramayanas. Today, we have at least three major versions of Valmiki Ramayana in Sanskrit. The first and most popular one is the Southern Recension, which was more prevalent in south India. The second one is the Gaudiya or Eastern Indian version, which was more popular in Bengal and the eastern parts of India. The third one is the North Western version. There are major differences in many shlokas; some differ by at least 30 per cent between versions. The sequence of the shlokas also widely differs between these three major versions. The Indian language versions have borrowed generously from each of these three major Sanskrit versions, but the borrowing

has not been strictly on the basis of geographical proximity. For example, many events in the Kamba Ramayana are more common in the Gaudiya version than in the south Indian version. Scholars say that the Southern Recension is the oldest and the Southern Recension of the Valmiki Ramayana in Sanskrit could be relatively close to the original. A few examples are as follows: In the Gaudiya version and the North Western version, Shanta is mentioned in greater detail. It also has a reference about Sita being the daughter of Janaka and the celestial nymph Menaka. In the North Western version, the incident where Angada seizes Mandodari's hair is mentioned. The story we know now as Ramayana is a mix of many of these versions. So, even when we say that Valmiki Ramayana is the authentic Ramayana, we should remember that there are many Valmiki Ramayanas. Even in the Ramayana, Valmiki is not the first one to write it as per Valmiki. Before him, Hanuman, Kakabhusundi, Narada and others had written the Ramayana. So, there was no one authentic Ramayana even during the time of the Ramayana. In other words, all Ramayanas are authentic.

3

The Epic Begins to Unfold

THERE IS ALWAYS A REASON FOR EVERYTHING. A SMALL SEED GROWS INTO A huge tree. To understand the tree, one must know the seed. Why was Rama born? Why was Ravana born? The story starts with a curse.

The four sages known as the Sanaka Kumaras arrive in Vaikunta, the loka (world) where Lord Vishnu dwells, also called Vishnuloka. The Sanaka Kumaras are the 'manasputras' (mind-born sons) of Brahma the Creator and they eternally appear as four little boys. Lord Vishnu is asleep when they arrive. He has instructed his doorkeepers, Jaya and Vijaya, that he must not be disturbed. So, when the diminutive sages who barely reach the doorkeepers knees appear and demand to be let in, Jaya and Vijaya are in a quandary.

Jaya, the elder, says to his brother Vijaya, 'They want to go in. How can we allow that? Our master, Jagannath, the Lord of the Universe, Lord Vishnu himself, has instructed us not to let anyone in while he is resting.'

Vijaya, the younger but wiser of the two, replies, 'But these are the Sanaka Kumaras, the four holy sages. Brother, they could curse us if we do not let them in.'

'But our master said no one was to enter. It is our dharma, our duty, to follow our master's instructions and not worry about the consequences,' Jaya argues.

'But laws are made to keep order,' replies Vijaya. 'If a law threatens that order, the balance, we must discard it. The concept of dharma is subtle. That is what I have understood, brother, and there is no greater dharma than self-preservation. If we do not let these holy sages in, they will curse us. So, for our safety, I think we should let them in.'

'Should we fear their curses when our master is Lord Vishnu himself?' asks Jaya. 'I will do my duty,' he says, 'and you as my younger brother must follow me. I'll take the responsibility.'

Reluctantly, the younger brother agrees. Accordingly, Jaya and Vijaya deny entry to the Sanaka Kumaras. The angry saints curse them to become demons and stalk off without meeting Lord Vishnu.

When Vishnu awakens, he finds his two bodyguards standing before him, ashen-faced.

'We have been cursed for doing our duty. My Lord, help us ...' Jaya pleads.

'The Sanaka Kumaras came to meet you while you slept, but we stopped them as per your instructions,' Vijaya explains.

Vishnu shakes his head in dismay. 'Do you not know that every rule in life has exceptions? Those who are rigid will face many difficulties. You must use your discretion to choose which rule to follow, when and where and which rule to ignore.'

Jaya is shocked. 'But Swami, is that not adharma? One must do one's duty without worrying about the consequences—is what you keep advising the whole world.'

Vishnu smiles. 'Not worrying about consequences does not mean there will be no consequences. For every action, there will be the fruit of that action. Karma always leads to karmaphala.'

'So not even you, the Great Lord of the Universe, can save us from having to eat the fruits of our action?' Jaya asks fearfully.

Vishnu nods. 'I too must eat the fruit of my actions, but I am not affected by it.'

'But Lord, this is unfair!' Jaya cries in anguish. 'You are God. You gave us instructions. Is it not your fault that you made us act this way? It is said that not a leaf moves without your knowledge. You are the Supreme God. So, the responsibility for our action is also yours. Is it fair that we have to eat the fruits of our action while the responsibility lies with God?'

Vishnu laughs in genuine amusement at this outburst. 'Son, I am Kala, I am the embodiment of Time, Kalapurusha. I am the one who ripens the fruits of your action. I don't ask you to choose in any particular way. I have given you the discretion to choose and to enjoy the good or suffer the bad that comes with that choice.'

Vijaya, who knows there is no point in arguing further, asks, 'Swami, when will we finish eating the fruit of our actions?'

Vishnu looks at him. 'You have two choices. You can take a hundred births in the world and be the most virtuous of men in every birth. As virtuous men, you may wallow in poverty, face many miseries in life, be tortured and killed, yet you will be hailed as the most virtuous of men. The world will praise you. You can return to your duty as my doorkeepers after that.'

'And what is the other option?' asks Jaya.

Vishnu replies, 'You can take three births as brothers and be reviled as the evilest of men. You will commit atrocities, torture others, wallow in luxury, be kings and the rulers of the fourteen worlds, and only I can kill you. But remember, as long as the universe exists, you will be hailed as evil.'

The brothers consult together, their faces creased with worry. Vishnu watches them, knowing already what their decision will be.

Finally, Jaya says, 'We have considered both options deeply. We asked ourselves, what is our goal? It is to return to Vaikunta as early as possible. So, we have decided that the first opinion does not matter to us. We choose the second path—that of three lives as evil men.'

Vishnu nods. 'Understand that there is no absolute good or evil. Even when you do evil to many, some good is also accrued, and vice versa. But whatever you do . . .'

'. . . there will be the fruits of our action waiting to be eaten,' Jaya and Vijaya cry in unison.

Vishnu smiles at them. 'And remember that it is I or, in other words, Time who ripens the fruits you must eat.'

Vijaya says, 'Lord, it seems that for you, the cycle of life is but a divine play, a leela.'

'It is so for all,' Vishnu replies, 'but only some know that life is but play. Others take life too seriously and suffer in their ignorance. Now, go to earth and play the parts you have chosen.'

We can learn many lessons from this simple story. How many times have you had to grapple with choices? Everything in our life is due to the choices we have made. We are the creators of our destiny. At any given point in time, we are confronted with multiple options. We decide, based on our fears, a false sense of duty, aspirations, desires, impulses, emotions, and so on. But whatever the choice, we must eat the fruits of it.

Not making a choice and allowing things to take their own course is also a choice. It does not matter what an action is based on, the fruit of karma always ripens. The Ramayana, like many Indian stories, emphasizes the principle of karma or action. As Lord Vishnu mentions to Jaya and Vijaya, even he is not free from the results of his actions.

In Indian thought, God is Time. That is why God is known as either Mahakala (Shiva) or Kalapurusha (Vishnu). The definition of right and wrong changes according to Time. That is also why there are no absolutes in Indian schools of thought. Time is considered infinite and cyclical. Consider the symbolism of Vishnu lying on Ananta. The word 'Vishnu' comes from the word 'expansive'; thus, expansive Time lies upon the snake Anantha (infinity). In Indian philosophy, snakes are often the symbol of infinity, or of zero (nothingness), the Buddhist concept of shunya. A snake eating its own tail is also the symbol of zero in tantric teachings.

The Western or Semitic concept of God is He who acts as a judge. He is the Father, with or without form, depending on which religion you follow. The Heavenly Father judges us based on our actions. The concept of 'sin' in India has emerged from its interactions with Semitic religions like Islam and Christianity, that is judged by an external agent who gives rewards or punishments. On the contrary, in the Jaya-Vijaya story, we find the foundation of the Indian Puranas to be based on karma—action and the choices we make. We create our own rewards and punishments depending on enlightened or ignorant choices.

Interestingly, India also has alternate streams of thought that negate karma and karmaphala. One such school believes all things are predetermined and happen because they are destined to happen so. Another believes that anything that happens is the will of God. If good happens it is because it is written in your destiny or vidhi. Hence the name 'Vidhata' for Brahma the Creator. The Bhakti tradition takes this route. Everything is the will of God. This is not dissimilar to Islam or Christianity.

There is yet another school, the Ajivika, that denies both the karma and the predetermined destiny theories, and holds that things happen purely by chance, at random. For a brief period in history, till about the time Emperor Ashoka converted to Buddhism, the Ajivikas were a prominent force in Indian thought. Ashoka's father, Bindusara, was an Ajivika. Until the fifteenth century, we find references to Ajivikas living in south India. The Kalabharas, who ruled in the south for three centuries until Tamil Shaivism revived, were also believed to have been Ajivikas. Sadly, their books have been lost to time. Goshala, the most famous of the Ajivika philosophers, was a contemporary of Buddha.

As per the Ajivika philosophy, even the universe was created by chance. If we meet someone on the street, it is by chance. We are born in a particular place and time by chance. We die by chance. There is no meaning to life and no need for purpose. Stuff happens. We exist because of the chance marriage of various natural elements that come together for a brief period. We die when a chance grouping of elements breaks. Why do elements behave the way they do? Because it is their nature to do so. The world is made of an infinite number of atoms. Each has its own properties. They interact and create different forms by chance. Life happens. So does death.

Jainism has many similarities with this school of thought. The earlier Ramayanas also bore the influence of such beliefs. Like most things Indian, none of these different paths have been invalidated. All are acceptable and incomplete. All three represent various methods to understand life.

Ancient Indians taught their children a game called Chaturanga. It was not similar to modern chess as many people believe, but rather like Ludo. It was a game of chance and skill. The player would throw the dice and move coins strategically, depending on the dice number obtained. No player could win by sheer luck, as one can in Snakes and Ladders. Nor could one win only by skill. Hence, Chaturanga was said to reflect life: throw the dice and chance determines how it falls. We use our talents to negotiate the board of life, depending on what points we obtain. Other players also throw the dice and move their pieces. Sometimes, another player's piece eliminates ours, sometimes we stop theirs. Just like life, it is a combination of skill and chance.

Jaya and Vijaya were cursed because they were at the wrong place at the wrong time when the Sanaka Kumaras came. They could not have done much about it. But once the event occurred, they made their choice, which combined with various chance events, determined their future lives. Karma and karmaphala are as crucial as chance. We cannot control how the dice falls, but we can learn to choose which piece to move where and how.

4

Dasaratha's Boons to Kaikeyi

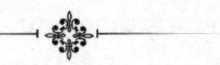

Jaya and Vijaya thus come to earth to play their parts as Ravana and Kumbhakarna, the two Asura (demon) brothers. Each acquires great boons from Brahma. With the help of these boons, Ravana begins to rule the world with an iron fist. But we will come to Ravana's story later. The stage is now set for Lord Vishnu to take birth as Rama of Ayodhya.

For a Rama to be born, a Ravana is required—Rama and Ravana represent opposing world views. They are prototypes of what we see in our day-to-day lives. It is only in the presence of Ravana that Rama has relevance, and vice versa. Many Ramayanas say that Rama and Ravana share almost all the same qualities. In fact, Ravana is more accomplished in many respects. What differentiates Rama and Ravana are the choices they make at each juncture of their lives. This difference becomes more apparent as we delve deeper into the Ramayana.

To know Rama and what drove him, one must first know Dasaratha. We are all defined by our childhood circumstances, our parents' values and the place and culture we grow up in. Hence, understanding the father is vital to understanding the son. Let us consider a few defining moments in Dasaratha's life. Dasaratha,[11] king of Ayodhya, has three wives—Kausalya,[12] Kaikeyi[13] and Sumitra.[14] Kaikeyi is the most beloved. She is an accomplished warrior besides having many other accomplishments. Born to King Aswapati, the ruler of Kaikeya, she was a fine equestrienne. After her marriage to Dasaratha, she often accompanies him to the battlefield. It so happens that in one such battle, Dasaratha is fighting the powerful Shambrasura, who has a flying machine that can carry thousands of warriors. The conflict goes on for days and missiles rain upon Dasaratha's army.

The king of Ayodhya is famed for his ability to control ten chariots at once, but busy fighting off Shambrasura's attack, he hands the reins to Kaikeyi. Soon, one of the flying arrows hits Dasaratha, and he falls unconscious onto the chariot floor. Shambrasura's next arrow breaks the pin of Dasaratha's chariot wheel. What Kaikeyi does next goes on to become an example of legendary courage. She uses the index finger of her left hand to replace the broken axle pin, thus keeping the wheel in place, while controlling the panicked horses with her right hand. In this way, she smashes through Shambrasura's ranks, scattering them like scared chickens and taking Dasaratha to safety.

When Dasaratha returns to consciousness, he sees Kaikeyi's broken finger and asks how it happened. She remains silent, but Dasaratha's soldiers tell him of the extraordinary courage exhibited by his wife. Overwhelmed with admiration and love, Dasaratha impulsively offers Kaikeyi two boons.

Kaikeyi declines the boons saying she has merely done her duty, that his love is all she desires. As he has offered the boons in public, in front of everyone in his camp, his ego and pride are hurt by her refusal. He insists she accept his offer. Kaikeyi, to pacify her agitated husband, says she will ask for the boons when she requires them. Dasaratha's thoughtless offer will come back to haunt him later.

How many times have we found ourselves in a similar situation thanks to our own rash words or actions? Dasaratha owes his life to Kaikeyi. To reward her is the right thing to do, perhaps, but Kaikeyi has not saved him expecting anything in return. Her love for her husband and her inherent courage are what caused her to do what she has done. But Dasaratha's ego puts a price on Kaikeyi's devotion. Even when she refuses a reward, he insists on it.

This is tantamount to a post-dated blank cheque. Such grandiose promises made on the spur of the moment often return to haunt us. The story of Mahabali also illustrates this.

Mahabali and Vamana's Three Steps

A great Asura emperor, Mahabali rules with justice for all, and his empire is founded on dharma. The gods can neither defeat him in battle nor find any fault in him to trigger a revolt or coup in his kingdom. But, despite all his greatness, Mahabali has one great flaw. He is proud of his sense of fair play and his commitment to what he calls the truth.

The gods thus go to Vishnu to find a way to defeat Mahabali. Vishnu takes on the avatar of a dwarf named Vamana and goes to a yagna (ritual fire sacrifice) that Mahabali is conducting on the banks of the Narmada River. When the time comes for Mahabali to give alms, Vamana asks Mahabali for three feet of land.

Mahabali's guru, Shukracharya, suspects foul play. Why would anyone patiently wait the whole day for such a trivial gift? If something appears to be so simple, it is wise to check for hidden deceptions. He warns Mahabali that the dwarf could be Vishnu, come to trick the Asuras into forfeiting their empire.

But Mahabali declares, 'I will not go back on my word.'

Many kingdoms, empires, families and lives have been lost at the altar of great ego. This is the same rigidity that Jaya exhibited when the Sanaka Kumaras visited Vaikunta. He was so sure that he was doing the right thing and that there would be no adverse outcomes. But there were.

The most excellent dharma is self-preservation. Rigidity in a self-proclaimed truth always results in failure and disaster. Despite Shukracharya's warning, Mahabali goes ahead and grants Vamana the permission to take three steps. The very next moment, Vamana grows to touch the sky. With one step, he measures the earth, and with his next, the sky.

Then Vamana turns to Mahabali and says, 'Fulfil your promise. I have taken but two steps, where shall I place the third?'

Mahabali has no choice but to offer his own head. Vamana's foot pushes him down into the netherworld. Thus, the most righteous Asura falls due to his own ego. The most excellent dharma is self-preservation. Rigidity in a self-proclaimed truth always results in failure and disaster.

This story, rich in symbolism, should have been a lesson to Dasaratha. But past wisdom seldom comes to one's aid in moments of passion, when one is gripped by ego. Dasaratha fails to realize that his promise, like the one Mahabali gave, can be his nemesis, and that the problem can grow sky high at the most inopportune moment in his life and push him down to his doom.

Dasaratha's rash act is what propels the Ramayana story forward. But, as it turns out, this was not his first indiscretion.

5

Shanta: Dasaratha's Eldest Child

THIS STORY APPEARS IN THE VANA PARVA SECTION OF THE MAHABHARATA, and is known as the 'Ramopakhyana'. It consists of seven hundred verses and forms one of the earliest versions of the Ramayana. According to the Ramopakhyana, Dasaratha's firstborn is not Rama, but a daughter named Shanta.[15] Dasaratha, however, yearns for a male child who will carry on his dynastic lineage and his queens are under tremendous pressure to produce an heir.

Though Princess Shanta is brought up in the palace in Ayodhya, she grows up with a sense of alienation. Home is a place where her father and his three wives are always busy with various ritual sacrifices and prayers to obtain male progeny. Shanta feels unwanted and uncared for.

Meanwhile, the country of Anga, ruled by Dasaratha's friend Romapada, is in the grip of a drought that has lasted twelve years, and famine now rages through the land. Various sages have advised Romapada to get Rishyashringa, a hermit living in a remote Himalayan jungle, to perform a ritual sacrifice to appease the rain gods. 'People are starving to death in my kingdom,' Romapada tells Dasaratha. 'If only Rishyashringa could come and conduct the sacrifice, we would be saved!'

But getting to Rishyashringa is a problem and Romapada tells Dasratha why this is so. Rishyashringa's father, Vibhantaka, in his youth fell in love with an apsara (celestial nymph) and broke his vow of celibacy, thus halting his spiritual pursuit. To ensure that his son does not commit the same mistake, Vibhantaka now keeps Rishyashringa insulated from women. No female of any species can enter the jungle because of the spell Vibhantaka has cast. Hence, getting Rishyashringa out of the hermitage is a dangerous proposition.

'I need your help, my friend,' King Romapada pleads. Then he adds something that piques Dasaratha's interest: 'The sages have prophesied that Rishyashringa is the only saint capable of performing the rare Putrakameshti Yagna, the ritual sacrifice that can help you obtain male progeny.'

As soon as he hears this Dasaratha gives his daughter to Romapada to adopt, in the hope that she may prove fruitful in bringing Sage Rishyashringa to Ayodhya. For this, she must first bring him to Anga, the home of her adoptive father. It's a dangerous task, not only because of the spell cast over the jungle by Vibhantaka to keep females out but also because she is asked to commit one of the greatest sins imaginable in those times—breaking a monk's brahmacharya (vow of celibacy). For this she can be cursed by the monk.

Yet Shanta takes on the task as a challenge to help the people of her adopted land. She manages to enter Rishyashringa's jungle and fortunately for her, he falls in love with her and chooses to leave his life in the hermitage and marry her.

When his father Vibhantaka questions him about this decision, Rishyashringa replies, 'Love is the greatest spirituality. In fact, spirituality is nothing but finding love. One can love another person or the whole world or God. Everything is but different forms of spirituality. One of the four great aims of life, according to the Hindu scriptures, is kama or passion. Without passion, there is no salvation.'

Vibhantaka—though sad that his son has fallen in the same way he had—blesses the couple. And so Rishyashringa marries Shanta and leaves for Anga. There, he performs a sacrifice which brings rain and prosperity to the parched land. Dasaratha then invites Rishyashringa to Ayodhya to conduct the Putrakameshti Yagna. Thus, to obtain sons, Dasaratha first sacrificed and then depended on the daughter he gave away.

Rishyashringa conducts the Putrakameshti sacrifice. From the fire appears a pot of payesa (rice cooked in sweetened milk), as delicious as nectar. Dasaratha gives Kausalya and Kaikeyi a portion each, but forgets about his middle wife, Sumitra. So Kausalya and Kaikeyi share their portions with Sumitra. In due time, Rama is born to Kausalya and Bharata to Kaikeyi. As Sumitra received two portions, one from Kausalya and the other from Kaikeyi, she gives birth to twins—Lakshmana and Shatrughna. As the boys grow up, Lakshmana becomes devoted to his half-brother Rama, and Shatrughna becomes Bharata's shadow.

Here again, we see how Dasaratha's choices play a part in developing the main storyline in the Ramayana.

We find another king in the same Ramayana who acts in precisely the opposite way to Dasaratha. This king is still considered to be one of the most learned people in all of Hindu literature. His name is Janaka.

6

Rama: Dasaratha's Most Beloved Son

DASARATHA SOON BECOMES OBSESSED WITH HIS SONS, ESPECIALLY RAMA, the eldest. All his dreams, ambitions and hopes are concentrated in him. He prefers Rama to his other sons, and this is obvious to everyone.

Dasaratha ensures the learned Rajaguru, the royal preceptor of Ayodhya, teaches Rama and his brothers. When the princes come of age, a new mentor, Sage Vishwamitra, whose rivalry with the royal preceptor Vasishta is legendary, comes to Dasaratha with a request. He wants Rama to go with him to protect his forest hermitage from the attacks of the demonic Rakshasas.

Dasaratha refuses to send Rama. He pleads with Vishwamitra saying, 'My Rama is too young. How can I send him to the forest alone? What if something happens to him? What if he does something rash—an indiscretion of youth?'

Vishwamitra replies, 'Dasaratha, once children grow up, parents must let them be free. They have to chart their own destiny.'

Dasaratha expresses the timeless fears of all fathers, proud of their sons' accomplishments yet fearful for their safety. They do not wholly trust their sons' ability to look after themselves, even when they are grown. The same Dasaratha had no qualms about giving away his firstborn, Shanta, to be adopted, nor did he worry about her fate in going into a forest. He had no care for the repercussions she might face in getting Rishyashringa to break his vow of celibacy, just so that he could be brought back to perform the yagna Dasaratha required to beget sons. Now Dasaratha is terrified of sending his son, trained as a warrior, out in the company of a great sage.

Vishwamitra is livid. 'You are too attached to your son, Dasaratha!' he thunders. 'And this will bring misery upon you one day or another. Once they grow up, children do not belong to their parents alone, they belong to society.'

Dasaratha pleads once again, 'I will come with you instead, Maharishi. I will fight the demons for you. My Rama is too young.'

When Vishwamitra threatens to ruin Ayodhya if Dasaratha does not comply, Vasishta intervenes and persuades Dasaratha to send Rama. Lakshmana, who is his half-brother's loving shadow, insists on accompanying Rama.

This is the first time we see Rama emerging from the shadow of his illustrious father.

Many of us have faced such situations in our lives, as sons and daughters, or as parents. At the age of seventeen or eighteen, when most of us leave the safety of the nest, we are brimming with enthusiasm for our new, great adventure. Parents are inevitably fearful. Dasaratha's behaviour is thus typical of most fathers. The only thing that has perhaps changed from the times of the Ramayana is that open discrimination against girls has somewhat reduced. Daughters are now fortunate to be born in a modern era when such patriarchal mindsets are slowly but surely being eroded.

The dilemma faced by young men and women today is twofold. On the one hand, an exciting world of opportunities beckons. One is beginning a new adventure, meeting new people, living in a new environment. All of life beckons with arms wide open to embrace one. On the other hand, there is the secret fear of leaving the comfort of one's home, missing their mother's cooking, the caring anger and scolding of their father, and the love-hate relationship with one's siblings.

I was a fussy eater in my teens. I craved food from restaurants, preferring it to my mother's delicious dishes. Then I left my home to study engineering and lived in the college hostel. Three days of the hostel mess food was enough for me to crave for home. Despite all the difficulties, this separation is easier for the young than for their parents. Once the young have left the nest, the constant reminders—posters on the wall, carelessly thrown shoes, piles of books, clothes hanging in the closet—bring back a thousand sweet memories. If it is tough on the father, it is doubly so on the mother.

Dasaratha is in just such a state. He is proud of his son's accomplishments but fears what his son might face in the jungle with the old sage.

The jungle is a dreaded place, where demonic creatures such as the fierce Asuras and Rakshasas roam. Thus for the first time, Rama and Lakshmana leave the protective walls of Ayodhya, with its regimental protocols. We see Rama go away with Vishwamitra as an enthusiastic youth and returning years later as a mature and poised young man. He also brings back a wife with him. But before all that, here are a few words about some of the essential lessons Vishwamitra teaches Rama and Lakshmana.

Real learning often begins once formal education has ended. Rama and his brothers have been well taught by Sage Vasishta, but the education Vishwamitra provides to Rama and Lakshmana is what prepares them for the future. It shapes their world view. These are not theoretical lessons learnt in the safety of the palace. Vishwamitra takes them into the wild, where different rules apply. There is no retinue of servants to wait on the princes. The first lesson Vishwamitra teaches Rama is about hunger. Only a person who has suffered real hunger can have compassion, he says. A ruler without compassion is merely a tyrant and worse than a demon.

For days, Vishwamitra makes the princes walk through the jungle without food or water, to teach the future ruler about the horrors of famine and drought. When Rama and Lakshmana fall down exhausted, too weak to even stand, Sage Vishwamitra teaches them the empowering Bala-Atibala mantras.

7

Three Interpretations of Two Mantras: The Freedom to Choose

WHEN RAMA AND LAKSHMANA FALL DOWN EXHAUSTED IN THE JUNGLE, Sage Vishwamitra gives them two divine mantras called Bala and Atibala, meaning 'strength' and 'supreme strength'. These mantras contain deep meanings, and various schools have interpreted them in different ways.

The wonderful thing about Indian culture is the freedom it gives us to pick and choose whichever stream of thought suits us. There is no dogma, no commandments to follow, and no concept of blasphemy. We are free to reject all scriptures or accept a part and reject the rest. There is no one authentic version of any of the Hindu scriptures. Over many centuries, many thinkers, sages and social reformers have translated, reinterpreted and rewritten them according to the society they lived in. Though there are modern disciples of the lineages of these great sages, who claim that only their version is authentic, that is like missing the wood for the trees.

Our stories have an unbroken and unending tradition with numerous deletions and understandings to them. If you do not care for a particular part, you are free to have your own version. What works for me may not work for you. What works today may not work tomorrow. That is why we do not have one holy book which never changes. We have a whole library of books, and we are free to add more books at any time. In other words, you can create your own way of life and it becomes part of our traditions.

The availability of so many interpretations and versions gives us immense freedom—a freedom that is the hallmark of the Indian civilization. Having narrated the Bhagavad Gita to Arjuna, Lord Krishna says, 'I have given you the most subtle of all wisdom. Now it is for you to reflect on it and accept what you want using your discretion and reject the rest.' This has been the basis of Indian thought for thousands of years. There is no one holy book. Every book is sacred. It is your choice that makes a book holy.

Thus I present here three interpretations of the Bala and Atibala mantras.

The first interpretation is the one that I personally find most attractive.

When Vishwamitra and the princes walk through the jungle without food or water and Rama says he is hungry, Vishwamitra explains that the hunger Rama feels is a function of his body, not his soul. Thus, hunger is impermanent, though illusory and real at the same time.

It is illusory because it is impermanent and real because Rama can feel the hunger in his body. Vishwamitra asks Rama to reflect on this. Vishwamitra explains this principle to Rama to prepare him to make wise choices in life. He teaches Rama to train his spirit to overcome rather than succumb and to do so, an understanding of 'impermanence' is essential.

This was further explained to me by my father when I was a child. Like so many Indians steeped in our country's timeless traditions, he told me that he had heard this interpretation from his father and chose to accept it over the many versions he subsequently heard. He did, of course, add his own perceptions to the acquired tradition. It is not wrong to add new views to age-old thoughts. It is necessary, even mandated by our traditions. Whatever I relate below are my own interpretations and reflections piled upon what my father taught me.

Vishwamitra is talking about hunger here. He says food is necessary for the body. Food nourishes and sustains life. So where does the food come from? It comes from the sun. The sun sustains life on earth. The heat from the sun evaporates the water on earth—this forms rain clouds that release rain and help sustain all life, including plants. Plants give us food, and food sustains life. For food to nurture life, it needs to be burnt in the stomach. This conversion of food to energy (represented as fire), is what sustains life. In Sanskrit, the word for 'metabolism' is 'jadaragni' or 'fire in the stomach'.

As per ancient Indian theory, all living beings are made of five elements, the panchabhootas, a primary classification of the five elements—vayu (air), jala (water), agni (fire), prithvi (earth) and akasha (space)—that make life possible on earth. The body and its processes too are made up of these five elements. Thus, when we say we are made of the panchabhootas, we are saying that we are part of the universe itself. It is eternal and infinite, hence by extension we too are eternal and infinite.

Nothing can be created or destroyed in the universe. Creation or destruction is only the changing of form, not of substance. Life is just another form and manifestation of the universe, a function of Time and form. The following poetic metaphor is often repeated in the

Upanishads: 'Time cooks everyone, and Time changes everything; Infinite Time, Mahakala'.

Hence, as Vishwamitra explains to Rama, understanding the impermanence of all things helps one overcome adverse situations and make wise choices in the present moment.

The second interpretation of the meaning of the Bala and Atibala mantras is found in Tamil folklore, where the bards speak about real issues that concern the common man. Thus, Vishwamitra makes Rama go hungry to make him understand the pangs of hunger.

Vishwamitra asks Rama, 'Are you hungry?'

Rama replies, 'I am.'

Vishwamitra says, 'One day when you are king, will you ask this question to each and every person who is your subject?'

Rama says, 'Yes, I will.'

Vishwamitra asks, 'Will you ask all the cows, buffaloes, ants, birds, worms and all living creatures whether they are hungry?'

Rama says, 'Yes, I will.'

Vishwamitra asks, 'And if you hear even a small voice, an insignificant voice that says, "I am hungry," what will you do?'

Rama replies, 'I will not eat until I satiate their hunger. I will not drink until I quench their thirst.'

Vishwamitra asks with a smile, 'Why?'

Rama replies, 'Because that is the dharma of the king.'

Vishwamitra then says, 'That is the dharma of everyone. If the king follows that dharma, everyone else will follow it too. The thought that no one should go hungry or thirsty is your Bala and Atibala, your strength and supreme strength. Son, now look around and ask the birds, ants, trees, the earth, are they hungry or thirsty?'

The third interpretation is the simplest and the shortest (and is famous in devotional circles as it reflects complete surrender to the divine): Bala and Atibala are mantras that magically quench hunger and thirst.

This is the beauty of the Indian storytelling tradition. It has something for everyone. For those who want to ponder deep existential problems, the first interpretation reflects on the unity of everything, on non-duality, that we, the stars and the universe, are one and the same. It also helps us reflect on our own insignificance in the larger scheme of things and above all on 'impermanence' so that we may learn to overcome and not succumb.

The second interpretation, which stems from Tamil folklore, is rooted in the soil. It is about compassion. This interpretation has reached people through stories, breaking barriers of caste, religion, language and time. You can see the impact of such folk interpretations in your day-to-day life. We may think we have lost touch with ancient wisdom in the rush of modern life, but as Gandhiji once said, 'India lives in its villages.' The majority of Indians do not live in urban centres or the few metro cities. To see this India, one needs to occasionally travel in a second-class unreserved compartment and see perfect strangers sharing a meal. No one eats without asking their neighbour whether they have eaten.

In my childhood, homes in Kerala would practise a beautiful ritual—before closing the compound gate, the lady of the house would ask loudly, 'Is there anyone hungry out there?' Perhaps a beggar would be waiting, or a hungry dog sitting, wagging its tail, or a cow that had ambled by and stopped. The gate would be shut only after ensuring there was no hungry soul left in the vicinity. That no one should go to sleep hungry forms the basis of this ritual of compassion.

If you have grown up in rural India, you will perhaps have seen your mother giving the first fistful of rice to the crows every day.

Rangolis using rice powder are still drawn in the courtyards of rural Indian homes. They serve two purposes—they are an aesthetically pleasing art form at the doorstep, and they keep ants away from the kitchen and pantry house by feeding them in the courtyard. This is pest control with compassion. Now we use chemicals that kill all creatures that come to our homes to satisfy their hunger. Such simple acts of compassion, an all-pervasive kindness, we scarcely notice, yet it is what makes India the country we love. It is what makes us human.

Such tales told by folk artistes and bards, many of whom are illiterate, have shaped the Indian conscience over thousands of years, more than any holy books or scriptures filled with deep philosophical thoughts. So, even as simple a story as this presents us with choices. We can choose the way we want to live.

We can even embrace all three interpretations—the first being that we are all one, as we are all built of the same panchabhootas or five elements and hence should address others' needs as we would our own; the second that Vishwamitra made Rama go hungry to teach him what it means to go hungry so that he ensures nobody goes hungry under his rule; and the third and simplest, which reflects complete surrender to the divine which makes chanting the mantras Bala and Atibala to miraculously quench hunger and thirst.

We can wonder about the intricate web that connects us with everything in the universe, and the impermanence of things. We can also think life itself is magical, which indeed it is, and live accordingly. We can learn to be compassionate to every living thing, and most importantly, to ourselves.

8

Tackling Tadaka:
A Life Lesson for Rama

TADAKA IS HEARTBROKEN WHEN THEY BRING IN THE BODY OF HER SLAIN husband, and she says to her sons Mareecha and Subahu, 'We must take revenge! The fire of revenge is scorching my heart and can only be put out when I have killed Agastya.'

And so Tadaka, Mareecha and Subahu attack Sage Agastya and he angrily curses her, saying, 'Your rage will make you ugly. It will consume you and others. You are cursed to roam this world, devouring others.'

As her rage grows, the Yakshini Tadaka, once famed for her beauty, indeed turns ugly and repulsive. Day by day the death of her beloved husband and the loss of her beauty compounds her bitterness, and soon she begins to harass the hermits in the forest. Powerless against Agastya, she vents her rage by killing others who are helpless. She has a valid reason to feel bitter against Agastya, but she has no reason to be cruel to the weak and vulnerable. Consumed by hate, she eventually becomes a cannibal.

Meanwhile, seeing no end to Tadaka's attacks, Vishwamitra rushes to Ayodhya to seek Dasaratha's help and returns with Rama and

Lakshmana to the forest. When Tadaka next attacks Vishwamitra's ashram, Vishwamitra tells Rama to kill Tadaka. Young Rama now has to resolve the most difficult dilemma he has ever faced—killing a woman. This is a critical turning point in Rama's life as it goes against everything he has learned from his guru, Vasishta. But if he does not end her life, she will kill those he has vowed to protect.

In life, it is easy to choose between right and wrong if we know which is which. Here, Rama confronts a reality that is far from a simple definition of good and evil. Is it right to kill a woman who is attacking sages and their disciples, not because she is evil but because fate has mistreated her and also because she has been cursed? She is a victim, but showing her mercy will result in the deaths of many innocents.

Seeing Rama perplexed, Vishwamitra says, 'You are not responsible for what happened to Tadaka. She may have her reasons for attacking, but those she kills are also not responsible for what happened to her. She has turned her wrath into cruelty against innocents. Perhaps it is for her own good that she be killed. She is leading a miserable life. You will not only be fighting for the people who have sought your protection, but also helping the poor woman herself.' With great reluctance, therefore, Rama fights Tadaka and kills her.

In many south Indian folktales, Tadaka is a beautiful woman who falls in love with Rama. When Rama is asleep, she comes to him, immersed in love. When Vishwamitra sees this, he wakes Rama up and asks him to kill her because she is the same woman who has been harassing the hermits and even devouring a few. So, in the folk version too, Tadaka's is a story of unrequited love. The dilemma over what is right and wrong is a continuous debate in the Ramayana, regardless of which version you are reading.

One of the most challenging decisions we face in life is deciding the right thing to do. The word 'right' is misleading. When you stand facing another, your right is their left. What is right to you might be wrong to another, and vice versa. Rama is confused about his dharma. Killing a woman is adharma. Tadaka has been cursed to devour others. It can be argued that even she is doing her dharma as a cannibal. A more straightforward analogy to sort right from wrong would be that of a forest guard who protects wildlife, but shoots dead a tiger that has turned a man-eater. In normal circumstances, a tiger hunting its prey is considered a natural phenomenon of the forest. The tiger is doing what nature intended it to do. It is merely following its instinct. Once the tiger becomes a man-eater, the guard's duty changes from protecting the tiger to killing it. There could be many reasons why a tiger becomes a man-eater. The tiger may be old or has been injured in a fight with another tiger, but the guard is left with no choice other than to kill it to save other lives. What constitutes dharma changes depending on the circumstances.

Vishwamitra's advice to Rama is similar. The decision on what is right or wrong is based on the good of the maximum number. Rama learns an important lesson here. He has made a choice based on what is suitable for the largest number of people. However, even this choice has consequences. Every karma will bear fruit.

When Rama kills Tadaka, her sons Mareecha and Subahu attack him. Subahu kills many rishis and attacks Rama. Rama kills Subahu in the conflict. Mareecha, though offering help for Subahu, doesn't directly participate in the carnage that his brother unleashed after their mother's death. Rama defeats Mareecha but does not kill him. There is no reason for Rama to kill Mareecha at this time. He could have done so, but he chooses not to because

Mareecha is not a threat to society at the time. Instead, Rama expels Mareecha from the jungle using a blunt arrow that lands the Rakshasa many thousand miles away to the South. Mareecha takes asylum with Ravana in Lanka. These two actions of Rama—that of killing Tadaka, and then sparing Mareecha's life—trigger a chain of events that affect Rama's own life. Karma spares no one, not even an avatar of Lord Vishnu.

9

Rama Redeems Ahalya, and the Mahabharata's Story of Nalayani

As THE TWO YOUNG PRINCES AND SAGE VISHWAMITRA MAKE THEIR WAY through the forest towards Mithila, the kingdom ruled by Janaka, they come across an abandoned hermitage. The Valmiki Ramayana states that Rama finds it pleasing to the eye, and asks Vishwamitra whose it is and why it is in this state. 'It belongs to the great sage Gautama,' replies Vishwamitra, and tells them why it now lies in ruins.

He tells them that Gautama was married to Ahalya, who was young enough to be his granddaughter. Having heard of her ethereal beauty, Indra, the king of Deva Loka, decided to seduce her. He kept an eye on the ashram and came to her when Gautama Maharishi stepped out one day.

Gautama returned just in time to spot Indra scurrying away from the hermitage. Indra was captured by Sage Gautama's disciples. He cursed Indra with festering sores all over his body. Gautama's disciples castrated Indra and stitched the testicles of a goat on his body.

In the Valmiki Ramayana, Ahalya is aware of what is happening and she too falls in love with Indra, if we go by Bala Kanda. In many

later-era Ramayanas and in the Valmiki Ramayana Uttara Kanda, which was written much later as per many scholars—following the change in the position of women and societal mores—Ahalya is portrayed as having been deceived by Indra when he comes to her disguised as her husband and makes love to her.

As per Valmiki's Ramayana, Gautama also curses Ahalya—to become invisible. Only when Rama's footsteps fall on the soil of this forest and purify it, can Ahalya's curse be lifted, he says. In other Ramayanas, she turns into stone. Both are metaphors for Ahalya being socially ostracized.

As he enters Gautama's ashram, Rama sees the huts have crumbled and the forest has encroached on the hermitage. Somewhere, invisible and lost among the vines and creepers is the woman who dared to sin. She lives unseen, shunning the society that shunned her. Rama's footsteps on the ashram's soil lift the curse on Ahalya. Rama reconciles her with her husband, Gautama. She had become stone; his presence melts her. She had become invisible to the world; he brings the world back to her. Rama gives Ahalya her dignity back. Following her redemption, Ahalya bows in gratitude before Rama. He tells her it is his dharma.

Ahalya's action, unlike that of Tadaka discussed in a previous chapter, does not and should not concern society. It is her choice as a woman. If the husband is ready to forget and forgive, as Gautama eventually was, and the woman chooses to return to her husband, it is not for society to pass judgement. This is the argument Rama makes when he redeems Ahalya. It is as if Rama is doing penance for the karma of killing Tadaka, another wronged woman.

Ahalya is one of the panchakanya (five virtuous maidens) in the Puranas; the other four are Sita, Mandodari, Tara and Draupadi.

Four—Ahalya, Sita, Mandodari and Tara—are mentioned in the Ramayana, while Draupadi is mentioned in the Mahabharata. In certain scholarly circles, Sita is placed among the 'panchasati' (five women who immolated themselves) and Kunti of the Mahabharata takes Sita's place among the panchakanyas.

Regardless of which list mentions them, each woman is fiercely independent, never just a mere shadow of her husband. These women are famous for the choices they make, and these choices define them. They are also famed for their wisdom and learning.

Society judges a woman for whom she chooses to love, unable to tolerate her independence of choice. All cultures from time immemorial have been afraid of women's sexual preferences. Later-day attempts by poets to make Ahalya's infidelity appear as the result of deception also underline this fear. Ancient literature abounds with the insecurities of men who have tried to glorify the blind devotion of women to their husbands. Through such stories, they have attempted to control their women.

The Story of Nalayani

The term pativrata or 'one who is devoted to her husband like a slave' came into prominence in medieval literature. The story of Nalayani, which appears in the Mahabharata, is a case in point. Nalayani was married to Sage Maudgalya, who was notorious for his temper tantrums. He was afflicted with leprosy and emitted a foul odour from the sores that festered on his body. Despite this, Nalayani served him with extreme devotion.

One day, when Maudgalya wished to visit a prostitute, he demanded Nalayani's gold ornaments to pay the prostitute. Nalayani handed over all her ornaments. Her husband then asked her to carry him to the prostitute's house. The dutiful Nalayani carried her leper husband in a basket and waited patiently outside the prostitute's house for him to return. By dawn, the prostitute was fed up with the insatiable passion and temper tantrums of her client and threw him out, keeping Nalayani's gold ornaments as a fee for her services.

Nalayani carried her husband home on her head. In a foul mood due to being thrown out by the prostitute, her husband vented his frustration on poor Nalayani. He repeatedly kicked her head and abused her with filthy curses. Nalayani the pativrata, the chaste and devoted, bore everything. She even expressed concern that he would hurt his feet with the continuous kicking. This infuriated her husband further and he started punching her face. Nalayani bore all the abuse without a word of protest and kept walking, carrying her husband on her head. The basket brushed against the legs of Sage Mandavya, impaled on a trident, awaiting death. The local king had caused him to be impaled thus in a moment of anger. When Sage Mandavya witnessed Maudgalya's unbridled behaviour and unabashed passion even in old age, he was enraged and cursed Maudgalya that he would die before sunrise.

Nalayani was shocked that her beloved husband was going to die. She prayed, 'If my devotion to my husband Maudgalya is true, let the sun not rise tomorrow.'

By virtue of her slavish devotion to her husband, the sun did not rise the next day. Nothing, not even the sun, can withstand the power of a devoted wife, says the story. The devas (gods), worried that the world would end, begged Nalayani to take back her prayer. Nalayani pleaded that her husband's life be spared. The devas went to Sage Mandavya and requested him to dispel the curse. On the point of death, he did so, and Nalayani's obnoxious husband was spared.

Impressed by her devotion, Maudgalya asked Nalayani what boon she would like to have. Nalayani asked that his leprosy be cured and that he turn into a handsome man. Maudgalya did this through his powers of penance. Nalayani then demanded that he make love to her in five different ways. Maudgalya obliged. But after a few years, he found his wife's passion overpowering. He tried to dissuade her, but she kept demanding that he make love to her in five different ways. Maudgalya became exhausted and cursed Nalayani to die and be reborn as a woman who would marry five men. Nalayani was thus reborn as Draupadi.

To a society that idealized Nalayani as the model of a devoted wife, Ahalya's independence was horrifying. No wonder she was shunned.

> Many versions of Ahalya's stories can be found right in Vedic literature. In the Satapatha Brahmana, Indra is called Ahalayayara, the abductor of Ahalya. Ahalya, the land that has not touched Hala or plough, and Indra, the god of rains, have an agrarian connection, which could be an allegory. Gautama, the rishi, has let the land go barren. Indra, the rain, takes the land that has been untouched, and wilderness grows in the land until civilization in the form of Rama steps in and the land is rescued. It should also be noted that one of the Vedic names for Indra is Gautama. In the Uttara Kanda of the Ramayana, Brahma created a woman using the best features of all creatures, and since she has no defect (Hala), she was called Ahalya. In the Ramayana, Gautama and Ahalya have a son named Satananda, who is the Rajaguru of Mithila. In the Mahabharata, Gautama and Ahalya have a son named Cirakari and a daughter. Saradvan is also mentioned as Gautama's son. In many Ramayana folk versions, Anjana, Vali and Sugriva are Ahalya's children.
>
> In the Shanti Parva of the Mahabharata, Ahalya's story has a different spin. When Gautama finds out that Ahalya has cheated on him with Indra, he orders his son Cirakari to kill her

and leaves for the forest. Cirakari thinks over his father's order and concludes that his mother is blameless because Indra had approached her in the guise of his father. Meanwhile, Gautama repents his order and returns to find that his son has not carried it out. Gautama praises Cirakari for his wisdom and reunites with Ahalya. There's no need for Rama to give redemption to Ahalya in this story. This contrasts with the story of Parashurama, who cuts off his mother Renuka's head on the orders of his father.

In the Valmiki Ramayana, in Uttara Kanda, it is said that Ahalya is blameless. In contrast, in the Bala Kanda (shloka 48), it is said that Ahalya knew it was Indra in Gautama's form but was carried away by desire. In the Krittivasa Ramayana, Indra doesn't even need disguise to convince Ahalya to sleep with him. In the Kamba Ramayana, Ranaganatha Ramayana and others, Ahalya commits adultery knowingly. However, later Ramayanas showed Ahalya committing the mistake unknowingly. The tale of Indra assuming the cat form first appears in the Kathasaritsagara and then in the Kamba Ramayana and the Padma Purana.

10

Janaka: A Saint among Kings and a King among Saints

WITH TADAKA VANQUISHED AND AHALYA REDEEMED, RAMA AND Lakshmana have performed all the duties for which Vishwamitra had brought them to the forest. The young princes are now more than ready to return home, but Vishwamitra tells them that they must now go to Mithila. Rama and Lakshmana are surprised. Vishwamitra does not tell them why they must go; instead he tells them about the king of Mithila, Janaka.

Janaka is a generic name. All kings of Mithila are called Janaka. Many stories about Janaka are scattered in the Upanishads, the Mahabharata, and various other Puranas. In the Mahabharata, Krishna and various sages narrate the virtues of many Janakas to Yudhishthira. One of the most famous stories is about compassion.

Janaka is once invited by Yama, the God of Death,[16] to his abode, says Vishwamitra. On his visit to Yama's abode, King Janaka passes through the vastness of hell and hears the pitiful cries of many people. They call out to him, 'Oh King, please stay! When you pass, we can feel a cool breeze. It is some consolation in the scorching heat of hell.' His heart is filled with compassion on hearing their cries and he stands facing the fire of hell, shielding the inmates from its heat, getting singed himself. But he does not budge an inch.

Seeing that King Janaka has not yet reached his abode, Yama comes in search of him and finds him standing in front of hellfire, shielding its wretched victims from the heat. 'Virtuous Janaka,' says Yama, 'why do you stand there? It is not fair what you are doing. The people who are suffering are but eating the fruits of their karma. That man you are shielding raped his friend's wife. And this woman killed her stepson. You are interfering with the cycle of karma. There is no undeserving man or woman in this hell. I am Kala, the God of Time, I am also the God of Dharma, and I know what punishment or reward to give. I am the judge, I am the jury, I am Time.'

Janaka says, 'I feel that as king I must stand with my people in their time of suffering. If they have sinned when they were my subjects, then part of their sin is my responsibility because I could not guide them properly. If I am standing here being burned, and my action can give some solace to these people, I do not mind being turned to ash.'

Yama offers him a choice. 'You can give away all your virtues,' he says, 'whatever good deeds you did in your life, to these people. They will then be saved. However, once you do so, it is you and not they who will burn eternally in hellfire.'

King Janaka replies, 'So be it. I take responsibility because I am their king, and if they stray from the correct path and cause injury to others, the primary responsibility is mine. Hence, I choose to be in hell. Please free them. They have suffered enough.'

Pleased, Yama says, 'This was a test for you because I have heard you are famed for your compassion. Now I understand why they call you the Wise Saintly King. You are a true Rajarishi.'

Janaka finds that hell has vanished and he is standing in Yama's abode. He asks Yama, 'I understand that you ensure everyone pays the price for their actions, yet you call me a virtuous king. If I am virtuous, why was I made to go through this test? Why did I have to suffer, even though it was an illusion created by you?'

Yama replies, 'In all your actions as a king, even in this, performed during an illusion, there is still a shadow of evil. No action is all right or wrong. When you punish a culprit as king, you act for the good of the maximum number of people, but when that culprit is killed for his own misdeeds, others suffer because of your judgement. His family suffers, his sons suffer. Similarly, for all actions, even this test in which you gave away all your virtues to save these people, there was an element of evil. As a father you left yourself no virtue, so the lives of your wife and children would have become difficult. To save these sinners, you denied that which your next generation deserved. Similarly, even in the most evil deed, there is some element of good. It is this that runs the cycle of dharma. Every action bears its own fruit, and every fruit has its own taste.' Saying this, Yama sends Janaka back to Mithila.

Janaka thus gains enlightenment from this encounter as he henceforth rules his kingdom without getting attached to any of his actions, says Vishwamitra. Soon Janaka becomes famous as Stithapranja.

In the Bhagavad Gita, Lord Krishna tells Arjuna the same thing, that all actions bear fruit. We must eat that fruit one day or another. The only difference is that if you act in a detached manner, the taste of the fruit will not affect you. Thus, Janaka rules as a nishkama yogi, who does his duty without worrying about the results. There are numerous arguments for and against this, but that is a subject for another discussion. Janaka rules his kingdom in the way the God of Time has instructed him to do. Drawn by his fame, a yogi comes to the palace to meet this saint among kings. He finds Janaka seated on a throne just like any other king.

The yogi thought that being a saint, Janaka would not live in luxury but in poverty and would have withdrawn to a life of solitude, living perhaps in a remote cave. Instead, Janaka is holding court, giving orders and handing out judgments. Whatever Janaka did before his enlightenment the yogi feels he has continued with it post enlightenment too. He can't fathom why the Maharishis call Janaka an enlightened king.

Meanwhile, Janaka, seated on his throne, has spotted the yogi and orders his guards: 'Arrest that yogi. I am going to behead him tomorrow.' The soldiers catch hold of the startled yogi and drag him to the dungeon. The yogi is terrified; he knows not what crime he has committed. That night, Janaka sends a delicious feast to the yogi, with 108 varieties of sweets, rice with ghee, and many exotic delicacies that only kings can dream of. The yogi, terrified that he is to be executed the next morning, does not touch a morsel. The following day, soldiers drag the yogi to the gallows.

King Janaka asks him, 'Yogi, how was the food?'

'I am going to die, why should I worry about food? I did not even taste it,' the yogi cries.

Janaka laughs. 'Who isn't going to die? Life is a game from which no one gets out alive, yet we all live as if we will live for eternity. The difference between you and me is that I know this truth. I can die at any moment. There is no guarantee of the future, yet I act by living completely in the moment. I do not worry about my past; I don't think about my future. I choose to live and act in the moment without worrying about the consequences. Yogi, I spare your life. I threatened to take it away so that you would understand how difficult it is to enjoy even a small luxury like food when you are sure you will die the next day. I want you to reflect on the fact that why the next day, one can die the next moment. Yet a wise man will *live* the moment. The only truth is now. The past is fiction, the future a dream. The truth is now.' So saying, King Janaka sends the yogi away with gifts.

Thus, says Vishwamitra to the two princes, the yogi finally understands that King Janaka is genuinely an enlightened king.

The Janaka of the Ramayana is also known as 'Ksheeradhwaja'. Janaka was so named because one day, while ploughing a field as part of a ritual he found a baby girl in a furrow. He named the foundling 'Sita' (furrow), adopted her and brought her up as his own daughter. Hence Sita, being the daughter of Janaka, is called Janaki. And since she belonged to the kingdom of Videha, she is also called Vaidehi.

Various other Ramayanas have different stories about Sita's origin.[17] Many early folk and south Indian Ramayanas, as well as the Jain Ramayana, talk of Sita being the daughter of Ravana and his wife Mandodari. In some versions, Mandodari is not the mother. In a Kannada folktale, Sita is born out of Ravana's nose. One common element in most of these stories is that astrologers state that Sita will be the cause of Ravana's death. So Ravana's Asura ministers take baby Sita and throw her into the sea. The current carries her to the shores of Mithila. There Janaka finds her, nestled in the sand.[18]

I too, have used the south Indian folk version in my first book *Asura*, where Sita is born as Ravana's daughter.[19] Sita being Ravana's daughter may be disputable or even unpalatable to many who hail from northern India, where such an idea is sacrilegious. The Valmiki Ramayana is silent on Sita's origins. However, south Indian and east Asian folk traditions assert that Sita is Ravana's daughter. I was fortunate to witness a traditional, nearly 400-year-old opera from the Philippines, performed during the 2019 Ramayana Week celebrations in Mumbai. I was surprised to discover that this tale has long been prevalent in the Philippines.

Returning to our story, when Vishwamitra and the two princes arrive in Mithila, they learn that a swayamvara is being conducted to find a husband for Sita. In ancient India, princesses had the freedom to choose their husbands and usually did so at a gathering of suitors; the event was called a swayamvara. Often, this included contests between prospective grooms such as archery using heavy stringed bows, shooting at challenging targets, or even duelling matches.

The contrast between Janaka and Dasaratha is evident when we look at their families. King Janaka never yearned for sons, unlike Dasaratha who was willing to give away his firstborn, a daughter, for the sake of a son. True to his enlightened nature, King Janaka makes no differentiation between a son and a daughter, nor is he anguished over whether he has any progeny at all. In many Ramayanas, Sita is Janaka's only daughter, a foundling, and not his biological child. But he never thinks to run around conducting rituals and sacrifices to have male progeny. Sita is enough for him.

He brings her up as other kings do their sons.

So Sita, by the time she is of marriageable age, is as accomplished as Rama. She is a great archer, a warrior, and has knowledge of the Vedas and scriptures, music and drawing, and she is also a fine equestrienne. She is, in fact, one of the most accomplished women of that era.

Some Ramayanas say Urmila is also Janaka's daughter, while others claim that Urmila, Mandavi and Sruthakeerthi are the daughters of Janaka's brother, Kushadhwaja. Of all the female characters in our Puranas, Sita is the strongest of all. If we take Sita as one of the panchakanyas, she stands taller than the others, Mandodari, Tara, Ahalya and Draupadi. If we consider her to be one of the panchasatis, as some scholars do, Sita appears more virtuous than the rest. Sita's life is defined by the great choices she makes. One can even say that Sita's choices drive the story of the Ramayana. She enters Rama's life and changes it forever.

11

Sita's Swayamvara

ONE OF THE MOST REPEATED EPISODES IN THE INDIAN ORAL STORY-telling tradition is that of Sita's swayamvara. Ironically, in the Valmiki Ramayana, Rama and Lakshmana do not attend the swayamvara.

King Janaka declares that Sita would take the man who can lift the divine bow of Shiva and string it as her husband. None of the kings and princes attending the swayamvara are able to do so. Enraged, the royal suitors attack Janaka, who uses the power of his penance to manifest an army and defeat them. The defeated and disgruntled kings claim that Janaka has placed an impossible condition for marrying his daughter as no one can lift the bow. In some versions, since it is Shiva's bow, it is the Shivaganas or bodyguards of Lord Shiva who defeat those who attack Janaka, a great devotee of Shiva.

By the time Vishwamitra reaches Mithila with Rama and Lakshmana, almost a year (a long time in the Southern Recension) has passed since the swayamvara and Janaka is a worried man. No one has been able to lift the 'Shaivachapa', the bow of Shiva.

> The Narasimha Purana, Bhagavata Purana, Adhyatma Ramayana, Kamba Ramayana, Dvipada Ramayana, Maithili Kaylana, Surasagara, Ramakerthi, and other texts mention the swayamvara more or less as it is popularly known today. In these works, it is a ceremony attended by many kings who fail to lift the bow, and finally Rama is able to string it and break the Shaivachapa. In earlier works like the Mahaviracharita and Satyapakhyana, instead of Ravana, an envoy reaches with a marriage proposal for Sita on his behalf. In the Devi Bhagawatha Purana, the envoy named Suskala reaches the court of Janaka exactly at the moment Rama breaks the bow. But in later-day Ramayanas, Ravana himself is present in the swayamvara. The first work that mentions Ravana's presence during Sita's swayamvara is the play Bala Ramayana by Rajashekhara. In this, Ravana, out of respect for Shiva, refuses to string the bow. In south Indian folk versions, Ravana knows Sita is his daughter and comes to watch who is marrying her. Hence, he refuses to string the bow. In the Padma Purana, not just Ravana but Banasura also arrives at the swayamvara and is unable to string the bow. Ravana vows to kidnap Sita one day and leaves. Many later-day works have made this story more and more colourful.

How Janaka came to place such a condition is also a fascinating story. It is said that as children Sita and her sister Urmila were one day playing with a ball made of cloth and string that rolled under a divine bow Janaka had received from Lord Shiva himself. The bow required the combined efforts of hundreds of soldiers to lift, but six-year-old Sita lifted the bow with one hand and retrieved the ball. Seeing this, the astonished king realized that Sita was no ordinary child. He decided that only a man who could lift the bow and string it would marry her.

These versions of the story also consider Sita an avatar of Lakshmi and Shakti as she combines the powers of both. These are the Shakteya versions of the Ramayana, where Sita, a great devotee of Mother Parvati, is said to possess her power. In later-day versions such as the Tulsidas Ramayana, and many other folk Ramayanas, the swayamvara (which lasted almost a year in the earlier versions) is compressed into a one-day event to which all the kings are invited, and even Ravana comes to take part. In some versions Ravana comes to lift the bow at the swayamvara, and everyone thinks that the man who once raised Mount Kailasa will surely lift the bow too. However, when he lifts it up, it falls upon him. When the kind Sita rushes to save him, Ravana is enraged and insulted at being saved by a woman.

In folk versions of the Ramayana where Ravana is Sita's father, he comes to the swayamvara to see who his daughter will marry and is not pleased when Rama succeeds in lifting the bow. In other versions, Ravana does not know that Sita is his daughter, and comes intending to marry her. Lord Shiva prevents this incestuous mishap by pressing his toe on the bow Shaivachapa, crushing Ravana under it. In many folk versions, where Ravana is an ardent devotee of Shiva, the Great God repeatedly tries to save him from committing such mistakes.

In the Valmiki Ramayana, however, Ravana does not see Sita until he comes to kidnap her. Indeed, it has no mention of Ravana coming to the swayamvara. However, later poets added it in for dramatic effect and to add to the plot of the story.

In both the Tulsidas and Kamba Ramayanas, Rama and Sita fall in love before the swayamvara occurs. Sita sees Rama and Lakshmana from the palace balcony following Vishwamitra into the city and is enchanted by the dark, handsome Rama. There are versions, including the Tulsidas Ramayana, where they accidentally meet in the palace garden when Rama is picking flowers for his morning puja and Sita is on her way to pray at the Parvati temple.

These are all later-day additions to give a romantic angle to Rama and Sita's love story, and it is such diversions that make reading different Ramayanas a fascinating experience. However, an essential aspect in all these versions is the emphasis on Sita's freedom to choose her husband. Sita's character comes alive as a strong and fascinating character not just in the Ramayana but perhaps the entire Hindu Puranic world because of the vital choices she makes. The Ramayana can, in fact, be told as a story of Sita's choices. As we progress, we will see that at every critical point in the story, it is Sita's decision that moves the plot forward.

When the two princes and Sage Vishwamitra reach Mithila, neither Rama nor Lakshmana knows that Vishwamitra has brought them to Mithila to forge an alliance between Ayodhya and Mithila. Vishwamitra does succeed in this, though not without a glitch or two.

To begin with, Rama easily lifts the bow but when he tries to string the Shaivachapa, Shiva's bow breaks in two. As per Janaka's condition, the suitor must not only lift the bow but must also string it. Technically, Rama has failed to string the bow as it has broken in two, so some of Janaka's ministers argue that Rama has not fulfilled the condition. Janaka turns to Sita and asks whether she wishes to marry Rama. Hence the choice to accept Rama or not falls upon Sita. Brought up to think and act independently, Sita takes her stand—she decides to marry Rama.

King Janaka then sends a messenger to inform King Dasaratha of their children's impending nuptials. The messenger reaches

Ayodhya in three days, also carrying proposals of marriage between Dasaratha's other three sons with the other princesses of Mithila. Dasaratha gladly agrees and thus Bharata marries Mandavi, Lakshmana marries Urmila, and Shatrughna marries Sruthakeerthi—forging a deep and strong alliance between Ayodhya and Mithila.

After all the ceremonies are done, the four grooms, their brides and the rest of the marriage party set off for Ayodhya with much fanfare. En route, they get a rude surprise when they are stopped by an angry Parasurama (the fifth avatar of Vishnu and a great devotee of Shiva). As Rama has broken Lord Shiva's bow, Parasurama challenges Rama to battle.[20]

Parasurama, whose name means 'Rama with an axe', is a very strange avatar. He does not have any one enemy, unlike the other avatars of Vishnu. All the other avatars take birth to vanquish a particular enemy such as Hiranyaksha, Hiranyakashyapu, Ravana, Kumbhakarna, Kamsa and Sishupala. There are specific enemies for each avatar. Parasurama alone, among all the avatars of Vishnu, is driven by anger and an equally powerful sense of duty. When his father Jamadhagni commands his sons to kill their mother Renuka because she disobeyed him, Parasurama's brothers refuse but Parasurama chops off his mother's head with an axe. Jamadhagni is pleased and offers Parasurama a boon. Parasurama asks that his mother be restored to life. Having given his word, Jamadhagni cannot refuse and restores Renuka to life.

Parasurama also considers the entire Kshatriya (the ruling) class an enemy and kills them indiscriminately, eventually dispatching twenty-one generations because he thinks they are perpetuating violence. He chops off the 998 hands of Karthiveerarjuna, a powerful Yaksha king, who defeated and imprisoned Ravana. Though famed for his valour, Parasurama is notorious for his rage.

> Though Rama and Sita are considered an ideal couple, many in rural India refuse to bless a bride and groom to live as Rama and Sita. This is because their life as a couple was full of trials and tribulations. The Krittivasa Ramayana offers an interesting explanation for this. The purpose of the Rama avatar was to establish maryada and to teach people about dharma through his life. In this grand play, it was essential that Rama and Sita be separated. But their astronomical charts matched so perfectly that there was no possibility of them ever being separated. Also, Rama and Sita are very much in love. They are divine beings in human form, as Vishnu and Lakshmi respectively. Seeing their love, the gods become worried and wonder what would happen if Vishnu forgets about his leela and refuses to be separated from Sita. If they lived happily ever after in marital bliss, there would not have been the kidnapping of Sita, the killing of Ravana and other events. In other words, there would not have been any Ramayana. So the devas grow apprehensive and they decide that Rama should marry Sita in an inauspicious moment. To delay the marriage, Chandra Deva, the moon god, comes as a danseuse to dance. Enchanted by this beautiful woman's dance, everyone forgets the muhurta, the auspicious time for the marriage. Thus, the events of Rama's life are set to unfold as per the script of Vishnu's leela.

From Parasurama to Lord Rama is a progression in how the avatars have been conceived. Consider all the Dasavatara, the ten divine incarnations of Lord Vishnu, and you will find—from Matsya to Koorma, from Varaha to Narasimha, from Vamana to Parasurama, from Rama to Sri Krishna—a step-by-step progression in the levels of consciousness.

Parasurama's father asks him to kill his mother, and he does. Rama also does what his father asks, but he uses his discerning mind. Rama is an ideal man in the Ramayana, who follows all of society's rules and does what his father demands. Once we reach the Krishna avatar, we find a playful and independent-minded man, immersed in life but not affected by it. Rama is considered the purna (complete) avatar, while Krishna is regarded as the paripurna (perfect) avatar. Thus the meeting of Rama and Parasurama is a point of transition.

Having confronted the joyous marriage party returning to Ayodhya with a demand to know why Rama has broken Shiva's bow, Parasurama refuses to be appeased when Rama apologizes. Handing Rama Vishnu's bow, which he carries, Parasurama says that if Rama is good enough, he will be able to string it. Rama strings Vishnu's bow with ease. Parasurama understands that Rama is an avatar of Lord Vishnu and peace is restored.

This incident is like the transition of powers from one avatar to the next. Why does the transition happen at this point and not before? It is because the Rama avatar attains meaning only after Rama's union with Sita. Rama and Sita's marriage is considered the union of prakriti (nature) and purusha (universal consciousness).

> Rama's monogamy is one of his most praised qualities, particularly his devotion towards Sita. The Eka Patni Vruta, the complete devotion to one wife, is repeatedly stressed in many Ramayanas. However, like any aspect of the Ramayana, this too has exceptions in various versions. In the Bhusundi Ramayana, Rama has two chief queens and thousands of wives. Bhusundi, the crow saint in the Ramayana, has the boon to be

present during every Ramayana and can travel across time and universes. Bhusundi says that countless Ramayanas have happened, are happening and will happen in various times and universes, and all are different and the same at the same time. So there could be apabhramshas or minor deviations in each of these Ramayanas.

In the Khotani Ramayana, which evolved in the Middle Asia region (now in China), Sita marries Rama and Lakshmana. The Ramayana has been written as per the social and cultural norms of the society that writes it. When this Ramayana came to its final form in central Asia by the middle of the eleventh century, Buddhism was the most popular religion, and its influence can be seen in these Ramayanas. These variations can shock readers who are used to the devotional Ramayana that evolved in medieval India, but these too are part of the Ramayana tradition. The Khotani Ramayana is so removed from other Ramayanas that Indians are usually familiar with it.

In this Ramayana, Dasaratha steals Parasurama's father's cow. Parasurama does twelve years of tapasya, obtains a boon, and exacts revenge by killing Dasaratha. Dasaratha's queen hides Rama and Lakshmana in a cave. As they grow old, they seek out Parasurama to avenge their father's death. Meanwhile, a daughter is born to Ravana, but she is abandoned because of her astrological predictions. She is brought up by a saint in a jungle. Rama and Lakshmana meet Sita and both fall in love with her. They come face to face with Parasurama, and Rama kills him. Meanwhile, Ravana sees Sita, doesn't recognize her as his daughter, and kidnaps her after fighting and killing an eagle trying to protect Sita. Rama and Lakshmana go in search of Sita and reach the kingdom of monkeys, which is ruled by

> the evil Sugriva, a friend of Ravana's. Sugriva has an identical twin brother, Nanda, who is very powerful. Rama becomes friends with Nanda and promises to kill Sugriva. During a duel between the twins, Rama is unable to recognize who is who. Nanda ties a mirror to his tail, and in the next duel Rama is able to kill Sugriva. With the help of the monkeys led by Nanda, Rama then challenges Ravana. By this time, Rama has become a Buddhist, as he meets a monk who converts him to the path of ahimsa. In the war, with the help of Nanda, Rama defeats Ravana, but forgives him when Ravana promises to become a Buddhist monk. Rama and Lakshmana marry Sita, return to their kingdom, and rule for a hundred years. Here, there is no Hanuman; instead, a new character, Nanda, is introduced who embodies all the qualities of Bali, Sugriva and Hanuman of the conventional Ramayana. The Buddhist values of ahimsa and compassion are stressed as the story progresses, and everyone, including Ravana, reforms and takes refuge in the Buddha.

As the story progresses, we find that only when Sita is with Rama, is he happy. When she is not with him, Rama is always in misery. It is only in the balance of prakriti and purusha that the bliss of life can be experienced. With Sita, Rama is now complete. They arrive in Ayodhya and after a few months, Dasaratha decides it is time for him to retire from worldly duties and take sanyasa (lead the life of an ascetic).

Sankhya philosophy is based on this concept.

Let us delve a little into the basics of the Sankhya philosophy. Purusha or universal consciousness is considered infinite. It neither has a beginning nor an end. Indian thought considers the entire universe to be nothing but a spandana or vibration of universal consciousness. We see or feel the manifestation of this eternal vibration, the sound represented by pranava or Om.

How does this consciousness or energy manifest? It does so in physical form through prakriti. It is only through prakriti that we can understand there is infinite consciousness. What we see or feel are mediums that keep this consciousness hidden. But without prakriti, we would not be able to feel or understand the existence of this consciousness. Prakriti or nature provides us with the tools to see, feel, hear, taste and understand. Prakriti is the foundation of 'vikaram' or emotions. Interestingly, emotions are considered feminine in gender.

In the Upanishads, this is explained through a metaphor: imagine a lake reflecting the sun. When the water is turbid, you see the sun as turbid. If the water is clear, you see the sun as clear and bright. If a breeze is creating ripples on the lake, you feel the sun is moving. However, it is just a reflection. The sun is real, the reflection is unreal. But we are seeing the movement of the sun through the water—the water is prakriti.

Another metaphor used is that of crystal. A pure crystal appears coloured if an object is brought near it. It reflects the colour of the object. The crystal seems disfigured if a disfigured thing is brought near. Similarly, we find the various abrasions around us through this object's medium, which is prakriti. Purusha is consciousness, prakriti is that through which we know purusha. This is the simplest definition.

Shankaracharya summarizes Advaita philosophy in one shloka that begins with the words: Brahmasatyam (Brahma is consciousness) Jagatmithya (the world is an illusion). This is a famous shloka but its second part is not often mentioned. It goes like this: Jivobrahmam Naparah. It means that life, Brahma, consciousness, God, Time, whatever you call it, are not different. The shloka '*Brahmasatyam jagatmithya jivobrahmam naparah*' thus implies that the entire universe is filled with universal consciousness.

In modern scientific language, it means that the entire universe is nothing but information (Brahma) stored in matter (prakriti). We can know Brahma hidden in the universe through the manifestation of prakriti or matter. That is why Shankaracharya says that only Brahma is truth, consciousness is truth, and the world is an illusion. The world, which keeps changing, is illusory, hiding the truth of consciousness inside it. Hence, in the shloka, they are *Jivobrahmam naparah*, not separate.

This has parallels in fundamental physics. Matter can neither be created nor destroyed; it only changes form. But the very changing nature of matter or prakriti makes it illusionary. As we know, everything is a function of space and time. Time is infinite. Humans have divided time for measurement, but time is neither measurable nor does it have a beginning or end. In simple terms, it is Brahma. This forms the basics of Sankhya philosophy from which Advaita is derived.

The other famous Advaita mantra—*Aham Brahmasmi* (I am Consciousness) talks about the same thing: I am the universe. What is stored in me as information is part of what is stored in the entire universe. Every atom is nothing but a reflection of the universe. It also says 'thatwamasi' (you too are that), meaning there is no difference between you or me or anything in the world, animate or inanimate. We are different manifestations of the supreme consciousness.

Imagine an infinite lake with a full moon in the sky. The full moon is supreme consciousness; the moonlight is all-pervading. The ripples of moonlight are life forms. Life is as transient as the ripples that come and go. Life is an illusion because it is a mere reflection. It is real for that moment when it appears and becomes unreal when it disappears. This is a simple explanation of Sankhya philosophy. There is a counter-argument to it which I will come to later as the story progresses.

Coming back to Rama and Sita, Rama is purusha or consciousness. But purusha without prakriti is indecipherable, hence Rama can be reached only through Sita. Rama is considered the manifestation of supreme consciousness, but he is complete only when Sita is with him. So, the entire Ramayana can be explained as Rama's (man's) search for meaning in life when Sita is taken away by Ravana. Without Sita, Rama has no meaning. It is in the union of prakriti and purusha that completion happens. Sita is the path that takes us to Rama.

Gandhiji was once asked, 'Who is your Rama? What proof do you have that Rama lived and ruled over Ayodhya?' He replied, 'Rama is the name of the light inside my consciousness. It is what is lighting my mind. It can be called Allah, it can be called Jesus, it can be called Shunya, it can be called anything. Names don't matter. It is the light inside my mind.'

'But how do you see the light inside your mind?' asked the critic.

Gandhiji replied, 'By uttering the name of Sita.'

That is the reason Rama's name is always taken with Sita's name first. Traditional people never speak Rama's name alone. It is always Sita-Rama, Siya-Rama, Janaki-Rama, because Rama has meaning only with Sita; otherwise, Rama is an entity that cannot be known. And what cannot be known is meaningless.

'Look within' is also the message of Buddha, Shankara and countless Indian saints and philosophers. The emphasis instead is on knowing something that is already within you. When Buddha was asked what enlightenment was, he answered simply, 'It is nothing but knowing oneself.' To know oneself, one need not look outside; one must look within. That is why Gandhiji also answered, 'Rama is the light inside my consciousness'.

A similar concept can be seen in the union of Shiva and Parvati. In Shaivite belief, the Uma-Maheshwara concept is about 'ardhanareshwara', half man-half woman. It talks of the feminine aspect of a man and the masculine aspect of a woman and the equality of both—one completes the other. A Hindu marriage is incomplete without songs praising the union of either Sita-Rama or Uma-Maheshwara. They are considered the perfect male-female relationships, based on equality, one completing the other, a union of prakriti and purusha.

An advantage to understanding the Sankhya concept, which leads to Advaita, is the mental peace it brings. Advaita teaches humility and knowledge (realizing our insignificance) as well as the divinity of our existence. We are as insignificant as a particle of dust in this vast, expansive universe. 'Anantham, ajnyatham, avarnaniyam' is how the universe is described—infinite, indecipherable, indescribable. On a new moon night, go into the countryside. Look up at the night sky and the millions of stars. You are looking deep into time, deep into space.

What you are seeing as stars may not exist at all because they are many light years away and the light reaching you now started millions of years ago. That star may have died, but you see it, so for you it exists. Is that not illusion, maya? You see what does not exist, what has already died. You also see empty spaces, but a star may already have been born there. Its light has yet to reach you. But how can you conceive it? You think there is nothing there, only empty space. You cannot see anything, whereas there is a star perhaps in the empty space you are staring at, the light of which may reach earth after thousands of years.

So, what you see is not present there, and what is present there, that you cannot see. Is this not what is meant by 'jagatmithya'? You see through the manifestation of prakriti. You are made of atoms, of star particles that have come together in a particular form to give you the senses through which you understand whether there is a star or not. This happens because you have consciousness, you are aware, and that is the function of purusha. That is why Brahma is satyam (truth), but prakriti or jagat is mithya (false). And so we arrive at the second stanza of Adi Shankara's *Jeevobrahma naparah* (no separation).

You understand that there is no difference between you and the sky or any other particle in the universe. Everything is made of particles and matter and matter does not undergo death or birth as it can neither be created nor destroyed. It keeps changing form, just like the ripples on a moonlit lake. Life keeps happening, transient and illusionary, and it keeps happening again and again.

You need not grasp this concept intellectually. If you grasp it through your feelings, through your emotions, using prakriti, that is enough. Once you grasp this, you understand how insignificant you are. And once you know that, all the problems and worries that assail you in daily life begin to look insignificant, even laughable. How does it matter whether you did not get that promotion you thought you deserved? How does it matter whether you got fewer marks in your exam? In this vast, infinite world, these are minor pursuits.

A star-studded sky fills us with awe. Even though our life is short and transient, even though we are so insignificant, the very fact that we can conceive this makes us unique. Once we understand there is no difference between us and the universe, a sense of immortality comes to us. There is no end, there is no beginning, we are just ripples and must make the best of our short lives. This is how we can make practical use of Sankhya and Advaita in life.

In the Hindu way of life, there are four purusharthas or stages of life. The first is Brahmacharya, and it is not, as many people think, just about abstinence from sex. It is about knowing oneself. Education in the Indian system is not learning about worldly things.

Hindu philosophy is about knowing oneself. There is no seeking, only understanding and discovering. So education in the Brahmacharya stage is about knowing oneself with the help of a guru. 'Teacher' or the term 'master' is not a correct translation of the word guru; I am using it for ease of comprehension.

Once you discover yourself, you find the essence of your purusha. Then you have a choice. You can become a typical householder. Your guru will have made you understand your inherent passion, swabhava (nature), gunas (strengths) and weaknesses. You choose your profession based on your gunas and swabhava. You might discover you are a warrior and join the army, or that you are an artist, and pursue that field. If you find your taste is in the building business, you should follow that.

In the brahmacharya phase, you also get to know your dharma—not as a religion but the dharma that is your own, personal ethical, moral code. It is not about society's ethical or moral principles. Your dharma could be influenced by it, but your dharma is your own. 'Moral' or 'ethical' codes are poor translations of the word dharma, which is not translatable. But once you know yourself, you know what your dharma is.

Based on your dharma and discovery of yourself and your nature or prakriti, you start earning your livelihood and enter the grihastha or householder phase of life. In this phase, you seek artha (meaning in life and wealth in life. Only wealth acquired in a meaningful way is consonant with dharma) and kama (livelihood must be earned with kama. Unlike popular perception, kama is not merely sexual passion but any kind of passion, like for the arts, adventure, sport, and so on). Through kama based on dharma, you acquire artha or wealth. This is the time when you marry, have kids and raise them, do your duty as a householder, and as a husband or wife. You look after your parents and become a contributing member of society.

After this is the stage of sanyasa. You have reached the stage of self-actualization. You have achieved *many* things in life. No one can ever acquire *all* things or even sufficient things, but somewhere during the journey, we find that enough is enough; we have done enough, and it is time to live for ourselves. When we start doing this, our circle expands from our family's small unit to encompass all of society. So, in the sanyasa stage, you begin living for the community, becoming slowly detached from your kama or passion. You do what you do for the well-being of all. This is when you devote yourself to charitable works, go on pilgrimages, find time to connect with nature, and pursue minor passions. You volunteer in the community and do things that are beyond making money and acquiring material things. In sanyasa, you guide youngsters regarding their dharma, artha and kama. You become a guru to the younger generation, a milestone showing direction.

After a few years of this comes the fourth stage, vanaprastha or forest existence. It does not mean you must go and live in a jungle, only that you stop being a burden to society. You withdraw into yourself to think because your capacity for action is waning. You were once sturdy, but time has caused you to become frail. You know the time has come to give way. The time is approaching when you will decompose into the soil or turn to ash in the fire. You will dissolve into nature, only to return again and again in an unending cycle of life.

You start thinking about moksha. Unlike what many people believe, it is not about going to heaven or some heavenly place, to Vaikunta or Kailasa. Of course, you can think about whatever brings you contentment. There is no dogma attached. But moksha as such is about knowing oneself and understanding the nature of the world. It is living every moment with gratefulness, with a childlike sense of wonder. It ensures that you do not become a burden on anyone and find peace with whatever you have done in your life. I have heard old people in my village murmuring the word 'swasthi' when they reach this life stage. Swasthi means peace. Peace to you, peace to the world. It also means forgiveness. We forgive others, and we forgive ourselves, for we finally understand at this stage of life that there is no time to harbour petty grievances. We are grateful for every breath we take. We are thankful for every sunrise and sunset and everything in between.

It can be debated if this is the right way to live. This is, however, the way traditional Hindus have conceived of life for thousands of years. There are other schools of thought in Hinduism, which reject these purusharthas. The Charvakas say that everything is for kama, '*kamarthamitham jeevitham*' (life is about fulfilling passions). There is no yesterday, no tomorrow. Eat, live and enjoy. Live life as if you are going to die the next moment. Nothing is immoral, nothing is adharma. There is no dharma, no karma, no afterlife. There is only one life, and this is it. There is only this moment. There is no caste, no religion, no bias based on gender, wealth, the circumstances of birth or race. Everything is for enjoyment.

This philosophy is also called Asura Marga. You live every moment drunk on the nectar of life. If all of society thought in this way, civilization would collapse. But if all of society lived following the purusharthas, that too would be dull. We need followers of the Charvaka school to make this world interesting. No path is invalid once you find what works for you. As mentioned before, the various Hindu schools of thought can fill a library. You can choose the book you wish to read. And if you do not like any of those in the library, you are free to write your own and follow it.

Thus, Dasaratha thinks of sanyasa after completing his duties. He has been a great king and has raised four illustrious sons. Sanyasa begins when your children are married. Until then, it is your duty to look after them and live for the family. But once your children are married, the entire world becomes your family, and you start living for the world. And so Dasaratha declares Rama will be the next king of Ayodhya. This triggers a new chain of events, as we will see.

12

Manthara's Machinations and Rama's Exile

THE DAY DASARATHA DECIDES TO CROWN RAMA AND RETIRE FROM HIS kingly duties, two of his sons, Bharata and Shatrughna, are away from Ayodhya, having walked to Kaikeya, the land of Kaikeyi's birth. The decision comes as a bolt from the blue, even for Rama. One can assume that Dasaratha will not have planned a coronation when two of his sons are absent, unless there is some compelling reason.

The ceremony is set for the very next day. Once the announcement is made, Ayodhya erupts in celebrations. Rama is immensely popular with the public and is known for his compassion and calm demeanour. The people look forward to an era of peace and prosperity.

But one person in Ayodhya is petrified that Rama is to be king. Her name is Manthara. She is described as a hunchback who came to Ayodhya with Queen Kaikeyi as her maid. It is she who has brought up a motherless Kaikeyi like her own daughter. There is a story behind this: while strolling in the garden with his wife, Kaikeyi's father hears two birds talking. Having the ability to understand the language of birds, he laughs aloud when he hears their chatter. One of the birds warns the king, 'Don't tell the world what I have been telling my mate. If you do, your head will blast into pieces'.

He nods and carries on walking. His wife, walking beside him, is curious and wants to know what the bird has told him. Though she insists, he refuses saying that if he tells her he will die. However, she insists on knowing what the bird said that made him laugh and says she will not be able to sleep without knowing. Annoyed by her insistence, Kaikeyi's father abandons his wife for life. As a result, Kaikeyi and her brother Yuddhajit are brought up in their father's palace by Manthara, and when Kaikeyi marries Dasaratha, Manthara follows her to Ayodhya.

Now hearing of Rama's impending coronation, Manthara is worried. She thinks, 'My Kaikeyi is the favourite queen now, but the moment Rama becomes king, she will become a junior queen, and Kausalya will become the Queen Mother.' Manthara has held a grudge against Rama from the time he, as a boy of six, shot a blunt-tipped arrow at her hunchback as a prank. Though he apologized, all those around him laughed loudly and Manthara felt insulted. Being a servitor to the temperamental Kaikeyi is an insecure life and her ugly appearance added to her sense of inferiority and bitterness. She always suspects people make fun of her, whereas in reality no one bothers about her one way or another.

Often in our own lives, we worry about what other people think of us. But the truth is that most people have no time to think anything about us. They have better things to do than worrying about what we are doing.

Manthara tells Kaikeyi, 'The king has decided to make Rama the next king.' Kaikeyi is happy. From childhood, Rama has been very close to her. She loves Rama as she does her own son, Bharata. There is no discrimination between the princes, and Rama refers to her as 'mother'. But when Manthara begins to feed her insecurities to Kaikeyi, she grows fearful.

Fear makes us do things we usually would not. It is a primaeval emotion that makes us susceptible to manipulation. Creating fear is an age-old technique of politicians, religious indoctrinators and fake gurus. Even mothers use the fear of ghouls and ghosts to make children eat, behave or sleep.

Manthara fuels this primaeval fire of fear in Kaikeyi. Manthara talks of the bleak future Kaikeyi will face once she loses her position of power and influence. She is able to eventually convince Kaikeyi to ask for the two boons Dasaratha had promised her so long ago. His impulsive promise comes back to haunt Dasaratha.

As a prelude to extracting her boons, Kaikeyi retires to the 'kopavana', a part of the palace where anyone angry can vent their anger. Kopavana means 'forest of anger'. Many ancient palaces had such a place so that queens could convey their displeasure to their husbands, who might be otherwise preoccupied.

Dasaratha reaches the 'forest of anger' to pacify his favourite queen and Kaikeyi asks him for the two boons he'd promised her long ago. For the first boon, Kaikeyi asks that her son Bharata be made king of Ayodhya. This devastates Dasaratha, who protests saying, 'That is not just, for Rama is the eldest.'

Kaikeyi replies, 'He is eldest by a few hours, and you gave me any boon. Now keep your promise. You are the scion of Ikshvaku, of the famed Raghuvamsha. You cannot go back on your promise.'

She traps Dasaratha in his own ego about his lineage and clan. For her second boon, Kaikeyi asks Dasaratha to exile Rama to the forest for fourteen years, to ensure he will not be a challenge to her son Bharata. Kaikeyi fears that Rama's popularity will cause dissent among the people, who will rise to overturn her son. So Kaikeyi wishes to ensure Rama is not around.

Why fourteen years is a puzzle that has given rise to much speculation. It could be that Kaikeyi thinks that in fourteen years people will have forgotten Rama. Public memory is notoriously short. By then, Bharata will have had enough time to prove himself. Also, Kaikeyi does not hate Rama, nor does she wish him bodily harm. If she had, she could have easily asked Dasaratha to behead Rama.

One folk version talks about Kaikeyi asking for Rama's exile because it will help him fulfil his life's mission. Rama, sitting in Ayodhya, cannot achieve his mission of killing Ravana and Kumbhakarna. He must go out to the forest where the Asuras dwell.

The original purpose of the Ramayana is to play the game of life, where Jaya and Vijaya take birth as Ravana and Kumbhakarna, and Vishnu comes as Rama to kill them. Kaikeyi is the tool destiny uses. Folk artistes raise Kaikeyi to heroic proportions for this act, because she takes the blame for expelling Rama, knowing she will be reviled for generations as the manipulative stepmother.

In the Valmiki Ramayana, when the news reaches Rama, his initial reaction is one of shock. Kaikeyi, the mother he has loved more than his own, has betrayed him. Rama does not take it stoically. He feels anguished, but calms down after some time. In other Ramayanas, however, he accepts the decision stoically, thus representing the moral values of society. As the son of his father, he is obliged to follow his father's orders. If he refuses to do so, he will be breaking societal mores and setting a bad example. So, on the eve of his coronation, he accepts his father's diktat and agrees to go into exile in the forest.

Dasaratha is devastated by the turn of events and falls ill. He is afraid that the curse of Sravana Kumara's parents is about to come true. Bharata and Shatrughna are absent from Ayodhya, and now Dasaratha hears the news that Lakshmana has decided to accompany Rama into exile. Lakshmana says he is Rama's shadow. Where Rama goes, the shadow must follow. He will go as Rama's brother, his servant, his friend. While Dasaratha is still reeling from this second blow, there comes another—Sita's choice. She decides to accompany her husband into exile.

Rama, who has not objected to Lakshmana accompanying him, objects to Sita's decision. He says, 'Mother Kaikeyi only wants Rama to go away from Ayodhya, not Sita. For fourteen years, I will be wandering in the forest, which is full of danger. I order you to stay in Ayodhya, Sita.' But Sita refuses to obey. A blindly obedient and devoted wife would have followed her husband's command. But Sita is not the demure wife that medieval literature has made her out to be. She cuts down every objection Rama raises. The argument goes on till finally, Sita puts forward a clincher. She says, 'In all the Ramayanas that have happened before, Sita has always accompanied Rama. So why are you not allowing me to come with you in this Ramayana?'

This is one of the most critical aspects of the Ramayana and represents the Hindu world-view. This dialogue is repeated in all the Ramayanas. It tells of the continuity of the Ramayana tradition. Even the so-called Adi Ramayana is not the first Ramayana, but just one among countless Ramayanas happening again and again. With this argument, Rama agrees to let Sita accompany him. The stage is set.

The Ikshvaku prince is to go into exile for fourteen years. Sita removes all her ornaments and Rama his princely garments and ornaments. They don deerskin and the simple clothing of hermits.

Lakshmana's wife, Urmila, stays on in Ayodhya. Unlike her sister, the free-spirited Sita, she does not insist on accompanying Lakshmana. She fits the description of the ever-obedient wife who does not question her husband. She is not the fiery, independent-minded Sita, who does not baulk at making her own choices. In folk versions, and even in the Tulsidas Ramayana, Urmila asks one boon from the Goddess of Sleep, Nidra Devi, that she remain asleep for fourteen years so that her husband can remain awake and serve his brother and sister-in-law.

These are all beautiful metaphors and not to be taken literally. Sleep is a metaphor for death too. Without her husband, she is as good as dead, she believes. Lakshmana goes away leaving Urmila behind so that he can serve his brother and sister-in-law.

> Kaikeyi's early life is told in the Southern Recension of the Valmiki Ramayana. In this, Kaikeyi's father abandoned her mother, and Kaikeyi was raised by Manthara. Kaikeyi's father, Aswapathi, had the ability to understand the language of birds. Once, while strolling with his wife, he overheard a conversation between two sparrows in which the male sparrow, trying to woo the female, said he had defeated Garuda in a fight. Aswapathi laughed at this empty boast, and the male sparrow cursed him, saying he would die if he revealed the bird conversation to any human. Aswapathi's wife wanted to know why he laughed. But Aswapathi refused to divulge the reason, leading to a huge argument between them. Aswapathi gets rid of his wife. Since his children were still young, his ministers advise him to marry again. But Aswapathi hadn't abandoned his wife for another woman. Instead, he asked his guards to find the ugliest-looking woman who could be a servant maid and foster mother to his daughter Kaikeyi. Thus, Manthara was found, and became both mother and maid to Kaikeyi. That is why she had so much influence over the queen.

Before Rama leaves, one of Dasaratha's ministers, Jabali, confronts Rama and asks, 'Why are you leaving Ayodhya? When your father gave these boons to your stepmother, he did not use his discretion. It is his mistake; you are not responsible for it.' Now Jabali is an interesting character in the Ramayana. He is a materialist and realist. He subscribes to the Lokayatha school of thought. Lokayatha means 'popular amongst people'. It is also known as Charvaka Siddhantha. The Charvaka Sidhantha or Lokayatha philosophy is pure materialism. In modern parlance, one may call it atheism. In simple words, it can be explained thus: There is no tomorrow, there is no yesterday, there is only today. There is no heaven, there is no hell, there is no sin, no virtue, and no soul. The entire world is made of matter. There is no Brahmman. Jagathsathyam, the world is true. Brahmman is mithya. Brahmman or super consciousness is an illusion. The only thing real is the world and today. Yesterday and tomorrow are illusions. All relationships are illusional.

A follower of the Charvaka philosophy, he tries to convince Rama that there is no compulsion to follow this order of his father. 'You are Rama by chance,' he says. 'You were born into the Ikshvaku family by pure chance, yet you speak of family tradition. It is just a matter of chance that all of us are here. Dasaratha is your father by chance. You could have been born in some other clan, race, country, or time. What is there to be proud or ashamed of regarding the things we are not responsible for? So why are you worried about some promise your father made?'

Jabali tells Rama he is lucky to be born a prince and is fortunate because his father declared him the next king. 'But now he has taken back his word to you and the public, so that he can keep the word he once gave his wife. Is that fair?' asks Jabali.

'He is placing his own ego above the public good,' he says. 'What sort of king does that? Is it not your duty to rebel against such adharma? Forget adharma, what about your self-interest? In your own interest, you should seize the throne and rule the kingdom. If your intention is to do good for the people, this is your chance to do so. If your purpose is to enjoy royal life, this is your chance to do so.'

Rama is angered by these words.

In a later addition to the Valmiki Ramayana—for anachronistically, there is a reference to Lord Buddha—Rama says to Jabali, 'Buddhists like you are misleading the world. If people follow people like you, there will not be any ethics or morality in the world, and no maryada. The world will be ruled by the law of the jungle. People like you should be eliminated.'

Seeing that he has angered the crown prince, Jabali withdraws from his position. Jabali acts according to his philosophical beliefs and choices, where there are no rigid positions. If arguing with Rama can result in injury to himself, he will retreat and shift his stand.

'I was just testing you,' he says, 'but perhaps, one day you will know that what I say is true. The people of Ayodhya want you to be king. It is your dharma to follow the will of the people. But you are choosing your father's will against that of the people. Perhaps a time will come when you will eat the fruit of this action when you have to bow down to the will of the people against your personal dharma. Your personal dharma is to obey your father; your raja dharma is to obey the will of the people. Now you are choosing your personal dharma over your raja dharma.'

Rama retorts, 'I am not the king, just a prince, so I do not have a raja dharma. I am merely the son of my father, hence I follow the dharma of a son.' And so saying, Rama prepares to leave Ayodhya.

When Rama, Lakshmana and Sita finally leave, the entire population of Ayodhya follows them with tears in their eyes. Even Kaikeyi is shocked to see what unfolds. But the die has been cast and nothing can be changed. The royal trio reach the banks of the Ganga after crossing the Sarayu, Vedasruti, Gomati and Syandika rivers. Waiting to help them cross the river is Rama's friend Guha, the boatman. A beautiful verse describes what the boatman feels: 'Rama, you are the boat that ferries us across the ocean of misery that the world is. Yet now you are coming into my boat, and I am helping you to cross this river. That is the irony of life.'

Before they cross, Rama turns to the multitudes waiting on the banks and says, 'Men and women of Ayodhya, please go back. I will return after fourteen years.'

In folk versions, Rama forgets to mention the transgenders, so when Rama returns from exile, he finds them still living on the banks of the Sarayu, where they saw him off to exile. When he asks them why they are living outside the city, they say, 'You said "men and women", but you, whom we consider our God, failed to mention us. We are perhaps the unfortunate people whom even God forgets.' Moved by their words, Rama apologizes to them saying, 'You will always have a special place in my heart and in society. Your blessing will be equal to my blessing.' That is why we often see transgenders come to bless a newborn child or on auspicious occasions. People believe that the blessing of transgenders is indeed the blessing of Rama himself. This is how folk tradition has woven marginalized people into the social fabric, compelling those who would otherwise have shunned them to show them respect.

Rama, Lakshmana and Sita enter the forest and from here begins a new epoch in Rama's life. A great misfortune strikes the land they have left behind.

The Jabali incident is only available in the Southern Recension of the Ramayana. In my childhood, I often heard the temple storytellers emphasize this incident. In this version, Rama calls Buddha a thief and an atheist. This is definitely anachronistic, as Buddha is a historical figure who lived many centuries after the Ramayana period. Many incidents in the Ramayana have been added by people to further their propaganda and agendas, possibly using Rama as a tool to propagate their criticisms against their opponents. The entire episode of Jabali reads as a criticism against atheism, Buddhism and materialism. Just like how the Buddhist Ramayanas used plots like Rama becoming a Buddhist, other Ramayanas used plots to mount criticism against Buddhism.

13

Dasaratha's Deathbed

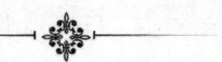

Having collapsed at the sight of Rama, Lakshmana and Sita leaving, and haunted by the injustice he has done his son, King Dasaratha lies on his deathbed lamenting that fate is punishing him cruelly. 'What wrong have I done in my life to deserve this?' he asks, holding the hands of his wife Kausalya.

Then it all comes back to him—

The Curse

'What wrong have I done to you to deserve this?' the teenage boy asks, bleeding from the arrow Dasaratha has shot.

Though this event took place long ago, when Dasaratha was just a prince, even then he had no answer. He'd heard a deer drinking at the river's edge and shot an arrow in the direction of the sound. It was not a deer but this teenager, filling his pot of water. Dasaratha had committed a terrible crime, prompted by pride in his own hunting skills. He had been trained as a great warrior and had learned the trick of aiming and shooting by ear. Even in pitch dark, he had the incredible skill of hitting his target, identifying it just by sound. Pride had resulted in this tragedy.

'Forgive me,' Dasaratha says in a trembling voice.

Sravana Kumara, the wounded boy, whispers, 'I understand it was a mistake. I forgive you.'

Dasaratha is moved by the boy's nobility. People do not forget even minor insults and carry the burden of bitterness in their minds for long periods. But here is a boy, barely into his teens, forgiving his killer with no sense of resentment.

'How can I make amends?' Dasaratha asks the dying boy.

'My blind parents are waiting for me,' he replies. 'I came to fetch water to quench their thirst.' Sravana Kumara dies with these words on his lips, his head in Dasaratha's lap.

Dasaratha sits immobile, too numb to think, too weak to act. The guilt of his mistake crushes him. As the boy's body goes still, he remembers the boy's blind parents are still waiting for water. With a heavy heart, Dasaratha picks up the fallen pot and drags himself to the river. He fills the pot, wishing some other hunter would make the same mistake he has. He does not know how to face the parents of the boy he has killed.

Then he climbs the hill carrying the pot of water and sees the blind couple sitting under a tree, waiting for their son to come. He thinks of running away. But he has given his word to the dying boy. Dasaratha must give the blind parents water and tell them what he has done.

As Dasaratha approaches, their faces light up. 'Where had you been, my son? Your mother is thirsty,' says the old man from between parched lips.

'Let your father drink first,' insists the blind woman in a hoarse voice.

Dasaratha controls his tears and pours water into the mother's cupped palms. A tear falls from his eye onto her wrinkled wrist.

'Son, why are you crying? What has happened?' The mother grabs Dasaratha's arm before he can withdraw. Her gnarled fingers fumble on his gem-encrusted bracelets. She draws back, saying, 'You are not my son. Who are you, kind stranger?'

'Oh, we have a guest,' the blind man cries. 'He must be a friend of Sravana. Do you have anything to give him?' he whispers in his wife's ear.

She is silent for a moment, then fumbles in the folds of her sari and brings forth two small mangoes. 'We have only this, my son. Share it with Sravana,' she says, smiling.

Dasaratha, the scion of the Ikshvaku dynasty, the Crown Prince of Ayodhya, takes the mangoes with shivering hands.

The old man says with a rueful smile, 'Taste them son, they are delightful.'

Perhaps the mangoes were their meal, thinks Dasaratha, yet they are sharing them with their son's killer.

The old woman asks, 'Where is Sravana?'

Dasaratha falls on his knees and hugs the mother's feet, crying, 'I ... I killed your son.'

The old woman chuckles as if he is joking. 'Sravana...' she calls, looking around with her blind eyes. 'Stop playing tricks on your old parents.'

Dasaratha chokes on his tears.

But the old man gives a gasp. He has understood the truth. He prises away Dasaratha's hands from his wife's feet, holds her close and whispers something into her ear. Dasaratha stands up, the momentary silence weighing him down. The anguished cry of the mother will haunt him forever. He stands with his head bowed before the blind couple.

'You have killed our only son!' the mother weeps. 'We have no one left in the world.'

The father curses Dasaratha saying, 'May your end be as miserable as ours. May you die when none of your sons are with you.'

The woman puts a hand over her husband's mouth and says, 'He too is someone's son. Do not curse him.'

Suddenly, the old man falls backwards, like a tree whose roots have been hacked. A heart-wrenching cry comes from his wife and Dasaratha rushes to the fallen man crying, 'Forgive my mistake!'

But the old woman holds him back with a trembling hand. 'Go away, son, and leave me to my grief before I utter a curse,' she says. 'Let me not die with a curse on my lips. Let me die in peace with the memories of my beloved son and husband.'

Dasaratha stands in silence as if turned to stone.

After some time, the woman wipes her tears and says, 'I do not know who you are and why you killed my Sravana, but whoever you are, forgive my husband for the curse he uttered. May you have sons like Sravana, beautiful and loving, who will spread light in the world. That is all this poor woman can do for you. Take this as my blessing.'

Dasaratha, the richest prince in Bharata Varsha, the scion of Ikshvaku, the future king of Ayodhya, stands before the grieving mother, feeling as low as a worm. Her blessing is more scathing than her husband's curse. And as he stands watching, the woman falls upon her husband's bosom and breathes her last—

Now, as he lies dying, Dasaratha holds Kausalya's hand and weeps. 'I am eating the bitter fruits of my karma,' he cries. 'I know why I am dying without my Rama beside me. I have four illustrious sons as the woman said, but I am alone when my end approaches. The old man's curse has come true.'

Dasaratha's words fade away as he slips into unconsciousness. Kausalya stands by his bedside, watching her husband. Then another woman walks into the chamber and stands beside her. Kausalya looks up and with a shudder, looks down again.

The woman says, 'Mother, go and rest. I will stay with my father.'

Shanta, Rama's elder sister and Dasaratha's firstborn, the girl child he gave away to have a son, has come to be at her father's side in his time of need.

When Kausalya goes away weeping, leaving the daughter they never wanted alone with her father, Shanta says to an unconscious Dasaratha, 'Your illustrious son will make you proud, father. Now let me hold your hand. Is that not why God made daughters?'

> In Buddhist and Jain Ramayanas, Rama voluntarily leaves for the forest like the Buddha or Mahavira. In the Pauma Chariyam, Rama feels he is not needed in Ayodhya but among the people to spread Dharma, so he leaves the palace by himself. In the Tibetan Ramayana, Rama hears about his father's predicament in choosing an heir. He quietly walks away, detached from worldly pleasures, in search of enlightenment. In the Indonesian Ramayana, Bharata is crowned while Rama is marrying Sita in a swayamvar. So Rama, Sita and Lakshmana never return to Ayodhya and leave for the forest. In the Sinhalese Ramayana, Rama has Shanidasa, an inauspicious time caused by Shani, and he decides to stay away from Ayodhya for seven years, which gets extended by another seven years due to the kidnapping of Sita by Ravana.

14

Tales of Brotherly Ties in the Ramayana

Rama, Lakshmana and Sita travel further. They cross the rivers Vedasruti, Gomati and Syandika and reach the banks of the Ganga. Sumantra, the loyal minister of Dasaratha, follows them until this point. The place where Rama, Lakshmana and Sita meet Guha on the banks of the Ganga is called Srivengapura. Beyond it lies a deep forest. As Rama bids everyone goodbye, the sun has set. The royal chariot that has brought them to the riverbank will also return to the palace tomorrow at dawn. With it will depart the last of the royal comforts and luxuries that Rama, Lakshmana and Sita will experience for fourteen years.

In folk versions of the Ramayana, since a multitude of Ayodhya's citizenry has come to see their beloved princes and princess off, Rama chooses to cross the river at night while they are all asleep. The people awaken the next morning and see the chariot in the distance returning to the city. Thinking that Rama has changed his mind, they joyfully follow it back to Ayodhya.

Guha, the one who takes Rama across the Ganga, is the Nishada King of the Rivers and Rama considers him an equal.[21] Guha is both Rama and Dasaratha's friend. In the Valmiki Ramayana, he brings many delicacies for Rama and orders his people to serve him the food. But Rama refuses everything and says he is a hermit now and has forsaken all luxuries. He does not eat cooked food as hermits eat only what can be derived from nature, just as they dress not in spun cloth but deerskin.

In the medieval Bhakti-era Ramayanas, the relationship between Guha and Rama undergoes a change. Instead of the proud Nishada king of the Valmiki Ramayana, Guha is a poor boatman and a great devotee who says to Rama, 'I only have a boat and nothing else. I am afraid that if I take you into this boat, it will change into something else, and I will be deprived of my livelihood.' He is referring to Rama's action of saving Ahalya. Rama laughs and hugs Guha.

This reflects societal changes. The medieval Bhakti poets wished to stress that Rama considered a low-caste Nishada his equal and was prepared to hug him. The proud Nishada king of Valmiki's Ramayana, with hundreds of servants ready to serve Rama, is replaced in the medieval era by a poor boatman.

The Bhakti tradition also has a fascinating conversation between Rama and Guha. When Guha ferries Rama, Lakshmana and Sita across the Ganga, Sita gives Guha a gold ring as the ferry fare. He refuses it saying, 'I do not take fees from my equals. A barber does not take fees from another barber for doing his duty. I will not take any money from Lord Rama as we are in the same profession.'

Sita is surprised. 'How can the Prince of Ayodhya and a boatman have the same profession?' she asks.

Guha replies, 'Rama is the boat that ferries people across this illusion of life and takes them to liberation. He is a boatman like me. We do the same job. So I cannot accept a fee from him.'

After crossing the Ganga, Rama visits Valmiki's ashram in Chitrakoot. Lakshmana, who is always vigilant about protecting his brother and sister-in-law, alerts Rama that a large army is arriving from Ayodhya. Lakshmana is livid. He implores Rama, 'Allow me to fight this battle! Bharata is coming from Ayodhya to finish us off! I can see the imperial flag of Ayodhya. Not satisfied with exiling you, Bharata wants to kill you! I will finish him now.'

Rama pacifies Lakshmana with the words, 'Brother, we should not do anything in haste. I do not think Bharata would do anything to harm me. Let us have patience.'

The moment Bharata sees Rama, he runs to his brother and falls at his feet. He begs for forgiveness for what his mother has done. Rama says he has no grudge against Mother Kaikeyi. Bharata conveys the heartbreaking news of Dasaratha's death. Rama is devastated.

Bharata says to Rama, 'I am so angry with my mother. I never wanted the kingdom. It is yours. I had gone with Shatrughna to visit my maternal relations. Without asking me, my mother created all this misery and trouble. I have brought Manthara with me, the maid who influenced my mother. Punish her, Rama.'

Shoving a trembling Manthara forward, Bharata cries, 'This is the evil woman who has created so much mischief and is responsible for our father's death.'

Rama lifts Manthara up and hugs her. 'Manthara too is like a mother to me,' he says. 'This poor woman has never been loved by anyone in her life. The only person who has ever shown her some kindness is Mother Kaikeyi, so when she thought Mother Kaikeyi's interests were being harmed, she acted. Her fear and love made her do what she did. I have nothing against her. In some other life she must have done something to warrant her actions, and I to warrant my suffering.'

Rama makes an interesting point. He alludes to what he has done in one of his previous avatars and the price he is paying for it now. This is repeated in the Mahabharata in a series of verses called the 'Ramopkhyana', in the Vanaparva section.

In one of the wars between the Devas and the Asuras, the Asuras are protected by Sage Bhrigu's wife, Kavyamatha. Due to her extreme piety and devotion, the Devas are unable to harm the Asuras. To win the war, Lord Vishnu deceives Kavyamatha. He appears to her in the form of her husband and beheads her. Kavyamatha's son Shukra is the guru of the Asuras. For the crime of beheading a pious and devoted woman who was only doing her duty, Shukra curses Lord Vishnu saying, 'You will suffer in the avatar of Rama. You will wander in the forests. Your wife will be abducted by a Rakshasa. You will pay for your karma.'

Rama thus alludes to the fact that the fruits of his past karma have ripened now. Manthara's action also yields the fruit of her karma. She is later born as 'trivakra' or a woman with three deformities in Mathura and is cured when she meets Krishna. The cycle of karma rolls on without pause.

After he is told of his father's death, Rama conducts the funeral rites as the eldest son but refuses to return to Ayodhya despite Bharata's pleading. When Bharata finally understands that Rama will not relent, he asks for Rama's padukas (wooden slippers), saying, 'The kingdom does not belong to me. I got it through the manipulation of my mother. I will not sit on the throne of Ayodhya. Until you come, your padukas will remain on the throne, and I will rule on your behalf.'

Even this noble declaration does not move Rama, who says, 'That is your choice, my brother. The kingdom has been given to you by

our father. Maybe our mother's words influenced him, but it was our father's decision. What you do with what you have is your choice. I will not return till my fourteen years of exile are over.'

A heartbroken Bharata takes Rama's padukas and leaves with his entourage. Rama, Lakshmana and Sita continue their journey. They travel to the hermitages of various saints and meet sages like Atri and his wife Anasuya. Sita is given guidance by Anasuya, one of the most revered women-saints of ancient India. Some folk versions tell of Sita meeting Rama's elder sister Shanta, now the wife of Sage Rishyashringa, who coaches Sita on how a hermit's wife should live.

But even while travelling to various hermitages and living like hermits, Rama does not forget his duty as king. He protects various ashrams from the attack of Rakshasas and Asuras. This contrasts with how another king, who became a hermit, acts. Vishwamitra is now a hermit, but was once a great king. He uses Rama, the Prince of Ayodhya, to eliminate his enemies when his ashram is attacked by the Asuras. He does not take up arms himself as he believes it is not his dharma to do so. It is a king's duty, and he is no longer a king.

Vishwamitra has chosen to be a sanyasi and live as a hermit. Rama's choice has been forced upon him. Ayodhya has never left Rama even though he has left Ayodhya. Rama is not a hermit who has left everything behind. If he were, there would be no Ramayana. Why would a hermit carry a bow and quiver full of arrows into the forest? A hermit carries a kamandalu or some holy water, or a prayer mat. Even though Rama and Lakshmana have discarded all the trappings of royalty, they still carry weapons because Rama has been sent into exile; this hermit life is not of their choosing.

Along the way, they meet an eagle or vulture (depending on the Ramayana version) called Jatayu—a giant bird who is King Dasaratha's friend. In many versions of the Ramayana, Dasaratha summons Jatayu to fight beside him when he is battling the hordes of

Shambrasura. Jatayu is one of the twin giant birds of the Ramayana, the other being his brother, Sampati.

> In the Valmiki Ramayana, Kaikeyi is clearly portrayed as wicked and cunning. Rama is apprehensive of her intentions and wonders whether his father would be safe in the palace with Kaikeyi dwelling there. Sita also criticizes Kaikeyi in harsh terms. However, once Rama settles in the forest, he absolves Kaikeyi of her crimes. Sage Bhardwaja says Rama's exile will prove to be beneficial to all, and one should thank Kaikeyi's karma for it. In Chitrakoot, Rama openly takes Kaikeyi's side against Bharata.
>
> In Bhavabhuti's *Mahaviracharita*, Surpanakha disguises herself as Kaikeyi and gives a forged letter to Dasaratha demanding Rama's exile. Kaikeyi is not even aware of this forgery. In the Bala Ramayana, this plot becomes more fantastic—Surpanakha, Mayamaya and a female servant take the forms of Dasaratha, Kaikeyi and Manthara to deceive Rama into exile. In this version, not just Kaikeyi, but even Manthara is blameless.
>
> In the Mahabharata's *Ramopakhyana*, Manthara is a Gandharva named Dundhubhi sent by the Devas to trigger Rama's exile so that Ravana can be killed. In the Torave Ramayana, Manthara is Vishnu Maya, whose purpose is to cause the exile as part of the grand plan. Tulsidas says Ma Saraswati was sent to delude Manthara to trigger the events. In the next birth, Manthara is born as Putana according to some versions of the Ananda Ramayana, which also states that Manthara was born as Kubja in Kansa's palace.

There is a fascinating tale about Jatayu and Sampati competing to see who can fly higher. As they soar into the sky, Jatayu, the younger, is very competitive and also envious of his brother's superior strength and tries to out-fly him. Sampati, however, soars higher and higher. Jatayu tries hard but cannot overtake his brother. In frustration, he starts pecking and mauling his brother. Still Sampati does not let Jatayu fly above him. As they soar even higher, Sampati's wings catch fire and he plummets down. Jatayu finally understands that Sampati was not competing with him but protecting him from the sun's blazing rays by spreading his vast wings above his younger brother.

Caught up in competing, Jatayu failed to see the kindness being shown by his elder brother. He dives down and finds Sampati has lost both his wings. He is heartbroken, but Sampati says, 'If I do not do this much, how can I call myself your elder brother?'

This story of compassion and brotherly love forms one of the critical cornerstones of the Ramayana. Often, we are angry at our well-wishers, unable to fathom their actions. We misunderstand kindness and compassion. The discipline our elders impose is often seen as unkind acts by the young. Sometimes it is too late by the time we understand the real intentions of those who love us. The tale of Jatayu and Sampati is a reminder that one should never jump to conclusions. It is a beautiful story about brotherly love. The Ramayana is often said to be the tale of brothers.

Folk songs often say that love flows like a river, from a higher plane to a lower level. It never flows upstream. Love flows in the same way from parent to child, from elder sibling to younger, says folk wisdom. Though this may not always be true, such ancient songs also tell of the elders' timeless grouse about the ungrateful young. I have heard folk artistes emphasize the selfless love of elder brothers for ungrateful younger brothers, an idea that connects with rural audiences, where obedience to elders is the only accepted behaviour.

Even when acting in a seemingly unsympathetic manner towards their juniors, the family elders are working for their good. Such tales help joint families live together harmoniously.

The relationship between Rama and Lakshmana emphasizes brotherly love. Lakshmana is wholly devoted to his brother. The interesting sibling relationship between Bharata and Rama is based on Bharata's staunch principles. He does not want anything he does not deserve. He does not wish for a kingdom that has been given to him through palace intrigue. He refuses to sit on the throne he thinks is not his. Bharata is a mirror image of Rama. Shatrughna, the youngest, is devoted to Bharata as Lakshmana is to Rama.

The Ramayana is also the story of other sets of brothers with an entirely different sibling relationship. We will soon reach Kishkindha, the city where the Vanara brothers Bali and Sugriva dwell, and to the far south in Lanka, we will come to Ravana, Kumbhakarna, Vibhishana and Kubera. Ravana rules Lanka, but how has he got to the throne of Lanka? By seizing it from his stepbrother Vaisravana Kubera. Kubera, a rich merchant, was the king. It is he who originally owned the Pushpaka Vimana, the flying machine that Ravana forcefully seized. In the case of Bali and Sugriva, and Kubera and Ravana, the lust for power drove one brother to seize the throne from the other. Rama's relationship with his siblings, on the contrary, is projected as the ideal one.

Ravana's relationship with his siblings is closer to reality. Having got the throne and exiled Kubera for good, he sees no threat from his other brothers Kumbhakarna and Vibhishana and has loving ties with them until Vibhishana betrays him (becoming one of the causes of Ravana's defeat and death at the hands of Rama). This family's politics are pretty much like that of any ordinary family, though on a far grander scale. Ravana's relationship with his kin represents how people actually live, straying from the ideal.

Valmiki uses Ravana, Bali and Sampati to show how things happen in the world, while Rama represents the ideal. He uses Rama and his siblings to demonstrate what the ideal sibling relationship should be. Ravana is not evil per se, he is like any of us. Rama is the model, the perfect brother. Yet this ideal relationship too faces its challenges as the story reaches its climax. We will discuss that in a later chapter.

After meeting Sage Agastya, Rama sets up his own ashram at Panchvati, near modern-day Nashik. Along the way, he kills many Asuras and Rakshasas who threaten the peace of the jungle. Rama tries to bring the 'maryada' (the moral order) of Ayodhya to a place where there are no rules, where might is right. This sets off a chain of events in which contradicting ways of life clash. Which way of life is evil and which is virtuous depends on how you view it.

15

Surpanakha, Who Triggers the Final Battle

Surpanakha was known as Lalita and Meenakshi because of her fish-shaped eyes but came to be called Surpanakha because of her nails, shaped like the talons of an eagle. She has three brothers—Ravana, Kumbhakarna and Vibhishana. When she falls in love with a Rakshasa called Vidyutjihva or 'lightning-tongued'—who often appears in folk-tales as a man with a giant tongue, which he uses to swallow entire cities—her brothers bless their marriage.

Vidyutjihva initially supports his brother-in-law Ravana in his conquests, but later grows jealous of him. In many versions of the Ramayana, Vidyutjihva uses his gift of the gab to arouse the common Asuras against Ravana. Perhaps he earned the name 'lightning-tongued' for his exceptional oratorical skills. Ravana eventually kills Vidyutjihva when he becomes a threat to his own power.

In an old Malayalam folk-tale, Vidyutjihva swallows Ravana using his long tongue, and his wife tears open her husband's belly with her talons to save her brother. This earns her the name

Surpanakha, for the sharp nails with which she killed her husband. But in most versions of the Ramayana, Ravana kills Vidyutjihva for eyeing his empire.

After dispatching her husband, Ravana pacifies his sister by promising her that she can choose any man she wants and her powerful brother will ensure she gets him. He also promises her that her infant son, Jambukumara, will succeed him instead of his own son Indrajit (as he gains victory or 'jit' over Indra, king of Deva Loka), who is also known as Meghanatha (lord of the clouds) and Meghanad (the roar or the thunder of the clouds). However, when Indrajit and Jambukumara grow up, Ravana forgets his promise and discriminates against Jambukumara. He refuses to teach Jambukumara any skills and treats him no better than a servant.

Surpanakha is enraged that Ravana has gone back on his word and fears for her son's life. She decides to move away from Lanka for the sake of her son's future and takes refuge in the Dandakaranya forest. There she encourages her son to do penance. Ravana and Kumbhakarna both received their special powers this way, and she sees no reason their nephew cannot do the same. She tells Jambukumara, 'Son, many years ago, your uncle Ravana did penance before Brahma. When Brahma did not appear, your uncle started cutting off his own heads one by one. When he was about to cut off his last remaining head, Brahma appeared and prevented him from committing suicide. Brahma asked Ravana what boon he wanted and Ravana asked for immortality.'

'But did my uncle get the boon of immortality, mother?' Jambukumara asks.

'Brahma never gives anyone immortality. Long long ago, my son, the great Asura twins, Hiranyaksha and Hiranyakashyapu, also prayed for immortality. But all they got was the option to choose the way they would not die. Hiranyakashyapu asked not to be killed by any man, animal, Yaksha, Deva, Kinnara, Gandharva or woman, during day or night, inside or outside. He thought he had covered everything and for all practical purposes he would be immortal. However, Vishnu encountered him as Narasimha, half-man half-lion, and killed Hiranyakashyapu on the palace threshold—neither inside nor outside. Narasimha placed Hiranyakashyapu on his lap, thus fulfilling another condition, that he could not be killed on earth, in the sky or in water. Narasimha killed Hiranyakashyapu at dusk, thus fulfilling the last requirement, not to be killed during the day or night.'

She told him the story of another Asura, Mahishasura, who asked for the boon that he could not be killed by any man, Yaksha, Kinnara, Gandharva, or any other species. 'But, my son', she said, 'he forgot to mention "woman" in this list. So, Parvati or Shakti appeared as Durga and killed him, thus fulfilling all his conditions. Your uncle Ravana was also given the choice to define all the ways he should not die. He told Brahma that he must not die of old age or disease, at the hands of any god, Yaksha, Kinnara, Gandharva, Rakshasa, Asura or animal.'

'But he forgot Humans!' cries Jambukumara.

'Yes, he thinks Humans are too insignificant,' replies Surpanakha. 'So, my son, when Brahma appears and you ask for immortality, be careful what you ask for. Do not leave a loophole the cunning Vishnu can exploit. Be careful of the tricks the Devas play. Your uncle Kumbhakarna was tricked by them. When he was offered a boon, he decided he would ask for Indrathva (to attain, to be, to live like Indra). But the gods played mischief and Indra, king of Deva Loka, took the form of a fly and entered Kumbhakarna's mouth when he was about to ask for the boon. Kumbhakarna blabbered that he wanted Nidrathva instead of Indrathva. Nidrathva means a permanent condition of sleep. Realizing the mistake, Ravana pleaded with Brahma to change the boon. Brahma partially modified the boon. That is why your uncle sleeps for six months and is awake for the next six months every year. Under no circumstances can Kumbhakarna be woken from his sleep.'

'These Devas are full of trickery and deceit!' says Jambukumara angrily.

'Yes, they are,' agrees Surpanakha. 'As deceitful as Asuras like your uncle Ravana. There is no point bemoaning how evil the world is. It is for us to play our game smartly. Ask for two boons instead of one. Pray for a man who will help you kill your uncle, and for me and you to be the cause of your uncle's death. For the second boon, ask for unconditional immortality without any loopholes.'

Jambukumara starts an intense period of penance on his mother's advice. He prays for a man who will help him and his mother kill his uncle. Due to the scorching heat of his penance, the forest around him dries up. Famine affects all forest dwellers, animals and birds start dying of hunger and thirst. Rama, Lakshmana and Sita find it difficult to feed themselves.

In a folk song, Indra is afraid Jambukumara will receive a boon from Brahma and take his position as Lord of the Devas. He lures Lakshmana into killing Jambukumara. Indra, in the form of a leopard, attacks Sita and Lakshmana gives chase. The beast hides in the bushes where Jambukumara is doing penance. Lakshmana spots the leopard and swings his sword at it. Indra vanishes and Lakshmana's sword accidentally chops off Jambukumara's head. The boy dies with the prayer that he and his mother will cause his uncle's death. In a Malayalam folktale, Lakshmana knows it is Surpanakha's son, yet he kills Jambukumara because he is an Asura.

But in most Ramayanas, Lakshmana is devastated by the mistake he has committed. He has killed an innocent boy doing penance and not troubling anyone. When he tells Rama, his brother says that even though it was an accident, it was a committed action, and every karma will have its consequences. We do not know how this will turn out, but we know there will be some consequence or the other. Lakshmana is a worried man. In a few months, he commits another mistake that will change the course of the story.

The loss of her only son and her hope in life makes Surpanakha mad. She does not know who has killed her son. She has two non-biological brothers, Khara and Dushana. In many folk versions, they are referred to as her sons. Most probably they were her adopted brothers or adopted sons or followers. In many tribal societies, the matriarch is often referred to as Amma or Mother. They could be her sons in the sense that she was the chief of their tribe in Dandakaranya.

Aided by Khara and Dushana, Surpanakha begins her search for the man who has killed her son Jambukumara. In the course of her search she stumbles upon Rama, Lakshmana and Sita. Having lost her husband and son she decides it is time for her to remarry and beget a son to take revenge on Ravana. So she goes to Rama with an unexceptional request in her society, but one that shocks Rama and Lakshmana. As per the Asura ethical and moral codes, it is not considered immoral or amoral for a woman to express love. But Rama and Lakshmana come from Ayodhya and a society where cultural norms are different. Surpanakha shocks them by proposing marriage. She shakes them further by saying that either brother can marry her. She expresses her plight and says she wants a son. She tells them that the son she had placed all her hopes on has been killed.

In folk versions, Lakshmana realizes that the boy he has killed is none other than Surpanakha's son. But Surpanakha herself is not aware that her son's killer is standing before her. Lakshmana does not respond to Surpanakha's request and stands like stone. Sita is amused when Surpanakha asks Rama if he will marry her. He replies that he is already married and has his wife with him. Why does she not approach Lakshmana instead? There is an element of playfulness in the way Rama says this, even in the Valmiki Ramayana. Does Rama not know this is the same woman whose son was killed by Lakshmana?

So Surpanakha turns to Lakshmana, but he refuses to marry her saying he has vowed to serve his brother. He also suggests that she ask his brother again. Surpanakha turns to Rama and pleads for marriage. Rama sends her back to Lakshmana. When this is repeated a few more times, Surpanakha becomes enraged. She assumes her fierce form and her talon-like nails come out. In many folk versions, Surpanakha is able to change her appearance and become as beautiful or as fiercely ugly as she wills. Now, she assumes the form of a Rakshasi and roars at Sita, 'You laugh at me? Because of you, these men are mocking me.'

In a fit of rage, she attacks Sita, whereupon Lakshmana draws his sword and chops off her nose. In many south Indian versions, he chops off her breasts too. Surpanakha runs away, screaming in pain. Her face mutilated, her breasts chopped off, she wonders what she has done wrong. She had only asked to marry one of the two brothers, both of whom she found attractive. She had merely acted according to the social norms of her community. 'What did I do to deserve such a cruel punishment?' she laments.

Sita is deeply unhappy about the treatment Lakshmana had meted out to a woman. 'I am afraid,' she says, 'what you did was wrong, and I fear we will all pay a heavy price for our karma.'

Neither Rama nor Lakshmana reply to this though each knows it is so.

Surpanakha runs to Khara and Dushana and narrates what has happened—that two men have entered her forest and insulted her, making fun of her reasonable request. And then, when she insisted that one of them marry her, the younger one chopped off her nose and breasts. By this time, Khara has discovered that it was Lakshmana who killed Jambukumara. When he tells her this, she cries out in fury.

Dushana says, 'We know that these same men killed your grandmother Tadaka years ago.'

'Kill those men and bring their heads to me!' Surpanakha commands.

Khara and Dushana rush off to attack Rama and Lakshmana. When he sees the two brothers, Khara roars, 'You have come to our forest: our forest, our rules. Here it is not wrong for a woman to ask a man to marry her. Why did you mutilate her? If you did not want her, you could have told her so. You had no business insulting or mutilating our sister. You are the same people who killed our grandmother Tadaka and our Uncle Subahu. They did not come to your place or attack Ayodhya. They did not seek anything that did not belong to them. We are sons of the forest. Yet you come into our forest and impose your rules. How fair is that? This woman's son was killed, and you must pay the price.'

A fierce battle ensues and Rama and Lakshmana eventually slay Khara and Dushana. Surpanakha flees from the scene. With her mutilated nose and breasts, she reaches Lanka. She, an Asura princess, sister of the man who has conquered the fourteen worlds, the aunt of Indrajit, who has even defeated Indra, cries to Ravana, 'Look at my plight! You killed my husband. Now these men have killed my son and mutilated me. I suffer for no fault of mine.'

Ravana is enraged. To instigate him further, Surpanakha taunts him saying that if he was truly a man, he would do to those men what they have done to her. She tells him that they have a woman with them who is as beautiful as any celestial being. She suggests to her brother that he take the woman.

Surpanakha is more a victim than an aggressor. For thousands of years, the debate has raged on about Lakshmana's action being right or wrong. Even the Bhakti-era poets, who consider Rama the Supreme God, were uncomfortable about dealing with this episode.

If we look at it from the angle of purely right or wrong, we can easily conclude that Surpanakha has more right on her side. She was wronged and let down by her brother and the two human males—Rama and Lakshmana—who came to her forest and took everything she considered precious.

Many folktales, especially the subaltern ones told by illiterate bards in the south, are highly sympathetic to Surpanakha, even while acknowledging Rama's divinity. They use this as a tool to say that even God is not fair to women and the downtrodden. If God were fair, would there be so much misery in the world? In folk versions, the lamentation is sharper. Surpanakha's words echo those of India's common women:

'One, a Rakshasa, is my brother. He kills the one I love and makes me a widow. One is a divine snake, Ananta, on whom Lord Vishnu lies. He kills my son and chops off my nose and breasts, while God stands smiling. A female is neither safe with God nor the Rakshasa. Whom shall we pray to and whom shall we hate? Where shall we go and stay forever? We have nowhere to go except the womb of the earth. That is where Sita went to be safe from the males, both Rakshasa and Deva. Why are we born as females?'

These are questions subaltern folk narratives keep asking, and Surpanakha becomes one of the critical fulcrums around which these arguments revolve. Why was Rama—the 'maryada purushottama' (epitome of dharma), the avatar of Vishnu whose dharma was to show people how to behave—silent on the crime committed by Lakshmana? Could he not have used less force even if Surpanakha was attacking Sita? Indeed, the two warrior princes who had defeated so many Rakshasas and Asuras could easily have restrained Surpanakha, instead of chopping off her nose and breasts.

These questions have always disturbed poets and philosophers. As per the poet-writer's dharma, one must stand with the victim, and in this incident the victim is Surpanakha. One way to explain her suffering is through the circle of karma and rebirth. The chopping off of Surpanakha's nose is Rama's karma too. He chooses not to condemn or punish Lakshmana.

A counter-argument is that Rama had blinded Jayanta, the son of Indra, in one eye, when Jayanta had molested Sita. He is punishing Surpanakha for the same crime. Just because the one committing the crime is a woman, the punishment need not differ.

Whatever the reasons, from that moment on, Rama, Lakshmana and Sita know no happiness in life. This incident keeps haunting them. The story takes a darker turn from here. Rama may be victorious again and again, but he can never again be happy in life after this incident.

> The incident of Surpanakha's disfigurement appears differently in different Ramayanas. In the Bhagwata Purana, the Devi Bhagwata and the Narasimha Purana, Rama sends a written message to Lakshmana to sever Surpanakha's nose. In the Seri Rama, Lakshmana not only chops off her hands and nose, but also kills her son who had accompanied her. In some Ramayanas like the Bhattikavya, Mahanataka, Champu Ramayana only her nose is cut. Her breasts are cut off in the Kamba Ramayana, Ananda Ramayana and Malayalam

Adhyatma Ramayana. As per folk-tales of western India, leeches emerge from the blood oozing from Surpanakha's severed breasts. The Jain Ramayana avoids this incident as Rama is considered non-violent and an enlightened being. As per the Brahma Vaivarta Purana, Surpanakha is born as Kubja in her next life. She is also called Trivakra as she has three bends in her body and is mocked for looking ugly by everyone. Krishna embraces her and makes her beautiful. Later, after killing Kamsa, Krishna spends a night with her, thus fulfilling the cycle of karma. Some tribal communities in Kerala believe they are descendants of Surpanakha and worship her.

16
The Kidnapping of Sita

SURPANAKHA GOES TO RAVANA AND DEMANDS THAT HE GET HER JUSTICE. She also tempts him with a description of Sita. In folk versions, wherein Ravana is Sita's father, he is horrified that the man who has married his daughter has behaved in such a way with his sister. He thinks his daughter is not safe and that he must bring her back.

There are multiple versions, as mentioned earlier. In the versions in which Sita is Ravana and Mandodari's daughter, Ravana brings Sita to Lanka with Mandodari's permission. There are other versions in which Sita is the daughter of Ravana and Vedavati. As Sita is not Mandodari's daughter, he does not tell Mandodari that the female he has kidnapped is his daughter. But in most versions of the Ramayana, Sita and Ravana are not related, especially in the Valmiki Ramayana. Valmiki is silent on the origins of Sita. For him, she is the representation of prakriti, the nature she is born from. She is nature's child, a foundling.

Whatever the various versions, Ravana decides to bring Sita to Lanka. Logically, if revenge was Ravana's aim, he could have gone and fought Rama and Lakshmana. Nor would he have gone alone. He was the king of Lanka, the emperor of the Asuras. He had a large army with great warriors like Indrajit, Kumbhakarna and many others. He could have gone with an army to take revenge on Rama and Lakshmana. The fact that he goes with his uncle Mareecha instead, is proof that his motive was not revenge.

So why did he kidnap Sita? Depending on the geography where the tale is told, the period, and the poet who tells it, the reasons are varied. That Ravana goes to Panchavati to abduct Sita is common to all Ramayanas. Mareecha, who was once spared by Rama when he attacked Rama to avenge his mother Tadaka, warns Ravana about confronting Rama and Lakshmana. However, Ravana insists that Mareecha must help him, so uncle and nephew depart from Lanka to kidnap Sita.

Mareecha is a shape-shifting Asura, a master of disguise, and the duo play out a ruse. In south India, many tribes are experts at imitating animals and birds, their cries and how they move. They use this skill to hunt. Mareecha was perhaps an expert in this kind of camouflage hunting. Though he knows his end is near, he owes much to Ravana and is fond of his nephew. So, despite his own misgivings, he camouflages himself as a golden deer. Sita, Lakshmana and Rama are in their hermitage when suddenly Sita sees this beautiful deer in the bushes. She immediately wants the golden deer.

In the oral storytelling tradition, the deer symbolizes human desire. We are always attracted to shiny things without even knowing what we will do if we get them. Often, this kind of chase after illusory shiny things ends up in disaster. Sita is obsessed with the golden deer that flits away and vanishes into the forest.

Rama asks Sita, 'What do you want it for? We are hermits. We don't eat meat. Nor can you have it as a pet. That is not a tame deer.'

Sita has no answer, but she is possessed by the desire to have the golden deer, dead or alive. She says its skin is so shiny, it looks so beautiful, and even though she cannot answer why, she wants it.

Whether Rama, Lakshmana and Sita ate non-vegetarian food is a debatable topic. As Kshatriyas, there were no scriptural sanctions against eating non-vegetarian food. In the Ramayana era and in Vedic and Upanishadic times, everyone ate non-vegetarian food. There are verses that talk about the qualities of meat. Many Ayurvedic preparations require non-vegetarian ingredients. The obsession with vegetarianism and the purity thus derived came after Buddha and Mahavira's time. Of course, many shlokas hail the nobility of ahimsa in the Vedas, Aranyakas and Upanishads, but there is no explicit proscription against eating flesh.

Later, in the Bhakti-era Ramayana, when the habit of associating purity with vegetarianism took root, the poets and storytellers who dealt with the Ramayana became uneasy about this episode. But if Sita wanted the deer simply as a pet, why did Rama shoot and kill it? A difficult question to answer.

At Sita's request Rama takes his bow and quiver of arrows and runs off behind the deer. Before going, he warns Lakshmana of the dangers lurking in the forest. Rama knows they have committed a wrong by mutilating Surpanakha and killing Khara and Dushana. Every karma inevitably bears fruit. Sometime, today or tomorrow, their deeds will yield bitter fruit. So, with much apprehension, Rama leaves Sita with Lakshmana to stand guard over her.

Sometime before, there had been a kidnapping attempt on Sita by an Asura named Viradha. When Rama killed Viradha, he discovered

Viradha was a cursed Gandharva, who had taken the form of a Rakshasa. The only way he could rid himself of his curse was to die at the hands of Rama. These kinds of stories, where Rama kills Asuras and Rakshasas, are justified by invoking the story of some curse. Anyone who dies at Rama's hands attains liberation and escapes the cycle of birth and rebirth, becoming one with the whole. The whole being universal consciousness or brahmam, of which Rama is the epitome. Dying at Rama's hands is thus one way of becoming one with universal consciousness, proclaims the Bhakti-era Ramayana.

After a long chase, Rama is still not able to catch Mareecha. Frustrated, he shoots an arrow to kill. The moment the arrow pierces the deer's heart, it transforms into an Asura who shocks Rama by crying out in Rama's voice, 'Lakshmana! Help me, I am dying!' Even as he dies, the Asura Mareecha performs his duty to his nephew-and-king, Ravana, and stays true to his dharma. He had given his word that he would ensure both brothers moved away from Sita so that Ravana could kidnap her. Even in his dying moments, Mareecha performs a deception to fulfil his promise. Some traditions say Mareecha is later born as Shakuni of the Mahabharata because as he is dying, he commits an act of duplicity. Thus, in the Mahabharata period, he is a master deceiver. When Sita hears this cry of anguish in Rama's voice, she is terrified that her husband is in grave danger. She urges Lakshmana to go help his brother.

Lakshmana replies, 'No one can touch my brother. It is that Asura trying to deceive us. My brother has instructed me not to move away from you. I am here to protect you.'

Sita, in her anguish, utters the unspeakable. There is an underlying sexual tension because of the tradition of those days. She accuses him of waiting for an opportunity to marry her once she is widowed (in that era it was considered acceptable, even desirable, for the younger brother to marry his elder brother's widow).

Lakshmana is heartbroken by her accusation. He has left his wife, left Ayodhya, and followed his brother like a shadow, and here the woman he has treated like a sister is accusing him of having sexual designs for her. He faces the most significant conflict of his life—whether to stay true to the word he has given Rama to protect Sita at any cost, and in doing so perhaps confirm Sita's fears; or defy his brother's orders and go in search of him, even though in his heart he knows that nothing can happen to Rama. When Sita repeats the accusation, Lakshmana breaks down and leaves her, warning her to be careful.

> In the Valmiki Ramayana, Rama, Lakshmana and Sita behave freely. The concept of a younger brother-in-law not looking even at the face of his brother's wife had not evolved. Sita treats Lakshmana as a devoted younger brother and Lakshmana is devoted to both Rama and Sita. In the much older Southern Recension, Lakshmana makes one hut in Chitrakoot where all three live, and he is Rama and Sita's devoted kid brother. In the Gaudiya and North Western Valmiki Ramayana, Lakshmana builds a separate hut for himself. In the Southern Recension, Sita and Lakshmana freely banter like how a sister would with her younger brother. Curiously, it is only in the Southern Recension that when Hanuman shows Sita's ornaments, Lakshmana says that he cannot recognize the bracelets or the earrings, but only her anklets, as he has only seen her feet. Scholars say this could be a later-day interpolation.
>
> In the medieval Ramayanas, the relationship is different. Extreme care is taken to maintain the propriety of Sita and Lakshmana's relationship. In the Aranya Kanda of Bhavartha Ramayana there is a tale about Lakshmana's innocent devotion

to his sister-in-law and brother. One day, Rama had gone out while Lakshmana was meditating. Sita had fallen asleep in the room, and her clothes got disordered in her sleep, uncovering her body. But Lakshmana did not notice it at all. Rama comes back and sees this and wonders aloud, 'Who can remain so steadfast in his sadhana, while seeing such a woman's beauty?' Lakshmana replies, 'A Rama bhakta will always remain steadfast.' However, like every story in India, there is a counter-telling to this tale too. According to the Skanda Purana, Nagara Kanda, during Pitru Kalpa Theertha, Rama decides to conduct shraddha, a ritual feast in honour of his father. However, Sita has a fight with him the previous night, and she hides in the jungle during the rituals. As a result, Lakshmana is forced to do all the household chores, including feeding the Brahmins. Sita returns only after the ritual ends, and Lakshmana is enraged by her behaviour. Now, it is Lakshmana's turn to sulk, and he walks away, leaving Sita to do the rest of the chores. Rama is unperturbed by their act and sleeps peacefully. Lakshmana sees Rama asleep, and evil thoughts start affecting him. He thinks of killing Rama and taking Sita. The next day, he follows Rama and Sita at a distance, fighting with his evil thoughts. When they reach Gokarna, Lakshmana suddenly comes to his senses. He is filled with remorse. He rushes to Rama and falls at his brother's feet. He confesses he had such evil thoughts and asks for punishment. Lakshmana asks for the death penalty and pleads with Rama to behead him. Rama is amused, and he refuses. He says he has forgiven Lakshmana. But Lakshmana is inconsolable. He prepares a pyre and is about to enter it when Sage Markandeya arrives. The sage teaches Lakshmana about human nature and says every human has such evil thoughts once in a while as the mind is an uncontrollable horse. It runs where it pleases. However, as long as one doesn't act on such evil thoughts, no sin has been committed. Lakshmana has repented already, and with that, he has atoned for his thoughts. Markandeya asks Lakshmana to bathe in Balamandana Teertha to calm his mind.

In the Padma Purana, the same tale is repeated, but there is no instance of Lakshmana being momentarily infatuated with Sita. In folk narrations, the oral storytellers often use this tale to create lighter moments. They will say Rama, Lakshmana and Sita were passing through this village (wherever the bard is telling the story on that occasion), and the devoted Lakshmana suddenly had evil thoughts of killing Rama and marrying Sita. The moment he stepped out of this village of sinners, such thoughts vanished and Lakshmana repented. I heard this story for the first time when a bard narrated this while passing through my village of Tripunithura, drawing much laughter from the listeners. I was a kid then and thought the bard had just made up a story to pull our legs, and it was only much later that I found a basis for this story in the Skanda Purana and Padma Purana.

In the Valmiki Ramayana, there is no concept of the Lakshmanarekha. But in folk traditions and later-day Ramayanas, Lakshmana draws a line around the ashram and tells Sita not to step beyond it, before leaving in search of Rama.

This is the opportunity Ravana has been waiting for. He comes in the guise of a hermit asking for alms. He cries, '*Bhavathi bhikshamdehi* (Lady of the house, pray feed me, give me alms).' Sita hurries inside to get some food to give him. As per the folk versions of the Ramayana, Ravana tries to follow her in, but is unable to cross the 'Lakshmana rekha', the line drawn by Lakshmana at the threshold of the dwelling. Ravana knows that as long as Sita stands behind that line, he cannot get to her.

Sita brings a fistful of rice and puts it into Ravana's extended hands, careful not to cross the line Lakshmana has drawn. To get her to cross it, Ravana, a great Vedic scholar who knows customs and rituals well, tells her it is inauspicious to give someone anything standing on the threshold, for it shows indecision and that the giver is not giving wholeheartedly. If Sita wants to give alms, she should cross the threshold or he will go away empty-handed. Sita is caught in a dilemma, and not wanting to offend the hermit she chooses to step forward. Ravana grabs her by the waist and carries her away in his Pushpaka Vimana.

> In the Southern Recension of the Valmiki Ramayana, Uttara Kanda, Ravana abducts Sita to attain moksha at the hands of Rama. Ravana hears from Sage Bhrigu that the demons and Rakshasas killed by Vishnu attain moksha. However, he asks how he can be killed by Vishnu, since as a Shiva bhakta he is protected. Bhrigu explains that the only way to warrant his death at the hands of Vishnu is to kidnap Sita. To get such a death, Ravana abducts Sita. *Aparhrto Sita Tatto Maranakanksaya* (Canto 5.43): He protects Sita and treats her like a mother in this version. In the other two versions of the Valmiki Ramayana, one can find hints of this, though it is not explicitly stated. When Kumbhakarna scolds Ravana

> for kidnapping Sita, Ravana tells him that he did so to attain salvation at the hands of Vishnu. The same theme is repeated in the Adhyatma Ramayana, Anand Ramayana, Padma Purana, Balaramadasa Ramayana and others.

In the Valmiki Ramayana, Ravana grabs Sita by the waist and carries her away in the Pushpaka Vimana. In southern recensions, Ravana catches her tresses with his left hand and clasps her thighs with his right hand. He carries her away in his arms. The Pushpaka Vimana is described as being drawn by miraculous mules with the faces of pishachas or ghouls. In the Central Indian tribal tradition, it is usually referred to as an ass-drawn chariot.

Ravana does not wait for his uncle Mareecha to join him, as he knows Mareecha has died at Rama's hands. Sita cries out for help, but no one hears. As they fly on, Jatayu the vulture (as per many traditions) or eagle (as per the south Indian tradition) hears Sita's cries and attacks Ravana to save Sita. Rama, Lakshmana and Sita had met Jatayu when they first began their exile. Jatayu is a close friend of Dasaratha's and considers Sita as his own daughter-in-law. When Jatayu comes to rescue Sita, they are in the thirteenth year of exile. Jatayu fights Ravana, injures him and also kills the asses and destroys the Vimana.

Unable to fight the powerful Jatayu, Ravana unsheathes Chandrahasa, the divine sword Lord Shiva had gifted him, and chops off Jatayu's wings. But Jatayu has already effectively grounded the Pushpaka Vimana, so Ravana uses his special powers to fly on to Lanka grabbing Sita by the waist. In other Ramayanas, Pushpaka Vimana can reassemble itself even when it crashes, so Ravana carries Sita away in the Pushpaka Vimana.

Following his battle with Ravana, Jatayu falls to earth. There are many places associated with Jatayu's fall. One is in Kerala, called Chadayamangalam or Jatayu Paara, and the other is in Andhra Pradesh, in Lepakshi. There are also claimants for the place where Jatayu fell in Maharashtra and Madhya Pradesh.

> Bhasa, the famous dramatist of ancient India, gives a different spin to this tale. In the play *Pratimanatakam*, Rama wants a priest to do the annual shraddha of Dasaratha. Ravana comes as the Brahmin priest and shows off his knowledge of the scriptures and the Vedas. Impressed, Rama asks him to conduct the rituals for his father. Ravana says that if Rama gets the golden deer that lives in the Himalayas, the ancestors would be pleased. Rama goes in search of the deer. Lakshmana was not in the ashram at that time as he had gone to invite other rishis for the ritual. Once Ravana is alone with Sita, he assumes his original form and kidnaps her.
>
> In the folk Ramayana of Kerala and Tamil Nadu, Ravana himself takes the form of a two-headed golden deer. Sita sees this curious animal and wants it. Rama goes in pursuit of it and kills it. Ravana's soul enters the body of a saint in Samadhi. The saint comes to the ashram and tells Lakshmana that Rama is being attacked by many Rakshasas. Lakshman rushes to save Rama, while Ravana kidnaps Sita.
>
> In the Narasimha Purana, Ravana comes in the form of a sanyasi on a chariot and says that Bharata has sent him to fetch Sita. Rama is becoming the king of Ayodhya and is also being summoned. Hearing this, Sita enters the chariot, and suddenly it flies away, revealing Ravana's form. There are versions where Ravana and Mareecha disguise themselves

> as Rama and Lakshmana and take Sita to Lanka cunningly, promising her they will take her to Ayodhya.
>
> In folk versions, Ravana loses Shiva's protection when he kidnaps Sita in the guise of a sanyasi. More than the crime of kidnapping Sita, the crime of disguising as a mendicant is what makes Shiva angry in such versions, as people would lose their belief in doing charity.

Ravana is now carrying Sita away after defeating Jatayu. She continues her struggle and tries her best to be free of Ravana. In her struggle, a bejewelled anklet of gold falls from her feet and hits the ground. Her necklace of pearls also drops down. She cries for Rama and Lakshmana. She beseeches Ravana to leave her. She tries praising him, blaming him, and appealing to his valour and goodness, but to no avail. Sita now knows that she should give some sign for Rama to follow her, for follow he will, and rescue her from the hands of Ravana. When she looks down, she sees a group of five monkeys sitting on a mountain peak. Sita tears off a piece of her upper garment, wraps her jewels in it and throws it down. Below, Hanuman of the Vanara (monkey) tribe is in his prayers. It is into his cupped hands that the ornaments fall. When he looks up, he sees a woman being carried away by an ogre.

Rama and Lakshmana return to find Sita gone. Rama is devastated and Lakshmana, guilt-ridden. He has disobeyed his brother's orders in considering his own honour. Lakshmana is further filled with guilt for he knows that he and his brother are paying the price for what they did to Surpanakha. Devastated, Rama goes about crying Sita's name, asking every plant and flower and bird where she is.

The curse of Ushana Kavyamatha, Shukracharya's mother, thus comes true. Lord Vishnu had deceived her, and in this avatar as Rama, Vishnu is paying the price for his choice, his actions. Rama does not know where to look for his wife. There are no clues about what happened and where she has gone. Rama and Lakshmana stand amid the vast jungles of Central India, not knowing where Sita has vanished.

Was Lakshmana right in reacting to Sita's accusations by leaving, when his duty was to protect her? Was he right to disobey his brother? Was his honour greater than his duty? But what if Sita was right? What if he had stood there, ignoring her pleas to help Rama, despite her accusations, and Rama really had been in danger? Was Rama important, or was following Rama's orders important?

Similarly, was it right for Sita to ignore Lakshmana's advice not to cross the threshold? Was following the right custom more important than her own safety? Knowing what is right and wrong at any given moment is a tough choice. This is perhaps where the hand of destiny plays a role. Why do we make mistakes? Why would a learned woman like Sita be tempted by a golden deer? Why would a great king like Ravana choose to kidnap Sita instead of attacking Rama with his massive army? Why would Lakshmana act in a cruel way towards Surpanakha, a woman who had only expressed love, and why would the ever-compassionate Rama remain silent about such an atrocity?

There are no easy answers.

Life is often inexplicable. We make choices, succumbing to temptations and emotion rather than relying on reason. Such questions are usually answered by those who subscribe to the karma theory, with back stories like Kavyamatha's curse. The other school of thought that contradicts karma answers such inexplicable quirks of life with a standard reply: It is niyati. Things happen as they are destined to. Alternatively, things happen by sheer chance. We get random thoughts and act on impulse. That is how the world is. That is its swabhava or nature. Once we understand the randomness, we neither feel pleased about our fortune nor unhappy about our misfortune. Like day and night, like rain and sunshine, stuff keeps happening in life. This is a passive way of looking at life.

The karma theory prods us to make choices and think about our actions. Though the karma theory is often stretched to accommodate unexplainable things, it is a more functional theory. In practice, we use both. We explain away things using karma and the rest we say is our destiny. Understanding life is a complicated exercise. Living life is a simple process. Just live.

17

The Interjection of an Illusory 'Maya' Sita

IN MANY LATTER-DAY VERSIONS OF THE RAMAYANA, THE VERY IDEA THAT SITA was touched by the demon Ravana is horrifying to those immersed in devotion to Rama. Over time, we find the concept of the Ramayana itself undergoing a change. In the original versions, both the Ramayana and its companion epic, the Mahabharata, were tales of karma and its result, the karmaphala. Over time, as the Bhakti cult spread in the medieval period, women's chastity became a central theme in medieval literature. This period also saw the advent of Islam in India. Contact with Semitic religions influenced storytelling in a fascinating manner.

Medieval poets were uneasy about Ravana touching Sita, which he did when he held her to his side and flew with her to Lanka after the Pushpaka Vimana crashed. We find a curse is added to these Ramayanas, to the effect that if Ravana touched any woman, he would die. In the Valmiki Ramayana, Ravana grabs Sita by the waist. Raja Ravi Varma's famous painting also depicts this scene.

Valmiki is not uncomfortable with this fact because he lived in a different era. He also shows Ravana in a more positive light because Ravana never forces himself upon Sita. But the moment the curse angle is added, it justifies the vilification of Ravana. We can see how slowly the story turns from a story about karma and karmaphala into a tale of good versus evil. So Ravana no longer has any redeeming qualities. He desists from forcing himself upon Sita not due to any noble intent, or because he knows she is his daughter (according to the folk and Jain versions) but because of the curse upon him.

The Concept of Maya-Sita

The touching of Sita by any other male other than Rama, and Rama's demand after the war that Sita undergo a trial by fire to establish her chastity—since she has lived in another man's abode for so long—are two of the most uncomfortable events as per many in the Ramayana. The concept of the Maya-Sita very effectively takes care of the discomfort factor in both cases.

As per this concept, the moment Sita crosses the line drawn by Lakshmana—the Lakshmana rekha—she vanishes and a new illusory 'Maya' Sita takes her place. Some Ramayanas state that Sita disappears when she sees Ravana in Panchavati, and a Maya-Sita takes her place.

It is this Maya-Sita who is taken away by Ravana.

When Rama, after defeating Ravana, asks Sita to undergo an agnipariksha (trial by fire) ostensibly to prove she is still chaste, it is actually to send this Maya-Sita back to Agni Deva, the God of Fire and allow the real Sita to return. However, in the Uttara Ramayana, Rama asks Sita to undergo a second agnipariksha as well, and there the concept of Maya-Sita is not mentioned.

We see how various authors of the different Ramayanas have tried to interpret and define it according to the ethics and morality of the times and the society they lived in.

As mentioned above, this explanation assuages the discomfort that many Vaishnava- and Rama-devotee poets felt and feel on reading the original Valmiki Ramayana. By creating a Maya-Sita, the demon does not touch Sita, an avatar of Lakshmi, the consort of Vishnu. Secondly, Rama's insistence on Sita undergoing an agnipariksha is explained away beautifully.

But this does not answer some other questions which arise.

If it was indeed the Maya-Sita whom Ravana kidnapped, then the entire Ramayana becomes meaningless. Why did Rama fight for a Maya-Sita? If it was an illusionary Sita, why was Rama chasing an illusion?

The evil Ravana had already been tricked by the Maya-Sita. So, when Rama returned after killing Mareecha, the real Sita could have easily appeared before him, and everyone would have been happy. Ravana got a Maya-Sita, an illusionary Sita, and Rama had his real Sita. So there was no need to kill Ravana at all, as he had already been tricked. Rama, Sita and Lakshmana could have had a good laugh at Ravana's expense and gone home to live happily ever after. But if that were so, there would have been no further story. That is why Valmiki did not go down this route.

One of the most important aspects of the Valmiki Ramayana is that he never hides any of Rama's flaws or mistakes. He is clear that Rama is a human avatar of Vishnu. As no human is perfect, Rama too has his failings. As a storytelling tool, a flawed hero is far more real and fascinating. Hence, Valmiki, the great poet that he was, conceived Rama in this fashion. He could have hidden every wart and mole; why indeed bring in an episode such as the agnipariksha, the trial by fire? Why make his hero suffer by having his wife abducted by Ravana? But Valmiki's Rama expresses deep anguish like any ordinary mortal. This is one of the most beautiful scenes of the Ramayana, where Rama openly shows his love for Sita. This often happens in our lives too. How often do we take our loved ones for granted? Only when they are absent do we admit how much we love or miss them.

The Maya-Sita concept is a straightforward addition to the Ramayana, introduced by Bhakti-era poets. In versions of the Mahabharata, in the Vishnu Purana, in the Harivamsha Purana, and even in the Kamba Ramayana, which is perhaps the earliest non-Sanskrit classical rendition of the Ramayana, the Maya-Sita concept appears. It is used as a tool to say that Sita remained unblemished. But in the Uttara Ramayana, even this argument falls apart. We will discuss that in greater detail later. The poem 'Ramacharitamanas' deals with the problem differently as the saint-poet Tulsidas would have been aware of the flaws in the amended versions.

In the Kamba Ramayana, Ravana scoops up all the ground upon which the ashram is situated, as well as Sita, and places it in the Pushpaka Vimana, when he abducts Sita. This is because Ravana has been cursed that he cannot touch any woman without her consent. Here, the Maya-Sita concept does not exist, but Sage Kamba is nevertheless uncomfortable with another man touching the divine Sita, hence this device. Medieval literature extols the chastity of women and their devotion to their husbands.

The Maya-Sita concept is central to the Rama cult, but not to the Valmiki Ramayana or even the story. Thus, it is contrary to the karma and karmaphala principles of the original Ramayana and sits as an addition that does not really merge with the storyline.

18

Jatayu's Funeral

WITH SITA HAVING VANISHED, RAMA AND LAKSHMANA ROAM THE FOREST in search of her. They have no idea where she has gone. There is no trace, since she was carried away in the Pushpaka Vimana and when that crashed, Ravana clasped her to his side and flew on using his own powers or in Pushpaka Vimana that reassembled itself. There are not even any footprints to follow. In the Valmiki Ramayana, Rama's anguish is portrayed beautifully. He asks every blade of grass, every flower, tree and bird that his eyes alight upon whether they have seen his Sita. He weeps like any other man separated from his beloved.

In later-day Ramayanas, Rama slowly becomes a stoic, omniscient god. But the Valmiki Ramayana is more relatable because Rama appears like other human beings. He cries when he is sad, becomes enraged when something occurs to anger him, and is loving when he wants to show affection. Valmiki's Rama is as flawed as any other character in the Ramayana.

The vulnerable Rama we see after he loses Sita forms the basis of a great love story. In Sanskrit literature, all poetry has its rasa or essence. Here it is 'viraha' or separation, and Valmiki uses nature to effectively convey this rasa. The sky is overcast and it reminds Rama of Sita's complexion. The chattering of the birds reminds him of her lively speech. The slowly flowing river reminds him of her serene nature. The relationship with nature is emphasized because Sita is the symbol of prakriti, nature.

Now, the purusha or universal consciousness embodied as Rama has lost contact with prakriti, manifested nature, that makes him whole. Various sages have explained this separation in the following manner: the Ramayana is what is happening in every person's mind. When the union of prakriti and purusha occurs, there is happiness. Ravana here is not represented as the evil Tamasa guna or darkness, but by the Rajo guna or virility. He is the epitome of all the senses.

Ravana's ten heads represent human emotions. Emotions are powerful. Hence, Ravana too is depicted as a mighty person. When emotions blind us, purusha becomes separated from nature. Ravana's abduction of Sita represents how our prakriti or nature is overpowered by our emotions, and purusha or true consciousness is clouded. Rama's quest for and the finding of Sita is the reunion of prakriti and purusha by overcoming emotion.

If this is accepted as the more profound meaning, there is no need to be uncomfortable about Ravana abducting Sita. The Ramayana here is thus not a devotional story about Rama but a tool to understand oneself.

As Rama and Lakshmana continue their search for Sita, they find a bird in its death throes. When Jatayu tried to stop Ravana, his wings were slashed by the Asura emperor. Jatayu is the son of Aruna, as is Sampati. In some Puranas, Jatayu is the son of Garuda, but usually Jatayu and Sampati, the twin eagles or vultures, are the sons of Aruna, Garuda's brother. Whether Jatayu and Sampati are vultures or eagles is a debatable point. Valmiki uses the word 'gridhrah', which means 'vulture', but they are represented as eagles who hunt elephants and other mammals in various other stories. Vultures are scavengers, but Jatayu and his brother are not scavengers. Another argument for considering them to be eagles is that they are the sons of Garuda, an eagle. Aruna too is eagle-faced, being Garuda's brother.

Rama and Lakshmana come upon Jatayu as he lies dying. Rama is shocked. He remembers meeting Jatayu at the start of his exile, thirteen years ago; now he finds his father's friend in the final moments of life. Jatayu tells Rama that Ravana has taken Sita in a flying machine and vanished, that he tried his utmost to stop him, but the Asura emperor chopped off his wings. Saying this, Jatayu dies. Rama is devastated. Even with the news of who has taken Sita, he stays to perform the funeral rites.

Here, the question arises of whether the rules of human civilization apply to animals and whether it is right or wrong for Rama to impose his own cultural norms on a bird. Is imposing our dharma on others the correct thing to do? However, Rama does so in a spirit of respect, to show his love and affection for a bird who died to save Sita.

The question about Rama's action being right or wrong in this instance has been long debated, even in ancient India. The fundamental problem is, whose dharma is it? This dilemma is brought forth in the Vishnu Purana's story of Sibi. The oral retelling has a much more powerful impact than the written version in the Vishnu Purana, where an attempt was made in the medieval period to make it wholly devotional. I narrate here the oral version.

Emperor Sibi is conducting a sacrifice when, to test him, Indra, King of the Devas, takes the shape of a hawk, and Agni the God of

Fire, that of a pigeon. The hawk chases the pigeon, and the pigeon comes to Sibi, sits on his lap and pleads, 'My life is in danger, please save me from the hawk.' Sibi, thinking that he must save the weaker one, promises to save the pigeon from the hawk.

The hawk arrives to find its prey now under the protection of the emperor. It asks for the pigeon, which is its food.

Sibi replies, 'He is under my protection, and it is my dharma to save the poor bird.'

The hawk asks, 'How can your dharma be to stop me from eating? If you save all my prey, I will starve to death. Are you not being unjust to me?'

Sibi is confused. Saving the pigeon from the hawk is an injustice to the hawk. The hawk is right.

The hawk continues, 'I did not chase this pigeon for fun. I am a hawk; I do not kill for pleasure. I kill for food. If I do not kill the pigeon, my chicks will die of hunger, and the sin of it will fall upon you, king.'

Sibi says, 'Do not worry, hawk, I will give you food.' In a burst of magnanimity, he orders his servants to, 'Feed the hawk a chicken.'

The chicken then asks, 'How fair is this, O king? To satisfy your ego that you are a righteous person, you are sacrificing me. To protect the pigeon, you are killing me. What kind of dharma is this?'

Sibi is flummoxed. After some thought, he says, 'I do not wish to hurt anyone, but I must keep my word. I will be the sacrifice. I will cut the flesh from my thighs and give it to the hawk.'

The hawk laughs. 'Do you think your body belongs to you? It belongs to your wife, your parents, and your children. Should you not ask them?'

So Sibi asks his wife whether he can do this. She is horrified. Sibi pleads with her, and finally she agrees. He seeks permission from his parents and from his children too. Sibi says, 'Now I have everyone's permission to cut off a chunk of flesh and feed it to you. With that, you can feed your children, and save this pigeon.'

Then the hawk asks, 'But you are the king, you belong to the country. Will your subjects agree to their king being lame?'

So Sibi summons his subjects and asks them. There are many objections, and then one person asks, 'If the king is lame, how will he protect us?' Finally, Sibi persuades everyone that what he is doing is an act of dharma. He goes to the hawk and says, 'I went to my subjects and they say they do not want a lame king. So I have decided to relinquish my kingship, but I will not go back on my word because I am a righteous person.'

Then the hawk asks, 'Today you will feed me, but tomorrow when I am hungry again, can I eat this pigeon?'

Sibi replies, 'Until I die, I submit myself to you. This is my ultimate sacrifice.'

The hawk replies, 'You are both magnanimous and righteous, but does it solve my problem? I can eat you for a week or two, perhaps a month. After that, what will my chicks do? And when they grow up, neither you nor I will be there to feed them. They will have to hunt pigeons. Who will sacrifice themselves like you? Can you ask others to sacrifice their bodies? Is it dharma to do so? And even assuming everyone sacrifices themselves like you, what makes you think your life is either inferior or superior to that of a pigeon, hawk or chicken?'

Sibi is confused again. He says, 'I do not know what to do. I wish to protect this pigeon. It is an act of compassion, an act of mercy.'

The hawk says, 'Even compassion is relative. All dharma is relative. An act of kindness towards the pigeon is an act of cruelty towards me. An act of cruelty towards the pigeon is an act of compassion towards me. There is a cycle of life. There is a web of life, and no one is supposed to interfere with it. If you interfere in what nature has intended, you create karmaphala. One day or another, you will have to eat the fruits of that action.

'That is why wise men do not interfere with what is happening in nature. That is why there are no absolutes, no absolute ahimsa paramodharma ("non-violence is one's primary duty"). While non-violence is the most excellent dharma, it has its flaws because violence is also a part of nature. Something must die for something else to flourish. That is the cycle of life.

'Man, with his limited understanding of what is right and wrong, sits in judgment. He judges the hawk to be cruel and the pigeon to be wretched. He thinks the hawk is the aggressor and the pigeon the victim. Now ask the worm which the pigeon has just eaten. The worm will say, "The pigeon is the aggressor and I the victim." Ask the leaf the worm has eaten, and the leaf will say, "I am the victim and the worm the aggressor." Ask the soil and the soil will say, "The plant has taken water and minerals from me, I am the victim and the plant the aggressor."

'Understanding this eternal, unending cycle of life and acting accordingly is the sign of a wise man.'

Sibi asks, 'But then how can we live? How will we know what is right and what is wrong?'

The hawk replies, 'The greatest dharma is doing minimum harm to others. Nobody can live without doing some harm, and every action sets up a chain of reactions. Even when you walk, you unknowingly crush many creatures underfoot. All these sins accumulate as fruits of your karma. It is called prarabdha, the weight, and this weight of your actions you carry from life to life. Escaping this burden is called moksha or liberation. The actions you do knowingly or unknowingly weigh you down and trap you like a fly in a cobweb. In this web of life, you struggle, free yourself, only to be caught in the web of another spider. Understand this—there is no action without reaction, and without the fruit of that action.'

———◆◆◆———

Rama, like any other human being, acts according to his discretion or viveka. He thus performs funeral rites for the bird Jatayu, denying food to the many creatures that would otherwise have fed on the bird's carcass. Does he pay the price for this? Yes, he does, as we will see in the next chapter.

19
Rama's Karmic Debt and the Slaying of Kabanda

WHETHER RAMA DID THE RIGHT THING BY CREMATING JATAYU MAY appear to be a strange question, but in folk Ramayanas, this too has been dealt with. In the folk songs of northern Kerala, scavenging animals and birds come to Rama and say, 'You have denied us our food by cremating Jatayu. You have done us an injustice.'

Rama replies, 'I did it because I am Rama of Ayodhya. But I understand your point. I understand that I will pay the price for my choice and one day I must eat the fruits of my karma.' Rama then tells the creatures who have come to complain, 'In your next birth you shall be my brothers and friends.'

The hyenas say, 'But we eat by stealing. You are a God, the avatar of Vishnu. Would you steal with us?'

Rama smiles and says, 'If I am playing a part that requires me to steal, I will do that too.'

Folk bards then relate how Rama is born as Krishna in Vrindavan, and all the forest creatures that lost their food because of Rama of

Ayodhya's maryada are born with Krishna in Vrindavan. These are the gopakumaras, Krishna's cowherd friends, who are his companions in mischief. Krishna steals butter and shares it with his friends.

The Ramayana is incomplete without the Mahabharata, which emphasizes the choices we make and the price we pay— the eternal cycle of karma and karmaphala. Through his action, Vishnu shows that even an apparent act of compassion can be considered cruelty to someone else. Ponder this: to uphold the moral values of Ayodhya, Rama goes to the forest. He imposes his values of that morality in the jungle, even on the living beings there. Rama cremates Jatayu, denying food to scavenging creatures.

In his Krishna avatar, he does precisely the opposite of what he did in his Rama avatar. During the eighteenth and nineteenth centuries, when Westerners began reading the Indian Puranas, they were shocked to see a God as playful and mischievous as Krishna, who breaks codes of morality with ease. Krishna steals; he loves other men's wives. Where Rama made Sita undergo an agnipariksha, Krishna is in love with Radha, someone else's wife. Every action Rama did, he did the opposite in his avatar as Krishna. Both sets of actions are valid as far as life is concerned, but every choice gives birth to new karmaphala. Depending on choice and actions, the fruits of the actions keep multiplying in an unending chain reaction.

After learning from Jatayu that Sita has been abducted by Ravana, Rama and Lakshmana still do not know where Ravana is, except that he'd travelled in a southerly direction. Jatayu tells them that Ravana was in a flying machine and he could have turned course and gone north, east or west. With the first flicker of hope that Sita is still alive, Rama and Lakshmana continue their search and go south.

The Slaying of Kabanda

Just as they are nearing Kishkindha, the city of the Vanaras, they are confronted by a headless Asura called Kabanda, who attacks them. Kabanda is notorious for devouring humans. He has two massive arms which he uses to catch and shove his prey directly into his stomach. He is perpetually hungry. Kabanda's nature is an allegory for those who live only for sensory pleasure. They do not even enjoy the indulgences they seek. They do not have eyes, noses, ears or tongues. They merely exist. They hunt what they want and devour it. They digest and excrete it, then repeat the process.

Kabanda catches Rama and Lakshmana, and a battle ensues. Rama chops off both the Asura's hands and kills him. At this point Kabanda turns into a Gandharva and says he had been cursed for going in search of mindless pleasure and pursuing other men's wives. He had indulged in gluttony and was never satisfied. He kept filling his belly mindlessly and soon evolved into a monster that merely existed without experiencing any of life's pleasures. He ate, excreted and ate again, repeating the process mindlessly. With his death at Rama's hands, he gets back his old form and promises to live with moderation.

This tale is often told by bards as a warning to those who pursue pleasure mindlessly. They ask us to pause and reflect. How are we leading our lives? Have we become like Kabanda, just eating, procreating and excreting, doing nothing fruitful? We have eyes, but do we see? If we have a nose, when was the last time we appreciated the fragrance of life? When was the last time we paused to hear something meaningful? When did we last hear a soul-stirring song, a moving tale or even what our dear ones said? Kabanda ate but did not have a tongue to taste. How many of us take the time to enjoy the food we eat? When was the last time we ate without looking at our mobile phones or talking to someone or reading a book?

One of the habits my father taught me was never to talk while eating or eat while talking. In traditional families, food is eaten in silence. We sat on the floor, and the food was served on banana leaves. Nothing was wasted. One of the rituals was to sprinkle a circle of water droplets around the banana-leaf plate and place a few grains of cooked rice beyond the ring of droplets. This was meant for the ants and small creatures that came in search of food. The circle of water droplets, sprinkled while chanting mantras, was meant to keep them away from the banana leaf. The few grains of rice were a tribute to them, meant to remind us to care for even the tiniest creatures and be aware that they too experienced hunger.

Before eating, we were told to think about the farmer who made the food, visualize the green fields, the sun, the rain, the rivers that irrigated the fields, the bullock that had taken the sacks of grain to the market, the shopkeeper, and our mother who had cooked the food. They all had to be thanked in the mind. Mantras were uttered in thanks before eating. Of course, you don't need to chant them in Sanskrit, or even speak any mantras, but you can think of these things too when you next eat and visualize them in your mind.

We were not allowed to drink water while eating, and nothing was ever wasted. The used banana leaf was thrown into a basket from which the cows ate. Even that was not wasted. There was no need to wash the banana leaves; even if the cows did not want them, they were anyway biodegradable. We washed our hands under the banana tree, thus watering it.

We talk today about sustainable living and eco-friendly products, but this has been inherent in Indian culture for centuries. If you go into rural India, you will see that some of these rituals are still followed. We often perform rituals without knowing their importance and how close Indian traditions are to nature. We have always lived a sustainable life, preserving our resources and respecting nature.

Compare this with modern urban living. Consider the act of eating. We stare at our mobile phones, read a book, and do not concentrate on the food before us. We do not spare a thought for the farmer who has grown the food, nor care about how it reached the market, who prepared the food, or the effort expended in making the meal. We devour the food mindlessly, like Kabanda. We carelessly put the dirty plate into the kitchen sink or dishwasher. To clean each vessel we use detergents and plenty of water. Where does this go? The water does not seep back into the soil but is piped away to pollute the sea through city drains. Even a simple meal, instead of sustaining life, ends up polluting the earth.

When the animals complained to Rama that by cremating Jatayu he had denied them food, Rama paid the price for it. Imagine the kind of choices we are making now by breaking the laws and cycles of nature. We collect water from its source, pump it unnaturally over hundreds of kilometres to towns and cities. Water is rarely recycled. These are the choices we have made in our modern life. The fruit of our actions is ripening and we will all soon taste how bitter it is.

Sabari's Story

Walking south, Rama and Lakshmana enter the forest of a tribal woman called Sabari. In the Valmiki Ramayana, Sabari is a tribal chief who has heard about Rama's exploits and is filled with admiration. She provides him with food and rest. Rama thanks her and goes away.

In folk and latter-day Bhakti-era Ramayanas, this scenario is rewritten to bring out Rama's divinity. Sabari is turned from a matriarch and chief of a tribe into a destitute untouchable. This also reflects how society treated women and tribals in the medieval era. Rama's meeting with Sabari is emphasized to show Rama's kindness. To a modern reader, this might sound highly patronizing, but in the period when it was written, the compassion Rama showed moved devotees to tears.

The illiterate, destitute Sabari of the Bhakti-era Ramayanas does not know the social rituals of purity and caste. Numerous poets, sages and storytellers have contributed to the considerable corpus of Ramayana tales. Some had noble intentions, others less so, when they tinkered with Valmiki's epic. In the Bhakti-era Ramayanas for instance, Sabari serves Rama wild berries after biting each to see whether it is ripe enough. Lakshmana is horrified that an untouchable woman gives Rama berries that have been sullied by her saliva. This reflects medieval India, where notions of purity about what could be touched, who could be seen, who could come near, and so on had made life increasingly difficult and complicated for everyone, and miserable for those pushed to the lower rungs of society. This naïve act by Sabari is exasperating and endearing at the same time. But Rama has no qualms about eating the berries.

The medieval Bhakti poets point to Rama's compassion, saying that if Rama did not believe in the purity of caste or the caste system, who are lesser mortals to impose these on society? Conservatives, uncomfortable with this egalitarian Rama, added their own versions, like the killing of a Shudra ascetic Shambuka, for reciting the Vedas. In doing so they were able to use Rama's name to strengthen the caste system.

All this while, as Rama and Lakshmana move through the forest in search of clues to find Sita, the Vanara Hanuman has been spying on the brothers from a distance. He becomes increasingly convinced that these two men can prove useful in helping his friend Sugriva gain the throne of Kishkindha.

Sita's hairpin (chudamani) is in Hanuman's possession, having fallen into his hands when she flung it from the Pushpaka Vimana. Hanuman understands that Rama is full of compassion and is searching for his wife. But he decides to test Rama before he reveals himself.

20
Stories of Hanuman's Origins, Early Years and Youth

Hanuman is the original superhero of the Puranas. He is one of the most beloved of all characters and rivals Rama, Krishna, Shiva and Devi in popularity. Who was Hanuman? Various Ramayanas give different explanations of his origin. One of the earliest Ramayanas talks of Hanuman being the son of Shiva and Vishnu—it is during the Mohini avatar of Vishnu that Hanuman is born, in union with Shiva.

It all begins with a curse that causes the Devas to lose their immortality. As the Asuras have never been granted immortality, the curse makes them equal. In a rare show of cooperation, both groups decide to churn the ocean of milk together to find 'amrita', the elixir of immortality. Mandara Parvata, a massive mountain, is used as the churning rod, and Vishnu assumes the avatar of a kurma or turtle and holds the mountain in place on his back. Vasuki, the giant serpent that adorns Shiva's neck, is used as the churning rope.

As the churning begins and picks up pace, many things emerge from the ocean of milk. Mahalakshmi appears from the ocean and

Vishnu makes her his wife. Airavatha, the white four-tusked elephant, emerges and is taken by Indra, the King of the Devas, as his mount. Similarly, other precious beings and things emerge from the ocean. But along with these, a dangerous poison that could destroy the entire universe called Halahala also emerges.

It emerges not from the ocean but from Vasuki, the serpent being used as the rope to churn. Exhausted, Vasuki spits out the Halahala and it falls into the ocean of milk threatening all creation. To save the world from the poisonous effects of the Halahala, the Devas and the Asuras pray to Lord Shiva, who consumes the poison. The venom is so potent that Shiva himself can turn evil if he swallows it. Afraid for her husband, Parvati stops the poison from going below Shiva's neck by choking him. If Shiva spits out the poison, the universe will be annihilated, so the Devas and the Asuras close Shiva's mouth so he cannot spit it out. The Halahala thus settles in Shiva's neck, turning it blue. Therefore, another name for Shiva is Neelakanta, the blue-throated.

The churning of the ocean continues, and finally, after millions of years, the elixir of immortality, the amrita, comes out and there ends the cooperation between the Devas and the Asuras.

Now begins a battle as neither side is ready to share the pot of elixir. Vishnu takes on the form of Mohini, a beautiful seductress, and offers to split the pot of elixir equally between the Asuras and the Devas. She makes them sit in two rows, one on either side of her, and starts doling out the amrita. But she gives it only to the Devas. When she turns to the Asuras, she pretends to pour the elixir into their hands but never empties the ladle. Bemused by her charm and beauty, the Asuras do not notice her deception.

One Asura, however, does see what is happening. Instead of making a hue and cry and starting a war, he decides to trick the Devas. He sneaks into the row of Devas and sits down. Mohini serves this

Asura the amrita too, and he gulps it down. Surya, the Sun God, and Chandra, the Moon God, see this and cry out that an Asura has gained immortality by drinking the elixir. Mohini immediately summons the Sudarsana Chakra, the weapon of Vishnu, and decapitates the Asura, separating his head from the rest of his body. But, since the Asura has already consumed the elixir of immortality, he does not die. Instead, both parts of the Asura come alive as Rahu and Ketu.

The ancient beliefs regarding solar and lunar eclipses come from this story. Enraged by Surya and Chandra's warning, Rahu and Ketu decide on revenge. Hence the solar eclipse is Rahu swallowing the sun, and the lunar eclipse is Ketu swallowing the moon. Since Rahu and Ketu are no longer one whole body, the sun and moon come out of these separated entities after some time.

Stories of Hanuman's Birth

The Devas, powered by the elixir of immortality thanks to Vishnu's Mohini avatar, defeat the Asuras in an all-out battle. Peace reigns once again in the universe, for a while. Then Shiva sets eyes on Mohini and is enthralled by her beauty. Following their union, Vishnu sheds his Mohini avatar and reverts to his original form. The seed of Shiva and Mohini's union is carried by Vayu, the Wind God and deposited in the womb of a Vanara woman, Anjana. So, according to these Ramayanas, Anjana gives birth to the son of Shiva and Vishnu, with the help of Vayu.

But in other Ramayanas and Puranas, the story differs.

In the Bhavishya Purana, Anjana is a beautiful celestial nymph who is cursed to be the wife of the Vanara Kesari. Shiva is enticed by her beauty, as is Vayu the Wind God. Shiva and Vayu together enter the body of Anjana's husband Kesari and make love to her. From this union, Hanuman is born. However, since Vayu and Shiva had competed to make Hanuman, the boy is born deformed. When

Anjana sees him, repelled by his ugliness, she flings the baby from a cliff. He falls onto a rock, which shatters into pieces while Hanuman remains unharmed. Anjana then understands her son is a divine being. Guilt-ridden, she decides not to return to heaven but remain on earth as Hanuman's mother.

In another version of the same Purana, Anjana leaves Hanuman as an orphan immediately after his birth. The back story to this is that Anjana was a celestial nymph called Punjikasthala, a servitor in Sage Brihaspati's ashram. Sage Brihaspati is the guru of the Devas. One day, Punjikasthala sees a group of young men and women making love in a grove. Her passion is aroused. When she reaches the ashram, she sees Brihaspati in meditation. Punjikasthala embraces Brihaspati. Disturbed in his meditation, Brihaspati opens his eyes and sees this inmate of the ashram in the throes of passion. When Brihaspati scolds her, Punjikasthala argues that she is a beautiful woman and what is wrong with a woman having passion?

Enraged, Brihaspati curses her to be born as a Vanara since she is so proud of her beauty. She has shown an animal-like desire, and her karma will yield the fruit of an animal birth. She will then marry a Vanara with an insatiable passion for making love, so much so that even the gods will try to enter his body to enjoy the pleasures of love. That is how Shiva and Vayu enter Kesari, and Hanuman is born.

In this version, Anjana is relieved of the curse the moment Hanuman is born, and she regains her beautiful form as an Apsara. But she is devastated to see she has given birth to a Vanara. Ashamed of her Vanara-faced son, she tries to kill him. But she soon discovers the baby Vanara has superpowers. But since her curse has ended, she is duty-bound to return to heaven.

Hanuman pleads with his mother to stay, saying, 'Why are you leaving me, mother? How will I survive? Who will teach me? Where will I get a proper education?'

Anjana, who is in a hurry to get back to Deva Loka, tells Hanuman, 'If God has given you a mouth, he must feed you. I did not choose to have you. You happened because of a mistake I committed. I am going back to my home, and this earth is your place.'

Hanuman tells her, 'Since you made a mistake of passion, and I am paying the price for it, I promise that I will never look at any woman with the eyes of passion. I shall remain eternally celibate. My brahmacharya (celibacy) will be my strength. I will remain the protector of all men, women, bees, birds, and everything that seeks my protection.'

Anjana blesses her son before leaving. 'Son, I am moved by your lack of rancour,' she says. 'You are not angry that I am leaving you. You are an obedient son, and you are not holding your mother with the ties of emotion. You have overcome emotion and passion from birth. Let your name be known until the end of the universe. May you be immortal.'

Hanuman asks, 'But who will teach me, mother? How will I get my education?'

Anjana replies, 'The sun is the provider of all life on earth. The sun is the guru. Observe the universe, look at the sky and see how vast and infinite it is. Everything to know is already there. From the sun you will learn everything.'

Hanuman is thus a castaway.

Ramayana's Orphans, Castaways and Foundlings

Rama is in a way abandoned by his parents when he is exiled to the forest because of a promise given by Rama's father to his stepmother before he was born. Lakshmana and Sita cast away royal life and all its trappings. Bharata too casts away the throne and never speaks to his mother Kaikeyi after what she has done to his beloved brother Rama. Kaikeyi herself is a castaway, because her mother was cast away by her father and it was the servitor Manthara who raised Kaikeyi and her brother Yuddhajit.

Sita is a foundling who has never known her biological parents. Hanuman is also is a castaway. Bali and Sugriva, the Vanara brothers, are orphans. Their story and the various accounts of their origin will be dealt with in subsequent chapters. Jatayu and Sampati, the bird brothers, are also orphans and look after each other. Ravana and his siblings, though descendants of Brahma, are orphans because their father does not provide for them and they are left to fend for themselves. Surpanakha is orphaned when her husband is killed by Ravana, and her son by Lakshmana, and she has no one to turn to.

Everyone in the Ramayana, whichever side of the spectrum they find themselves, is self-made. Dasaratha is brought up as an orphan. His father Aja is described as deeply in love with his celestial wife. So much so, that he neglects his kingly duties, leaving them to his Rajaguru Vasishta and his ministers. But tragedy strikes. Sage Narada is travelling through the skies with his veena, which is attached to a garland slung around his neck. Unfortunately, the garland snaps and the veena falls from the sky onto Dasaratha's mother, killing her on the spot. Heartbroken, Dasratha's father Aja also dies.

Dasaratha, a small boy when the tragedy occurs, is brought up by Vasishta. He has hardly known the love of a father and mother. He continues to admire the love his father had for his mother, which is why he in his turn loves his wives blindly. This blind devotion to Kaikeyi makes him give her an unthinking promise, which triggers the chain of events. The beautiful way in which Sage Valmiki has crafted each character of the Ramayana is fascinating.

Hanuman's Early Years

In the Bhavishya Purana, the story of Hanuman continues and we see that he must fend for himself. What a Vanara does not know by instinct, it learns from other Vanaras. Hanuman yearns for education, which is unnatural in a Vanara. He decides to follow his mother's advice and learn from the sun. Using his superpowers, he flies to the sun and pleads with the deity Surya to teach him. Surya is the knower of all knowledge in the universe. In his chariot, he allows the souls of great saints to sit and understand the wisdom of the universe as he traverses through the sky. But the wise saints in Surya's chariot laugh aloud when they see the little Vanara.

Surya asks Hanuman, 'I have given all the knowledge required for animals, so why do you take the trouble of coming so far in search of more knowledge?'

Hanuman replies, 'If I think I am just a Vanara, I shall remain a Vanara. We become what we aspire to be. I aspire to be great. I want to learn the secret of the universe. I want to learn the secret of universal consciousness.'

Surya says, 'You are the universe. There is no need to seek it outside. Look deep into yourself. I have put all the wisdom of the universe inside you. Discover the wisdom within you.'

Hanuman says, 'But I want to learn even mundane things. Supreme knowledge may get me liberation, but how will I help everyone if I attain moksha and leave the earth? Is that not selfish? I want to help anyone in distress. For that, I need not the wisdom of Brahma, but knowledge of life.'

Surya invites Hanuman into his chariot. The sages cry foul. 'How can the great Sun God allow a mere Vanara into his holy chariot? A Vanara does not need education. Education is for people like us, who teach the world how to live. We are Brahma Gyanis (knowers of Brahma), Brahmins who have reached the Surya Mandala through thousands of years of penance. It is unfair that a lowly little Vanara gets the same treatment as us. Knowledge is the privilege of sages and saints. We don't want to sit with a Vanara.'

Surya is caught in a dilemma. He looks at Hanuman helplessly.

Hanuman smiles. 'Knowledge cannot be exclusive to anyone. Everyone has the right to knowledge, for with knowledge they acquire wisdom. I think the Brahma Gyanis have neither acquired wisdom nor knowledge. However, they are all my elders and I do not wish to disrespect them, so I shall learn standing outside the chariot.'

Surya says, 'Son, I travel at high velocity. From earth, it may appear that I am taking a day and night to travel. In fact, it is the earth that travels along with me as I travel across the universe at great velocity, circumambulating the centre of the universe. If you are not sitting with me in my chariot, you will not be able to keep pace with me.'

Hanuman says, 'I will keep pace with you.'

The sages laugh. 'Little Vanara, you cannot show your back to your guru. You must face him when he is giving you knowledge. Nor can you stand behind him, so how are you going to learn?'

Hanuman smiles at them. 'I shall travel backwards, never showing my back to my guru. I shall be in front of the chariot and travel at the same velocity as my guru.'

So, Hanuman stands in front of Surya's chariot. As the chariot progresses at high speed, he walks backwards in space, never allowing the chariot to overrun him, nor going so fast that he is too far from the chariot. Surya gives Hanuman all the knowledge of the world and a piece of advice too. When his education is finished, he tells Hanuman, 'My son Sugriva is being harassed by his brother Bali. Be his protector until Vishnu takes birth in the Surya Vamsha, my dynasty.'

In the folk version of this story, there is an addition. As Hanuman is leaving, a small blob of arrogance comes into his mind—the thought that 'I know it all'. On the way back he meets Narada and says, 'I have learnt everything there is to be known.'

Narada merely smiles knowingly. Hanuman is assailed by self-doubt and asks, 'Why are you smiling?'

Narada says, 'I know another person who said the same words. He also knows everything, or so he claims.'

Hanuman is annoyed and demands, 'Who is he?'

Narada replies, 'Oh no doubt he is a great scholar. He is Ravana, emperor of the Asuras. When I told him about you, he said he would vanquish you.'

Hanuman laughs. 'He can never vanquish me.'

Narada smiles again. 'Perhaps he cannot. But you too have some arrogance. Unless you change, we will have two Ravanas to deal with. Two people, full of power, full of knowledge, who don't know how to use either.'

Hanuman is annoyed at being compared to the Asura king, Ravana. He reaches Kishkindha. Aged just eight, a mischievous age, he is aware of his superpowers and starts using them on others, creating trouble wherever he goes.

One day, he enters the ashram of Saint Trinabandhu, a sage so humble that he treads the earth on soft feet for fear of hurting even a blade of grass. Trinabandhu means 'friend of the grass'. The little monkey Hanuman enters his ashram and starts his mischief. The destruction he causes is unimaginable. Hanuman uproots trees, hurls boulders and flattens huts, stomps over crops, chases cows and destroys Trinabandhu's beautifully crafted garden.

A heartbroken Trinabandhu curses Hanuman that he will lose all his powers. Vayu, the Wind God appears and pleads with Sage Trinabandhu to give Hanuman back his powers. Trinabandhu says that Hanuman has to pay the price of his actions. Then Vayu reminds Trinabandhu that Hanuman has come to earth to play a role in the coming days and by cursing him, Trinabandhu is interfering with his destiny.

Trinabandhu says, 'I do not know or care about destiny. Hanuman has harmed innocent creatures, and he must pay the price. His powers must be checked, or else he will become another Ravana. He shall henceforth forget he ever had superpowers, unless someone reminds him of them. Besides, he will always remain a servant, never a master.'

Thus, Hanuman, perhaps the most beloved of all gods in India, is an eternal servant. At first, he is a servant-friend-protector-minister to the exiled King Sugriva. Later, he is a servitor to Rama. Later, when Rama abandons Sita, the folk Ramayanas say Hanuman goes to play with Sita's sons, Lava and Kusha, and becomes a servant to Sita.

In the Kamba Ramayana, the story of Brihaspati and Punjikasthala (as Anjana) is explained differently. Here, Anjana does not leave Hanuman immediately. Bali, the king of the Vanaras, is told by Narada that his reign as the most powerful Vanara king is about to end, because Anjana's son will be more powerful than him. Bali tries to kill Hanuman when he is still in Anjana's womb. He captures her and forces her to drink a molten mixture of five metals or 'panchaloha'. Instead of killing Anjana, the five metals strengthen Hanuman's body, and he emerges with more power.

When Hanuman leaves Anjana's womb with a body made of five metals, Bali decides to have him cursed somehow. So he befriends Hanuman and encourages him to be mischievous. One day, Bali shows Hanuman the rising sun and says, 'Every day that red fruit blooms in the sky at dawn, and every evening it withers away. It goes to waste if no one eats it. All fruits are meant for Vanaras. It is the Vanara dharma to eat fruit.'

Hanuman starts to cry for the red fruit in the sky. Encouraged by Bali, he rushes to eat the sun. When he gets close to the sun, he finds the four-tusked white elephant Airavata that belongs to Indra, the ruler of Deva Loka, and tries to gobble it up. Indra uses his a thunderbolt to strike him down and Hanuman falls to earth dead.

Hanuman's father Vayu, the Wind God, takes the little body away from earth, mourning that his son has been unfairly killed. All the Devas come to plead with Vayu to return to earth, because without air all life will end. In return Vayu asks for immortality for his son. The Devas have no choice but to grant his wish. Vayu also seeks immunity from karma for Hanuman and receives it. According to the Kamba Ramayana, the Devas also grant him various powers.

Thus Bali finds Hanuman has returned even stronger. So he tricks him into entering Trinabandhu's ashram where he creates happy mayhem. Exasperated, the sage curses Hanuman to forget his superpowers until reminded at the right time by others. Thus when Hanuman meets Rama, he doesn't know he has superpowers.

Living with his friend and master Sugriva in the Rishimoolachala Mountain, Hanuman observes Rama and Lakshmana entering his forest and decides to test them. He has seen Rama's actions when he killed Kabanda earlier, and when he met Sabari. Is this the man the sages had predicted he would serve and so fulfil his life's purpose, Hanuman wonders. Is Rama really the avatar of Vishnu? Hanuman decides to find out.

21

Hanuman's Ties with Sugriva and His Meeting with Rama

HAVING SEEN RAMA AND LAKSHMANA IN ACTION WHILE SPYING ON THEM all this while, Hanuman decides that these two young men can help his master and invites them to meet Sugriva. However, when Sugriva sees the duo approaching, he runs away in fear. Hanuman asks why he is running and Sugriva exclaims, 'My brother Bali has sent two warriors to kill me!'

Hanuman explains that these are not Bali's men. 'I have seen them do good work,' he says. 'They killed the Asura Kabanda and helped him abandon his Asura form. I have seen how they behaved with Sabari. They are compassionate and righteous. It seems they are in search of someone. The black-skinned one is grieving. I will go and enquire.'

Hanuman takes the form of a Brahmin and goes to Rama and asks, 'Oh black-skinned warrior, who are you? You wear the dress of a hermit, and you roam in our forest doing good deeds, yet you carry a bow and arrows. Are you a hermit or a warrior? Or are you some Deva disguised as a human?"

Lakshmana whips up his bow and points it at Hanuman. 'Are you an Asura in disguise? Brother, permit me to kill him.'

Rama restrains Lakshmana saying, 'We should never act in haste. If he were an Asura in disguise, he could have attacked us from behind. There was no need for him to come empty-handed before us. We should always think all are good and noble unless they prove to be otherwise. Even if they commit some mistake, we should not punish them in haste, but try to understand why they committed such a mistake and what we can do to help them. He has neither committed a mistake nor threatened us. It seems he belongs to this forest and we have intruded. He has treated us with respect.'

Rama turns to Hanuman. 'I am Rama, prince of Ayodhya, and this is my brother Lakshmana. We are in exile because of a promise my father gave my mother Kaikeyi. My wife has been abducted by the Asura Ravana, and we are searching for her. I know you are no ordinary Vanara, kindly introduce yourself.'

Hanuman introduces himself as Sugriva's minister and tells Rama that his master is suffering just like Rama. 'Sugriva's brother Bali has thrown him out of the kingdom and forcefully taken his wife, Ruma.'

Hanuman then takes Rama and Lakshmana to Sugriva. This tale is as per the Valmiki Ramayana. However, in various other Puranas, such as the Skanda Purana and folk Ramayanas, Hanuman and Rama meet in childhood. Hanuman grows up with Rama until Rama sends him to Kishkindha (the city of the Vanaras) to serve Sugriva.

In the Valmiki Ramayana, Rama retains his human form in all but two chapters. He is a great prince and warrior, a righteous man, but he is rarely seen as the avatar of Vishnu. However, in the Bhakti-era Ramayanas and in many folk versions (discussed below), everyone, including Rama, is aware that Rama is Vishnu the Supreme God, who has taken birth on earth.

One of the fascinating folk-tales about how Rama and Hanuman first met goes like this. Shiva, Hanuman's father, is anxious to see how Rama, Ayodhya's boy-prince, is faring. He goes in various disguises to the Ayodhya palace to watch the mischievous Rama. Sometimes, he takes one of his disciples, called Kakabusundi, and at other times he goes with his wife, Parvati, and Hanuman, then a very young Vanara, in the disguise of a tribal. Shiva makes the little Vanara perform tricks in the street, and the children crowd around to watch. Little Rama insists on watching this entertainment with the other children.

Dasaratha does not wish Prince Rama to go out into the streets and instead invites the Vanara to perform in the palace. Rama asks for some time alone with the Vanara. Dasaratha is afraid he will harm the little boy, but the Vanara's master assures him he is very tame. So Rama picks up the little Vanara and carries him to his chamber and closes the door. The Vanara jumps on to a chair, a table and a cot, and starts playing pranks. He tries to get Rama angry by tearing up the bed, pulling down the curtains, and toppling the chairs. But Rama is merely amused. When the Vanara is exhausted and the chamber a mess, Rama calls the Vanara's master in.

Shiva, who is disguised as the master, is aghast at the mess and apologizes to Rama, saying, 'Prince, I am a poor man. I don't know why he has played all these pranks. He is always well-behaved.'

The young Rama smiles at him. 'Lord Shiva, you think I cannot see through your disguise? If your son cannot play pranks on me, who can?'

Shiva laughs aloud and removes his disguise. Rama too reveals himself as Vishnu. The two gods discuss the growing menace of Ravana.

Vishnu says, 'As long as Ravana has the grace of Lord Shiva, it will be impossible for Lord Vishnu to defeat him.'

Shiva says, 'The moment my disciple Ravana does something that is inherently cruel, he will lose my grace, and this Vanara, my son, will be responsible for his downfall. Hanuman will do what he has done in this room. He will go to Ravana's abode and destroy it. And how Ravana reacts to that will determine how much of my grace he will continue to possess. If Ravana reacts as you did, which I am sure he will not, it will be difficult for me to deny him my blessings.'

Vishnu says, 'I understand. I only pray that I will always have your son's help. I am sure that when the time comes, everyone will choose according to their nature, and those choices will decide their destinies.' He tells the little Vanara, 'You don't belong in the city, you belong in the forest. Go to Kishkindha, and when the time comes, we shall meet.' He hugs Hanuman and sends him away. This is the folk version, reminding us about choices and consequences.

There are other versions of the Ramayana, in which Hanuman grows up with Rama in the palace in Ayodhya, and they do many heroic things together. However, from a story point of view, the Valmiki Ramayana has more logic to it. Here Hanuman behaves as if he is seeing Rama and Lakshmana for the first time, and though he is shown as suspecting them to be Devas in disguise, the word Deva is just a figure of speech for men of noble bearing and temperament. Hanuman serves as a wise minister for his exiled master Sugriva and takes Rama and Lakshmana to him.

Bali and Sugriva's story is another fascinating tale within the Ramayana. As I mentioned earlier, the Ramayana is also the tale of brothers. Bali and Sugriva are the half-brothers of Jatayu and Sampati who are the sons of Aruna (the charioteer of Surya the Sun God). But in the case of Bali and Sugriva, Aruna in his female form,

Aruni, is their mother (Bali's father was Surya, and Sugriva's father was Indra).

In the Puranas, the difference between male and female is very fluid. Hindu thought considers male and female as different aspects of a whole. A day contains both day and night. Similarly, the term man includes woman too, and the term woman holds man. Many characters take the male-to-female form or vice versa seamlessly. This is better expounded in the concept of ardha (half) nareshwara, the half-male half-female form of Shiva, which is Shiva and Parvati together. In many temples, this form is worshipped to emphasize the whole. Like the concept of prakriti and purusha, the ardhanareshwara concept plays a significant part in the Hindu way of life. The sex of characters changing seamlessly is a common theme in the Puranas, for instance, when Vishnu takes the female form in his avatar of Mohini.

As per the Mahabharata's folk versions in Tamil Nadu, Krishna too takes the form of Mohini and marries Aravan for a day. Aravan is the son of Arjuna, who must be sacrificed to ensure the victory of the Pandavas. Transgender people consider Aravan their deity because he made Krishna take the female form and marry him. Similarly, in the union of Shiva and Mohini, Lord Ayyappa is born. It is thus not surprising to find that Aruna is Jatayu and Sampati's father, and as Aruni is Bali and Sugriva's mother.

22

Bali and Sugriva: Their Origins and Rivalry

IN AN EARLIER CHAPTER, WE TALKED ABOUT THE STORY OF NALAYANI, THE virtuous woman in the Mahabharata whose husband was cursed by Sage Mandavya. Bali and Sugriva's tale is linked to this. Remember, Sage Mandavya had cursed Nalayani's husband saying he would die before sunrise. However, the sun was not able to rise the next day because of Nalayani's great virtue.

Aruna, the Sun God's charioteer, arrives on duty and finds that his master has not arisen yet. After waiting for quite some time, he gets bored. He can hear sounds of merriment coming from Deva Loka, and knows that Indra is watching the Apsaras like Menaka, Rambha, Urvashi and Tilottama dance. Aruna decides not to wait for Surya Deva to arise and goes to Deva Loka to watch the dancers. However, Indra's bodyguards stop him. No male other than Indra can view the performance. So with his magical powers, Aruna takes the form of a dazzlingly beautiful woman and enters Indra's harem and enjoys the performance.

When it is over, Indra summons him. Aruna, worried that he has done something wrong, is sure he will be cursed or punished. When Indra asks who 'she' is, Aruna heaves a sigh of relief. The king of the Devas has not seen through his disguise. Aruna says his name is Aruni, and 'she' has come from Surya Loka, the heavenly world of the Sun God. Indra is drawn to this beautiful woman and forces himself upon her.

By this time, Nalayani's curse has been lifted and Surya is ready to rise. In a panic, Aruna as Aruni rushes to perform his duty and jumps into his chariot. An impatient Surya is waiting for his charioteer, and is surprised to see a dazzling beauty jump in instead. Aruna, having forgotten to change back, mumbles an apology for being late and Surya bursts out laughing when he realizes that this beauty is none other than his charioteer. But he too is smitten by Aruni's beauty and forces himself on her.

From the union of Indra and Aruni, Bali is born. So Bali is the son of Indra. From the union of Surya and Aruni, Sugriva is born, hence he is the son of the Sun God.

In other versions of the Ramayana, Bali and Sugriva's origin story is different but it still involves a male turning into a female. After their birth, one version states that Bali and Sugriva are given to Ahalya, the wife of Sage Gautama, to bring up. When Ahalya is cursed, the two brothers are left on their own. A eunuch Vanara called Riksharajas or Vriksharajas adopts them and teaches them everything they need to know to build the Vanara empire. Bali, the more powerful of the duo, builds the empire with Sugriva's help.

In an alternate version, Riksharajas is not their adoptive father but their birth mother. The story begins with a mighty Vanara being born from one of Brahma's tears. His name is Riksharajas. Everyone in heaven laughs at this Vanara avatar. Brahma, in trying to create humans, had ended up with a creature that was neither Vanara nor human. The young creature is sad that he is the butt of ridicule and asks Brahma why he is so unfortunate. Brahma blesses him, saying, 'You will rule the forest. You will be more powerful than any human and more intelligent than any animal.'

Riksharajas is happy with the boon but does not pause to reflect on the catch. Brahma has not said that he will be more intelligent than any human. Riksharajas starts ruling the forest and brings the Vanara clan together.

One day, he comes upon a magical lake. He remembers the ridicule he once faced in heaven when his father Brahma created him. Curious to see what he looks like, he gazes at his reflection in the lake but does not understand it is his own reflection that is staring back at him. He sees an ugly Vanara glaring back. He shouts at the Vanara; it echoes back. He tries to punch the Vanara; it disappears. Like many of us who fight with the world without knowing that it is our own reflection, Riksharajas does the same. Deciding to kill this Vanara who dares to grin at him, he jumps into the lake. The lake is a magical one. Whoever enters it becomes female.

Some folk-tales say this lake was located near Rishyashringa's home. Rishyashringa's father, Vibhantaka, had cast a magical spell around the forest and lake where his son lived to protect his son's celibacy. His efforts, however, were in vain, for Shanta, Rama's elder sister, had succeeded in turning the ascetic Rishyashringa into a householder.

When Riksharajas comes out of the lake, he is surprised to find that he has turned into a beautiful woman. He cries to Brahma, 'Father, I was a powerful male, where has this female come from?'

From the skies, Brahma says, 'That female was always in you. In every male there is a female, and in every female there is a male.'

Riksharajas, who has more intelligence than any other animal but not as much as humans, wonders what Brahma means. As he sits contemplating the complexities of life, Indra, who has been travelling through the sky on his mighty white elephant, Airavata, sees the reflection of a beautiful woman in the lake. He flies down and scoops Riksharajas up and makes love to her. In some versions, his seed falls on Riksharajas's hair and from that Bali is born. In other versions, Bali is simply said to be born of their union.

Meanwhile, the setting sun also happens to spot the female version of Riksharajas and is so entranced that he too makes love to her and from their union Sugriva is born. After giving birth to Sugriva through his neck ('grivah' in Sanskrit), Riksharajas assumes his manly form once again. From that day onwards, he is both father and mother to Bali and Sugriva.

The brothers grow up to become great warriors. In the Valmiki Ramayana, Bali is considered the most powerful of warriors, who even defeats Ravana. In latter-day folk Ramayanas and the Bhakti-era Ramayana, Bali has a unique power. Whoever confronts him loses half their strength, which then accrues to Bali making him even stronger. That is why Bali remains unvanquished in the Ramayana, till his death.

Once, when Bali is praying in the evening, Ravana sees him. He remembers what Sage Narada has told him, that the greatest and most powerful warrior in the world is a Vanara called Bali. For Ravana, who has even lifted Mount Kailasa in the Himalayas, this is an insult he cannot bear. He searches for Bali and concludes that the Vanara praying by the sea is the famed warrior.

Ravana lands his Pushpaka Vimana and walks towards Bali, who is immersed in his prayers and does not hear the danger approaching. Ravana considers using his famed sword Chandrahasa on Bali, but then thinks better of it. It is not fair to use a weapon on an unarmed opponent, especially when he is not facing you on a battlefield. He decides to test Bali's strength by wrestling with him. Ravana sheaths Chandrahasa and sneaks up behind Bali, grabs him and whispers in his ear, 'I challenge you, Vanara, to a duel.'

Ravana thinks he has locked Bali in a deathly hold and the Vanara will not be able to wriggle out of his powerful grip. But Bali winds his tail around Ravana and dives into the sea still in deep prayer. Gasping for breath, Ravana is unable to free himself from the coils of Bali's tail. Then Bali leaps out of the water and leaps to the Western Sea. He prays there, even as Ravana lies tied down in the coils of his tail. Then he emerges from the Western Sea, takes another dip in it before leaping to the Northern Sea and then to the Southern Sea. Through all this, poor Ravana lies trapped in Bali's tail, crying piteously to be freed. Bali finally opens his eyes as if surprised to see something trapped in his tail. He releases Ravana and apologizes to him. Ravana, feeling insulted and worthless, asks Bali to kill him.

Bali says, 'I have nothing against you. I want nothing from you. Why should I commit a violent act when I can neither eat you nor want your territory? I am no human, Asura or Deva. I am a being of the forest, whom you call a Vanara. No animal attacks anyone unless it is fighting for food, territory or mate. I have no dispute with you, so it is not my dharma to kill you.'

Ravana is moved by the Vanara's generosity and logic and swears eternal friendship to Bali. Ravana and Bali become the best of friends and promise never to harm each other or attack each other's kingdoms.

Bali and Sugriva too remain close. Bali is affectionate towards his brother, treating him more like a son. But everything changes when they meet Tara, the beautiful daughter of Vaidya (healer/doctor) Sushena. They both fall in love with her, but she falls for the elder brother, Bali. They get married, while Sugriva is forced to marry

Ruma, though he covets his sister-in-law. Bali remains unaware of this.

Folk-tales narrate in detail the dangers to domestic life when a younger brother yearns for the elder brother's mate. However, Sugriva does not act on his feelings as long as Bali is alive, even though he remains conflicted between his love for his brother and lust for his sister-in-law. Bali is short-tempered and Sugriva knows that if Bali were to get even a hint of what is in his heart, Sugriva would be finished.

As fate would have it, an Asura, in the form of a wild buffalo called Dundhubi, attacks Kishkindha. Bali kills the Asura in a duel. Dundhubi's brother Mayavi seeks revenge and challenges Bali. Bali is said to have been eating when he hears of this challenge. Not one to back down, and despite his wife Tara's warning, he does not finish his meal but runs out with his club to duel with Mayavi. Sugriva follows his brother.

The battle begins and after a while Mayavi understands that he is no match for Bali and runs for his life, abusing Bali. Enraged, Bali follows him. Sugriva follows both. Mayavi enters a cave and hides. Bali tells his brother, 'Sugriva, it is dangerous to leave this Asura alive. He does not listen to even his emperor Ravana. He is full of rage and seeks revenge. For the safety of our people, I must kill him. We all know that Mayavi has many magic spells. If I am killed, I do not want him to come back and wreak havoc in the city we have built. I must protect my people. It is my dharma to put their safety above mine. So brother, close the mouth of this cave with that boulder. If I die, red blood will flow out because I am a mere animal. If the Asura dies, the blood will be some other colour, perhaps white or blue. So, for our safety, close the entrance of the cave and stand guard.'

Accordingly, Sugriva moves the boulder to close the cave once Bali enters. In the folk versions from northern Kerala, Bali has a pet wolf too. All hunter-gatherer tribes in south Indian forests usually have dogs with them or perhaps tame wolves. Sugriva waits for a long time and hears sounds of fighting from inside the cave. Suddenly, to his horror, red blood flows out. Sugriva remembers Bali's words and leaves, assuming his brother is dead. He does not wait to confirm this because he is afraid of Mayavi coming out of the cave. But the wolf refuses to leave. Ironically, Sugriva, the brother Bali has looked after all this while, abandons him and leaves for Kishkindha.

Bali understands that the colour of blood is red, irrespective of caste, creed, religion or species. But it is too late. He is trapped. He tries to come out, but a landslide locks him inside the mountain. The patient wolf waits for him outside, while Sugriva goes to Kishkindha to tell everyone about the tragedy that has befallen his beloved brother.

Following a period of mourning, Sugriva becomes the king of the Vanaras and marries Bali's wife Tara. Sugriva thinks he has achieved his life's ambition. However, Bali claws his way out of the landslide and the cave and one fine day returns to Kishkindha. There he is shocked to find that his brother didn't even try to rescue him nor has he waited for him. When he challenges Sugriva to a duel, Sugriva falls at his feet asking for forgiveness. But Bali is in no mood to forgive; he thinks Sugriva has cheated him. A brother who betrays one is not worth protecting and deserves death, he decides. But just as he is about to kill Sugriva, he realizes this is the younger brother he has brought up. He cannot kill him. So Bali expels Sugriva from Vanara society.

However, Sugriva refuses to go. He pleads for mercy, entreating Bali to take him back. Bali no longer trusts Sugriva and chases him out of Kishkindha. Whenever Sugriva tries to enter the city, Bali chases him out again. Eventually, Bali gets so enraged at this behaviour that he decides Sugriva will remain nowhere near

Kishkindha. Hanuman, who arrives at this time, remembers that he must stand with the powerless and the downtrodden. He attempts to advise Bali, telling him to forgive his brother. But Bali does not relent and in vengeance takes Sugriva's wife, Ruma. Angry with Bali's arrogant attitude, Hanuman decides to support Sugriva. Thus, the Vanara Bali, a brave and noble creature, is corrupted by the rancour he builds within himself.

Sugriva fails in all his attempts to either defeat Bali or achieve reconciliation and moves to Rishimoolachala Mountain, where he lives in eternal fear, even though Bali has been cursed to die if he enters this mountain. When he was young, he had placed a dead snake on a saint doing penance there. The sage had cursed him that his head would burst if he stepped on to this mountain. So, this is the only place where Sugriva is safe from Bali. One fascinating folk-tale, however, states that Bali leaps up from the valley, kicks Sugriva on the head without touching the mountain, and leaps down. He continues to do so to harass his brother.

Hanuman wants to help Sugriva, so one day when he spots Bali in the valley, he hides near Sugriva in a bush. When Bali leaps up and lands on Sugriva's head, Hanuman grabs his legs and tries to ensure Bali's feet touch the mountain so that he dies. But Bali escapes while unsuccessfully trying to take Hanuman with him so that Sugriva is left without his bodyguard. Since Hanuman and Bali are equally matched in strength, neither is successful in doing what they want. Bali declares a truce—as long as Sugriva lives in Rishimoolachala Mountain and does not come to Kishkindha, Bali will leave him alone. So, Hanuman, Sugriva and three of his ministers live on Rishimoolachala Mountain, waiting for someone to help them get justice.

Sugriva tells Rama this story, painting himself as the faultless victim and Bali as the oppressor. He pleads with Rama to help him. Rama, who is suffering the pain of anguished separation from Sita, identifies with Sugriva's sorrow. He too has lost his wife to another man. Rama and Sugriva make a pact before a raging fire to help each other. Thus, Rama becomes aligned to the Vanara kingdom.

Thus Lord Vishnu's avatar must take the Vanara clan's help to defeat Ravana, which is also a tale of choice and its consequence.

23

The Day Narada Almost Got Married

This chapter is about why Rama is compelled to take the help of the Vanaras. In the Bhagavatham, this tale starts when Lord Vishnu pays the price for a prank he plays on Narada. He does so because Narada too has to pay the price for a choice he once made. This never-ending cycle of action and consequences forms the basis of Indian thought.

The story goes like this: Narada goes to do penance in a forest in the Himalayas. He is unaware that this particular forest has the protection of Lord Shiva as it is where the Lord did penance after losing his wife Sati in her father Daksha's sacrificial fire. Lord Shiva becomes a vairagi, a renunciate. This worries the Devas as a god who is a brahmachari (celibate) cannot be a compassionate god. Indian thought has always emphasized that earthly and heavenly rulers must be householders. Hanuman is the only exception to this. Having a family is one of the requirements for balance in the world.

So the Devas ask Kamadeva, the God of Love, to shoot Shiva with his arrow. Kamadeva uses a sugarcane as his bow, bees as the string, and five flowers as his arrow. When Kamadeva's arrow strikes Lord Shiva, he opens his eyes and sees Parvati, who has come to pick flowers, and falls in love with her. He then realizes that thoughts of passion have entered his mind and he has failed in his penance. It is said that the most potent force in the world is love. Even Shiva in his grief could not stop the power of Kamadeva's arrow. But, angered by this interruption, Shiva destroys Kamadeva, who is burnt to ashes. With passion gone, Shiva returns to his penance. But when love disappears from the world, life collapses. There is no procreation. Life as we know it stands still.

So the gods plead with Shiva to bring Kamadeva back to life. Shiva revives Kamadeva, but since he was burnt by the powerful rays of Shiva's third eye, he never regains his body. Hence, Kamadeva is called 'Ananga' or 'one without a body'. Shiva blesses Kamadeva to be present in an invisible form in places where love blooms. Kamadeva is blessed to live in rainbows, in the fragrance of flowers, in the moonlight, in the drone of the bees, in the chirping of birds, in music, in dance, in painting, and in heroism. With Kamadeva's return, the world resumes its normal functions, and Shiva's love for Parvati ignites once again. Kalidasa describes this scene beautifully in his poem 'Kumara Sambhavam'.

Shiva returns to the life of a householder and Lord Kartikeya is born. Shiva also blesses the forest where he has done penance saying that whoever does penance there will not be struck by Kamadeva.

It is to this forest that Narada comes to do penance. But this worries Indra. He can understand Asuras doing penance. It is usually to gain boons. Sometimes they ask for immortality, which they never get; other times they ask for divine weapons to conquer the world. When humans do penance, Indra knows they ask for ordinary things like a good life, money or love. But why is Narada, a sage who needs nothing and who has no use for anything, doing penance?

Narada is, in fact, praying to become the greatest devotee of Narayana or Lord Vishnu. Not knowing this, Indra wishes to disturb Narada's penance and sends various Apsaras to disturb Narada's concentration. But since he is sitting in a forest blessed by Lord Shiva, the celestial nymphs are ineffective. Eventually, Narada achieves his aim and goes back triumphant. He boasts to everyone saying, 'Nothing could tempt me. I am beyond all temptations. Even the great Lord Shiva was tempted. Other sages like Vishwamitra and Vasishta have been tempted by various Apsaras, but I can control my mind. I am greater than Shiva and all the Maharishis.'

The news of these boasts reaches Shiva, who is amused. Does Narada not know that he was able to concentrate on his penance because he, Lord Shiva, blessed the forest? Lord Shiva narrates this amusing tale to Lord Vishnu, saying, 'Your devotee has become arrogant. He thinks he is responsible for his own success. I am not taking anything away from his efforts, but circumstances always play a part in anyone's success. Narada was successful because so many other things came together. One should be grateful for whatever they achieve in life.'

Lord Vishnu replies, 'It is time to teach Narada a lesson he will not forget.'

As soon as Narada reaches Vaikunta, full of confidence and brimming with joy, he excitedly tells Vishnu that he has achieved something that even Lord Shiva failed to do.

Lord Vishnu tells Narada, 'If you start thinking about something, the mind has the power to manifest it.'

Narada is confused. Vishnu explains that if he keeps boasting that he cannot be tempted, his own mind will play a trick on him, and soon the sage will find that whatever he has shunned so far will attract him with a vengeance. Narada is confident that no such thing can happen and takes leave of Vishnu.

As Narada walks on, he sees a beautiful woman taking a bath. She is a princess and Narada finds that he is attracted to her. Kamadeva has played his tricks on Narada. To his dismay, Narada learns that the princess's swayamvara is to take place the next day and she is sure to become the wife of some king. Narada rushes back to Vishnu and asks for his help. Narada sheepishly says that he wishes to be married.

Vishnu tries to dissuade him, saying, 'With great difficulty, you have reached this position. You had chosen the life of a hermit. You know it is best for you. Why are you now succumbing to temptation?'

Narada replies, 'Lord, you have always said we are free to choose. I choose to cast aside the life of a hermit and take on the life of a householder. I do not want to live if I am not able to marry the princess.'

Vishnu says, 'Then go and marry her.'

But Narada is filled with doubt about his own worth. He says, 'I am not confident she will choose me. I don't look good. She is so beautiful. There will be great warriors and handsome princes who will come for her hand. Why should she marry a person with a face like mine?'

Vishnu asks, 'What is wrong with your face?'

Narada says sadly, 'I am not handsome.' Then, after a moment's thought, he adds, 'I wish I had a handsome face like yours.'

Vishnu says, 'Love yourself for what you are. Do not try to be like anyone else. There is nothing wrong with you as long as you do not think there is something wrong.'

Narada pleads, 'Please give me a boon. Let my face look like Hari's.'

Vishnu smiles, amused. 'You want to look like Hari? That is your choice? So be it.'

Narada leaves, his heart brimming with confidence and happiness. He is to look like Hari, his beloved deity. Hari is another name for Vishnu. But Hari also means 'monkey', a Vanara. Vishnu has played a prank on Narada to teach him that arrogance is not a quality a sage should have. Narada goes to the swayamvara and waits patiently for the princess to come with the garland. He is confident she will choose him because he is as handsome as Hari. He cannot understand why all the kings and princes present are laughing at him. When the princess comes, she sees Narada. He looks at her with deep expectation. She smothers her laughter and passes on.

Narada is crestfallen and yells at the assembly, 'What is wrong with me? Or rather, what is wrong with all of you? Am I not the most handsome man here?'

The assembly of kings and princes laugh uncontrollably at this comment. One of the kings yells at him, 'Hey monkey-faced man, go and look in a mirror.'

Narada is shocked. He rushes out to look at his reflection. A monkey stares back at him. Vishnu had played a trick on him! He rushes to Vaikunta and finds Shiva and Vishnu waiting for him. They laugh at his plight.

Angered by this, Narada curses Vishnu, saying, 'I went in search of love. I trusted you and asked for a boon for the first time in my life. I lost the girl I loved. May you be born as a man on earth and may you lose your beloved to another man. And to regain her, may you be forced to take the help of Vanaras. Let a Vanara be your protector and servant. Without the help of the Vanaras, you shall remain a helpless wanderer who has lost his wife to another man. Let the world know that the mighty Lord Vishnu too must take the help of mere Vanaras. And Lord Shiva, may you be born as a Vanara and serve Lord Vishnu in his human avatar.'

Vishnu replies, 'When I am doing something, I do it with deep thought. It was not my intention to make fun of you but to make you understand that you are already on the right path. When you want something desperately and don't get it, you may feel disappointed. But be aware that I am looking after you and I know what is good for you. You would never have been happy with that woman. You have devoted your life to me, yet you do not trust me.'

Narada is devastated when he hears this and falls at Lord Vishnu and Lord Shiva's feet, begging for forgiveness.

Lord Vishnu says, 'I am happy that you cursed me because it again proves every action will bear its fruit. I could have chosen to teach you in some other way, but I thought this was the most harmless. Being ridiculed is a minor thing compared to suffering for many lives. However, it was a choice I made, and it has hurt you. Your curse will also do me good, and I am happy that Lord Shiva will be there with me as my protector and servant in that avatar. Together, we will deal with the power of Ravana and Kumbhakarna.'

In many versions, Hanuman is the avatar of Lord Shiva and not just his son. Due to Narada's curse, Rama is separated from his wife, and Shiva leads a hermit's life in the form of Hanuman. Again, the cycle of karma is at work. As predicted by Narada, Rama is forced to take the help of the Vanaras. He is taken to Sugriva by Hanuman, and they take an oath to help each other. However, Sugriva is assailed by doubt. Bali is a huge Vanara and his powers are legendary, whereas this dark-skinned human looks lean. Can he possibly match Bali's strength?

Rama senses Sugriva's doubts and decides to clear them. As they are walking together, they come across the corpse of a wild bison called Dundubhi, who has been slain by Bali. Rama kicks the carcass, and it falls at a great distance.

Here, one pauses to reflect why Rama did not conduct Dundubhi's funeral as he did for Jatayu. The reason many folk artistes give for this strange omission is the fact that in Jatayu's case, the bird was killed by Ravana, an Asura. In Dundubhi's case, an animal (Bali) killed another animal (Dundubhi). Rama does not wish to interfere with the cycle of life.

Sugriva has yet to be convinced of Rama's strength. Sensing Sugriva's doubt, Rama shoots an arrow. It chops off the heads of seven palm trees that Bali has nourished. Convinced at last of Rama's strength, Sugriva tells Rama that he will challenge Bali the next day.

24

The Slaying of Bali

Sugriva and Rama make a pact, with the fire as holy witness, to help each other. Accordingly, Sugriva challenges Bali to a duel. Hearing that his brother, who has been living in Rishimoolachala Mountain for so many years, has come back to challenge him leaves Bali both surprised and angry.

Nevertheless, he picks up his club to fight his brother, but his wife Tara stops him, saying, 'There must be a reason why Sugriva has returned. He may have powerful allies. Otherwise, your brother is not so brave as to challenge you again. Neither is he fool enough to attempt to defeat you when he has lost to you so many times before.'

Bali says he is a warrior, and it is his dharma to fight. When he is challenged, he cannot remain mute. Despite Tara's premonitions and warnings, Bali rushes out. Tara knows something disastrous is going to happen to her husband. Tara is one of the pancharatnas or five jewels (virtuous women) of Hindu mythology. Her life is a fascinating one. She first marries Bali and then Sugriva, after a brief period of mourning following Bali's alleged death. When Bali returns, they remarry and she has a son called Angada. Tara has always been in

love with Bali. She had married Sugriva out of a sense of duty. She embraces life and takes it as it comes. She chooses not to live the life of a widow, but that of a powerful and independent woman.

When Bali came out of the cave and returned to the palace, Tara told Bali to be merciful to Sugriva, saying that Sugriva did not take her by force; she married him willingly. This enraged Bali, not because he suspected Tara, but because he thought Sugriva was well aware that he was not dead. Bali accepted Tara back even though she had been living with Sugriva in his absence. Tara is considered the wisest of all the women in the Ramayana, and more beautiful than Sita, Ahalya or Mandodari.

So Tara sits in her cave palace, worried about both Bali and Sugriva's fate. In the courtyard, the Vanara brothers face each other. Sugriva's courage dissolves when he sees Bali's fierce form. Then he remembers Rama, standing behind a tree waiting for an opportunity to shoot an arrow through his brother's heart, and attacks Bali with his gada (mace). Taken aback by Sugriva's sudden confidence, Bali fights with all his might, beating Sugriva to an inch of his life and says, 'I would have killed you but you are my younger brother. I am sparing your life once again. Go to Rishimoolachala and stay there, and I will not touch you.' Turning his back on Sugriva, he walks to his palace.

Sugriva, bleeding and bruised, is carried back to his hiding place by Hanuman. He frets and fumes, saying Rama has betrayed him. When Rama comes, Sugriva vents his anger upon him. He trusted Rama, but Rama did not kill his brother as promised. Rama apologizes to Sugriva saying that since both Bali and Sugriva are so alike, he could not make out who was who. Rama suggests that when Sugriva next challenges Bali to a duel, he should wear a garland of flowers. Rama can then identify him and know whose heart to shoot at.

The next day, Sugriva challenges Bali again. This time, Tara is sure her husband is in grave danger and begs him not to accept the challenge. But Bali is adamant. He believes that if he does not accept the challenge, he will have forfeited his right to rule the Vanaras. Tara holds Bali tight, saying she will not let him go. Bali pacifies her saying that a warrior must face death one day or another on the battlefield. It is better than growing old and dying in bed. Tara tells him that she has made enquiries and found that two princes from the north have befriended Sugriva. They are Rama and Lakshmana, and they have killed many Asuras and Rakshasas on their way. It is they who must be Sugriva's allies. Tara senses a trap.

But Bali says that Rama is also a warrior and will expect him to fight face-to-face. Has Bali not defeated the mighty Ravana in a duel? Bali says he will defeat Rama too. Tara then says that if Rama wanted to fight him directly, he would have come out and done so the previous day. The fact that he did not is proof of some conspiracy.

Bali replies, 'I have heard the bards tell of the virtues of Rama. They say he is the incarnation of Lord Vishnu himself. Hence, I do not think he will do something ignoble. And if he must go against the code of warriors and Kshatriya dharma, that would be the greatest tribute he can pay to my valour. If he must use trickery to defeat me, it shows I am a greater warrior than he. I will be in the league of the great Asura emperor Mahabali, who had to be deceived to be defeated. My time has come, Tara. And if it is my destiny to die at the hands of Rama, let it be so. As long as the world lasts, people will remember me as much as they will Rama.'

This conversation is part of many folk versions, especially in southern India, where Bali is still held in awe. And so Bali and Sugriva face each other yet again. Sugriva wears a garland, as advised by Rama. The brothers fight and Sugriva is on the verge of another defeat, when an arrow comes flying from behind a tree and pierces Bali's heart. Bali turns to see who has shot him and finds Rama coming out of hiding. Like a chopped banyan tree, the mighty Bali falls to the ground.

Sugriva is struck by remorse at what he has done to the brother who brought him up. Tara comes running, wailing for her dying husband. She takes Bali's head on to her lap and hugs him close. Sugriva beats his chest, crying for his brother.

Rama looks down at Bali, lying on the ground, facing him for the first time. Bali asks him, 'Why did you shoot me?'

Rama replies, 'Because you are an animal.'

This argument stands on very shaky ground. For thousands of years, writers, poets and sages, including those of the Bhakti era, who considered Rama the Supreme God, have grappled with the morality and ethics of Rama's action in killing Bali. Like Surpanakha's mutilation at the hands of Lakshmana, Rama's act of killing Bali in Valmiki's version has always raised questions. If Bali was an animal, to be shot and killed, why was his funeral conducted as per human customs? Bali's son Angada performs the death rituals according to Aryan traditions. As in Jatayu's case, Bali's funeral negates the argument that he was an animal.

In folk Ramayanas, Bali's words ring with uncomfortable vigour through the ages. He asks Rama, 'Animals hunt for food, for a mate or for territory. Why do you, a prince, say it is your dharma as a Kshatriya to hunt? If you have hunted me, I wish to know whether you are hungry. Will you be eating me to satiate your hunger? If you are not going to eat me, what then is your hunger for? Is it for my territory? Are you going to rule as king here? Or is it for my mate? Are you going to marry my wife?'

Rama has no answer to any of these questions. In some folk Ramayanas, the explanation given is that it is the king's duty to hunt dangerous animals. Bali had become a danger to society, and just as one would hunt down a mad elephant or a man-eating tiger, Rama kills Bali. However, in the same folk tradition, where subaltern views have prominence, this justification is ripped apart. They say that Bali was not creating trouble for anyone except his brother, whom he believed to have betrayed him. Bali neither attacks Rama's nor Ravana's kingdom. Both Ravana and Rama come at various times to Bali. Ravana fights a duel in which Bali defeats him. Rama does not fight but shoots him from behind a tree.

The fact that Bali, a Vanara, follows human customs indicates he is like any other king. So, the argument that he is a dangerous animal and thus can be killed by Rama, gives rise to another question: Does a human have the right to kill animals? Can he interfere with the rhythm of nature? Bali had taken Sugriva's wife Ruma forcibly, acting as per the dharma of the Vanaras. If Rama's argument that he can hunt animals is correct, then animal dharma must reign supreme in the animal kingdom. Bali taking Ruma is not an immoral act if we accept the logic that Bali is a Vanara. So, the argument about morality or dharma in Rama's action falls flat.

However, if we read the Valmiki Ramayana, along with Vedavyasa's Mahabharata, we get a simpler and more elegant explanation for Rama's act. Rama must choose whether to support Bali or Sugriva. Bali tells Rama when he lies dying that he could have got Sita for him much quicker than Sugriva. For one, Ravana is his ally and friend. He could have persuaded Ravana to give Sita back, or he would have defeated Ravana once again for Rama.

He says, 'I am the king, and I would have rendered you justice. You have come to my kingdom as a mendicant, not an invading prince. The right thing would have been to come to the king and ask for help. I would have given you justice. Instead, you decided to perpetuate an injustice.'

Rama does not wish to ally with Bali because he thinks that one who has taken his brother's wife (i.e., Bali) will not be sympathetic to his own cause. If Bali believes that might is right and one can take the mate of another by force, this does not sit well with the moral values Rama has learnt. In Aryan society, it is not uncommon for a younger brother to marry the elder brother's widow. From Rama's perspective, what Sugriva has done is not wrong. He has taken his brother's wife thinking his brother is dead, and Tara voluntarily accepted him. But Bali taking Sugriva's wife Ruma is immoral because in Aryan societies the younger brother's wife is considered a daughter. Rama is thus imposing the human moral values of Ayodhya society on Bali's Vanara kingdom of Kishkindha.

From Bali's point of view, he has acted as per the ethical code of the Vanaras. It is not an immoral act; it is natural. Bali's mistake, which he confesses to Tara as he is dying, is that he spared Sugriva's life in the first place. Had he acted as per Vanara dharma, he would have killed Sugriva the day he returned. The choice of showing compassion to his brother has resulted in his own death. Bali is confused about whether to follow the ancient moral code of the Vanaras or the morality they have acquired through their education. His choice proved fatal for him. But even though this explains Bali's act, it does not explain Rama's.

The explanation for it comes not in the Ramayana but in the Mahabharata. To understand, we must put aside the Bhakti-era Ramayana, where Rama is always right. In the Valmiki Ramayana, Rama is not eternally right. He chooses specific actions based on time and circumstances. Since Rama is a human avatar in the Valmiki Ramayana, he has some human failings. Just as Rama decided not to chastise or punish Lakshmana for what he did to Surpanakha and paid the price for it, his action of killing Bali has its own consequences.

The Ramayana and Mahabharata, before the Bhakti-era versions, are stories meant to emphasize the importance and consequences of our chosen actions. In this dharmic world, logic is quite simple. Rama kills Bali by hiding behind a tree. He kills because he does not wish to ally with Bali and chooses Sugriva. He thinks it is the right choice at the time, and he is neither right nor wrong. It is just a choice. He pays the price for it in his next life as Krishna. In the Mahabharata, Bali takes birth as Jara, a hunter. Jara also means 'old age', 'time' and 'judgement'. As the incarnation of Bali, Jara kills Krishna in the same way that Rama chose to kill Bali.

Actions and their consequences are emphasized elegantly and beautifully in the Puranas, with none of the convoluted and contrived justifications the Bhakti-era poets struggle to bring.

> There are indirect references to Rama killing Bali in a straightforward battle. Hanuman repeatedly says in all versions of the Ramayana that Rama killed Vali (Bali) in a battle: *Valianam Samara Hatva Mahakayam Mahabalam*. Therefore, it is possible that the story of Rama shooting an arrow from behind a tree to kill Bali is a later-day addition. In the Ramopakhyana of the Mahabharata, Rama is quoted as saying, 'I will kill Vali in a battle.' In Gunabhadra's Uttara Purana, it is Lakshmana who beheads Bali with a sharp arrow, not Rama. However, in the Sanskrit play *Mahaviracharita*, Rama kills Bali in a duel. Many Ramayana-based stories like the Mahanataka and Janaki Parinaya claim that Bali and Rama dueled hand-to-hand, and Rama killed Bali in a straight fight.

25

Bali's Royal Funeral and Tara's Questions to Rama

RAMA ASKS BALI'S SON ANGADA TO PERFORM THE FUNERAL RITES. Once again, the logic that Bali is just an animal who was hunted down by a Kshatriya falls apart through this action of Rama's. On the other hand, it shows the respect Rama had for Bali. Tara, devastated by the death of her husband, wails piteously during Bali's funeral. She asks Rama whether his action is as per dharma. Rama gives many explanations, none of which satisfy Tara. Finally, Rama says it is an action he had to do for maryada, the ethical code.

Tara asks, 'The maryada of Ayodhya or of Kishkindha?'

Rama pacifies her by assuring her that when her son Angada is old enough, he will be king of Kishkindha. Sugriva will rule only till Angada achieves maturity. Tara the wise understands there is no point in crying over what is already past. She accepts her fate and Rama's suggestion that she marry Sugriva once again. Thus, Tara marries Sugriva for the second time, becoming a woman who has married two brothers twice.

And so, Sugriva is made king of Kishkindha and he takes Tara as his wife. Ironically, Sugriva thus acts according to the dharma of the animal kingdom. To get a mate and territory, he has resorted to killing his own brother, albeit through Rama's agency. We find that the concept of dharma is evoked as per the convenience of the characters. Valmiki shows us how difficult it is to define dharma, and Vedavyasa underlines the same in the Mahabharata. Through their characters, they demonstrate how subtle and flexible the concept of dharma is. That is why Krishna talks about the importance of 'swa' (one's) dharma. Swadharma does not mean one's religion, as has been interpreted in recent times, but one's understanding and definition of dharma.

We all justify our actions. It is a human tendency to claim we are right using various justifications, calling it dharma or the righteous thing to do at the time. But the consequence of what we do is not dependent on how we define dharma. The fruits of our actions, irrespective of all justifications and definitions, act independently, always binding human beings in a complex web of karma and karmaphala. Only animals, plants and bees are free of the web of karma because they act according to their instincts and not from conscious choice. Thus, whichever way Rama justifies killing Bali, he pays the price for his karma.

The rainy season arrives, and the Vanaras retreat into their cave palaces. Rama and Lakshmana wait patiently for Sugriva to fulfil his promise to help them rescue Sita. But Sugriva loses himself in wine, women and music. Even when the rainy season ends, Sugriva shows no inclination to start the search for Sita. Rama loses his patience and sends Lakshmana to remind Sugriva.

When Lakshmana reaches Sugriva's cave palace, he is horrified to see the king of the Vanaras in an inebriated state. Sugriva, driven by the guilt of killing Bali, has taken to excessive drinking, or that is the excuse he gives Hanuman when he tries to bring him back to the correct path. When Lakshmana requests Sugriva to start the search for Sita, the drunken Sugriva insults him and Lakshmana threatens to behead Sugriva.

Once again, the onus of resolving the crisis falls on Tara. She pleads with Lakshmana that Sugriva does not know what he is doing, that he has spoken without thinking. She assures Lakshmana that she will ensure Sugriva and her own son Angada and the other Vanaras go in every direction in search of Sita. Tara's wise words pacify Lakshmana, but before he goes, he warns her that if Sugriva does not start searching for Sita, all the Vanaras will pay a heavy price.

Tara advises and consoles Sugriva and brings him out of his self-imposed grief. She talks practical wisdom to him and warns him that the kingdom he has won by betraying his brother will be destroyed, and the Vanaras will be known as those who do not keep their word. She reminds Sugriva of his dharma and that those who do not keep their word are ridiculed for generations.

At dawn the next day, Sugriva goes to Rama and begs for mercy, promising never again to forget his duty. With Rama's blessings, Sugriva commands the Vanaras to go forth in all four directions to search for Sita. Hanuman, Angada, Nala and Neela go south, searching every nook and corner, but find no trace of her anywhere. Discouraged and despondent, they reach a valley where not a single blade of grass grows. The earth is scorched and the land is parched and barren as far as the eye can see. As they approach the valley, they can see the carcasses of birds and beasts and the air is putrid. Such a place in verdant south India surprises Hanuman. The others warn him of the magical creatures who live there and warn him not to enter this valley of death.

Hanuman tells the Vanaras that he must search every part of the world, including this valley. What if Ravana has kept Sita in this barren land? While the other Vanaras watch, Hanuman tries to enter the valley of death. But he is blown out by a great and forceful wind. Praying to his father, Vayu, he walks into the valley with incredible difficulty. His friends watch him vanish behind the clouds of dust, worried for his safety. Hanuman walks for many days, fighting the dust storm, and finally reaches the centre of the valley. There he finds a sage named Kandu, sitting without moving, as if cast in stone. Hanuman tries to break the sage's trance, even though he knows he can be cursed for this. But it is his duty to ask everyone about Sita.

Kandu opens his eyes and sparks of fire come out of them. He refuses to answer any of Hanuman's questions. Hanuman understands that the sage is suffering from some great grief, which has turned the valley into such a parched land. With great patience and compassion, Hanuman serves the sage. After a few days, the sage breaks down and starts talking. He says he had a son of sixteen years, whom destiny took from him. Grief consumed him, and he started hating the world. His hatred festered and parched the land. The more he hated, the larger the area of barren land grew. But this did not concern him.

Sage Kandu tells Hanuman that he wanted the world to end because it did not care about a sixteen-year-old boy's death. He berates Brahma, Vishnu and Shiva, saying they are just foolish imagination, not gods. If there is a Creator and the world is cruel, then is the Creator not also evil? If the world is self-created and still brutal, does such a world deserve to exist? Either way, Kandu cannot find meaning for the world to survive. Everyone is trapped in the web of illusion; he is doing everyone a favour by destroying the world.

Hanuman tells Kandu that he is right, life is an illusion. But to know this truth one needs to be alive, to be aware, to know that beyond the illusion lies the perpetual truth of time. Grief and happiness are but parts of life's illusion.

Sage Kandu asks that if supreme consciousness has no form, no beginning or end, why is it represented as Brahma, Vishnu and Shiva?

Hanuman explains that Brahma is nothing but the past aspect of Time, where creation occurs. We are all the creation of our pasts. The choices we have made have created us; that is why Brahma is the Creator. Vishnu represents the present and only the present is real. We know the world, prakriti, because Vishnu is where we are at any moment. That is why wise men tell us to always fix our minds on Vishnu, not because one form of divine representation is superior to another, but because Vishnu represents the present.

The choices you have made in the past, which have created you, cannot be changed. The future is Shiva, the destroyer. His job is to continuously destroy moments so that we are reborn again and again in Vishnu, the present. That is why the ancients divided Mahakala, the Supreme God, into three aspects—Brahma, Vishnu and Shiva—and said that one must dwell on Vishnu. It means one must live in the present. Only the present is real. The rest, the past and the future, are illusions. We are all functions of time and space, purusha and prakriti.

Hanuman says to Sage Kandu, 'By dwelling in the past, in the grief of losing your son, you are creating a present that is full of suffering. Your grief is not going to change what has happened. The past is gone, and the future will never come. This is the simple truth of life. This is the meaning of the primaeval sound Om that represents the vibrations of the universe. A pulse is relevant only in the present. This moment is always joyful; hence God or Time or the Great Consciousness is called Ananda or Bliss.'

Hearing Hanuman's words, Sage Kandu is pacified. The grief of losing his son slowly mellows to beautiful memories of bringing him up. He understands that nothing can change the past. He can only create the future by the choices he makes in the present. He decides to concentrate and dwell in Vishnu so that he can create a beautiful world.

As Kandu changes his thinking, rain falls on the parched land. Rivers starts flowing, and the valley becomes green again. Flowers bloom, birds and other species return, and Kandu finds peace in the present. He says that whomsoever thinks about Hanuman will never dwell in the past or the future, but always be aware of the present.

Accepting Kandu's blessings, Hanuman returns to his waiting friends. They are happy that he has been able to bring peace to a suffering sage, but their mission remains incomplete. So they continue travelling south until they reach a cave. Once again, Hanuman volunteers to enter the perilous-looking cave. This time his friends accompany him. They walk for many days through the dark and brooding cave, gradually losing hope. But Hanuman urges them on, saying, 'Let us not worry about the dark path we have traversed or how much further we must travel in this darkness. Concentrate on this present moment and think about what we can do to make it joyous.'

Hanuman starts singing and his friends join in, forgetting the past, not worrying about the future. As they sing, they hear a beautiful voice coming from the other side of the cave. Hanuman's friends warn him that it could be some Rakshasi trying to lure them away from their path, and that they should go back.

But Hanuman says, 'Never say no to life. If we go now without checking whether it is a Rakshasi or an Apsara, we will always regret the missed opportunity. What if Lanka is at the other end of the cave? What answer will we give Lord Rama if we go to him empty-handed, and to ourselves? Earlier, we were worried about the valley of death.

Now we are hearing a beautiful voice and are still afraid. Why should we fear either ugliness or beauty? Let us go and face whatever awaits us. If it is a Rakshasi, we will fight. If it is an Apsara, she may help us. Let us not assume what the future holds. Do not forget the lesson I taught you—fix your mind on the present, on Vishnu, and keep walking. Sooner or later, the darkness of this cave will give way to light. What we are thinking in our minds will manifest. Let us be Brahma and create something beautiful.'

Urged by Hanuman, the Vanaras conceive a kingdom that sparkles with diamonds and is fragrant with colourful flowers. Rivers flow with sparkling waters through verdant valleys where birds sing melodiously. The song they hear keeps beckoning them, and they walk on in search of it. Their search for beauty takes them to Swayamprabha's valley.

Swayamprabha, in folk tales, is a close friend of Tara. She falls in love with Sugriva, but he rejects her, obsessed as he is with Tara. Swayamprabha, heartbroken at the rejection, wanders aimlessly and stumbles upon the dark cave. She decides there is no meaning in life since she cannot have the one she wants. She walks on through the same path that Hanuman and the Vanaras are now traversing, and reaches a valley that is as parched as Sage Kandu's valley of death. She decides that her life can be useful after all and works on the valley day and night. She cultivates the land and plants beautiful trees that bear fragrant flowers and sweet fruits. Birds come, as do animals. She transfers her bitterness and disappointment into creating something beautiful.

When Hanuman and his friends arrive, she is happy to see her people once again after a long time. She feeds them to their hearts' content, and Hanuman's army is grateful. Swayamprabha, the one who had left the Vanara clan in disappointment and heartbreak, had created something beautiful out of her grief. This is the choice she made with her life, and now she helps her people. The choices we make are what define us. Swayamprabha means 'one resplendent in herself'. She shines because of the beauty of her mind. Swayamprabha gives the Vanaras directions to Lanka, advising them to go further south towards the sea.

26

Hanuman Awakens to his Siddhis and Flies Over the Ocean

H̲anuman takes leave of Swayamprabha and goes with his army of Vanaras towards the Southern Ocean, searching for Sita. They decide to rest for the night on the steep side of a mountain. As darkness falls, Hanuman is awakened by the screams of his friends. A giant bird had crawled out of a cave and picked up many Vanaras in its beak. Hanuman attacks the bird. It drops the Vanaras and picks up Hanuman instead and tries to eat him. Hanuman resists with all his might, but he is no match for the giant bird.

Thinking that death is near, Hanuman sighs sadly, 'One giant eagle died trying to protect my master Rama's wife. Another giant bird is trying to kill me when searching for her. Such is the irony of life.'

At this, the bird drops Hanuman and asks in a trembling voice, 'Did you just speak of a giant bird?'

Hanuman explains that he is speaking of Jatayu, who was martyred in trying to save Sita from Ravana. To his surprise, the giant bird breaks down in tears. He laments that his brother Jatayu has left him and Hanuman realizes the bird is none other than Jatayu's elder brother, Sampati.

The sacrifice Sampati had once made to protect Jatayu from being burnt by the sun's blazing rays was legendary. Hanuman bows down before Sampati and says that their story of brotherly love will be told again and again as long as the world exists. Sampati is inconsolable. Still devastated by the news of his brother's death, Sampati tells Hanuman that after losing his wings to Ravana's sword and the ability to fly, he did not wish to be a burden on his brother. So when Jatayu was sleeping, he had crawled away and eventually hid in this cave. Jatayu had, in fact, been searching for his elder brother when he saw Ravana taking Sita.

Full of admiration for Sampati's selflessness, Hanuman asks him how he survived when he couldn't fly. Sampati says that he trusts life. He never got food whenever he wanted it, but he always found it whenever he needed sustenance.

Hanuman is confused. He asks, 'What is the difference?'

Sampati tells him that want is the root cause of all misery. Wanting something is different from needing it. Desire is a way for the mind to fool the soul. Need is the way by which the body sustains life. So, food or anything else one needs is usually just an arm's length away, provided we know how to find it. But, forgetting that whatever we need is available, we roam around the world searching for what we want. The loss of his wings taught him that. This is the sweetness of life.

Sampati says, 'For many months I did not eat anything, and I thought life had gifted me food when you all arrived. I would not have eaten everyone, but only the few I require to sustain my life.'

Hanuman, moved by this simple vision of life, says he is willing to sacrifice himself if Sampati's life can be sustained. 'If God wants me to be your food, let it be so.'

Sampati replies, 'I have lost my will to live, for I have always lived for my brother. I am proud that he sacrificed his life for a cause that had nothing to do with him, but because he thought it was the right thing to do. As a bird, his dharma was only to kill or get killed, eat to sustain life, and mate to continue life. His decision to sacrifice his life for another has elevated Jatayu from being a mere bird.'

Hanuman tells Sampati how Rama conducted Jatayu's funeral without allowing his body to petrify or be eaten by scavengers. Sampati is moved to tears when he hears this and says that Rama has also sacrificed much. Sampati knows that Rama acted against nature by cremating Jatayu and will pay the price for it one day. Yet, Rama chose to give dignity and respect to Jatayu. Sampati asks Hanuman for permission to die and for forgiveness for not doing anything to help him. Hanuman pleads with Sampati that there must be some purpose to his life, and he should not give up.

But Sampati is not ready to live without Jatayu. Yet he says, 'Hanuman, perhaps you are right. I am a helpless old bird who cannot fly. But maybe, I can do something before I go.' Sampati flaps his chopped wings and tries to lift himself up. The old bird trembles with the effort as he has not flown for many years and the muscles of whatever is left of his wings are weak and malformed. Yet, with an iron will, he lifts himself up into the sky. Hanuman watches him in admiration. The bird becomes a dot in the sky and flies in a circle, scanning the whole earth.

And from above, Sampati yells in excitement, 'Hanuman, I can see the island of Golden Lanka in the south! I can see the great palaces and the mighty temple of Shiva. I can see the gold-paved pathways and gardens with fragrant flowers in the city. In one of those gardens, under an Asoka tree, I can see a woman of unimaginable beauty and serenity. I think it is Mother Sita waiting for her Rama.'

The word Rama lingers on Sampati's lips, and he repeats it three times before losing his strength and spiralling down to earth. Mother Earth accepts Sampati's body, and Hanuman weeps at the bird's selfless sacrifice. Then he rushes to his mates to give them the news.

'We have found where Sita is! One of us must cross the ocean and reach Lanka and bring her back to our Lord. The one who goes must carry this Mudra Motiram, Rama's signet ring, so Mother Sita will know he is not an Asura in disguise but Rama's servant.' Saying this, he pulls out a distinctive-looking pearl and gold ring.

The Vanaras dance with joy. After months of searching, they now know where Sita is. They praise God and praise the ultimate sacrifice Sampati has made to aid them. But soon their excitement gives way to confusion. The sea stretches between them and Lanka. It is a mighty challenge. Who will cross the choppy waters and penetrate Ravana's fort? The Vanaras discuss the perils of the task. There will be magical creatures guarding the fort. There will be great warriors like Indrajit, Ravana's son, who has defeated Indra himself. Who knows whether Ravana's giant brother Kumbhakarna is asleep or awake? And who can face Ravana himself, who has beaten everyone, except Bali?

Jambavan, the oldest among the Vanaras (in some versions, Jambavan is a bear, but in most versions he is an old monkey), says, 'I might be able to jump across the ocean, but I don't know whether I have the strength to leap back. If I am not able to come back, the mission will be a failure.' (In some versions, Jambavan is a 'Mareecha', a bear, but in most versions of the Ramayana he is an old Vanara.)

Angada, Bali's young son, volunteers to jump but is restrained by the elders, who tell him that he is too young for such a dangerous mission.

Hanuman is sitting in a corner when Jambavan approaches him and says, 'I think there is only one amongst us who can execute such a dangerous mission. Son of Anjana, only you can do it.'

Hanuman is surprised. He has just lost a battle with a bird and was almost eaten—how is he to fight the mighty Asuras? Hanuman says he does not have the powers to do so, but Jambavan reminds him that he'd once acquired many superpowers but had forgotten them because of a curse, since he misused those powers in his childhood. But now it is time to use them in the service of their master, Rama. Hanuman is not convinced.

Jambavan assembles all the other Vanaras and tells them to remind Hanuman how powerful he is. The Vanaras begin to recite his story, and slowly he starts growing in stature, transforming into a giant before their eyes. They remind him that all the power of the universe is within him, and that he can do whatever he sets his mind to.

Often, we too forget that the power of life, the power of Vayu or breath, Hanuman himself, resides within us. We think the task ahead is impossible to achieve. We concentrate on the difficulties we might face. We exaggerate them, just as the Vanaras thought of Indrajit's might, the unknown magic of the Asuras, the power and wealth of Lanka, the accomplishments of their opponent Ravana, and so became discouraged. Sometimes, it needs the wise words of one's friends to awaken the sleeping giant within us.

With fire burning in his eyes, bulging muscles and firm feet, Hanuman lets out a roar, looking towards Lanka. He towers over his friends. Now he knows that he has powerful siddhis. He remembers he has eight superpowers. One is anima, the ability to become as small as possible and to be humble when required. He can become as little as an ant or a blade of grass and be one with them. He has the power of mahima, the ability to become big when required. He knows that he can become as big as the mountains, as high as the skies, and large-hearted when needed. He has the power of garima, to be heavy and live with gravitas, the superpower to take words and deeds seriously and understand the gravity of life. He has the power of laghima, to be as light as a feather, be playful when required, not take life seriously, and enjoy the lighter side of living. Hanuman also has the power of prapti, to acquire anything he needs and never want for anything.

Prapti is the discernment to know what is needed and what is wanted. Hanuman has the power to acquire whatever is necessary at any given moment. He has the siddhi of prakamya, the ability to dream and realize those dreams. Hanuman first dreams about what he wants to achieve and then works to make them come true. Prakamya is the power to first create whatever we need, in the mind, and then watch the miracle of life unfold before us.

Hanuman has the capability of ishatva, 'lordship over everything'. Hanuman knows, like each of us, that he is lord of everything he perceives. Being lord is not about having unlimited power but having unlimited responsibility for everything in the universe. Ishatva means 'protecting everything with one's life'. The one who knows his ishatva knows that he has the responsibility not to rupture the rhythm of the universe. Hanuman also has the superpower of vasitva, the ability to utilize anything available for the good of the world. Hanuman is aware that all these powers were asleep within him, and now they have awakened.

Storytellers have always used Hanuman as a symbol of mental power. The words they associate with Hanuman are manobalam, the immense power of the mind—he is praised as one having maruthathulya vegam, the speed or velocity of the wind, jitendriyam, the one who has conquered the want of the five senses and is aware that need is different from want, and budhimatham prathistam, which means 'one whose opinions are rigidly fixed on reason and discretion'.

These are powers that every human being has. But not everyone is aware that they have these powers. The story of how Hanuman grows in stature when he uses his powers—not for his entertainment, as he did in childhood, or to create trouble for others, but in the service of another—is particularly important. The powers we all have come to fruition only when they are used to aid others.

Returning to the story, Hanuman leaves for Lanka. This scene has been vividly described in various Ramayanas.

The mountains tremble as he takes off. The wind blows, and the trees sway with the incredible power of his leap. It is his confidence that powers him. It is his devotion to the cause he has aligned himself to, the service of his master Rama, that gives strength to his limbs and meaning to his purpose. As he travels at great speed towards Lanka, the gods decide to tempt him. This is a common phenomenon in many journeys described in the Puranas.

The first phase of a journey is about knowing where to go. Hanuman and his friends, too, roam about with only a vague idea of what to do or where to go. They only know that Sita has been abducted by an Asura king called Ravana. Sent southward in their search, they wander into Sage Kandu's miserable valley of death. They could have easily lost their way and died there, instead Hanuman pulls Kandu back to life with infinite compassion. Hanuman and his friends then walk to the self-luminescent valley of Swayamprabha, who had converted her unhappiness to do good and created a beautiful place. Instead of succumbing to the beauty of the place, they resist the temptation to stay. As they move further they are almost devoured by a hungry bird, another hindrance on their journey. Again, Hanuman's compassion helps the distressed bird Sampati and in return they learn where Sampati has spotted Sita—in Lanka.

Now on his solo flight, Hanuman's first temptation comes in the form of Mainakam, the mountain, son of the Himalayas, who rises from the sea as Hanuman flies over him, and calls out, 'Son of Anjana! Hanuman! I know you are going for a good cause. I appreciate your commitment and sincerity. Please stop here and rest. I have a garden full of beautiful fruits and flowers. There is sparkling water here and cascades that create rainbows every moment. There is a cool breeze and cosy caves to sleep in. Stop and rest for a while.'

For a moment, Hanuman is tempted to rest. Then he remembers he is on a mission, not for himself, but to fulfil the word he has given to Rama. What defines me, he asks himself? Will the world know me as the one who was tempted to rest or the one who was only focused on what he had to achieve?

'O son of the Himalayas,' he replies, 'I thank you whole-heartedly for your kindness. There will be a time when I will come and enjoy all this. But now I have something great to achieve in the service of my Lord. For my sake, give all the fruits to the birds, preserve your honey in the fragrant flowers for the bees, and let pure water always flow, sustaining life. A time will come when I retire in my own garden of Kadalivana, the plantation of kadali fruits, but now is not the time.'

Mainakam bows to Hanuman's wishes and bids him godspeed. Hanuman has successfully dealt with the distraction that comes from the well-meaning but ill-timed efforts of our well-wishers.

Soon, a shadow-catching Rakshasi tries to stop Hanuman. Her name is Simhika or Chayagrahini. Hanuman tries to escape from her grip but cannot. Then Hanuman observes that his shadow is behind him, and Simhika is grabbing at it. The only way to tackle Simhika is to face her so that she has to run behind him to catch his shadow. Every time Simhika tries to grab his shadow, Hanuman boldly faces her and eventually Simhika gets tired of chasing his shadow, then Hanuman kicks her away and continues flying to Lanka.

This Rakshasi is like those who try to pull us back from completing our mission. The shadow represents our reputation and self-belief. Fearless Hanuman sees the Rakshasi for what she is—someone who can neither affect him nor stop him. So, he continues his journey.

In many Ramayanas, this shadow-catcher is the mother of the Nagas, called Surasu. As Hanuman fights the shadow-catcher, in some versions, a drop of his sweat falls and is swallowed by a mermaid. From that drop of sweat a son is born, called Makaradhwaja. He looks like Hanuman, and he is considered to be Hanuman. But since he was conceived while Hanuman was fighting the shadows, he is the dark form of Hanuman. Makaradhwaja faces Hanuman at another point in the story, and we shall talk about him when we reach there. Even the simple act of getting distracted from our mission creates karma that we will have to deal with at some point in life.

Surasu, who is also sometimes referred to as Mother of the Sea, rises before Hanuman to stop his journey. Surasu has always swallowed those who try to escape her. As Hanuman tries to fly over her, she becomes bigger and bigger. Hanuman does the same but when Surasu matches Hanuman's strength and opens her mouth wide enough to swallow him, he knows his ability to become big and bulky is not going to work here. So he makes himself small as a fly, enters Surasu's mouth and immediately flies out again.

As he flies away, he smiles at Surasu and says, 'I have fulfilled your need; I have entered your mouth. And I have come out alive. You could have swallowed me, but by becoming small, weightless and humble, I have won the challenge.'

Surasu blesses Hanuman, saying that nothing can stop him from achieving his goal.

Next, Hanuman faces the protector of Lanka, Lanka Lakshmi.

27

Hanuman Tackles Lanka Lakshmi and Locates Mother Sita

Having crossed the Southern Ocean and reached Lanka, Hanuman now tries to enter the imposing Lanka Fort. He goes to the entrance and finds no guards there but the gate is closed. This surprises him because he had expected the fort to be heavily guarded. This sets Hanuman thinking. If something looks so easy, it is usually deceptive. Nevertheless, he punches the gate. It cracks in two and, as expected, out jumps Lanka Lakshmi, a Rakshasi who is the guardian of Lanka. She slaps Hanuman and he staggers back. Without thinking about the right and wrong of hitting a female, a problem that made Rama hesitate when he had to deal with Tadaka, Hanuman slaps her back. At this point, Lanka Lakshmi turns into an Apsara and tells Hanuman that she had been stuck there because of a wrong life choice. His retaliation and her assuming her normal form show her that she has paid for her bad karma.

In another life, she was Vijayakumari, guardian of Brahma's treasures. She was tempted by the great riches Brahma had and, one day, stole something. She thought Brahma would forgive her.

After all, it was such a little thing among so much. However, when he found out, Brahma told her that she had to pay for her action. She pleaded for forgiveness, but Brahma said everyone must pay for the choices they make.

Lanka Lakshmi's karmaphala or the fruit of her action was to guard Lanka, the kingdom of Ravana. From being the guardian of Brahma's treasures, she became the guardian of an Asura ruler's kingdom. Since Hanuman's retaliation freed her of her karma, she lets him in.

He enters the fort and begins his search. In one of the chambers he sees a beautiful woman and wonders if it is Sita. Then Ravana walks in, and the woman treats him with love and respect. Momentarily, Hanuman is taken aback. If it is Sita, why is she behaving like this? Has she come with Ravana voluntarily? No, it cannot be her, he decides. This is confirmed when Ravana calls her Mandodari. Hanuman realizes it is Ravana's virtuous wife. Satisfied and relieved that Sita has not betrayed Rama, and berating himself for even harbouring such doubt, Hanuman goes in search of Sita.

Next, he finds a woman in distress sitting under an Asoka tree in a garden. He watches as female guards try to persuade her to marry Ravana. They speak of his virtues. The emperor of all Asuras is a scholar of all the Vedas and Upanishads. He is a master of sixty-four arts. He has conquered the fourteen worlds. He is a great musician, dancer, singer and composer. He has written books on astrology, and on Ayurveda for healing horses and elephants and children. Pleased with his musical skills, Lord Shiva has given him many boons, and he is the greatest warrior alive. Why is Sita then obsessed with a man who has neither kingdom nor done anything other than killing a few minor Rakshasas? Ravana, they tell her, will treat her just as he does Mandodari—with respect, love and dignity.

Sita refuses all temptation and tells them about Rama's virtues, that Rama thinks of no other woman but her. The very fact that Ravana wants to marry another woman, when he has a beautiful and virtuous wife like Mandodari, makes him evil. Sita also tells them she has heard about the various curses Ravana has acquired in his life.

Various folk tales and versions of the Ramayana do talk of Ravana's curses—how a great scholar and warrior weakened himself by the choices he made and had to therefore pay the price for his actions.

28
The Eighteen Curses That Destroyed Ravana

SITA NARRATES TO THE RAKSHASIS, THE EIGHTEEN CURSES CAST UPON Ravana. No matter how great their master might be, he will have to pay the price for his actions sooner or later, she says. Sitting hidden under the tree's canopy, Hanuman is overjoyed by her words and unflinching stance. Sita narrates them as follows.

1. Nalakubera's Curse

Nalakubera is the son of Kubera, Ravana's half-brother, the merchant-king from whom Ravana had wrested Lanka. Nalakubera is in love with the celestial nymph Rambha, and the couple is betrothed to be married. One day, Ravana stumbles upon them in the garden and, taken in by the Apsara's beauty, tells her to marry him instead of his nephew. Nalakubera curses his uncle, saying, 'May all your ten heads get blasted away one day when you face a man. May you die because of your insatiable passion.'

Sita tells the women guards that the time for Nalakubera's curse to be fulfilled is approaching.

2. Vedavati's Curse

Similarly, Ravana tries to molest Vedavati, the daughter of Sage Kushadhwaja. She has vowed to marry only Lord Vishnu. Ravana comes upon her doing tapasya in a forest and tries to force himself upon her. Vedavati jumps into a fire, but before committing suicide, curses Ravana that she will come back in her next life as the cause of Ravana's death.

Many Ramayanas consider Sita the reincarnation of Vedavati. In some folk Ramayanas, Vedavati was raped by Ravana and gave birth to Sita. Vedavati curses Ravana that this daughter will cause his death, so Ravana steals the baby, puts her in a reed basket, and sends her floating away on the sea. This basket is carried by the sea to the River Ganga, which deposits the basket on its banks in the kingdom of Mithila, where King Janaka finds her.

Another version talks of Vedavati and Ravana being in love and Sita being born as an illegitimate love child. The Asuras take away the child, put her in a reed basket, and send her drifting out to sea. In all these folk versions, Sita is Vedavati's daughter. However, this story is not found in any of the Bhakti-era Ramayanas nor in the Valmiki Ramayana.

---

3. The Brahmin's Curse

Lord Shiva gives Ravana an idol of Tripurasundari or Parvati. To consecrate this idol, Ravana seeks the help of a Brahmin. The Brahmin is late and the auspicious time for the consecration is passing, so Ravana, a great scholar and the son of a Brahmin, consecrates the temple himself. When the Brahmin finally arrives, Ravana has him imprisoned for seven months because he had the audacity to arrive late.

The Brahmin curses Ravana, saying, 'I am an old man, and it takes me time to walk this far. I am late because of my physical ailments. Instead of being compassionate to an old man, you choose to punish me. If you knew how to do the rituals, there was no need to call me. You wanted to insult me, which is why you asked me to do the consecration, despite your pride in the fact that you are the greatest Vedic scholar. I curse you for your arrogance. One day you will be imprisoned like me, for seven months.'

This curse fructified when Karthiveerarjuna imprisoned Ravana. This is described in folk versions of the Ramayana: Ravana tries to save baby Sita when the Asuras put her in a reed basket and float her on a river. Ravana is caught in the current and Karthiveerarjuna, the Yaksha (demi-god) emperor of Mahishmathi, captures and imprisons him.

In other versions, Karthiveerarjuna uses all his thousand arms to stop the flow of the river to create a dam so that his queens can enjoy bathing in the river. Ravana, performing his evening prayers further down the river, suddenly finds it drying up. He walks upstream on the dry river bed and finds the dam. He challenges Karthiveerarjuna over the dam and loses. Karthiveerarjuna ties him up and imprisons him for seven months. The Asuras pay a huge ransom to free Ravana and Ravana feels insulted by this.

The story appears in various forms in folk-tales and multiple versions of the Ramayana. The emphasis, however, remains on the original tale, on how Ravana chose to act towards the old Brahmin who reached the temple late. When Ravana tells the Brahmin that he is being unfair, for it was his duty to be on time, the Brahmin says he will pay the price for being late, but it is not for Ravana to punish him.

---

4. Nandi's Curse

Ravana's fourth curse comes from the bull Nandi, Shiva's vehicle. Visiting Mount Kailasa to pray to Shiva, Ravana sees Nandi resting at the gate. When the bull refuses to let Ravana in, he tells Nandi that Shiva has given him permission to visit whenever he desires. But Nandi replies that Shiva has instructed him not to let anyone in and that he is only doing his duty.

Ravana insults Nandi, telling him that he is behaving like a Vanara. He uses the term '*markadamushti*' or 'the fist of a monkey'. Monkeys, when they grip something, never let go. One way hunters trap them is by placing a sweet substance in a pot with a narrow opening. When the monkey tries to get at the sweet, its unopened fist gets caught in the pot's narrow mouth. Similarly, people hold on to unproductive beliefs and opinions instead of letting go like a monkey going after the sweet in a pot with a clenched fist. He does not understand that unless he lets go, he will get trapped. He will neither enjoy the sweet nor be free again. By calling Nandi as obstinate as a monkey, Ravana insults him.

Nandi therefore curses Ravana, saying that a Vanara will come and burn his palace down and kill his loved ones.

5. Vasishta's Curse

Ravana invites Vasishta, the guru of Rama's Surya Vamshi clan, to teach him the Vedas. But, instead of learning from Vasishta, Ravana starts debating with him. Ravana's knowledge of the Vedas is equal to Vasishta's, and his memory is phenomenal. Ravana can render all the Vedas in a hundred-and-one different ways. Vasishta understands that Ravana has not invited him to learn but to show off, and he curses Ravana, saying a man from the Surya Vamshi clan will be the cause of his end.

6. Ashtavakra's Curse

Ravana invites Sage Ashtavakra, whose body is bent in eight places, to debate the Upanishads. Ashtavakra is considered an authority on the Vedas and Upanishads, but Ravana defeats him in debate. Ashtavakra gracefully accepts defeat, saying there is no scholar like Ravana. In turn, Ravana, reputed for his handsome appearance, disgracefully mocks Ashtavakra's bent form, saying his knowledge is as deformed as his body. Then he kicks him, saying, 'I am a great Ayurveda scholar too. Let me see whether I can straighten your bends.'

Pained by Ravana's words and actions, Ashtavakra replies, 'You are a great scholar, yet you behave like a boor. You are no better than an animal. Let your arrogance end when you lose to the Vanaras. They will kick you as you have kicked me now.'

7. Dattatreya's Curse

Ravana, while travelling on the Pushpaka Vimana, sees a group of saints with a pot of sanctified water preparing to do abhisheka to their guru, Lord Dattatreya, seated nearby. Ravana jumps out, lands among them and asks them the reason for the ritual. The disciples say that Guru Dattatreya is the most knowledgeable man in the world and hence the abhisheka. Ravana says that as he is the most knowledgeable person on earth, he qualifies! And he grabs the pot of sanctified water and pours it over his own head.

Laughing, he tells the guru and his horrified disciples, 'Now the ritual to honour the most knowledgeable person has been done.' Dattatreya's disciples curse Ravana that the head on which he has poured the sanctified water will be defiled by a Vanara's kick.

8. Dwaivayana's Curse

Once, when Sage Dwaivayana was travelling with his beautiful sister, Ravana sees them and is attracted to her. Despite her protests, he forcefully tries to kiss her. She fights off his assault, and in the tussle her nose is injured. Ravana withdraws on seeing blood and Dwaivayana curses him, saying, 'You forced yourself upon my sister without her permission. I am a powerless man and you an emperor, but you too will be helpless one day when another man mutilates your sister.'

9. Mandavya's Curse

One day, when Ravana and Mandodari are enjoying themselves in a forest, Sage Mandavya arrives and requests them to move away as he wishes to do penance without disturbance. Ravana argues that they were there first. If Mandavya does not wish to be disturbed by Ravana's lovemaking to his wife, he can go elsewhere. Mandavya warns Ravana that he is disrespecting an elderly sage. Angered, Ravana slaps Mandavya. The sage then curses him saying that a Vanara will slap him in the same way one day.

10. Atri's Curse

The tenth curse is from Sage Atri, who is present with his wife while Ravana is conducting a holy sacrifice. Ravana recites a shloka from the Rig Veda and explains it. Atri's wife corrects him. Ravana argues with her about his interpretation of the shloka. However, she defeats Ravana in the argument. Enraged, Ravana grabs her hair and flings her away from the sacrificial altar. Atri curses Ravana that one day at a sacrificial altar, when Ravana performs a holy sacrifice to save his life, Vanaras will grab Ravana's wife in the same way and cause his own death.

11. Narada's Curse

One day, Ravana and Narada argue about the actual meaning of pranava or Om. The debate continues without end. Ravana finally loses patience and threatens to punish Narada by cutting off his tongue. Narada curses Ravana, saying that a man will one day cut off all his ten heads for his arrogance.

12. Rituparna's Curse

Ravana makes love to Sage Rituparna's wife by consent and without using force. However, the heartbroken sage curses him, saying that a man will kill him.

13. Maudgalya's Curse

Sage Maudgalya, doing austere penance, had propped up his chin on his wooden yoga staff. Seeing this, Ravana laughs aloud and mocks the sage, saying this is no way to do penance, that such penance is meaningless. Immersed in prayer, Maudgalya does not hear him. So Ravana uses his sword Chandrahasa to cut the staff from under Maudgalya's chin, and the sage falls on his face, breaking his nose and teeth.

He curses Ravana saying that since he had used the Chandrahasa not to protect people but to harm the innocent, the Chandrahasa will disappear from his hand when he needs it the most.

14. Curse of the Brahmin Mothers

A group of young Brahmin girls are bathing while their mothers pray at the riverside. Ravana steals their clothes and refuses to give them back unless they come out of the water naked with their hands above their heads, praying to Ravana. The mothers curse Ravana that Vanaras will strip his wife and insult her in front of him.

A similar incident is mentioned in the Bhagavatham too. Instead of Ravana, the same act was perpetuated by Krishna, on the gopikas.[22] However, Krishna was not cursed. Instead, the Bhakti-era poets remained in awe of Krishna's pranks and much medieval poetry was written about the same act for which Ravana was cursed.

15. Swaha's Curse

Ravana once molests, and according to some versions rapes, Swaha, the wife of Agni. She curses Ravana, saying that his palace will one day be devoured by her husband, Agni. And that a Vanara will cause the calamity.

16. Anaranya's Curse

Ravana attacks Ayodhya and conquers it during the reign of King Anaranya, a forefather of Rama. When Ravana enters his palace, Anaranya is praying. He asks Ravana not to defile his prayer room since Ravana's mother is an Asura. Enraged, Ravana cuts off Anaranya's head. Before dying, Anaranya curses Ravana, saying, 'The day will come when one of my descendants will chop off all your ten heads.'

17. Brihaspati's Curse

Ravana attacks heaven and ties up all the gods. He captures the celestial nymphs, arguing that as per the rules of war, he has not done anything that the Devas had not done when they defeated the Asuras. However, when Ravana grabs Brihaspati's wife, Sulekha Devi, Brihaspati curses him, saying, 'You have grabbed the daughter and wife of a Brahmin. You have conquered heaven, but Kamadeva has conquered you. You, who are under the control of kama or passion, will die at the hands of Rama.'

18. Brahma's Curse

Ravana sees Punchikadevi, the beautiful daughter of Brahma, and tries to abduct her. Thereupon Brahma curses him, saying that if Ravana touches any woman without her consent, his head will burst.

This curse generally appears in the later-era Puranas. In the southern versions, the curse is usually absent, and there are just seventeen curses.

Having molested so many women, why does Ravana not molest Sita too, especially now that she is his captive in Lanka? In the earlier southern renditions and Jaina Ramayanas, Ravana does not force himself upon Sita because he is her father. This logic works, because for someone who has been so richly cursed for forcing himself on other men's wives and daughters, to suddenly act noble towards Sita does not make sense.

The Valmiki Ramayana is quiet about Sita's origins, but even in Valmiki's version, Ravana does not force himself on Sita. There must be a reason he does not touch Sita. He does, however, grab Sita and drag her to the Pushpaka Vimana in Panchvati.

But if we consider earlier folk versions and many other Ramayana versions of Sita being Ravana's daughter, the Bhakti-era definition of good versus evil falls flat since Ravana is protecting his daughter. These versions explain the dichotomy by saying that Ravana did not touch Sita because of a curse. The Bhakti-era Ramayanas solve this issue by saying that Ravana took all the ground on which Sita's hut was situated. In this way, Ravana did not touch Sita.

29

Hanuman Meets Sita

Hanuman sees Ravana walking towards the Asoka tree, decked in diamond necklaces and gold jewellery. He comes to Sita and says, 'Stop thinking about your husband, who has nothing. Behold my Golden Lanka and be my queen.'

He uses all his persuasive powers to tempt Sita. He shows her his achievements and asks her to compare the grandness of Lanka with both Mithila and Ayodhya. Lanka is famed for its wealth. Ravana boasts that all his subjects are happy under his rule. He has brought equality and prosperity to his people. He says that just as he treats all Asuras as equal, he will also treat Sita as he does Mandodari.

Sita scoffs at Ravana's words, telling him that his end is near. Her husband Rama will soon arrive, and Ravana will pay the price of his karma. Ravana leaves in a huff, instructing the Rakshasis standing guard to convince Sita of his greatness.

After some time, Trijata, Vibhishana's daughter, arrives. Sita considers Trijata to be her friend, as she is the only one sympathetic to her plight and does not ask her to marry Ravana. Hanuman hears Sita narrate to her friend how she fell in love with Rama and the story of their first meeting.

When Rama came to Mithila, Sita first saw his reflection in the mirror in her chamber and then rushed out to the balcony to look. She saw Rama picking lotus flowers from a pond in the garden for his morning puja. He saw her reflection in the pond and looked up. Bashful, Sita ran inside. Later, Sita sent a letter to Rama, talking of her fears and insecurities about marrying the prince of a great kingdom like Ayodhya. Rama sought permission to meet her and they met away from prying eyes. Rama assured Sita that unlike his father Dasaratha, he would marry only her and there would never be another woman in his life.

Sita tells Trijata how Rama treated her in Ayodhya. Though bound by a conservative kingdom's rituals and customs, he was as much her friend as her husband. Trijata listens sympathetically, then seeing how weary Sita is, tells her to rest, saying she will not be disturbed.

Once Trijata leaves, Hanuman gets down from the tree and bows before Sita. She thinks it is Ravana, come once again in disguise. Ravana had earlier sent an Asura in the form of her father Janaka, to lament that the daughter he brought up was languishing in the forest. This Janaka had told her to marry Ravana and thus make her father happy. Sita had seen through the disguise and laughed at the Asura. Now, Sita is convinced that Hanuman too is another Asura come to trick her.

When Hanuman gives her Rama's pearl ring and the message Rama has sent her, she is finally convinced. Hanuman mentions an incident that only she, Rama and Lakshmana know of: when Rama, Sita and Lakshmana had reached a small jungle on the outskirts of Ayodhya, Sita had said, 'The condition is that we live in the forest. Why can we not live here? This is also a forest.' Rama and Lakshmana had laughed at her words.

Hanuman mentions a second incident when Sita accompanied Rama in the same clothes she was wearing in Anthapura, when they

were exiled. In this way, Hanuman convinces her that he is not an Asura in disguise sent by Ravana. He assures her that he can take her back to Rama and pleads with her to allow him to rescue her. Sita makes an important choice here. She says that if Hanuman rescues her, it will be an insult to Rama. People will say that Rama could not protect his wife and required a Vanara to save her. Ravana stole her from Rama. If Hanuman takes her back without Ravana's knowledge, that would also be stealing.

'I am not a thing to be stolen and retrieved,' she says. 'I am the wife of Rama. It is for Rama to come and rescue me. I choose to stay here until he comes for me. I will neither become Ravana's wife, nor will I escape even if I have the chance. It is for Rama to save me. If I act in any other way, it will be a blot on the reputation of the husband I love.'

Hanuman understands Sita, though he is saddened by her decision. Seeing his crestfallen face, Sita laughs and says she does not believe a mere Vanara can do the brave deed of rescuing her. Upset by the slight, Hanuman decides to prove to Sita that he can face Ravana's army alone.

30

Ravana's Son Indrajit Defeats Hanuman

Hanuman begins his rampage with the destruction of Ravana's beautiful garden, and when soldiers come to capture him, he beats them up. Ravana then sends his warriors, including his son Akshaya Kumara, after him. Hanuman defeats them and in the fight, Akshaya Kumara is killed. In the folk versions of south Indian Ramayanas, Akshaya Kumara is an eight-year-old boy who is killed later, when Hanuman sets fire to the palace of Lanka.

Ravana is devastated at the loss of his young son. His valiant older son Indrajit promises to capture the Vanara who killed his brother.

Indrajit's Birth and His Accomplishments

Many versions of the Ramayana say that Indrajit is the son of Shiva. As the story goes, a celestial nymph called Madura falls in love with Shiva. She sneaks into Kailasa when Parvati is absent and Shiva becomes enamoured of her. He accepts her request to be his wife for some time.

When Parvati returns, she sees that her husband has taken another wife and curses Madura, turning her into a frog. Madura pleads with Shiva to help her, arguing that if she is a culprit, he is too. So, Shiva gives her a way out, saying that after twelve years Madura will regain her beautiful form and be adopted by one of the world's greatest architects. Madura, now a frog, falls into a well and lives there for twelve years.

Meanwhile Mayasura, the architect of the Asuras, had been praying for a daughter. As a matrilineal society, the Asuras often desire daughters rather than sons. One day he finds a beautiful young woman inside a well and adopts her as his daughter. Since she transformed from a frog or manduka, she is called Mandodari. Ravana weds Mandodari, but the seed of Shiva is still in Mandodari's womb. Thus, Indrajit is born to Mandodari, but is the son of Shiva.

In the Valmiki Ramayana, Indrajit is the son of Ravana and there is no mention of him being Shiva's son. When Ravana goes away to do tapasya, Indrajit learns all that is to be known by a prince from Shukracharya, the guru of the Asuras. Indrajit conducts various ritual sacrifices and yagnas such as the Shaiva Yagna, a sacrifice to please Shiva, and the Aswamedha Yagna, the horse sacrifice, where he captures large territories, among many others. When Indrajit is completing the last yagna, which is for Vishnu and is called the Vaishnava Yagna, Ravana returns to Lanka.

He sees his son and is not pleased, for Ravana is the incarnation of Jaya, and it is his role in this life to be Vishnu's enemy. Ravana holds Guru Shukracharya responsible for misguiding his son. Shukracharya curses Ravana saying that Vishnu himself will take birth to finish both Ravana and Indrajit.

Indrajit, on Ravana's advice, prays to Shiva for more powers. Pleased with his penance, Lord Shiva gives him the boon of being invisible whenever he chooses. Ravana feels confident enough to attack Deva Loka, the abode of the gods, and defeats them. Their king, Indra, runs to Lord Shiva, but Shiva declines to help, saying it is Ravana's destiny to be killed at Lord Vishnu's hands. Indra then rushes to Lord Vishnu for help, who says there is still time for Ravana to die and that he is invincible for now.

Desperate, Indra hurls his famed thunderbolt, Vajrayudha, at Ravana and knocks him unconscious. Seeing his father thus, Indrajit uses the invisibility boon Lord Shiva had granted him and attacks Indra, ties him up and drags him to Lanka. Since he vanquished Indra, he acquires the name Indrajit.

For a year, Indra remains tied to the flagpole of Lanka. The Devas plead with Brahma to intervene. Brahma appears to his grandson Ravana, and requests him to free Indra. Indrajit asks him for the boon of immortality. But Brahma says such a boon cannot be given as anyone born must die one day. Brahma tells Indrajit to ask for any other boon. Indrajit then asks Brahma for invisible chariots and the capability to hurl the most devastating of all missiles, the Brahmastra, invisibly.

Brahma says Indrajit will have to perform a sacrifice for him and from that sacrificial fire, an invisible flying chariot and an invisible Brahmastra would emerge. However, if the sacrifice is interrupted, Indrajit must understand that his end is near. Indrajit is able to complete the sacrifice successfully. Hence by the time Hanuman reaches the Asoka Vatika garden, Indrajit has already acquired these weapons.

Indrajit Knocks Out Hanuman

Meanwhile, after Hanuman has vandalized the garden and defeated Ravana's soldiers, he remembers that he has been cursed to be affected by the Brahmastra once in his lifetime. Aware that Indrajit has this weapon, he has a choice to be trounced now, or in the coming war between Rama and Ravana. If he is defeated now, only he will bear the insult and shame. If the Brahmastra were to defeat him in the crucial war, it could result in failure for the whole army and his master, Lord Rama.

Hanuman chooses to be knocked down at this time rather than on the battlefield. So, when none of the other arrows has any effect on Hanuman, Indrajit hurls his powerful Brahmastra with its power to kill. In the case of Hanuman, it is only able to make him unconscious. Realizing he is not dead, the Asuras tie him up and carry him to the court of Ravana for the Asura king's ruling.

31

Lanka Dahan: Hanuman in Ravana's Court

Having dragged Hanuman to court, Indrajit presents him before Ravana and his courtiers. Ravana looks at the Vanara who killed his son Akshaya Kumara and damaged Asoka Vatika, his beautiful garden. Ravana's ministers ask for the death penalty, so Ravana orders Hanuman's execution. Vibhishana, Ravana's younger brother, stands up and states an unpopular opinion. He argues that Hanuman has come as a messenger, and as per the dharma of kings, a messenger cannot be harmed.

Indrajit, who had taken the trouble to capture Hanuman, argues that the intruder has not behaved like a messenger. Instead of sneaking into Lanka and creating damage, he should have come directly to the king and delivered his message. It could only be concluded that Hanuman was not a messenger but a spy, who had come to create trouble. According to raja dharma, a spy could be executed.

Vibhishana counter-argues that without hearing the culprit's version, one cannot punish him. He has the right to a neutral trial.

Ravana has immense respect and affection for his younger brother Vibhishana and gives importance to his opinion, overruling his son Indrajit and his ministers.

He asks the now-conscious Hanuman to state the purpose of his visit. Hanuman says he has come as the messenger of the king of Ayodhya, who is in exile. He praises Ravana as one who has acquired great wealth and fame and won many victories, thanks to his proper conduct and Lord Shiva's grace. However, by abducting Sita, he has committed a grave injustice. Hanuman warns Ravana that this act of adharma will affect him negatively and he will be forced to eat the fruits of his karma.

Prahasta, Ravana's uncle and minister, argues that Ravana has behaved reasonably with Sita. He could have avenged himself for what Lakshmana did to Surpanakha, princess of Lanka, but Ravana has neither forced himself upon Sita nor mauled and disfigured her as Lakshmana did. Hanuman responds by saying that everyone pays the price for their actions. Ravana too cannot escape the fruits of his choices.

This enrages the Lankan court, and the ministers and courtiers clamour for Hanuman's death. Vibhishana once again pleads that they should show clemency, saying it would be a blot on Ravana's reputation if he were to harm a messenger. Battered by differing opinions, Ravana seeks a compromise. He decides to spare Hanuman's life but to punish him in a way he will never forget.

Prahasta objects, saying Ravana must choose between pardoning Hanuman and being known as a compassionate king or killing Hanuman and proving that he is a decisive king. By vacillating between killing and not killing, Ravana is not making a proper choice.

Seeking to provide a resolution, Vibhishana says that there are many kinds of killing. Insulting someone is a form of killing. For

Vanaras, their tail is a matter of pride. Instead of killing Hanuman, why not set fire to his tail, so he will always remember how he was punished for the mischief he perpetrated in Lanka?

Ignoring Prahasta's protests, Ravana accepts Vibhishana's suggestion. Guards tie up Hanuman and wind reams of cloth around his tail and drench it with oil. Then they march Hanuman through the streets of Lanka, crying, 'Behold the spy of Rama who has been captured by the brave Prince Indrajit!' The Asura guards then set fire to Hanuman's oil-soaked tail.

Hanuman, using his superpowers, makes himself as small as a gnat and the rope that has bound him loosens, freeing him. Hanuman then becomes as big as a tree, and with his tail ablaze, he jumps from roof to roof, setting Lanka on fire. The residents run helter-skelter, like scared hares from a forest fire. The guards try to chase Hanuman, but he sets fire to the marketplaces, the stables, the temples, the ministers' houses, and even Ravana's palace. In folk Ramayanas, Akshaya Kumara is killed in this fire and not in the fight with Hanuman.

Having done a thorough job, Hanuman jumps into the sea and watches Lanka burn with satisfaction. Then a sudden fear grips him. Has he inadvertently killed Sita in the flames? He berates himself for giving way to anger, lamenting how fickle-minded monkeys are. In Valmiki's Ramayana, the poet talks of Hanuman's anguish when he thinks of Sita possibly dying in the fire.

He rushes back to Asoka Vatika and finds Sita protected from the flames. She praises Hanuman for his valour, saying she was worried when he was captured by Indrajit. She tells him that she is confident that her husband will be able to defeat Ravana with valiant Vanaras like him. Hanuman bids Sita farewell and jumps back to Mahendragiri, the hill from which he leapt to Lanka.

As the scene where Hanuman burns Lanka offers a bit of comic relief in the story, many folk-tales and many Ramayanas offer different versions of this incident. In the Adhyatma Ramayana, Hanuman asks Sita for permission to eat the fruits in Asoka Vatika. Sita says he can only eat fruits that have fallen down. So Hanuman shakes all the trees, makes all the fruits fall down and gulps them down in a trice. In the Assamese Ramayana, Sita gives Hanuman a tasty fruit. Wanting more, Hanuman disguises himself as a Brahmin, goes to Ravana, and says that in order to break his ekadasi fast, he wants some fruit. Ravana gives him permission to eat his fill from the Asoka Vatika. After receiving permission from the owner, Hanuman quickly eats all the fruits in the Vatika.

In the Bhavartha Ramayana, Hanuman sits atop the throne made of his own tail to be above Ravana's throne, and one can still find many wooden and clay toys depicting this incident in villages even now. In folk Ramayanas, Ravana is forced to strip everyone in Lanka naked to get clothes to cover Hanuman's tail. That is why people in south India and Lanka wear only their loincloths, as Ravana had used all the clothes. In the Ananda Ramayana, Bhavartha Ramayana and many folk-tales, Ravana's ten beards catch fire at the same time. Ravana had to slap his ten faces with his twenty hands, and thus, Hanuman made Ravana punish himself for his sins.

There is a huge Hanuman idol in the Suchindram temple, a few kilometres from Thiruvananthapuram. The temple is now in the Kanyakumari district of Tamil Nadu. Here, devotees apply butter to Hanuman's tail as it is believed that it is still sore from burning Lanka. Hanuman had jumped to this place near Thiruvananthapuram to cool his tail. The Ayurvedic

> vaidyas of the area applied butter to cool Hanuman's tail down. But since Hanuman's act had resulted in the deaths of many innocent creatures, the pain remained. It is upon the devotees to keep the tail cool, and the offering has continued for many centuries. The butter so applied is prasadam from this temple.

Hanuman's burning of Lanka has been dealt with in various folk-tales in a more subaltern way. They talk about the plight of ordinary Asuras who get caught in the fire and lose their lives and property. Folk-tales have lamented that common people are like ants that get trampled when elephants fight. Their fate is to be crushed under the elephant's feet, irrespective of what they want. When rulers make decisions based on their selfish needs, the common man is helpless—this is emphasized in the oral telling of the Ramayana, which sympathizes with the citizens of Lanka. Often, it is the innocents who suffer when war breaks out for reasons beyond their control.

When asked what the golden rule for free India's rulers should be, Mahatma Gandhi said that before taking any decision he hoped they would think of the poorest Indian they had seen. A ruler must protect the weakest. Ravana, an ideal king for Lanka residents thus far, fails for the first time to protect them. He built a prosperous Lanka, which is burned down because he makes a wrong choice yet again. Ravana achieves neither the fame of a compassionate and dharmic ruler, nor admiration as a decisive one.

Hanuman leaps from Mahendragiri from his return flight over the sea, worried about his action but also delighted at the success of his mission. When the Vanaras see Hanuman return hale and hearty, they cheer loudly. They can see from his face that he has had success. They rush back to Kishkindha to tell Rama. On the city's outskirts they come across Madhuvana, the garden of wine, and decide they deserve a celebration. Madhuvana is the property of the king of the Vanaras and its intoxicating beverage is reserved for royal guests. Common Vanaras are not allowed to enter.

Led by Angada, the jubilant Vanara army invades Madhuvana and starts quaffing the intoxicating royal drink. Madhuvana's keeper, Dandhimugha, tries to stop them, but Angada beats him up. He also kills his maternal uncle in the brawl that follows. Dandhimugha rushes to Sugriva, who is sitting with Rama and Lakshmana, and relates the chaos being created by the common Vanaras under the leadership of Angada. He asks Sugriva to pardon him for his failure to protect the royal garden.

But Sugriva only laughs. He hurries to the spot to see what his riotous army is doing and finds Hanuman sitting with a sad face. When Sugriva asks him why he is dejected among such merriment, Hanuman narrates how he met Sita and what happened in Lanka. Hanuman laments that he succumbed to anger for the first time in his life. It was not the right choice to make, and even he is not free of karmaphala. Thus, his return from Lanka was the cause of Madhuvana's destruction. Karma has caught up with him. He destroyed Ravana's Asoka Vatika, now the fruits of his action have caused the devastation of Madhuvana in Kishkindha.

Sugriva pacifies him saying that Madhuvana is a small price to pay for Vanara honour. They hurry to tell Rama and Lakshmana that Hanuman has seen Sita.

Hanuman hands Sita's chudamani over to Rama to prove he has seen her. He also narrates the personal story Sita told him, so Rama would be convinced. 'In Panchavati,' he says, 'a crow once harassed

Sita. The crow, a son of Indra called Jayanta, had come to molest her, enticed by her beauty. Rama lay asleep on Sita's lap. The crow pecked Sita between her breasts, but she shooed it away. When it did so a second time, Sita adjusted her garment and the string of her blouse came loose. Rama woke up, saw this and laughed at Sita, who was embarrassed and began to cry. When she told Rama that the crow had pecked at her, he invoked the Brahmastra and flung a blade of grass at the crow.'

'Then,' said Hanuman, 'the crow fled to his father Indra for safety, but Indra was helpless before Rama's arrow. Jayanta the crow then hurried to Lord Shiva and then to Brahma, and then to all the Devas, but no one could save him from Rama's anger. Helpless, the crow fell at Rama's feet and begged for forgiveness. Rama said that the Brahmastra once evoked could not be retracted without causing harm. Jayanta pleaded that his life be spared, and the Brahmastra struck his left eye. The arrow pierced and blinded him in one eye in retribution for his action of trying to molest Sita. Through this story,' concluded Hanuman, 'Sita wishes to remind Rama that when he could not stand even a crow molesting her, why is he waiting so long to take revenge on Ravana, who has abducted her?'

Hanuman adds that Sita has stipulated a month. If she is not rescued by then, she will leave the world.

Hearing of Sita's plight, Rama begins to weep. Hanuman says she is sitting in the open, surrounded by Rakshasis, wearing only a single cloth, covered in dust and filth. She refuses to groom herself so that she appears unattractive to Ravana. Rama weeps even more when he hears this and vows to rescue her and kill Ravana. The Vanaras, inspired by Rama's proclamation, decide to invade Lanka. 'If Hanuman can cause so much damage,' Angada roars, 'imagine what thousands of us can do to Lanka!'

Led by Angada, the Vanaras rush to the southern shore. There they find a rough sea separating them from Lanka. Hanuman is capable of jumping across the ocean, but no other Vanara has his superpowers. To reach Lanka, they need to build a setu (bridge) across the sea. Rama gives Nala, the architect of Kishkindha, and his friend Neela the charge of creating the setu. In the Valmiki Ramayana, only Nala is mentioned. However, in the various later-era Ramayanas, Nala is always mentioned with Neela.

With great enthusiasm, the Vanaras start building a bridge with rocks. However, the sea will not relent. Whenever the Vanaras fling in a rock, it sinks to the bottom of the sea. The Vanaras fear that it will take them many years to complete the bridge. Sugriva wishes the rocks would float instead of sinking, but he knows that is an unnatural thing. The Vanaras appeal to Rama to somehow make the stones float. Rama, the avatar of Lord Vishnu, evokes the Ocean God, Varuna. When Varuna appears, Lord Rama imperiously commands him to allow the rocks to float. But Varuna refuses. Everything in the universe has its own nature, he says, hence a rock, which is heavier than water, must sink.

An angry Rama says it is his command that the rocks float. Varuna refuses again. Lord Rama then points his arrow at Varuna and says that he will destroy him if he does not obey. This picture of an angry Rama aiming his arrow at the sea has recently been made famous. When this image became popular, traditional Hindus lamented that it was an inauspicious sign, for Lord Rama's action ended in a great disaster. Even he was not spared from eating the fruits of his actions.

In traditional Hinduism, evoking Rama without Sita is considered inauspicious. Rama is never mentioned alone because he is incomplete without Sita. Once Sita has gone away from Rama, he ceases to be a god and becomes a man. The poster of Rama angrily pointing his arrow at a raging sea evokes a sense of fear amongst traditional Hindus for this reason.

Eventually, Varuna has no choice but to obey. But Rama's karmaphala comes to haunt him in his next avatar as Krishna when the same Varuna returns to destroy Dwaraka, the city Krishna built of stone. It is believed that Dwaraka still lies submerged in the waters off the coast of Gujarat.

Rama's actions are driven by his desire to reach Lanka and rescue Sita. Whether his behaviour with Varuna is right or wrong is irrelevant. That is why the Ramayana must be understood with its companion epic, the Mahabharata. Each complements the other to emphasize the theory of karma and karmaphala. Whether it is the killing of Bali, the abandoning of Sita, or building the Rama Setu, each action has a reaction either in the Ramayana itself or later in the Mahabharata.

Rama watches as his army of Vanaras builds the bridge, now known as Rama Setu, with rocks that float. In folk-tales, a squirrel plays an integral part in this venture. As Rama is watching the bridge being built, he sees a small squirrel running into the sea, wetting its fur and rolling on the sand. The sand sticks to the squirrel's fur. Then it runs to the bridge and shakes off the sand against the bridge. It repeats this action many times. Rama is curious and picks up the squirrel to ask what he is doing. The squirrel replies, 'Lord Rama, I may be small, but I choose to give my own contribution. The small quantity of sand that I can carry in this way may perhaps speed up your work. I am doing what I am capable of. I cannot sit quietly thinking that I am small and cannot contribute like the mighty Hanuman or Sugriva.'

Rama is pleased by the squirrel's dedication and caresses its fur. Many Hindus believe that the three lines on the Indian squirrel's back are the marks of Rama's fingers.

The bridge is finally completed and Rama's Vanara army gets ready for battle.

32

The Defection of Vibhishana

WHILE RAMA IS CONSTRUCTING THE BRIDGE AT RAMESWARAM, RAVANA'S spies inform him of this development. He calls his ministers to discuss what they should do to prevent Rama from invading Lanka. Ministers like Dhumraksha and Prahasta advise Ravana to fight Rama at all costs. They talk about the insult a princess of Lanka has suffered and say it is better to avenge oneself and die in the process than take any other path. They remind him that Lanka has already suffered at Hanuman's hands because they underestimated him. This time they must be prepared to destroy Rama and his Vanara army.

Prahasta says, 'We should use the Pushpaka Vimana to destroy the bridge Rama is making.'

Vibhishana disagrees. He says to Ravana that by abducting Sita he has performed an act of adharma. He will have to suffer the fruits of that act. The only way Ravana can escape is by repentance. It is better to return Sita to her husband and beg his forgiveness.

Vibhishana's words anger Ravana. He roars at his younger brother, 'We listened to you when Hanuman came. Had I listened to Prahasta and killed Hanuman when Indrajit captured him, we would not have been in this plight. You are talking for the enemy. You are so confident of our enemy's divinity that you are trying to dissuade us from fighting for what we believe to be right. You have no concern for what happened to our sister, Surpanakha. If someone else had spoken as you have done, and tried to discourage my soldiers, I would have beheaded him. You are my younger brother. I brought you up. Whatever you enjoy in life is by my favour. Yet, having eaten my food, lived in my palace, and enjoyed all the luxuries that our brother Kumbhakarna, my son Indrajit and I have fought to acquire, you talk on behalf of the enemy! There is no one worse than a jealous family member. I ignored the warnings of my spies about you eyeing my throne. My wise ministers have warned me many times that you have evil intentions towards my wife. I do not want to see you anymore.'

Vibhishana storms out of the court, warning his brother that his destiny and karma will catch up with him. Ravana's ministers ask him to stop Vibhishana. Prahasta warns him that an angry relative can be a dangerous spy and tells Ravana to kill Vibhishana. Ravana once again chooses to spare his brother's life over the safety and security of his country. When Prahasta asks Ravana to hold Trijata, Vibhishana's daughter, as hostage, Ravana refuses. His ministers remind him how close relatives of earlier kings had betrayed them. Ravana's choice to show compassion towards his brother at this juncture returns later to haunt him.

Vibhishana leaves Lanka along with three of his supporters and arrives at Rama's camp. The Vanara army stops him and Angada rushes to Rama saying that a Rakshasa, Ravana's brother, has arrived seeking asylum. He says that Vibhishana could be a spy, or Ravana himself could have come in disguise as the Asuras are creatures of magic and intrigue. Angada says they are evil with dark skin and darker minds and this Asura must be killed immediately so that he cannot go back with information about their preparations. Jambavan, the old ape, says, 'We must not act in haste. But what Angada says may be true. It is best to send one of our spies to Lanka to find out about Vibhishana's character.' Sugriva suggests imprisoning Vibhishana and questioning him.

As various Vanara army leaders argue about what to do with Vibhishana, Hanuman stands up and tells Rama that Vibhishana can be trusted, that he has always been different from his brothers. He says he has seen Vibhishana performing puja to Lord Vishnu. He has also seen how well Trijata behaved with Sita. If the daughter has been brought up thus, surely the father must have inculcated such teachings in her. Hanuman asks Rama to take advantage of the information an insider can provide them.

Rama listens to all these arguments and opinions and says, 'My dharma is to protect those seeking asylum. I choose to trust rather than distrust. Raja dharma is about protecting even an enemy who seeks asylum. Even if it had been Ravana who had come here, I would have trusted and protected him. We should not judge someone by their origin, race, varna, caste or appearance. He might be of the Asura clan, but even Ravana is the great-grandson of Lord Brahma. It is neither kula nor varna that decides the character of a person. I have decided to trust Vibhishana. If he turns out to be a traitor, I will deal with that when the time comes.'

Rama thus offers asylum to Vibhishana, who begs forgiveness for what Ravana has done. Rama's companions praise Vibhishana for his honesty in acknowledging his brother's mistake. Vibhishana proves to be a critical ally for Rama in the days ahead.

Whether Vibhishana's changing camps was right or wrong has been the subject of debate for many centuries. Even the staunch Bhakti-era poets were uncomfortable about portraying Vibhishana as totally blameless. Amongst ordinary people across India, Vibhishana is often considered a traitor. In Bengali, the phrase *'gharer sotru Bhibhison'* (traitor within the house, Vibhishan) is often used to denote the worst kind of treacherous behaviour. And in most Indian languages there is a saying that means every home will have a Vibhishana.

So, what is Vibhishana's dharma? Is it to side with his brother at a time of crisis; the brother who brought him up and gave him everything? Or is it to side with what he believes to be right, and to switch over to Rama's side? Kumbhakarna, Ravana's other brother, also gives Ravana the same advice that Vibhishana does, but in the face of Ravana's decision, chooses to fight and die for his brother, despite believing that what Ravana has done to Sita is wrong.

Should our loyalty and love trump what we believe? Some folk versions say that Vibhishana was later born as Karna or Dushasana in the Mahabharata, and Kumbhakarna as Vikarna. Thus, in the Mahabharata, their roles are reversed. Dushasana dies for his brother Duryodhana, and Vikarna objects to his brother's actions. However, these stories do not fit into the Puranic logic of Kumbhakarna being Vijaya.

The Ananda Ramayana of the fifteenth century, which itself has multiple versions, contains many stories not included in the Valmiki Ramayana or prominent Bhakti-era ones like the Kamba Ramayana or the Adhyatma Ramayana. One of these is a fascinating story about the consecration of the temple at Rameswaram. 'Ramasya-iswaram' means 'God of Rama'. Shiva is known here as 'Ramanatha' or the Lord of Rama. This is an important temple for Shaivites, for it is here that Rama prayed to Shiva before the war. However, this temple is not mentioned in either the Valmiki Ramayana or the Kamba Ramayana. It is only in the Adhyatma Ramayana that Rama consecrating the Shivalingam at Rameswaram finds mention. According to various

Puranas, Rama consecrates this lingam after the war to atone for the sin of killing a Brahmin, Ravana.

As per the Ananda Ramayana, before crossing the setu, Rama decides to build a temple to Shiva and pray to him. This is to seek Lord Shiva's permission to fight a war against his greatest devotee, Ravana. Rama asks Hanuman to bring the lingam from the Shiva temple at Kashi (modern Varanasi). Hanuman flies to Kashi, but as time goes by, he does not return. The muhurta or auspicious time for the temple's consecration is passing, so Rama forms a lingam with his own hands and consecrates it. When Hanuman finally arrives, he finds Rama already engaged in the puja. He is crestfallen that his efforts have been in vain. Seeing this, Rama allows Hanuman to consecrate the Shivalinga that he has brought. A temple now stands on this site, just before one reaches the main Rameswaram complex.

After consecrating the lingam, Rama wishes to conduct a sacrifice to ensure success in the war. For this, he needs a learned Brahmin. When Rama enquires who the most learned Brahmin is, he receives only one answer—Ravana. So Rama sends an invitation to Ravana to officiate at the sacrifice as a priest. Ravana replies that as the son of Visravasa, he is a Brahmin, and as the son of Kaikasi he is an Asura. He agrees to perform the ritual but says that Rama must have his wife by his side for it to be fruitful. Since Sita is in Ravana's custody, this poses a dilemma.

When Rama gets this reply, he responds to Ravana saying that since he has agreed to be the officiating priest, it is his duty to ensure Sita is beside Rama for the sacrificial puja. Ravana gives his word of honour as a Brahmin to bring Sita to sit beside Rama and then to take her back once the rite was over. Rama agrees, so Ravana brings Sita to Rameswaram to conduct a sacrifice to ensure his own defeat and Rama's victory. This is his dharma as a Brahmin.

After the ritual puja, Rama and Sita must seek the blessing of the officiating Brahmin. So they bow down before Ravana, who is forced to say, '*Vijayibhava* (May success be yours).' Thus, Ravana signs his own death warrant. Thereafter, Rama permits Ravana to take Sita back with him. Rama must now fight and kill Ravana in order to get her back for good.

As mentioned above, this story is found in the Ananda Ramayana, but in no other Ramayana. The power of Indian thought lies in its diversity. Even this fantastic tale of Rama seeking Ravana's blessing is defined as an act of karma and dharma.

When Jaya and Vijaya are cursed to take three births, Jaya cries to Vishnu that life is unfair. For thousands of years, they have bowed and prayed to Vishnu. If the result of all their prayers is a curse, what then is the meaning of karma (that is, why is the fruit of their good actions not protecting them)? Vishnu pacifies them, saying, 'One day, I too will bow before you.' Rama bowing to Ravana after the ritual sacrifice at Rameswaram is explained with this tale.

Bhakti-era poets have questioned the authenticity of such stories. However, if we compare various Ramayanas, we find that even the greatest of the Bhakti-era poets sought to interpret, omit or add stories different to those in Valmiki's Ramayana to suit their own purposes. This proves that the Ramayana is a living, throbbing entity that keeps changing according to society's needs, and every era thus far has produced its own Ramayana.

Returning to the main story, with Vibhishana's help, Rama's Vanara army crosses the strait (known as Palk Strait today) and marches towards the capital of Lanka. Thus, the story moves towards a riveting climax, where Rama must face the might of Ravana's army and eventually Ravana himself.

33

Drums of War and Tales of Espionage

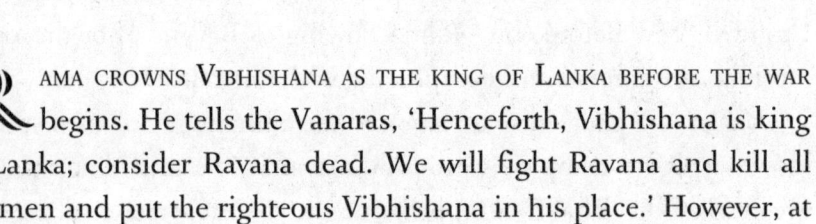

RAMA CROWNS VIBHISHANA AS THE KING OF LANKA BEFORE THE WAR begins. He tells the Vanaras, 'Henceforth, Vibhishana is king of Lanka; consider Ravana dead. We will fight Ravana and kill all his men and put the righteous Vibhishana in his place.' However, at the sight of Ravana's impregnable fort and hearing tales of Ravana and Indrajit's valour, the Vanaras begin to lose confidence. Every Vanara is not Hanuman. Many start to doubt whether they will return to Kishkindha.

Ancient Hindu wisdom encompasses the power of sankalpa (an intention or a resolution). Anything is created twice—first in the mind and then in physical form. Thus, by conducting an elaborate coronation ritual for Vibhishana, Rama creates a powerful image in the minds of the Vanaras and to further allay their fears, he delivers a rousing speech.

Had Rama only said their goal was to win against Ravana, it would have had little impact. But Rama creates the vision of a victorious future and delivers it to them. When we are working towards something, it is always good to know what we want to achieve. It is also a declaration to Ravana's army that they have a new Asura king to look up to. Rama also makes his own intentions clear by crowning Vibhishana—his aim is not to conquer Lanka and rule over the Asuras, but to reclaim Sita.

Rama's bold declaration does not go unnoticed in the opposite camp. One of Ravana's spies, who witnesses the elaborate coronation ritual, informs Ravana that Lanka now has two kings. Ravana is enraged by his brother's betrayal. Prahasta advises Ravana to send out spies to discover the strength of Rama's enemy. So Ravana sends his best spies—Shardula and Shuka.

Disguised as Vanaras they start spreading rumours that many Vanaras are going to die. They talk of the atrocity of Sugriva killing their beloved King Bali, and his bad judgement in siding with Rama against the valour of Ravana and Indrajit. Just as Sugriva betrayed his elder brother, they say Vibhishana has done the same. However, unlike Bali, who was killed by an assassin's arrow while fighting Sugriva, Ravana cannot be killed so easily. To kill Bali, Rama had to use deceit. The spies also tell the Vanaras that they are siding with an unknown man who claims to be a king in exile, but who has no kingdom, nor an army to fight for him.

By spreading such discouragement and sowing the seeds of doubt, Shardula and Shuka create dissent in the Vanara ranks. Many announce they wish to go back home. Sugriva knows that he is not popular after Bali's death among those who considered Bali their king and god. But he also knows that if he does not suppress the dissent, the war will be lost before it has even begun.

It is Vibhishana who comes to his aid. He suggests the growing discontent could be the work of Ravana's spies. In folk-tales, Vibhishana conducts a test to separate the Vanaras from the two disguised spies. He asks the entire Vanara army to climb a hill. They do so quickly, as monkeys will. However, the two Asura spies initially struggle to keep up and then use magic to reach the top first. This unmasks them. The spies had forgotten that this was not a competition they had to win. By being the first to get to the peak, they lose the larger purpose of their mission. Often, we get carried away in the spirit of competition and forget our real goal.

Sugriva thus catches the spies and Angada beats them to an inch of their lives when they claim they are mere messengers. They cry out that this is not how messengers should be treated according to raj dharma. Sugriva reminds them of how Ravana treated Hanuman when he went to Lanka as a messenger. Eventually, Rama stops the lynching and saves the spies. Shardula and Shuka tell him they have come with a message from the Asura emperor. Ravana wants Rama to hand over Vibhishana and leave Lanka.

Instead of answering them, Rama takes them around his camp and says, 'You have come to spy on our strength. You need not have used deception. You would not have been assaulted if you had come directly to me and asked about our strengths and weaknesses. I do not believe in unnecessary violence. I apologize for what my Vanara army has done to you.' Then he takes the duo around his camp and shows them the military preparations made to invade Ravana's palace. He treats them with compassion and kindness and feeds them. By the time Shardula and Shuka are freed they are ardent devotees of Rama. They have never seen such compassion amongst either the Devas or the Asuras. A spy who gets caught is always killed, after being tortured in the worst possible manner.

They return to Lanka and tell Ravana what happened. Ravana is further enraged by their praise of Rama. Shuka advises Ravana that he should give Sita back and offer peace to avoid unnecessary bloodshed. Rama desires nothing from Lanka but his wife. Ravana should return

Sita and part as friends. Ravana roars at them, 'I am not a beggar to plead before a man with a bunch of monkeys! I have taken what I deserve. I am honour-bound to avenge my sister. I do not need advice from my own lowly servants. I would have been proud of you had you been killed when they captured you. But you have sold your soul to the enemy, and you are no better than Vibhishana. I would rather kill you, but since I do not kill my own people, I will spare your lives. You are dismissed from my service. Never dare show your faces before me again.'

The two Asura spies depart in haste, relieved their lives have been spared. Ravana's spy network had already revealed that many common Asuras thought the king had erred by taking Rama's wife. If Sita were to voluntarily submit herself, then this popular perception would change. Ravana would then become Sita's protector from a husband she did not want. But how can he convince Sita that she should forget Rama?

Ravana finally calls a great illusionist named Vidyadhjiva to discuss his problem. Vidyadhjiva assures Ravana that he will be able to convince Sita through his methods. In any war, whether political or corporate, misinformation plays a significant role in influencing neutral people and killing the spirit of those who support the opponent. Vidyadhjiva plays just such a trick on Sita, by creating a life-like head of Rama.

Sita is sitting in a pensive mood under the Asoka tree, being consoled by Trijata, when they hear loud laughter and see Ravana hurrying towards them. As he nears them, Sita is horrified to see Ravana's sword, Chandrahasa, dripping with blood. In his left hand is Rama's severed head. 'Sita,' he says triumphantly, 'your wait is over. I have killed Rama. The fool tried to attack Lanka with a bunch of monkeys. It did not take me even a few moments to behead him.' He flings the head at Sita's feet and she cries out in shock.

'You are a widow now, but do not worry. Unlike Ayodhya, Asuras do not believe in widowhood. You need not spend a colourless life after the death of your husband. Here, women are free to marry according to their choice. I will give you a decent period of mourning, and then you can live as the queen of Lanka.'

Hearing Ravana's words, Sita faints. Just then, the alarm bell in Ravana's fort begins to toll and he rushes to the fort's ramparts where he sees Rama's army approaching. Meanwhile, Sita regains consciousness and begins to lament Rama's death. She beats her breasts and pulls her hair, asking how she will answer Mother Kausalya. She had come to the forest to look after her son, but her desire for a golden deer changed her destiny. Her temptation resulted in the death of her husband, and she was trapped amongst Rakshasas. She remembers the past and laments every harsh word, real and imagined, that she has spoken to Rama in their married life. She is filled with remorse and guilt and wants to die. Trijata pacifies her saying she must think calmly.

'Where is Rama's head?' Sita asks.

Trijata points to Ravana standing on the ramparts looking worried, and says, 'If Rama was indeed killed, would Ravana have come like this? He would have been celebrating his victory with a procession through the streets of Lanka. The entire palace would be celebrating the king's victory. Instead, there is a deathly silence. Why are the Asura soldiers arming their bows? It means it was an illusion. My uncle will play many tricks to influence you, and you must be alert. They are a part of war strategy. When you hear any news, do not take it at face value.'

Any news must be analysed against certain measures. First, who is giving the information? Is the person credible? What is their history? To know whether the news is fake or genuine, consider who stands to gain. If the information has come from a neutral person who has nothing to gain or lose, it is likely true. Here, Rama's death is advantageous to Ravana. Hence, he has a vested interest in propagating the news. Another measure is, how exaggerated is the news? Often, those who peddle fake news exaggerate it to show their strength and their opponent's weakness. They invoke the past mistakes of their opponents, mostly imaginary, and gloss over their own. Ravana is guilty of propagating just such false perceptions.

Trijata reminds Sita that if Rama can cross the sea and has the confidence to challenge Ravana in his own kingdom, she can be confident that Rama will win this war. Pacified by Vibhishana's daughter, Sita regains her composure and prays for Rama's victory.

Meanwhile, Sugriva watches Ravana standing atop the fort. In the light of the setting sun, the Asura king, bedecked with priceless jewels and diamonds, looks lustrous. Sugriva is unable to control his anger. He sees Rama polishing his bow. Rama does not have even a horse and chariot. Clad in simple deerskin, carrying a bow and quiver of arrows, Rama's image is in stark contrast to that of Ravana's.

Why would an Asura who has everything—the position of the emperor of all the worlds, the kingdom of Lanka, a beautiful wife like Mandodari, and an illustrious son like Indrajit—covet another man's wife, Sugriva wonders. The memory of Bali taking his wife Ruma still bothers him. He sees himself in Rama; he wishes he had had the same courage of conviction as Rama has shown in challenging Ravana. Instead, he remained holed up in Rishimoolachala Mountain until Rama came to his rescue.

All his fears and insecurities prompt Sugriva to anger. He loses his sense of discretion. Without telling anyone, he sneaks up the fort wall of Lanka, reaches Ravana from behind and hits him on the head, knocking his crown off. Ravana is surprised to see a Vanara standing behind him and hits back at Sugriva. Ravana's soldiers rush to save their king, but the Vanara holds on to him and bites off his ear.

Furious, Ravana lifts Sugriva and flings him off the fort wall. It is a great insult to Ravana that a Vanara has once again sneaked in and this time bitten off his left ear.

Rama is surprised to see Sugriva land at his feet with a thud. He calls for help and Vaidya Sushesna, the Vanara physician, rushes to aid Sugriva. After some effort, Sugriva regains consciousness.

Rama chides Sugriva for his reckless act. He reminds Sugriva that he is no ordinary individual, but the leader of the Vanaras. By acting in this manner, he has put the entire mission at risk. Initiative is a good thing, Rama tells him, but misguided initiative can bring disaster down on the whole team. If they are to win against the mighty Ravana, they cannot fight for individual glory. Sugriva begs forgiveness and Rama gracefully forgives him. However, Rama appoints Angada as commander of the Vanara army. Hence, Sugriva loses a position of leadership.

Ravana is angry with his ministers for the security breach. As he is deriding them, a messenger arrives from Rama. This time it is Angada, who asks Ravana to surrender Sita and beg Rama's forgiveness. Angada warns Ravana that if he does not heed the message, not a single Asura will be spared.

Enraged by the audacity of a teenager, Ravana orders Angada's arrest. 'You tortured Shuka and Shardula when they went as messengers, now I will do the same thing to you,' Ravana roars as soldiers rush towards Angada. Angada hits out at them, flinging them away.

In many folk Ramayanas, this scene plays out slightly differently. Angada plants himself before Ravana and challenges the Asuras to lift his feet. Try as they might, no Asura can lift Angada's feet from the ground. Angada knows that only Ravana or Indrajit can do so, but he also knows that they will not touch a Vanara's feet. Using this supposedly audacious act, Angada uses another trick in warfare—tying the enemy up using their own ego.

Ravana could have perhaps kicked Angada instead of using his hands to lift Angada's feet, but Ravana is also a prisoner of his beliefs. If challenged, he plays, at least in public, as per the rules of the game. Angada took a calculated risk. Ravana could have used his sword to chop off Angada's head, but Angada knows Ravana will not do any such thing. Hence, Angada dents the confidence of the other Asuras. If they cannot lift a teenaged Vanara off his feet, how are they to fight a Vanara army with great warriors like Hanuman amongst them?

Ravana knows Angada has trapped him and orders his arrest. Angada knocks down the soldiers who try to grab him and leaps out of the palace window to reach Rama's camp, victorious.

Neither side is willing to give an inch. Rama is fighting for his wife. Ravana is fighting as per the dharma of the Asuras, for whom might is right; among Asuras there is nothing wrong in taking another's wife, if you can defeat him.

As mentioned earlier, in many south Indian and Far-Eastern folk renditions, as in the Philippines, Sita is Ravana's daughter. This makes the war more intense and fascinating. Ravana is not fighting for another man's wife but for his daughter. However, the question about the daughter's wishes arises. Except for the Philippines Ramayana, no other Ramayana says Sita is willing to remain with Ravana as his daughter.

In most Ramayanas, including Valmiki's, there is no mention of Sita being Ravana's daughter. The Filipino version has a curious twist. Unlike the south Indian versions and the Jaina Ramayana, where Sita is unwilling to stay in Lanka as Ravana's daughter, in the

Filipino version she is close to her father and until her last breath she tries to avoid confrontation between the two men she loves.

In this version, Kaikeyi is related to Ravana and instigates him to take his daughter away from Rama by convincing him that Rama is not the right husband for Sita. When war becomes inevitable, Ravana asks Sita to go back to her husband, to avoid battle, but she chooses to stay with her father because she does not want his honour to be compromised.

I was witness to this Ramayana, performed as an opera by a Filipino troupe in January 2019 in Mumbai. Different countries, different stories.

34

The War Begins

Day I

WITH ALL HOPE OF COMPROMISE LOST, THE WAR BEGINS IN EARNEST. BUT before the battle starts, both sides agree not to use magical weapons. When the Asuras agree to this, the advantage clearly shifts to the Vanaras. The Asuras have now committed to fighting according to the ancient techniques of warfare. But their strategies go haywire when confronted with the Vanara army, which follows no traditional rules. The Vanaras fight with uprooted trees and boulders, and the Asuras find themselves helpless. The great Vanara heroes like Jambavan, Sugriva, Nala, Neela and Hanuman distinguish themselves by slaying thousands of Asuras. Facing defeat, the Asuras retreat to the fort of Lanka.

There is jubilation in Rama's camp. The Vanaras are happy to have beaten back such sophisticated opponents. The Asuras fought using chariots and bows and arrows; the Vanaras climbed into the chariots and bit the horses, driving them mad. In Ravana's palace, the scene is one of gloom and doom. The Asuras are afraid that their highly trained army could be easily routed by such crude opponents.

Rama and Ravana have not yet entered the fray; the Vanara army is being led by Sugriva and Angada.

Prahasta says to his king that it is foolish not to use the advantage they have. 'The enemy tried to tie you down with norms they decided. The concept of dharma yuddha is applicable only when you fight with equals. The Vanaras do not belong to any civilized society. When you are fighting animals, you do not fight as an equal because animals have superior strength. Man conquers animals because he is superior in intelligence. The magic, the spells, and the Asura technologies are all products of thousands of years of innovation and the work of many Asura rishis.'

Listening to Prahasta's wise words, Ravana feels he has been a fool to have agreed to a war without magical weapons.

Often in life we are bound by rules and limitations we have set for ourselves. What brings victory at one point may not bring the same result at another. Only a person or team that knows the opponent, continuously innovates and uses suitable strategies can win in battle or in life. Rules are made by people who want to take advantage of them. Agreeing to rules without thinking why the other side is proposing them is like signing one's own death warrant.

This wisdom comes too late for Ravana, and he decides to employ all the magic he can muster. That, too, is a mistake. Ravana summons Indrajit, his illustrious son, and orders him to use all the force and magical spells that he is master of.

Day II

Thus the next day's battle takes a sinister turn. Indrajit showers death on the Vanara army. He uses magical spells and becomes invisible using the ancient siddha art of samadhi. In an invisible flying chariot, he devastates the Vanara army.

When the Vanaras inform Rama and Lakshmana, the brothers enter the battlefield. Since Indrajit has already broken the pact about not using divine weapons, Rama and Lakshmana unleash their own powers. However, the invisible Indrajit is too fast for Rama or Lakshmana's arrows. He matches their divine weapons with incredible skill and dexterity and pushes back the Vanara army.

Finally, Indrajit, who has the power of Shiva in him, invokes the Brahmashakti spell, which causes an explosion above them, stunning the Vanaras and rendering Rama and Lakshmana unconscious. Indrajit descends from his chariot and rushes to behead the brothers. However, Vibhishana, who has miraculously escaped because Indrajit did not wish to hurt his uncle, stops him, saying that it is adharma to kill an unconscious enemy.

Indrajit looks at Rama and Lakshmana lying supine on the ground, sure they cannot hope to escape the devastating effects of his Brahmashakti spell. The entire Vanara army appears to be dead. All but Hanuman, who is dazed. Jubilantly, Indrajit returns to Ravana's palace to break the news that the Vanaras were unable to withstand the magical powers that Lord Shiva had bestowed on him.

A grand celebration breaks out in Lanka and the news reaches Sita. She is devastated but remembers Trijata's words. She decides not to worry until she sees for herself that Rama is dead. She trains her mind to dwell on Rama and imagines him victorious.

Amongst the Vanaras, Jambavan slowly crawls back to life. He revives Vaidya Sushena and asks him how they can save Rama and Lakshmana. The vaidya says there are only two herbs, Sanjeevakarani and Vishayakarani, found in the Himalayas, that can save them. But Hanuman is incapable of flying there to procure the herbs. As night falls, the few Vanara survivors huddle together, not knowing what to do. Hanuman, who is slowly regaining his strength, says they should not lose hope because they are fighting for a righteous cause.

As if giving meaning to his words, they hear a loud flapping of wings and from the sky, a lustrous golden eagle arrives and lands near Rama. Jambavan whispers, 'Garuda, Lord Vishnu's eagle.' Garuda is carrying the Vishayakarani and Sanjeevakarani herbs in his beak. As Garuda places the herbs reverently near Rama and Lakshmana, the brothers regain consciousness.

Garuda bows to Rama, saying, 'My Lord, I am happy I have this opportunity. You once saved us from annihilation and this is how I can repay you. Now you don't know who you are, for you are in the form of a human, but understand that you are Vishnu, and once you achieve the purpose of your avatar, that realization will come back to you.'

Hanuman is convinced that the appearance of Vishnu's eagle is proof that Lord Rama is none other than Lord Vishnu. He bows with deep reverence and requests Rama to revive all the Vanaras lying unconscious. Rama evokes all the powers of heaven and cries to Lord Shiva, 'If I am fighting a righteous war, let us not be defeated by the magic of the Asuras.'

One by one, the Vanaras rise as Indrajit's Brahmashakti spell disperses. The Vanaras cheer for Rama, and the wind carries the sounds of their jubilation to Lanka. Ravana is surprised and looks at Indrajit. Worried that Rama and Lakshmana have survived, Indrajit bows his head before his father and admits, 'I did not cut off their heads for I thought it was adharma to do so.'

Ravana explodes with rage. He asks why, when they are fighting a war with no rules. Indrajit says that his uncle Vibhishana advised him. This makes Ravana even angrier. He says that because of Vibhishana's advice Hanuman was able to destroy Lanka. Vibhishana had once again betrayed them.

'We had our reasons for abducting Sita—to take revenge for what they did to Surpanakha,' says Ravana. 'We too are in a righteous war. Rama has his reason to attack us, for we have kept his wife in captivity. There is only one dharma, and that is to ensure our own victory. If there is adharma, it will not fall upon you, for you are only following my instructions. Let the adharma fall upon me. Your instructions were to kill them, and you failed me.'

Indrajit, who deeply loves and respects his father, falls to his knees and begs for forgiveness. He promises to do whatever Ravana asks and to not act independently. Ravana, pacified by his son's words, hugs Indrajit and says that if every soldier in the army questioned what was right and wrong, the army would surely lose. Only the leader can decide the right course.

Day III

The next day's battle is more difficult for the Asuras. Hanuman leads the attack. Fortunately for the Vanara army, Indrajit withdraws to meditate and beg forgiveness for disobeying his father and does not come to the battlefield. The day marks the death of many great Asura warriors. Hanuman kills Dhumraksha, Angada kills Vajradamshtra, and Hanuman also kills Akampana and Maharathika with a boulder. By afternoon, Prahasta goes to lead the Asuras. A rock hurled by Neela hits his forehead, and he falls dead.

Prahasta's death affects Ravana significantly. He is consumed by grief and anger, more than what he suffered when he lost his son. Prahasta always spoke his mind and was never a sycophant. Ravana would say that all kings need ministers like Prahasta, who was a critical thinker. The loss of such a minister was more devastating than that of loyalists like Vajradamshtra or Akampana.

So Ravana dons his best armour and takes to the battlefield in a chariot drawn by high-speed stallions. Rama sees Ravana coming and for a minute pauses to admire the splendour of the Asura king. He tells Lakshmana, 'Behold the Indra of the Asuras. He may be evil, and he abducted my Sita, but he is a power to be respected. There is no one to match him in knowledge and learning. Alas, in his old age, his wisdom has failed him. He is a learned man, but wisdom has abandoned him. He is losing his trusted men and will soon lose his kingdom. He has a beautiful, virtuous wife, so why does he covet another man's wife? He has a brilliant warrior-son like Indrajit, who is dutiful to his father, as I am to Dasaratha. What more could Ravana want in life?'

But this is how destiny plays out when great men must fall. Ravana's is the power of anger. The death of his generals makes him blind with cruelty. He flings Hanuman far away when he tries to enter his chariot. He hits Neela and knocks him unconscious. Ravana has one target for the day, and that is not Rama. He roars, 'Vibhishana! Without you, these mere men can do nothing to me. You are the traitor, gifting my opponent all my state secrets. Today is your last day!'

Ravana finds Vibhishana hiding behind Lakshmana. He says to Lakshmana, 'Move aside, for even though I have a grouse with you, today is not the day to settle it.'

When Lakshmana refuses to move, saying he must protect one who has taken asylum at his brother's feet, a battle ensues between Lakshmana and Ravana. Both are fighting for their brothers—Ravana to kill his, and Lakshmana to protect his. Ravana skillfully deflects all the divine weapons that Lakshmana hurls at him; in return Ravana throws his Chandrahasa. The hilt of the sword hits Lakshmana's forehead and he falls down unconscious.

Vibhishana runs away, seeing his protector fall. Ravana barks at his charioteer to chase and catch the traitor. The chariot goes after Vibhishana at great speed but Hanuman comes rushing back and topples Ravana's chariot. Ravana falls to the ground, dazed by the sudden turn of events. Hanuman picks up Lakshmana from the ground and vanishes into the Vanara army. By the time the chariot steadies, Vibhishana too has disappeared.

As the day draws to a close, Ravana turns towards the fort, fretting and fuming, promising himself that Vibhishana will die the next day. As his chariot prepares to leave the battlefield, Rama comes to stand in his path.

Rama is angry at what Ravana has done to Lakshmana and what he has attempted to do to Vibhishana. They exchange angry words. A battle ensues and Ravana gets more and more enraged, while Rama descends into a state of calm. He concentrates on the job that must be done, while Ravana starts losing his focus and cannot withstand Rama's attack. Rama kills Ravana's horses and breaks his chariot with his arrows. Another arrow pierces Ravana's armour, yet another knocks off his crown.

Trembling with rage, Ravana does his best to defeat Rama but is unable to do so. Rama tells Ravana that the latter could have beaten him had he not been overcome by anger. 'When you act in anger, you forget to think and you commit mistakes. You have taken my Sita, yet I am willing to give you the benefit of the doubt. Perhaps your ego and passion affected your judgement. I am giving you the boon of a second life. I do not want to kill you today, for I want to give you the chance to repent. I do not want anything from you except my Sita. Give her back, and I shall be gone, and you can continue to rule Lanka and make it prosperous.'

Ravana says, 'I fight for my pride. I fight for my people. I fight for my sister. You are free to kill me. If I had the chance, I would not hesitate to kill you. If you leave me now, you will regret it. I am neither going to give you Sita nor am I going to change my ways. I am not led by my intellect, but by my emotions. Nature has placed those emotions in me. It is my swabhava that makes me who I am. If I lose my passion and become stoic, then I will become you. I do not want to be you. Once I dressed as you to tempt Sita. I took your form using magic, and I looked exactly like you. I went to Sita, thinking that perhaps she would start loving me. But as I was walking, I asked myself what I was doing. Why had I taken Rama's wife? I thought I should return her and ask for Rama's forgiveness. I paused, horrified by these thoughts. Why was I thinking like Rama? I am Ravana, and I should think like Ravana. I do not want to become Rama. I am Ravana, emperor of the Asuras.'

Rama laughs and says, 'It is not too late to be Rama. Go to your palace and love your wife, the virtuous Mandodari. Embrace your son Indrajit, who will do anything you command. Talk to your people, who adore you. Do what is right and return my Sita. If you choose to remain Ravana, this Rama will have no choice but to kill you.'

'I can choose to be what I am or what I should not be,' he retorts. 'I choose to be Ravana, and I shall die as Ravana.'

Ravana returns to the fort, his heart shattered by the humiliation he has faced at Rama's hands. He had almost killed Lakshmana and Vibhishana, yet anger overtook him, and he could not match Rama's skill. Such a defeat was worse than death. He misses Prahasta, who would have advised him on the right path to take. He does not wish to send Indrajit once again into battle, for he has a premonition that Rama will kill him too. He has already lost one son, Akshaya Kumara, and does not wish to lose his beloved Indrajit.

He decides it is time to wake up his younger brother Kumbhakarna.

35

Kumbhakarna Is Woken Up and Sent into Battle

IN SOME FOLK RAMAYANAS, IT IS SAID THAT KUMBHAKARNA WAKES FOR SIX months and sleeps for the next six months. However, in the Valmiki Ramayana, Kumbhakarna sleeps through the year and wakes for a day. His appetite is so huge that he eats whatever he requires for the entire year on that day.

When Ravana and Kumbhakarna had gone to Lord Brahma to receive their boons, Kumbhakarna had asked to be blessed with 'Indratva', to be like Indra. However, due to a slip of the tongue, the word came out as 'nidratva', being in a state of sleep. Brahma gives him the boon before Kumbhakarna realizes his mistake. Though in his heart of hearts Ravana did not want a rival in his own home and wanted the position of Indra for himself, he nevertheless pleaded on his brother's behalf. Brahma mitigated the boon by saying that for one day in the year, Kumbhakarna would be awake before going back to sleep again. Brahma told Ravana that this was advantageous for him too, for if Kumbhakarna had the same sleep-wake cycle as everyone else, nobody would be able to satisfy his appetite through the year.

On the designated day of his waking, he is invincible. But if his sleep is interrupted, he becomes vulnerable, just another powerful Asura. When Ravana decides to wake up Kumbhakarna, he is aware of his brother's vulnerability. However, he believes that he must use Kumbhakarna's enormous strength as a warrior, or else Rama could kill him, win the war and take Sita. What is the use of having such a powerful brother if he cannot help at the most critical time? Against the advice of his ministers, Ravana orders Kumbhakarna to be woken.

In many folk-tales, the waking of Kumbhakarna is often depicted with comical scenes and hilarity. The Asuras bring elephants to trumpet near Kumbhakarna's ears. They beat massive kettle drums. But the giant Kumbhakarna, as big as a mountain, does not even stir when elephants walk on his big belly. Finally, they bring roasted meat and place it near him, so the enticing aroma rises to his nostrils.

Kumbhakarna is a symbol of the great passion that lies dormant in every human mind. If this passion is awakened at the correct time, it becomes powerful and useful. But if the time is wrong, it can consume everything. The smell of roasted meats wakes up Kumbhakarna, and he starts devouring the food. After finishing massive amounts of rice, roasted meat and fruits, he starts devouring the elephants that had come to wake him. When he has finished with them, he starts eating the soldiers. The remaining men run off in fear as the giant stands up and stretches his limbs. With every step he takes, the earth trembles.

Kumbhakarna is annoyed that his sleep has been disturbed and asks Ravana why. His brother tells him of the danger at the gates of Lanka. When Kumbhakarna hears the story, he berates his brother. He tells Ravana that it was foolish to succumb to passion and invite danger to Lanka. Ravana is supposed to be learned and wise. Why did he need to take another man's wife? Are the king's personal passions a justifiable reason to bring danger to his subjects? If he cannot put the good of his subjects above himself, he does not deserve to be king. Who Ravana marries is Ravana's business, and perhaps Mandodari's. It should not become the problem of the Asuras. They have given their blood and sweat over a lifetime to build this kingdom, and Ravana is throwing it away for the sake of a mere woman.

In the folk versions where Sita is considered Ravana's daughter, Ravana says he is protecting his daughter to pacify Kumbhakarna. He appeals to Kumbhakarna as Sita's uncle that he must protect his niece from her vagrant husband.

To this, Kumbhakarna replies, 'You threw her away when she was a baby when some astrologers said she would bring destruction to the Asura race. As you too are a great astrologer, we all believed you. Knowing your daughter would bring destruction to us all, why did you bring her back? Are you willing to sacrifice your sons, ministers, brothers, and your people for the sake of a daughter you cast away? When did the king's personal relationships become more important than the welfare of the people? If you find your family a hindrance to conducting your dharma as a king, you need to either relinquish the crown or your family. My brother, you have not chosen wisely. You are mixing your personal relationships with the dharma of kingship. Since being a king is more important to you, and you have been a great ruler for Lanka, I advise you to give Sita back to Rama and make peace with him. Since Sita went into exile voluntarily with Rama, even though he was no longer a prince of Ayodhya, it is evident she loves him. As a father, you must ensure her happiness. By keeping her here against her will, you are not doing your duty.'

This is not what Ravana expected to hear from his brother. Ravana roars at Kumbhakarna, 'I thought I had raised two brothers who loved and respected me. I devoted my whole life working for the benefit of my family and my people. And now, when a crucial time has come, you are turning your back on me. All of you are cowards, thinking only of your safety while enjoying the benefits of living under my rule. You are my younger brother, but I am your king too. Your duty, your dharma, is to obey me without question. When your elder brother needs advice, he will ask you. When your king needs advice he will ask his ministers, not his relatives. If you want to go the way Vibhishana has gone, I will not stop you. I have decided I need Sita. If I give her back now after losing my son Akshaya Kumara and ministers like Prahasta, the world will laugh at me.'

'Many times we make choices without thinking of their consequences,' Kumbhakarna retorts. 'Sometimes our choices bring results we do not like; sometimes, they are even harmful. Those who are wise correct their choices. When we enter a river without knowing its depth or current, we can be washed away. It is always better to swim back to the safety of the shore instead of foolishly pursuing one's course. Perhaps, because of bad advice or misfortune, you might have chosen the path that is taking you to your destruction. But it is not too late. If you correct your action, the world will not laugh at you. Instead it will praise Ravana's wisdom saying he is great enough to understand his mistakes and repent for them. If you do not, you will sacrifice not only yourself, but those who love you, like me and your subjects. Think about your virtuous wife, Mandodari.'

Ravana slams his fist on the armrest of his throne and springs up. 'Kumbhakarna, you are a traitor like your brother!' he yells. 'I do not want to see your face again. Go with Vibhishana. When I am dead, my two brothers can share the spoils and divide my kingdom and be Rama's servitors. You are a shame on the Asuras.'

Kumbhakarna, with a heavy heart, bows to Ravana and says, 'Brother, it is my duty to warn you. But you are not ready to listen. I promise I will do everything possible to serve you. I am not like

Vibhishana, and I am pained that you doubt my loyalty. I am hurt, but I have no grudge against you. I do not judge you nor doubt your love for me. You have protected me all my life. A few harsh words spoken when you are agitated cannot erase the good you have done me. I am a burden to you, sleeping most of the year and devouring huge quantities of food. You could have cast me away, yet you chose to protect me, ensuring my sleep was not disturbed. I also understand that you want to protect your son Indrajit from Rama and that is why you have chosen to wake me, even knowing that I am vulnerable and no longer invincible when my sleep is broken. The strength in my body, every little bit of it, I owe to you. I will be loyal to you until my last breath. I will go to the battlefield knowing I will not return. If I die, I do so knowing my elder brother will take care of my family.'

Ravana is moved by his brother's words and hugs Kumbhakarna. Ravana knows he is sending his brother to his death. What he hopes is that Kumbhakarna will inflict sufficient damage to dishearten the Vanaras into abandoning Rama. So Ravana feeds Kumbhakarna with his own hands. When his brother touches his feet to seek his blessing, Ravana breaks down and weeps. Without speaking another word, Kumbhakarna marches into battle.

Both Kumbhakarna and Vibhishana understand that their elder brother is taking a perilous path, bringing doom and destruction to the Asura clan. How they choose to respond to the same crisis is what makes them fascinatingly different. Vibhishana decides what he thinks to be right. For him, family loyalty does not count. He chooses wisely too, as the story shows.

Kumbhakarna understands that he will never return, yet he chooses to stay loyal to his brother. Kumbhakarna is often depicted as a demon, a giant without compassion. However, as far as the Asuras are concerned, Kumbhakarna is a hero. The kingdom of Lanka and all its riches are within his reach. Like Vibhishana, he merely has to convince himself that what his brother has done for him over the years does not matter in the present circumstances. He too can claim Rama is God, and it is his duty to do whatever God says.

Kumbhakarna is the incarnation of Vijaya, the other doorkeeper of Vishnu. His destiny is to fight Lord Vishnu and die. The purpose of both Ravana and Kumbhakarna's lives is to play the roles assigned to them. If Kumbhakarna acts like Vibhishana, he ceases to be Kumbhakarna and becomes just another Rama devotee. What sets Kumbhakarna apart is his clear vision of right and wrong. When he gives advice to Ravana, he proves he is wiser than his learned brother.

In the Mahabharata, Karna resembles Kumbhakarna the most. Karna could have had the kingdom had he betrayed his friend and benefactor, Duryodhana. He knows he can even end the war, for he is the eldest amongst the Pandavas and Kauravas, but when Krishna offers Karna all of Bharat Varsha, Karna declines. He chooses to die a heroic death rather than become the ruler of Hastinapura. Similarly, Kumbhakarna decides to die for his brother rather than become another Vibhishana.

The debate on who is right, Kumbhakarna or Vibhishana, has raged for centuries. Until the Bhakti-era Ramayanas took prominence, even ardent Rama devotees considered Vibhishana a traitor. In Vaishnava tradition, Rama is not just the human avatar of Vishnu, but Vishnu himself. There is a subtle difference between the concept of Valmiki's Rama and the Bhakti-era Rama. In the Kamba Ramayana and the Tulsidas Ramayana, Rama is God, not just a human avatar of God. A human avatar of God will have human flaws. He is not all-knowing and omnipotent.

So, in the earlier-era Ramayanas, including the Valmiki Ramayana, Rama gets angry, feels jealous and is even arrogant on some occasions. He repents for what he has done. He weeps like any human being when he is separated from his beloved. Rama of the earlier Ramayanas is more human and endearing than the religious figure that the Bhakti era made him into. That is my opinion.

In the Bhakti-era Ramayana, Kumbhakarna is a fool who does not understand Rama's divinity. Vibhishana is a wise man who understands God has come in the form of Rama and abandons his evil brother. The later Ramayanas make the story into a purely good versus evil tale. They served the purpose of getting people more devoted to the concept of Rama as God at the cost of losing the subtle arguments on what dharma is.

The Bhakti era produced beautiful literature and poetry and soothed the caste system's bruises to an extent, but it was also a rebellion against free thought. It muffled the voices of reason and the questioning that the Vedas, Upanishads and Aranyakas espoused. Instead, by smoothening out the Ramayana's nuances and the play of myriad human characteristics and choices, it made the story into a one-sided affair where God is always right, and anyone expressing the slightest dissent is evil. The Bhakti era, like any other era, had its roots in the society of the time.

The age of the Upanishads and Vedas, or the early Sangha literature of the south, was an age of confidence, when Indian civilization flourished. Only a flourishing culture has the confidence to question, rationalize, discern and produce works such as the Valmiki Ramayana or Vedavyasa's Mahabharata, where there is no clear-cut distinction between good and evil. Both epics ponder various human conditions and allow readers to arrive at their own conclusions.

The preachy Bhakti-era literature caters to a different group of people. It must be noted that the Bhakti movement began when the caste system was at its peak. Bhakti united people and served as a bridge between the philosophical heights the Upanishads had reached and the common man's needs.

Amongst the different ways of living, the path of Bhakti is the easiest. It offers liberation by merely chanting the name of God. In rural India, especially in areas under Islamic rule, Rama became a symbol of righteousness. Valmiki's Rama and Ravana were changed beyond recognition. I believe this is the way a defeated society reacts.

> The Southern Recension of the Valmiki Ramayana elaborates on the Kumbhakarna-Ravana debate regarding the return of Sita. This is not mentioned in other versions of the Valmiki Ramayana. The comically exaggerated description of waking Kumbhakarna is also a speciality of the Southern Recension. In the Bhavaratha Ramayana, Apsaras like Rambha, Menaka, Tilottama and Urvashi come to wake Kumbhakarna at Ravana's command.
>
> In the Valmiki Ramayana, while asking Brahma for boons, Kumbhakarna, impelled by Saraswati, asked for sleep (nidratva) instead of the throne of Indra (Indratva). After receiving his boon, Kumbhakarna sleeps for thousands of years, as per the Uttara Ramayana. However, in the Yuddha Kanda, Kumbhakarna's sleep is said to last for six months. He wakes up for a day and hungrily devours anything he sees. In the Ananda Ramayana, Kumbhakarna sleeps for six months and wakes up for a day to eat food. In a few folk versions from the south, Kumbhakarna sleeps for six months and then wakes up for six months, during which he becomes invincible. In all Ramayanas, if Kumbhakarna is forcibly woken up before his quota of six months, he will still be powerful but can be killed.

In the Raghuvamsha, Dasavatara Charita, Skanda Purana, Maheswara Kanda, Padma Purana and Uttara Kanda, it is not Brahma but Shiva who gives the boons to Ravana and his brothers, including Kumbhakarna.

In the Seri Rama, Prophet Adam pleads with Allah to give boons to Ravana. In the Pauma Chariyam, Ravana obtains all his powers through Siddha practice and meditation, and not because of any boons.

36

Kumbhakarna: Death of a Mighty Warrior

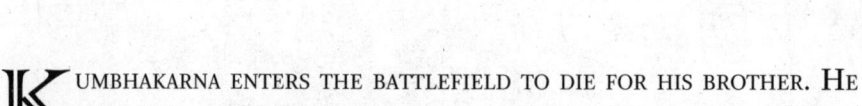

KUMBHAKARNA ENTERS THE BATTLEFIELD TO DIE FOR HIS BROTHER. He has nothing to lose. As he starts to fight, the Vanaras realize that this opponent will not be easy to tackle.

He fights the way they do, using his brute strength. He does not invoke magical arrows like Indrajit, nor deploy the army with a strategic plan. He towers over all on the battlefield and whatever they hurl at him has no effect. He catches Lakshmana's arrows and breaks them like twigs. When Hanuman tries to attack him, he flings Hanuman away like a pesky fly, with one swipe of his hand. Angada and Sugriva get caught in his grip, and he tries to gobble them up. Angada pokes his mace into Kumbhakarna's eye. As the giant yells in pain and loosens his grip, Angada and Sugriva fall to the ground and run for dear life.

The Vanaras rush to Rama, asking him to do something. If this continues, they will be annihilated. Rama tries to defeat Kumbhakarna, but even his arrows have no effect. When Lakshmana asks Rama why this is so, Rama says, 'Kumbhakarna is fighting for his dharma. He does not use deceit, nor has he done any adharma.

That is his strength. He is loyal to his brother, just as you are loyal to me. He is not fighting for himself, but for the idea that one must be grateful to the people who feed and help us.'

A similar situation arises in the Mahabharata as well. Arjuna finds it challenging to defeat Karna. Despite Arjuna having Krishna's help, and knowledge of all the divine weapons, Karna is invincible. When Arjuna asks why, Krishna replies, 'Karna's dharma, of being loyal to Duryodhana, is acting as a shield.'

To defeat Karna, Krishna goes to him as an alms seeker. Karna understands it is Krishna, but he has vowed never to send back anyone who asks for his help. Karna will help anyone who asks for his aid, even if it harms him. Knowing this weakness, Krishna asks Karna to give him all his good deeds and dharma. Karna knows it is a trap, but he is bound by his own principles. He gives Krishna the gains of dharma that he has achieved by being loyal to Duryodhana and generous to everyone. With that gone, Karna loses his protective shield and is killed by Arjuna.

In the parallel story in the Ramayana, Kumbhakarna remains invincible. Rama says the only way Kumbhakarna can be defeated is to make him act against his dharma. Lakshmana is perplexed; what Kumbhakarna is doing is adharma. 'He is killing our people,' he says. 'Isn't that adharma? Why is he not like Vibhishana, who understands right from wrong? By supporting Ravana in holding Sita, Kumbhakarna is also party to the crime.'

Rama answers with a smile, 'Kumbhakarna is obeying his elder brother. Let me ask you a question. If I ask you to commit an adharma, would you do it?'

That sets Lakshmana thinking. He would never disobey his brother, but if his brother asked for an act of adharma, would he obey? Lakshmana says the concept of dharma is exceedingly complicated to comprehend. Rama tells him that everyone acts as per their definition of dharma and pays the price for it. No one wishes to intentionally commit adharma. Even those whom we consider evil think they are doing the right thing. That is human nature.

Lakshmana cries, 'But how are we going to defeat Kumbhakarna?'

Rama replies, 'We have to wait for Kumbhakarna to make a mistake. His strength will then become his weakness, as usually happens in life. His strength is his blind loyalty to Ravana.'

As Rama predicts, Kumbhakarna does make a mistake. The trigger is Ravana, who, watching Kumbhakarna, suddenly yells, 'Kill Rama! Kill Rama!'

Kumbhakarna looks for Rama but cannot find him.

Ravana cries again, 'You are not fighting enough! You are not loyal enough! You must find Rama and kill him!'

Kumbhakarna is hurt by his brother's words. Why is Ravana questioning his loyalty? Kumbhakarna utters a cry of anguish and prays to Lord Shiva, saying, 'Oh Shiva, my brother suspects my loyalty and I am angry. Show me where Rama is.'

Shiva blesses Kumbhakarna with a vision of Rama. Kumbhakarna sees him everywhere he looks. All the Vanaras and Asuras look like Rama to him. When he turns back to look at Ravana, instead of his brother, he sees Rama. Kumbhakarna is confused. He asks Lord Shiva, 'Why do I see Rama everywhere?'

Shiva answers with a smile, 'Because everyone *is* Rama. Some people know it; some are yet to discover it.'

This confuses Kumbhakarna further. He thinks he sees Rama everywhere because he is thinking about Rama. One tends to see what one keeps thinking about. He shuts his mind and concentrates on what his brother is yelling. He hears only one word, 'kill'. The moment he ceases to think about Rama, he stops seeing him everywhere. Instead, he is consumed by rage. His mind recognizes only one word—'kill'. Anger consumes Kumbhakarna, and he starts killing indiscriminately. Soon, discretion leaves him and he kills whoever comes near him, whether Asura or Vanara.

The Asuras run to Rama, pleading for help. The weapon Ravana has unleashed upon the Vanaras is now turning against everyone. 'Now,' says Rama to Lakshmana, 'Kumbhakarna has lost his shield of dharma. He has lost his head, he is acting without discretion. As long as Kumbhakarna was doing his dharma, he was invincible. Now, consumed by anger, he has committed adharma by killing those he has vowed to protect. Now he is vulnerable.'

Rama takes on Kumbhakarna, and this time Rama's arrow finds its mark. Rama uses the weapon Shakteya against Kumbhakarna. The moment it pierces Kumbhakarna's heart, the giant Asura realizes his mistake. He had come to kill Ravana's enemies, but consumed by anger, he killed and endangered the lives of his own people. At the moment of death, Kumbhakarna loses his rage and gains clarity. He begs pardon and then increases his body to the maximum possible size. He reaches the sky and collapses onto the Vanara army, crushing many thousands to death.

Kumbhakarna has finally done his job. He acted as the leader of the Asuras and did his duty by inflicting maximum damage on the Vanaras. As he falls and life ebbs out of him, he sees Vibhishana. Kumbhakarna curses his brother for bringing death and destruction to Lanka. He says, 'Let no Asura child be named after you. As long as the world exists, your name will be associated with treason. You will be the eternal traitor, and may every man be wary of a Vibhishana amongst his brothers.'

Vibhishana falls to his knees weeping when he hears Kumbhakarna's curse. He tries to justify his actions by saying that he followed his conscience. Rama pacifies Vibhishana, saying one must choose one's own dharma and live by one's choices and consequences. Rama refuses to condemn Kumbhakarna and says that just like Vibhishana and Lakshmana, Kumbhakarna too is dear to him, for he is the one who has followed his dharma unto death.

This rendition of Kumbhakarna is seen in south Indian folk-tales. It is more or less similar to the Valmiki Ramayana, but the event of Kumbhakarna seeing Rama everywhere is an innovative addition in the folk-tales. A variation is where Kumbhakarna sees his own reflection in a pool of blood and finds that he too is Rama. In this oral Jain folklore version, Kumbhakarna refuses to fight and becomes a Jain monk. In the oral Jain versions of the Ramayana, Rama is a proponent of non-violence, ahimsa, and it is Lakshmana who fights and goes to hell because he has committed violence; it is Lakshmana who kills Ravana, while Rama remains the epitome of ahimsa.

Kumbhakarna's death is a big blow for Ravana. He knows that he sent his brother to his death to protect his son. Ravana weeps through the night in guilt and sorrow. He thinks that perhaps his final instruction to kill Rama might have caused Kumbhakarna's death. Until then, Ravana knew that Kumbhakarna had been winning the battle for him. Ravana need not have intervened when his commander was doing the right thing. A leader must know when to trust his people and to leave them alone, instead of giving instructions that can spoil a winning hand. But it is a lesson learnt too late.

37

The Death of Valiant Atikaya, and Kumbhakarna's Sons

After Kumbhakarna's death, Ravana is in a dilemma. He wishes to send Indrajit once again into battle, but his son pleads with him not to compel him to commit an adharma. Ravana has told Indrajit to create a Maya-Sita and slay her in front of Rama. Ravana is sure this will kill Rama's spirit and that of the Vanara army. However, Indrajit does not wish to commit the adharma of killing a woman, even using a mere illusion. Ravana does not have the strength of mind to compel Indrajit, for he knows that Indrajit's conduct in following his dharma is shielding his son from defeat.

Following much deliberation, Ravana decides to send Kumbhakarna's sons Kumba and Nikumba instead. Kumbhakarna's widow, however, is distraught at the idea. Is it not enough that her husband has sacrificed himself, she asks Ravana. Must her sons too be offered at the altar of Ravana's ego? Why does Ravana not send his illustrious son into battle instead of asking two boys who have just lost their father?

This sets Ravana thinking. Kumbhakarna's widow is right, he admits grudgingly. But he does not want to send Indrajit again. He recalls he has another son, Atikaya, his illegitimate son with Dhanyamalini, Mandodari's maid. Ravana summons Atikaya and tells him to lead the Asura army. For Atikaya, who has always been more a servant than a son, who has fought all his life for his father's love and affection, this seems like an excellent opportunity to prove his loyalty. He takes it as a great honour that Ravana has asked him, an illegitimate son, to lead the army. He bows before his father and marches to the battlefield.

Initially, the Asuras are not comfortable fighting under Ravana's illegitimate son by a maidservant or daasi. However, Atikaya surprises both Rama and Ravana's armies with his valour and capacity to lead strategically. He kills many Vanaras and defeats Angada and Sugriva. With Hanuman, he engages in a duel of equals and the Asuras start pushing the Vanara army back to the sea.

Finally, Lakshmana shoots Atikaya using the Nagastra, the potent weapon of the serpent clan. As the poison of the Nagastra courses through his veins, Atikaya cries out to his father that he has proved his worth and Ravana should call him 'son'. Ravana sees how the son he has ignored from birth has fought and died with valour and blesses him from atop the fort's ramparts. In death, Atikaya achieves what he has yearned for all his life.

Rama himself conducts Atikaya's funeral. When Lakshmana questions this, Rama says, 'An enemy who is slain ceases to be an enemy. If I do not respect him in death, how can I call myself a man?'

As the Vanaras converge and pray for Atikaya's moksha, the gods from heaven bless Rama with victory for showing compassion and respect.

Kumba and Nikumba Enter the Fray

Now, Ravana approaches Kumbhakarna's widow with a request that Kumba and Nikumba be sent to the battlefield. He has sacrificed yet another son but shielded Indrajit. Kumba and Nikumba seek the blessings of their devastated mother and march into battle. Like their father, they are convinced the war is not righteous. However, they fight because they are grateful to their uncle for what he has done for them.

They fight just like their father. They have magical powers and can rise high into the sky. The Vanara army is once again in retreat. Lakshmana finishes off Kumba with an arrow shot from behind. As Kumba lies dying, he warns Nikumba that the other side is not following dharma. Nikumba, angry at the way his brother was killed, begins to indiscriminately attack the Vanara army, just as his father did. But this time Lakshmana is unable to defeat Nikumba and so he runs to Rama to ask, 'Why am I not able to defeat Nikumba?'

Rama says, 'Nikumba's anger is justified, so he can be defeated only by someone who does not succumb to anger or hatred, but one who will kill with compassion.'

Lakshmana is perplexed by this. 'How can anyone kill with compassion?' he asks. 'The moment you choose to kill someone, compassion dies within you.'

Rama explains that for some, death is a relief. Nikumba is not looking for victory, but death. He misses his father and brother. Since his anger is justifiable, it makes him stronger rather than weaker. But a warrior like Hanuman can easily tackle him because he does not succumb to anger. He fights because he believes in the righteousness of his cause. He will approach Nikumba with compassion, who is weighed down by anger, by the loyalty he has for his uncle, and his conviction that this war is unrighteous.

'If you go, Lakshmana,' he says, 'you will fight with the same hatred towards the Asuras that they have for us. Anger against anger can only bring destruction to everyone. Anger must be dealt with understanding and compassion. We must relieve Nikumba of his pain. Even if he wins against us, he will live an empty and miserable life. By dying, he will have paid back his uncle. So, send Hanuman to fight Nikumba.'

Many hours later, as the sun is setting and waves lap at the shores of Lanka, the two warriors fight on. The entire Vanara and Asura armies stop the battle to watch this duel. Nikumba has the same siddhis or divine powers as Hanuman; he can become small or big, fly, become light as a feather or heavy as stone, and match Hanuman in strength. It is a fight between equals that can continue forever but for one factor. As Rama predicted, Nikumba is fighting with hatred and anger in his heart. Hanuman is poised and calm, convinced about the righteousness of his cause. Every blow he delivers is slightly more potent than the blows delivered by Nikumba.

Initially, the difference is so minute that nobody observes it. Hanuman can punch Nikumba at the right moment and at the right place, whereas Nikumba uses all his strength to beat Hanuman indiscriminately. As time progresses and the sun is about to set, a mighty punch from Hanuman knocks Nikumba down and he lies dead.

Rama tells Lakshmana, 'You might have observed that initially none of Hanuman's punches made any impact on Nikumba. It seemed that Nikumba would win because of the anger he was using as a tool. However, a calm and poised Hanuman wore him down slowly. Each of Hanuman's punches was equivalent to ten of Nikumba's. Just as persistent water falling wears out a rock, or a breeze flowing for thousands of years over a mountain can reshape it, Hanuman's punches made an impact at the right time. It was not the last mighty punch of Hanuman that killed Nikumba but all those punches that were delivered with precision that weakened him.'

Lakshmana learns another vital lesson. Anger, if not controlled, and not for the right cause, can consume one. Rama once again conducts Kumba and Nikumba's funerals with respect. This time, the Vanaras know that Rama treats his enemies with the same respect he accords them. They come together and cook a feast in honour of the slain heroes and invite the Asuras to eat with them. The Asuras, however, decline, saying that once they eat with the Vanaras, they will cease to be enemies and that would be disloyal to their king. They bow to the Vanaras and march back to Lanka, carrying the tragic news of the death of Kumbhakarna's brave sons.

In folk Ramayanas, the offer of food from Rama to the Asuras is given prominence. In rural India, sharing food is a sign of brotherhood. Rama is trying for peace with this gesture. The oral storytellers of rural India emphasize the importance of giving and sharing food, even with one's enemies. Food dissolves enmity. Eating together is a mark of the unity of the community.

This peace initiative by Rama, at this poignant moment, creates an impression in the Asuras' minds. They begin to wonder if their king is wrong. They question why they are fighting. Why is their king so obsessed with Sita? Is there any basis for the rumours that Sita is the king's daughter? If that is true, the Asuras are prepared to fight to the death to defend their princess. If the rumours—that Ravana kidnapped Sita because he was enticed by her beauty and wanted to marry her—are correct, then the war they are engaged in is not righteous.

The elders warn them not to overthink. As Ravana's soldiers, they must obey their superiors. But the conflict between duty and conscience plays heavily in the minds of the Asuras. What is more important, their duty towards their families or towards the country? Does 'the country' mean the king or the people? With all these dilemmas in mind, the Asuras end the day's battle and march back with heavy hearts to Lanka.

38

The Death of Indrajit

WHEN INDRAJIT LEARNS OF THE DEATHS OF KUMBHAKARNA, NIKUMBA and Kumba, he becomes enraged. He promises Ravana that he will kill Rama and Lakshmana. Once again, Ravana asks him to use deception to create an illusory Maya-Sita and fly her in the Pushpaka Vimana to the battlefield and behead her in front of Rama and Lakshmana. This will kill the fighting spirit of the Vanaras and Rama. Ravana explains to his son that using strategy and deception in war is not adharma. Indrajit says he cannot harm a woman, even as a ruse. Illusion or not, it is not in Indrajit's character to kill Sita.

So Ravana asks his son how he plans to defeat Rama and Lakshmana. 'The enemy will use deceit sooner or later,' says Ravana. 'People talk about dharma and ethics only when they have the upper hand. When they are cornered, they use any trick to win. I have lost Akshaya Kumara, Atikaya, Kumbhakarna, Kumba, Nikumba and Prahasta. The greatest dharma is survival. Observe nature, and you will find that it uses ruse and deception at every moment. Why does the tiger hide behind the bush, waiting for its prey? Even if the tiger is stronger than the bison, it attacks from behind. The snake lies waiting in the grass, camouflaging itself so that it can pounce on the rat. We are creatures of nature; morals and rules are made by men to control others. If you do not use strategy to win, your opponent will, sooner or later.'

Indrajit says he does not need any tricks to destroy Rama's morale. He reminds his father that he has defeated even Indra and dragged him back to Lanka. 'I will use the Brahmastra and finish off all the Vanaras,' he says confidently.

Ravana reminds him that the Asuras are Rakshasas. As Rakshasas, they have a duty to protect every creature (Rakshasa also means 'one who protects'; it comes from the Sanskrit word 'raksha', protect). Rakshasas stop the sacrifices of the maharishis because sacrificing animals to please the gods does not make sense to the Rakshasas. This respect for nature makes them enemies of those who conduct Vedic sacrifices.

Ravana reminds Indrajit that if he uses the Brahmastra, he will be going against his clan's dharma. The Brahmastra is a last resort. He asks his son whether he is aware of the weapon's destructive potential.

Ravana also tells his son that with its destructive power not only will it kill their enemies, but many Asuras as well. Even that could be justifiable, for death is a part of war. But the Brahmastra will kill all the creatures that fly, run on four legs, the tiniest creatures that cannot even be seen with human eyes, the fish in the rivers and the sea, and many other helpless creatures that have nothing to do with either the Asuras or the Vanaras.

'Is it not adharma to use this weapon to ensure our victory?' Ravana asks his son. 'Consider which is the greater adharma—killing innocent creatures to win, or creating an illusory Sita whom you slay in front of Rama and Lakshmana?'

Indrajit is confused. His nature does not allow him to use the ruse of killing Sita. He goes to his chamber to think it over. His wife Sulochana advises him to act according to his conscience, but adds,

'Since Ravana is not only your father but also your king, you should take his advice. It is because of his love for you that he has given you a choice. Had it been someone else, your father would have simply ordered him to do his will.'

After much deliberation, Indrajit says, 'I am not my father, neither am I Rama to think about everyone else. My duty is to win the war for my father. I must kill my enemies as I am a Kshatriya. I will not harm a woman, even if she is just an illusion created by me. I will take the sin of using the Brahmastra for my father's victory upon myself, rather than suffering the ignominy of being known as the molester of a woman.'

Indrajit goes to battle in the Pushpaka Vimana, his arrows wounding and killing Vanaras by the hundreds. The Vanaras are unable to withstand Indrajit's attack. He then makes himself invisible and attacks from everywhere and the Vanaras panic. An enemy who cannot be seen is impossible to fight. Rama and Lakshmana come to challenge Indrajit. They shoot many divinely powered arrows. When Rama's arrows start breaking Indrajit's invisibility barrier, he decides to use the Brahmastra.

The Brahmastra explodes above the Vanara army, knocking down lakhs of soldiers on either side. Lanka's earth becomes scorched, the sea, rivers and lakes boil and the sky is filled with deep purple smoke. The sun goes into hiding and darkness descends on all. High above the carnage, through the clouds, Indrajit sees Rama and Lakshmana lying immobile. He returns to the palace and celebrations begin in Ravana's court.

Ravana announces that Indrajit has saved Lanka; Rama and Lakshmana have been killed, and his great son has achieved what neither Kumbhakarna nor he could do. Ravana sends word of the victory to Trijata. When Sita receives the message, that Rama and Lakshmana are dead, she laments her fate. But she cannot free her mind of doubt. The last time, Ravana had conjured up an illusion of murdering Rama before her. Perhaps this too was a ruse. She refuses to believe Rama and Lakshmana are dead.

To convince her, Ravana tells Trijata to take Sita in the Pushpaka Vimana and show her Rama and Lakshmana's immobile bodies. At first, Sita sees many Asuras lying dead from the impact of the Brahmastra. But then she sees that most of the Vanaras are dead, and at their centre are Rama and Lakshmana's bodies. Sita faints, and Trijata takes her back to Lanka.

There are few survivors in the Vanara camp. Jambavan wakes up slowly and goes in search of Hanuman. He finds Hanuman sitting in one corner, lamenting Rama and Lakshmana's death. Hanuman, though dazed, appears to be unhurt. Jambavan tells him that this time he must bring four herbs to revive Rama and Lakshmana. They are not dead yet, and if Hanuman hurries, they can save Rama and Lakshmana. Sushena, the physician, gives Hanuman the names of the four herbs and Hanuman rushes to the Himalayas using his superpowers.

In folk Ramayanas, Hanuman flies over Ayodhya en route. Bharata, who thinks it is an Asura flying above, shoots him down. Hanuman lands at Bharata's feet with a thud, an arrow piercing his belly. He tells Bharata that he is flying to the Himalayas to save Rama and does not know which evil king shot him down. Hearing Rama's name, Bharata is shocked. Without enquiring, acting on prejudice, Bharata had shot down the one rushing to help his beloved brother.

Sage Vasishta is summoned and he heals Hanuman, who then flies on towards the Himalayas. As he arrives there, dawn is breaking. He sees Mount Kailasa and Manasarovar, but he cannot find the mountain Sushena had told him about, on which the herbs are located. After a frantic search, he finds a mountain illuminated with many magical herbs. Since he has lost precious time, in his panic, Hanuman forgets the names of the herbs. He lifts the entire mountain on to his shoulder and flies back. He lands on the battlefield of Lanka just as dawn is breaking. He is surprised to find that Rama and Lakshmana have revived, and so have all the Vanaras.

Hanuman is angry and perturbed. If they had been revived without the herbs, why had he gone to so much trouble? So, he lifts the mountain and flings it back towards the Himalayas. As the hill is hurled north, parts of it fall in various parts of India. Locals now claim that these hills, containing medicinal herbs, are present thanks to Hanuman.

Seeing Hanuman's strange action, Rama beckons to him. But Hanuman is not ready to speak to him. When Rama enquires why Hanuman is unhappy that he and Lakshmana have survived, Hanuman finally says that no one seems to appreciate his gigantic effort.

Rama laughs and says, 'What makes you think that your work was worthless? You were asked to bring four herbs, and you brought the entire mountain. You have done more than what was required. You should have just brought the four herbs, yet, confident in your great strength, and to show that you could carry it, you brought the entire aushadhi parvatha, the mountain of medicinal herbs. Everyone knows your strength, Hanuman. You need not keep proving it. And, after bringing the mountain and doing this great deed, you expect the world to notice. But the world never notices extra work done. It only notices the result. The result is that not just my brother and I, but all the Vanaras and Asuras who were struck down have revived. You threw away all your hard work, thinking you were not appreciated. People are happy they have come back to life. They are celebrating. To expect them to stop their celebration and appreciate you is unreasonable. None of your hard work has gone to waste. You have given life to all of us once again. There is not a single Vanara or Asura who is not grateful for what you did. But they will express their gratitude and love at the time of their choosing, not yours. Your dharma was to bring the aushadhi parvatha.'

Hanuman understands his mistake and asks for forgiveness with folded hands. Rama consoles him saying that everyone makes mistakes. 'It is part of life. The child falls down many times, but always gets up and tries to walk, again and again. Mistakes are the greatest gurus. The gurudakshina is paid in the form of success. Next time you feel angry or unappreciated, Hanuman, just think that you are far greater than all this. Remember who resides in your heart. Then there will not be such disappointments in life.'

When Sita awakens, she hears a familiar sound—the twanging of Rama's famed bow, Kodanda. She hugs Trijata, saying, 'I know my Rama is alive! He will kill Ravana and take me back to Ayodhya.'

Ravana too hears the twanging of Rama's bow and is terrified. Indrajit is shocked beyond belief. If a man can survive even the Brahmastra, what can kill him? Ravana scolds Indrajit for not completing his task, calling him an ungrateful son. A devastated Indrajit goes back to his chamber. His wife Sulochana once again advises him to act only according to his conscience. Indrajit laments that he did indeed act according to his conscience, but perhaps his father was right.

Sulochana says he should not do anything that goes against his nature. 'You are not your father. Your strength, your shield is your dharma. Even hurling the Brahmastra at Rama can be considered your dharma. You were doing it to protect your father and your country. However, if you do something against your nature, then it becomes adharma.' Sulochana also says she fears that dharma's protective armour will fall away if he acts against his nature.

Indrajit, torn between his convictions and his love for his father, finally decides to obey Ravana and flies back in the Pushpaka Vimana towards the battlefield. This time he uses his magical powers to create an image of Sita. He flies low enough for the Vanaras and Rama to see that he has Sita with him. He then grabs the illusionary Sita's hair with one hand and unsheathes his sword with the other. He roars, 'Rama! All your efforts have been in vain. There was no use building the bridge across the seas. Your killing Bali through deceit cannot yield anything good. All your valour in killing many of our great heroes is wasted, for I have your Sita with me and I will kill her.'

Indrajit cuts off the head of the illusionary Sita and flings it down to Rama. With a roar, the Pushpaka Vimana turns and flies away towards the hills.

Rama rushes to Sita's severed head and starts to weep. 'I was supposed to protect you but I failed, again and again. I cannot call myself an ideal husband,' he says, and then faints, holding Sita's head close to his heart.

Lakshmana cannot control his emotions, and he too breaks down. Gloom spreads over the Vanara army.

In the hills, Indrajit jumps out of the Pushpaka Vimana and rushes to his favourite Kali temple, inside a cave called Nikumbila. He cannot face himself for what he has done. For the first time in his life, he has acted against his conscience. Sulochana's words echo in his ears, 'Hurling the Brahmastra at your enemies is not adharma, killing the Maya-Sita is.' Now he understands why Vibhishana and Kumbhakarna acted the way they had. Even his father is dharmic in his own way. He serves according to his nature and his conscience. So does Rama. 'The only evil one is I,' laments Indrajit.

Meanwhile, the Asuras start massacring the dispirited Vanaras, who begin to retreat. Vibhishana, who has been watching, goes to Rama. As he touches Rama's hand, holding Sita's head, the head vanishes. Vibhishana had suspected it all along to be an illusion created by Indrajit, but knowing his nephew's character, he had never expected him to practise such deceit. He awakens Rama and starts laughing. Rama looks at his empty hands, surprised that Sita's severed head is no longer there. Vibhishana tells Rama that it was all an illusion. Rama understands the implications immediately.

He calls Lakshmana and says, 'Your sister-in-law is not dead. I understand why my friend Vibhishana is laughing. So far, Indrajit's dharma has protected him from my arrows. He has been a moral and dutiful son, and he, like me, has been following his father's orders. When my father asked me to go to the forest, I chose to because my conscience told me to do so. When Indrajit was fighting, he was doing so because his conscience told him to do so. Hence, he had the armour of dharma. But by succumbing to his father's deceit, he has destroyed his own armour. Lakshmana, now is your chance. Now he will be vulnerable to your arrows.'

Vibhishana promises Lakshmana that he will take him to his nephew. But he warns Lakshmana that Indrajit will be conducting a penance to wash off his sins. If he completes the sacrifice, he will once again have the armour of dharma, and it will be impossible to kill him.

Lakshmana knows the implications. He must kill a man in prayer. He has long harboured doubts in his mind about the righteousness of his brother killing Bali by hiding behind a tree. Though he had never spoken about it, he understands that it was the only way Rama could have killed Bali. And that Rama would pay the price for his choice. Now, Lakshmana knows that he too will pay the price for his choice. He must kill Indrajit while he is praying, and he will have to bear the consequence of his action. Lakshmana asks his conscience whether he can do it. After some deliberation, he knows that he will happily take whatever karma has in store for him to help his brother.

Vibhishana leads Lakshmana to the Nikumbila cave. They see Indrajit lying prostrate before the idol of Goddess Kali, shoulders limp from the guilt of what he has done. Lakshmana cries out, challenging him to a duel. Indrajit knows that if he stops his prayers, he will die. But the dharma of a Kshatriya is never to back out from a challenge. Knowing that he does not have much time to live, Indrajit picks up his bow and quiver of arrows. A fierce battle ensues.

Finally, Indrajit falls to Lakshmana's arrows, and a triumphant Lakshmana returns to Rama. The Asuras are devastated. When Ravana hears the news of his son's death, for the first time he thinks he has committed a grave mistake in bringing Sita to Lanka. Overcome by grief, and knowing that it was the illusion that Indrajit created that finally destroyed him, Ravana vows to make the slaying of Sita real. He rushes to Asoka Vatika with the Chandrahasa unsheathed.

'I am going to behead Sita!' he roars. 'She has caused the destruction of Lanka and everything I have built. I no longer care what adharma I do. For a year I have not touched Sita. I have treated her with respect, waiting to kill Rama to have her. But it seems defeat is staring me in the face. I will kill Sita and then go to Rama with her head. I will do what I asked my son to do. Let the world call Ravana an evil Asura.'

Sita sees the terrible form of Ravana approaching and trembles in fear. She closes her eyes in prayer and whispers Rama's name.

One of Ravana's ministers rushes up to him and grabs his feet. Ravana kicks him, but the man does not let go. He pleads with Ravana not to commit the evil deed. 'If you kill her, what did we all fight for? So many have sacrificed their lives for you, my king. Is it all to be in vain?'

After much pleading and cajoling, Ravana finally flings down his sword and walks back to his chamber. There, Mandodari, devastated by her son's death, pleads with him not to continue the war.

Ravana retorts angrily, 'What choice do I have? I have sacrificed so much! If I fall at Rama's feet now like a coward and give back his wife, there will be no bigger fool than I. For ten thousand years, Ravana has ruled the fourteen worlds. The emperor of the Asuras will not bow his head before a mere man. I am not a fool like Rama, who left his palace and kingdom to wander in the forest. Ravana has always lived like a king and will die as a king. To beg Rama's forgiveness now would be worse than death for me. I am Dasamukha, the one with ten faces, the one with all emotions intact.'

Mandodari knows that nothing is going to change her husband's mind. Having lost her child, she now braces herself for widowhood. The whole night Ravana prays to his beloved deity, Lord Shiva.

39

The Legend of Ahiravana and Mahiravana

Indrajit's death pierces Ravana like an arrow through the heart. His mother, Kaikasi, tries to console him. Like many others, she advises him to end the war by giving Sita back to Rama. Ravana tells his mother he has not sought her out to get the same advice being doled out by his wife. As his mother, she is supposed to protect him, he says. Kaikasi, though she knows her son is walking a dangerous path of no return, gives him one last hope. She reminds him of his half-brother Mahiravana.

In some folk versions, Mahiravana is Ravana's son. These legends are mostly found in eastern India and parts of south India. Such folk tales have a tantric base. Tantrism developed in India as a rebellious social movement, questioning every taboo society had enforced upon people. Human sacrifice also formed a part of occult tantrism. Kali or Mahamaya is the supreme goddess in the tantrism of eastern India.

Mahiravana is an ardent devotee of Kali. He refused to join Ravana's battle as he believed his half-brother had done wrong in abducting Sita. However, when Ravana pleads with him to save the Asuras, Mahiravana is undecided. Seeing his brother waver, Ravana reminds Mahiravana about his incomplete human sacrifice. To gain supreme power, Mahiravana had been sacrificing great kings. Thus far, he had sacrificed ninety-eight kings and princes. Ravana points out that Rama and Lakshmana belong to the Suryavamsha, the most illustrious dynasty amongst Kshatriyas. This gets Mahiravana's attention, and he agrees to participate in the battle.

The news that Mahiravana is going to join the battle creates panic in the Vanara ranks. Vibhishana knows Mahiravana's power and warns everyone that he is a master of disguise. He will not fight as Indrajit or Kumbhakarna have done. In fact, Mahiravana will not be interested in fighting at all. Instead, he will plan to kidnap Rama and Lakshmana. The security at the Vanara camp is strengthened.

Hanuman stands guard at the hut where Rama and Lakshmana are asleep. The folk version says that Hanuman makes a wall using his tail, which he can elongate to any length. As a sorcerer, Mahiravana's powers are stronger at night. If there is an attempt to kidnap Rama and Lakshmana, it is likely to happen before dawn. And indeed, Mahiravana tries many methods to breach Hanuman's security, but Hanuman sees through all of them and prevents him from entering.

As dawn breaks, Hanuman feels relieved that Mahiravana has not succeeded in entering the hut. Then Vibhishana comes to enquire about them, and Hanuman lets him in, while he waits outside. When Vibhishana does not return, Hanuman becomes suspicious. He rushes into the hut and is shocked to find Rama and Lakshmana missing. It is only then that he understands that Mahiravana had taken Vibhishana's form and kidnapped them, taking them to his empire in Patala Loka, the netherworld.

Often, danger comes in the form of one we trust. Hanuman believed no one could penetrate his security ring, but he himself let the enemy in. The Vanaras blame the guilt-ridden Hanuman for this slip. Vibhishana pacifies him but warns that it will not be easy to retrieve Rama and Lakshmana from Patala Loka. Hanuman promises he will bring them back.

Hanuman bores down into the earth in the form of a worm and reaches the netherworld. He is surprised to find that Mahiravana's empire is a complicated palace complex, with magical creatures standing guard at every corner. It is more challenging to penetrate Mahiravana's Patala Loka than Ravana's Lanka.

In the classical folk adventure tale format, Hanuman defeats many warriors and sorcerers using intelligence and sorcery. Having defeated almost all the sorcerers of Mahiravana's magical land, Hanuman faces the most significant challenge at the gate of Mahiravana's Kali temple. Standing guard is the exact replica of Hanuman himself. Hanuman is shocked to see this. The replica says he is Hanuman's son, Makaradhwaja.

Hanuman, a celibate brahmachari, is surprised. He denies having a son, but Makaradhwaja says he was born from Hanuman's karma. When Hanuman was crossing Lanka, a drop of sweat, indicating his efforts (karma), fell into the sea and a fish swallowed it. From this, Hanuman's karma took his form and was now standing guard in the netherworld.

Makaradhwaja is the result of the negative impact of Hanuman's karma. Hanuman had set fire to Lanka, thus acquiring a lot of bad karma. Even though he may have thought he was acting according to dharma, his actions produced some dreadful karma that strengthened Makaradhwaja. Since Hanuman is considered immortal, he cannot eat the fruits of his karma in his next births. Hence, the storytellers of eastern India devised Makaradhwaja as the image of Hanuman's karmaphala.

Hanuman finds that he must fight his son and alter ego and defeat him to gain entry. But even fighting his son is karma and will result in some karmaphala later. After a great effort, Hanuman defeats Makaradhwaja. The folk tradition says that since Hanuman was fighting to save Rama, he was able to defeat Makaradhwaja. (In a fascinating folk-tale, narrated in another chapter, Hanuman is forced to fight Rama himself!)

Meanwhile, having defeated Makaradhwaja, Hanuman enters the Kali temple and is shocked to see Rama and Lakshmana tied to a pillar. The sacrificial altar is ready, and Mahiravana is seated in meditation. Hanuman sees the statue of Kali or Mahamaya, the Great Illusion. He takes the form of a honeybee and flies towards it. In rural south India, Hanuman taking the form of a bee gave birth to the belief that the drone of a bee is the chanting of Rama's name.

Hanuman flies to the ears of the giant Kali image and asks the goddess whether she is thirsty for the blood of the noble Rama. Kali says she would be more satisfied with Mahiravana's blood.

There are two versions of this tale. In the Krittivasa Ramayana, Mahiravana is killed by a ruse. Hanuman hides behind the Kali idol and takes his original form. When Mahiravana opens his eyes, he asks Rama and Lakshmana to bow before Kali. Rama says he is a Kshatriya and has never bowed before anyone. He asks Mahiravana to show him how to bow so that he can imitate him. Knowing that dawn is approaching, and he must finish the sacrifice before sunrise, Mahiravana kneels and bows his head before Kali. Hanuman leaps from behind the idol and severs Mahiravana's head.

Mahiravana's pregnant wife then attacks Hanuman with a trident. Hanuman kicks Mahiravana's wife. The trauma causes her to deliver the baby, who is called Ahiravana. Ahiravana grows to a massive size as soon as he is born and starts fighting Hanuman. Ahiravana is slippery from the blood and mucus of birth, so Hanuman cannot grip him, and he slips away from Hanuman's grasp. As the time to close the doors to Patala Loka approaches, Hanuman manages to grab

Ahiravana's feet and slam him on to the floor, shattering his head. Hanuman, Rama and Lakshmana then hurry back to the battlefield to face Ravana.

In south Indian versions of the story, the goriness is less pronounced. After Hanuman reaches Mahiravana's Kali temple, he asks the goddess how he can kill Mahiravana. Kali tells him that Mahiravana's life is secured by five lamps placed in five directions. To kill Mahiravana, Hanuman must blow out all five lamps at the same time. Hanuman sprouts five heads and blows out the five lamps, thus killing Mahiravana. This image of Hanuman with five heads is called Panchamukhi Hanuman and is considered auspicious in south India.

The number five is also considered auspicious in the Hindu belief system. The Kamba Ramayana talks of Hanuman uniting the five basic elements or panchabhoothas: akasha (space), vayu (air), bhoomi (earth), jala (water), and agni (fire). Hanuman travels through space, over the sea, meets Sita, the daughter of earth, and sets fire to Lanka. Thus Hanuman, the son of Vayu, unites all five elements in his mission to reach Sita. Panchamukhi Hanuman also represents the sanctity of the number five.

These tales are not found in the usual Bhakti-era Ramayanas or even in the classical Ramayanas of Valmiki or Kamba. These are folk-tales mostly found in India's eastern parts and with some variations in the south. The myth goes on to highlight Hanuman's importance. Rama and Lakshmana have hardly any role to play in this myth. In some folk versions, Rama is shown as scared and fearful when Mahiravana is about to sacrifice him. His only hope is that Hanuman will rescue him.

The folk-tale motifs of eastern India have many tantric elements and the sacrificer getting sacrificed is a common theme in Bengal, Orissa and the Northeast. This shows how the Ramayana evolves according to the time and culture of the place where it is told.

Folk-tales and additions to the regular Ramayana are used to emphasize the importance of karma and karmaphala. The belief that one is responsible for one's own actions and must pay for the choices one makes is ingrained in the Indian psyche. Whether through sacred texts or in folk-tales, this idea is emphasized again and again. This phenomenon happening to an immortal like Hanuman is an innovative addition and a variant.

40
The Fall of Ravana

RAVANA SITS IN HIS DARK CHAMBER, DISHEARTENED AND DEMORALIZED. He has lost everything, yet he is not ready to accept his mistakes and move forward. Giving up is not an option for him. When Mandodari comes to advise him one last time, he argues that he will not hear about surrendering. Ravana was not born to give up, but to make others submit before him. Mandodari knows her husband will not return from this final battle. Ravana too knows it is a fight unto death, but he wishes to march on to the battlefield with his head held high and die a hero's death.

As Ravana bids Mandodari farewell, there is a huge commotion in the streets. War-ravaged Lanka does not want to fight anymore. The people have risen against their ruler, and they do not want war. Often, wars are started with great bombast and inflated pride. People come enthusiastically to die for the love of country, language, race and national pride. When the harsh realities of war are restricted to where unknown soldiers fight and die, it is easy to be jingoistic and patriotic. Only when war comes to one's own doorstep, one finally understands its futility; there are no winners, only losers. Now, war has come to the doorstep of every house in Lanka. The people question their mighty king for the first time.

Ravana is shocked and surprised that his own people, who once considered him no less than a god, are now revolting against him. When people start marching in the street against their ruler, the ruler must understand that his rule is ending. Ravana talks to his people with all the sincerity he can muster. He reminds them of the great things he has done for them. They were living like slaves under the Devas; it was he who brought them pride and dignity. For many years they ruled the world. He considered them as his children. 'I have nothing left to live for, except you. Do you want to live once again in slavery? Is it not better to die a glorious death?' he asks his people.

Inspired and moved by Ravana's speech, the Asuras change their minds and shout enthusiastically that they will fight and die for Ravana. Once again, Ravana's charisma works like magic. He does not promise them heaven or victory, only glorious death. He gives them a chance to redeem themselves by choosing an extraordinary journey.

'You will die today or tomorrow. The choice is to die as a nobody or a martyr who has done his dharma for his king and country. I promise to either win or not return alive. I will follow you to heaven,' Ravana tells them.

The more Ravana speaks, the more he moves the Asuras. Soon, even the soldiers who were injured, common men who had never held a weapon, teenage boys and old men assemble behind him. Ravana calls this army his 'moolabala', the foundation of his strength. 'My people are my strength,' he tells them. And with these heroic words, he marches his rag-tag army to take on Rama, Lakshmana and the Vanaras.

On the other side, Rama tells the Vanaras that they should prepare for the most devastating battle yet. Ravana has the armour of passion, which might prove even more challenging to penetrate than Indrajit's armour of dharma.

'Our cause is a righteous one,' Rama tells his soldiers. 'It was Ravana who took my Sita. I did not covet anything that belonged to him. When you are fighting a force of passion such as Ravana, you must fight with the strong belief that dharma is on your side. We are fighting not only to save Sita but to prove to the world that irrespective of the enemy's strength, if we believe our cause to be right, we will win.'

Ravana leads his army in a chariot drawn by six dark horses. There is no great strategy in his war formation, but the Asura army radiates a kind of energy that rattles the Vanara ranks. Ravana attacks Rama's army head-on, but it soon becomes evident that he is after neither Rama nor Lakshmana; he is targeting Vibhishana. Ravana shoots mighty arrows at the brother who betrayed him. He once again hurls the Shakti missile at Vibhishana. In trying to stop it, Lakshmana is knocked unconscious and Sugriva and Sushena carry him away from the battlefield. Ravana mocks Rama that it will be his turn next.

Enraged by Ravana's tremendous power, and by what has happened to his beloved brother, Rama declares, 'By sunset today, either you will live, or I will. There is no place for Rama and Ravana together in this world.'

Ravana roars with laughter. 'There is a place for everyone on earth, but Rama, in your self-righteousness, you are not ready to acknowledge that. I have not come to Ayodhya to conquer it, at least not yet. Many generations ago, I beheaded your ancestor. But I do not covet your kingdom. I stay on my land with my people. You are the invader; you have come with your army of Vanaras to destroy the Asuras and their civilization. And you talk about dharma!'

'I did not come to take Lanka from you,' Rama replies. 'I want nothing that is not mine. You took my wife using deceit, yet you are talking of righteousness. If you are not a coward, fight and face Rama's wrath.'

In folk versions, Ravana asks a pertinent question that will haunt Rama again and again in the time to come—whether he is sure Sita did not come of her own free will? In answer, Rama shoots an arrow and destroys Ravana's chariot. Ravana uses his magical powers and invokes the chariot of Brahma. This chariot has twelve black horses and is a force to reckon with. It comes at great speed at Rama, and Ravana is like the roar of thunder on a stormy night. The thunderbolts of his arrows fall on the Vanaras, and thousands of them die. Rama thinks it unfair that he is standing on his feet fighting while Ravana has such a fast chariot. As he wishes for a chariot, the gods give Rama a chariot of twelve white horses, levelling the field.

Rama is now all man, as the story reaches its climax. The Vishnu avatar's divinity ebbs away, as destiny has willed that only a man with many flaws can kill Ravana. As the final moment approaches, Ravana grows more and more powerful. He believes he is a powerful Asura, that we are what we feed to our minds. Just as our bodies respond to what we eat, our character reacts to what we think.

Rama understands what is going on and tries to break the robust chain of Ravana's thoughts. He says, 'You are a learned Brahmin. Why do you want to throw away everything for a woman? Few people in the world are blessed by the Tridevi (Saraswati, the Goddess of Learning; Lakshmi, the Goddess of Wealth; and Shakti, the Goddess of Power).'

Ravana roars back, 'I may be all that, but I am an Asura first. Asuras are forces of nature. I am driven by passion. I become enraged when I am angry, sorrowful when I am sad. I feel jealous. And if I want something I take it by force. Do not judge me by your definitions of what is right and wrong. You do not judge thunder, calling it good or evil. You do not judge a storm or a tidal wave. They are powerful because they are what they are—forces of nature. None can judge me. I am neither good nor bad. I am Ravana.'

Rama hurls a Brahmastra, saying, 'When forces of nature become a danger to society, a Kshatriya must protect his people. I am destroying you not because I hate you, but because it is my dharma.'

Rama's missile knocks Ravana unconscious. Ravana's charioteer flees from the battlefield, carrying his unconscious king. When Ravana awakens, he finds himself in a cave, deep in the jungles of Lanka. He yells at his charioteer for taking him away from the battlefield. He has come prepared to win or die, not to flee. He unsheathes his sword and threatens to behead his charioteer. The charioteer tells him calmly that his dharma is to protect his king. If his king wants to behead him for that, it is his king's choice. But in battle, the dharma of a charioteer is to ensure that his master is not hurt.

Ravana pauses for a moment to reflect on these words. Then he smiles and takes off a diamond-encrusted bracelet from his arm and gives it to his charioteer, saying, 'Though you have brought me infamy by taking me away from the battlefield, I appreciate your sense of duty. Your dharma has protected you from my wrath. This is a token of my pleasure and appreciation for your noble act. Now take me back and let me face Rama.'

The charioteer protests that Ravana is not strong enough to fight and it would be strategic to retreat for a few days, but Ravana forces him to return.

When Rama sees Ravana return like an approaching storm, he is taken aback. He knows he is slowly losing his divine powers as the hour of destiny approaches. Rama feels all the weaknesses of a common man. Then he remembers the 'Adityahridaya' mantra that Vishwamitra taught him, about the cycle of life. He remembers that everything that is happening in the world is linked through an infinite number of events. Life and the perspectives of good and evil keep changing. The time has come for the evil of his time to end.

Rama observes that there are signs around Ravana spelling his doom, but Ravana is ignoring all the omens and appears reckless. His defiance and his passion to fight are the only things keeping him alive. Inside, Ravana is broken, and his spirit has been crushed.

Rama seeks the blessings of all his ancestors. With a prayer asking the universe to aid him in ending this cycle of life while knowing that there is no real end and Ravanas and Ramas will keep returning to the universe, Rama once again shoots the Brahmastra at his opponent, severing Ravana's head. But another head sprouts up in its place, roaring with passion. Once again, Rama severs Ravana's head, only to find another head has taken its place.

As many times as Rama severs a head, Ravana grows a replacement instantly. Ravana's ten heads represent the passions and the emotions. Trying to conquer each individually is not working for Rama. When the head of anger is cut, the head of jealousy pops up, and when that is cut, the head of the ego appears. This goes on for a long time. The time to kill Ravana is passing, and Rama becomes desperate. Ravana seems invincible.

At this juncture, Vibhishana moves towards Rama and whispers that Ravana has the elixir of life inside his belly. He is a creation of passion, and the gut is where emotions and desires reside. Rama thus shoots Ravana in the stomach, and the arrow pierces his abdomen. With a roar, the mighty emperor of the Asuras falls to the earth. As he lies dying, he sees Vibhishana and laughs. His brother's laughter sends a chill down Vibhishana's spine.

Lakshmana rushes to sever Ravana's head, but Rama stops him, saying, 'With the death of the enemy, the enmity ends. Here lies Ravana, a great scholar and warrior. There has been no one like

him before, and there will be none like him again. Before he dies, Lakshmana, seek his wisdom.'

Lakshmana, surprised at his brother's words, obeys reluctantly. He goes to stand at the head of the dying Ravana and asks him to give him his wisdom. Ravana laughs mockingly, and Lakshmana turns away, affronted.

But Rama says to him, 'Brother, you are still treating him as your enemy. You are seeking his wisdom. He is your guru now. Would you stand at the head of your guru and seek knowledge? Stand at his feet, touch them with reverence and ask for wisdom.'

Lakshmana apologizes to Ravana and touches his feet, saying he considers him to be his guru. So Ravana summarizes his life philosophy. There are multiple versions of what Ravana says to Lakshmana, but I love this south Indian folk version: 'The choice to live as Ravana or Rama is up to you. There will be consequences of both. You cannot avoid them. The only thing you must remember is if you are Rama, be a complete Rama. If you are Ravana, be a complete Ravana. If you try to imbibe qualities from both, you will be born again and again in this world until you learn that lesson. Knowing whatever you are and being completely true to it is the secret of happiness and success.'

With these words, Ravana's role in the play with his master comes to an end, and he returns to become Jaya, the doorkeeper of Vishnu's palace in Vaikunta.

41

After the War, a New King in Lanka

Following Ravana's fall, Rama orders that his body be cremated with the honour due to an emperor. The Vanara army enters Lanka and begins to pillage and loot as per the war norms but is called back by Rama. He chastises them saying that enmity must end when one has conquered the enemy.

However, the damage has been done—once when Hanuman set Lanka on fire, and then after the war, when the Vanaras under Angada did the same. In various folk-tales, Rama quenches the fire using his arrows, thus symbolically ending the enmity. The Asura women who lost their men slowly emerge from their homes. Leading them is Mandodari. She comes to view her husband's body and weeps softly. Rama tries to pacify her, but she is not consoled. She says that Ravana might have been an evil Asura for Rama and many others, but he was always a loving husband to her.

The folk Ramayanas of south India and the Valmiki Ramayana reveal that during the war, Angada had entered Ravana's palace and dragged Mandodari away. In Valmiki's Ramayana, Angada and his

Vanaras dragged Mandodari by her hair, and some of them even tried to molest her. Ravana, who was performing a sacrificial ritual, was forced to abandon it and fight to save his wife. Thus, Ravana's sacrifice was interrupted, making him vulnerable.

This deplorable act of the Vanaras was justified as a reaction to the war. However, subaltern folk-tales do not spare Rama for his deep silence on this issue. Rama, who is supposed to be noble, is found wanting here, and Indian tradition never shies away from questioning even those we revere.

Thus, Mandodari puts a Deva on trial. Mandodari's words about Ravana accepting her even after she was sullied by the enemy brings sniggers to the lips of the Vanaras. Rama observes this and burns with shame. He promises Mandodari that no other Asura or Rakshasa will be harmed and apologizes for his army's conduct. 'If someone has committed adharma, they will pay the price,' he assures her.

Mandodari replies, 'The wise keep talking about the law of karma. They say everyone will have to eat the fruits of karma. However, in life, it does not happen like that. Good people suffer, and evil people flourish. There is no correlation between action and the fruits of action. It is our need to find some pattern to life that makes us think so. Things happen randomly; there is no one controlling it. Sometimes, when bad things happen, we console ourselves saying it is the result of prarabdha or what we have carried from our past lives' actions. Men perform actions for their selfish needs and justify them by talking about dharma. I would instead think it is my destiny to be the widow of a great warrior. I accept what life has offered me. Life has been benevolent to me till now. I had a courageous husband who looked after and protected me, showered me with love and luxuries. I have lived as queen of the Asuras. I never asked why I was lucky to be his wife, so now I have no right to ask why I have been widowed. Time throws its dice. We do not know how it will roll. Whatever it is, I accept with grace. It was my destiny to be Ravana's wife and widow. It was his destiny to be killed by Rama's arrow. I neither revere nor hate you. You are just a tool in the hands of the great God, Time.'

We see Mandodari giving here an alternate life philosophy that goes against the theory of karma and choice. In India, these two streams of thought have often conflicted and sometimes merged. Many schools of philosophy talk about destiny being supreme. The Ajivikas, who became prominent during Chandragupta Maurya and his son Samudragupta's reigns, were the last known adherents of this stream of thought. For them, there was no creator, sustainer or destroyer of the universe. It came into being by sheer probability and chance. Everything that happens in the world is because of the chance meeting of various 'sookshma', very minute particles. This gives birth to 'sthoola' or 'things that can be seen by the eye'.

Depending on the time, chance and nature of these infinite particles and how they interact, the universe manifests itself in various forms, sometimes as life, sometimes as non-life. So, there is no point in either rejoicing or despairing about life. As we have no control over events, we have no responsibility either. Everything is destiny or fate. As per the Ajivikas, an infinite number of chance events occur before even a simple thing like two people meeting on the street. The trail of chance events stretches into the infinite past.

Pause to think about it. Our every action has its trail stretching into the infinite past, anantakala, the endless future, also called anantakala, the infinity of time. Hence, the Ajivikas advised people to live in the moment and not worry about karma and karmaphala and to float in the river of destiny like a twig. Both these streams of thought had their adherents. Gosala, the last great philosopher of Ajivika philosophy, lived during the Mauryan period. For a brief period, Ajivika became the most prominent religion in India when Emperor Samudragupta became Gosala's disciple.

Rama does not offer any counter-argument to Mandodari, as he believes in the equality of all thought streams.

In a debate Swami Vivekananda had with his guru Ramakrishna Paramahamsa, the latter tells him, 'All paths are valid. We are trying to decipher the secrets of life using various tools. One cannot be dogmatic by saying that only one tool is true. We are the sculptors of our life. A sculptor will use various things to sculpt. If a sculptor insists that only a hammer is the right tool and refuses to choose the chisel, the sculpture will never get formed. Where the chisel must be used, the chisel is the truth. Where the hammer must be used, the hammer is the truth. Similarly, karma theory, the theory of destiny, the theory of atheism or agnosticism or the Vedas are all different paths humans use to understand life. Life is complicated and simple.'

Swami Vivekananda asks, 'Then what is the path of bliss?'

Paramahamsa answers with a smile, 'That which your conscience agrees upon at a given point of time is the path of bliss. Eeswara, divinity, is residing inside you and is speaking to you every moment. Don't drown its sweet whisper with the cacophony of complicated thoughts. Give space to silence, and you can hear the music, the symphony, playing inside you.'

Rama, coming from the great Indian tradition of considering all paths as valid, does not try to correct Mandodari. In her grief, if it is the belief in destiny that is consoling her, so be it. Human beings are different and what works for one need not work for another. That is why Sri Krishna says in the Gita to follow swadharma. This has been misinterpreted by many to mean caste duty. But Krishna is not talking about caste, nor is the Gita a book of advice for those belonging to a particular caste. Such twisted interpretations by selfish minds have turned the Gita into a philosophy to solidify an exploitative caste system. Swadharma is what one's conscience whispers. Rama remains silent and reverential, listening to Mandodari without offering her any further words of consolation.

After giving the Asura women time to accept the reality of their loved ones' deaths, Rama orders the coronation of Vibhishana as king of Lanka. Rama had crowned Vibhishana in Rameswaram before the war. That was an act of intention and resolution, visualizing Vibhishana on the throne, for his warriors. By bringing the goal to be achieved into visual form, Rama instilled confidence in his troops. Rama thus demonstrated a vital leadership lesson when he coronated Vibhishana at Rameswaram when there was no assurance they would win against the mighty Ravana. By first visualizing your goal, even enacting the result in your mind, ideally as a mock play, one connects with the hidden strength in one's mind. Ravana might have looked invulnerable, but by making Vibhishana king at Rameswaram, Rama filled his warriors' minds with confidence before starting the conflict. And now, after the war, it was time to bring what they then imagined and fought for, to fruition.

But Rama does not perform the coronation with his own hands this time. He does not even enter the city of Lanka. Following the victory, he gives importance to those who fought with him. He is a leader who does not grab all the credit. He asks Lakshmana to conduct the coronation.

When Vibhishana asks Rama to stay on as king of Lanka, the famous words, '*Janani janmabhoomishcha swargathapi kharidhasi* (Mother and motherland are more precious than heaven),' come from Rama's mouth. 'Lanka might be a more prosperous and bigger kingdom than Ayodhya, but it is not my motherland. Lanka belongs to the Asuras.' Hence, he does not even step into the palace of Lanka.

And so, it is Lakshmana who seats Vibhishana on the throne so long held by Ravana. In folk narratives, the bards are unforgiving towards Vibhishana. None of the oral folk-tales doubt Rama's divinity. Unlike Western or Semitic traditions, where criticism of God or his actions is considered blasphemy (and was punishable by death in medieval times, and is still so in some countries), India has never desisted from critiquing deities. The bards who narrate Rama's tales in the multiple tongues of India also do not spare Vibhishana. They hail him as a devotee of Vishnu, but at the same time condemn him as a traitor to his brother.

The debate on right and wrong in the Ramayana still rages on today. Some of the tales suggest a compromise—Ravana was wrong in abducting Sita; Kumbhakarna was right in supporting his brother and dying for him, even though he condemned Ravana's action in abducting Sita; Vibhishana was wrong in going against his brother, but did the right thing by joining Rama.

The theory of karma, as the Ajivikas believe, breaks down at many points in the story. Many of Rama's acts, which do not appear righteous, are also explained or justified by the punishment he gets in his next avatar as Krishna.

However, some actions like Hanuman's burning of Lanka and the killing of innocents, or Vibhishana's treason go unpunished. The Puranas deal with this anomaly by making such characters immortal; thus they are not punished for their actions. It is an uneasy compromise, and hence the karma theory gets criticized by many ancient sages, once again underlining that there is no absolute truth.

Vibhishana becomes the king of Lanka and argues that as king everything that belonged to the previous king, his brother Ravana, now belongs to him. He marries Mandodari. Again, the classical Ramayanas are silent on Mandodari's thoughts on this. Folk narratives say Vibhishana always planned to marry Mandodari, and Rama coming to Lanka to reclaim Sita allowed him to do so.

In Ravana and Vibhishana's case, Mandodari has remained a faithful wife to Ravana. Other than in the folk narratives, Vibhishana never brings up his intention to marry Mandodari before the actual wedding. The uneasy silence about Mandodari in the classical Ramayanas is proof that this made the many sages who rewrote the Ramayana think that Vibhishana was not right in doing this. Some explanations given are that in societies like those of the Vanaras and Asuras, marrying a widowed sister-in-law is an accepted practice. But then what was the sin of Bali in that case?

Rama and Lakshmana are ideal brothers, with Lakshmana considering his sister-in-law as his mother. Sugriva and Bali loved the same woman, and their antagonism had its roots in their love and lust for Tara.

In a later incident, when Rama is forced to order Lakshmana's death, the sages warn Rama that abandoning his brother is equivalent to killing him. If that logic is applied, Bali banished his brother Sugriva, which was equivalent to killing him as per the saints' logic. Bali then marrying his brother's widow Tara cannot thus be an act of adharma, nor can Rama killing Bali be justified.

This problem has also been debated and discussed for thousands of years. The continuing debates prove there is no agreement about what is right and what is wrong.

Following Vibhishana's coronation, Rama sends Hanuman to Lanka to ask Vibhishana to send Sita to him.

42
Sita's Trial by Fire

ONCE VIBHISHANA HAS BEEN CROWNED KING OF LANKA, RAMA ASKS Hanuman to bring Sita back. She is ecstatic when Hanuman narrates the tale of how Rama killed Ravana. She feels loved and worthy. Her husband did the impossible for her, and this is proof of his vast love for her, she tells Hanuman.

The Rakshasis who stood guard over Sita hide behind the trees when they see Hanuman. He sees them, however, and seeks Sita's permission to tear them limb from limb. He says, 'Mother, they have harassed you, tortured you, and told you evil things about Rama. Give me permission to kill them.'

Sita replies, 'With Ravana's death, I have no enmity towards them. They are but servants doing their duty. I request you to forgive and spare them, for I have no grudge or anger against them. I want to meet my husband without delay. Now when the time has come to see his handsome face, I do not wish to carry any grudge or evil in my mind.'

She calls to the Rakshasis and they come out of hiding. She embraces each of them and gives them the gifts Hanuman had brought from Rama for her. The Rakshasis are surprised by her generosity. They praise Sita for her large-heartedness and wish her a happy life.

Sita is ready to go, but Hanuman says she should be decked in the most beautiful clothes and ornaments. Sita, with her matted hair, unwashed clothes and sleepless eyes, does not appear attractive. But Sita says this is what she is. 'Rama must accept me as I am. This is how I have lived, worrying about him.'

So, Hanuman takes Sita to Rama as she is. Sita sees Rama standing at the head of the Vanara army, and a shiver of pleasure runs through her. Her eyes well up, and her vision becomes blurred. This is the moment she feared would never come. She yearns to rush towards him and embrace him and shower him with kisses. But as Sita walks towards Rama, she senses something amiss. Why were there no signs of happiness or pleasure on Rama's face? Why does he avert his eyes? This is not the reunion she had imagined. This is not the Rama she knew.

Sita can hear the clamour of the Vanaras as she walks. They are talking about her beauty or perhaps the lack of it. She stops before Rama, fighting the dread slowly rising in her mind, hoping that her beloved will break into his usual handsome smile. Instead, she hears harsh words she has not imagined even in her worst nightmares.

Rama takes a deep breath and, without looking at Sita, says, 'I came to avenge Ravana's insult. Like a man, I fought against him and won. I fought for my honour and the honour of Ayodhya. I have safeguarded the honour of the house of Ikshvaku. Do not think I came for any other reason. I have done my dharma.'

There is a pregnant pause. Sita looks at him with trembling lips, her vision blurred by tears. She cannot believe her ears. What is Rama talking about?

Rama continues, 'Do not think for a moment that I came for you. I did not fight the war for the sake of a mere woman. I did not let my

Vanara friends die for your sake. Your name is a stain on the Ikshvaku family name. How can I accept a woman who has lived in another man's abode? How can I believe she is still chaste? It pains me even to look at you. It is dishonourable for the scion of Ikshvaku to face a sullied woman. You are free, Devi. You may go wherever you want. As your king, I have rescued you. I did not fight the war to win back my wife. I am beyond that. The war was not my selfish pursuit, but was fought to establish dharma. I feel nothing for you.'

Tears flow down Sita's cheeks as she looks at the man she has loved ever since she set eyes on him. For thirteen long years, she accompanied him in the forest, being his shadow, taking care of his needs. Then she was taken away by force by an evil man. Her husband was not there to protect her. And now she is seeing a different Rama. The next words he utters are words she will never forget.

'You can go with whomever you choose,' he says. 'You may choose Lakshmana or Bharata or Vibhishana, or even the Vanara Sugriva. Seek your fortune since you have already been with Ravana for so long.'

As deathly silence falls, even the Vanaras are unable to believe what they are hearing. The Vanaras believed Rama to be God and fought for him because they thought he was fighting for Sita, moved by his deep love for her. They had never expected their hero to talk like this. What has Ayodhya's honour got to do with the Vanaras of Kishkindha? They shift their feet uneasily, not knowing what to make of Rama's words. Hanuman does not look at Rama, for he cannot even comprehend what is happening.

Sita shivers in anguish. No words come from her trembling lips. She was insulted by the man she has always loved, in front of strangers. The entire war has been rendered meaningless. Then Sita says, 'I am Janaka's daughter. I am the daughter of the earth. I was born an orphan, yet I thought I belonged to everyone. But more than anyone, I felt I belonged to you. Once you took my hand and called me your wife, I considered you my entire world. Have I been a bad wife to you? I swear I am chaste. I did not even think of any other man.

'Ravana did indeed touch me once when he carried me away forcefully. But after stepping on to Lanka's soil, he never laid hands on me. He kept his own honour, and preserved the honour of your wife. If an evil Asura can behave in such a manner, why is the scion of Ikshvaku so full of doubt? Why did you not tell Hanuman that you had no feelings for me, that your mind was filled with doubt? I would have killed myself at once, and we could have avoided this war. Is your honour worth more than the lives of the innocents who were killed? Instead, you sent him with a message and your ring. Not for a moment did I suspect how you really felt. You have ruined my peace and happiness with your suspicion. You have insulted me and questioned my purity. Rama, I have never thought about any man other than you. But now that you suspect my chastity, I do not want to live.'

She turns to Lakshmana and says, 'Make a fire, Lakshmana. I shall walk into it. If I am pure in thought and deed, let the fire not burn me. If the fire burns me, let the world know that Sita has sinned.'

There is a hushed silence among the Vanaras. Sita waits for Rama to stop her, to say it was just a cruel joke. But Rama remains unmoved. Lakshmana starts preparing the fire. Clouds roll in from the sea and fill the sky. Dark clouds swirl over them as Sita walks around the fire, circumambulating three times. Lakshmana prepares the holy fire and Sita walks into the flames with a prayer on her lips: 'If I have been true to Rama, let the fire not burn me.'

In the folk Ramayanas of south India, Sita walks around Ravana's cremation pyre. Remember that in these versions, Sita is his daughter. He had no sons left, so Vibhishana lights the pyre. Sita then whispers, 'Forgive me, father,' and walks into the flames. A poignant folk narration says she comes out unscathed as even in death, Ravana didn't want to harm his daughter.

In traditional Ramayanas, a granite-faced Rama watches the woman he has loved walking into a blazing fire. The skies open and torrential rain pours down. The traditional Ramayanas say that Sita emerges from the flames unscathed. The Vanaras break into a cheer, saying Mother Sita is unsullied. A reluctant smile breaks out on Rama's face, and he goes to embrace Sita, who faints in his arms.

In folk Ramayanas, the torrential downpour quenches the fire and Sita is left unscathed. She faints on the embers, and it is Hanuman who rescues her. This sets the stage for the second demand for agnipariksha in the later part of the Uttara Ramayana.

Many scholars believe the Uttara Ramayana is a medieval addition to Valmiki's original Ramayana. A woman's chastity becomes the fulcrum for social cohesion in a society that has slipped into rigid patriarchy by the medieval times. There is an inconsistency in Rama's behaviour in the early part of Valmiki's Ramayana and in the agnipariksha in the Uttara Ramayana.

In many Ramayanas, the agnipariksha is part of the section on the war, the Yuddha Kanda, but many scholars consider this a later-day addition. Remember the conversation between Rama and Jabali in Valmiki's Ramayana, where Rama refers to Buddhists? This anachronism clearly indicates that many hands have rewritten and reworked portions in later times, as convenient.

The obsession with a woman's chastity is a recurring theme in medieval epics. In the great Tamil epic Silappathikaram, the heroine Kannagi burns the city of Madurai, evoking her chastity. Kannagi is shown as an ideal wife who stood with Kovilan, the hero of the story, even when her husband visited prostitutes and gambled away his earnings.

She stands behind him like a rock despite his infidelities, thus showing the world how chaste a medieval Indian wife should be. When only her anklets are left to pawn, she gives one of them to Kovilan to resume their life. Unfortunately, the queen of Madurai's anklets are stolen around the same time, and the guards are on the lookout for the thief. They find that the anklet Kovilan has brought to pawn looks precisely like that of the queen's. They drag him before the king, who sentences him to death.

A widowed Kannagi comes to the court of the Pandyan king of Madurai and asks him whether he gave her husband a fair trial. When the king hotly retorts that the Pandyan kings are famed for their sense of fair play, and he was convinced that Kovilan was a criminal, Kannagi flings the other anklet on the floor, shattering it into many pieces. From it roll out pearls, whereas the queen's anklets had rubies.

Knowing he has conducted a travesty of justice to please his wife, the king dies heartbroken. But Kannagi's anger is not quenched. She evokes the power of her chastity and burns the city of Madurai and then turns her back on Madurai and walks towards the Chera kingdom. Various temples on the Kerala–Tamil Nadu border are identified as the places where Kannagi rested and became a goddess. Many believe the Kodungallur temple in the Chera capital of Muziris, also known as Muchiripattanam, is where Kannagi still dwells as Devi.

The Uttara Ramayana is also believed to have been written in the same period as this great Tamil epic. The chastity of a wife becomes an obsession for men in medieval India. It is the same Rama who once redeemed Ahalya, who had chosen Indra over her husband and been punished. Rama does not display medieval India's enforced morals when he is benevolent towards Ahalya and reinstates her in society. Why then does Rama have a problem with Sita?

Sita's trial by fire has always disturbed even the most devoted of Rama's devotees. Various stories have been added to justify it, including that of the Maya-Sita discussed earlier.

Valmiki never intended the Ramayana to be a play of good versus evil. The medieval Ramayanas turned it into a simplistic tale of good and evil, painting anyone opposing Rama as dark and Rama's every action as godlike. As I explained in the introduction, I am not alone in believing that the Ramayana is not a tale of good versus evil, but a poem about human frailties and choices. Sita's agnipariksha remains one of the most discussed ethical questions in the Ramayana over the last few thousand years. It remains, along with the killing of Bali, a tale that has been debated endlessly. Indians have long understood the nuances of right and wrong because of such open debates.

Life is under no obligation to make sense. Life just happens. Nothing explains life thoroughly. Hence no single book can provide a single answer, and no single theory can explain its frailties and complexities. Indian tradition has always emphasized finding what is right through discussion, debate, questioning and experiencing. By trying to explain away every character's acts in the Ramayana with convoluted justifications to make some good and others evil, we lose the great depths and richness that Valmiki envisaged.

> In the Valmiki Ramayana, Rama is angry when he sees Sita fully adorned. He starts suspecting her character and says, 'I have only avenged the insult of my enemy, but I have doubts about your character. The woman who has lived in another's house—how can a man accept her? No attraction for you remains in me. You may go wherever you want. You may choose Lakhshmana or Bharata at your pleasure. You may choose Shatrughna, Sugriva or Vibhishana. Ravana, having seen you so beautiful, would have never left you alone.' (Yuddha Kanda, Canto 114) However, once Sita undergoes the ordeal by fire, Rama's position changes. He says that Sita deserves this purification

among the people. People would have said Rama was lustful if he had accepted her just like that after living in Ravana's home. Many scholars believe this was an interpolation added in later years to the Ramayana when Indian society had become obsessed with women's chastity and purity.

In the Mahabharata's Ramayana, there is no fire ordeal for Sita. Sita swears that Ravana has not touched her, and Rama accepts her. An agnipariksha is also not mentioned in the Harivamsha, Vishnu Purana, Vayu Purana, Bhagavata Purana or Narasimha Purana. Neither is it found in any Buddhist or Jain works like the Anamakam Jatakam, Rama Jataka, Tibetan Ramayana or Gunabhadra's Uttara Purana. The Pauma Chariyam doesn't mention it at all. However, in the later part of the Pauma Chariyam, there is a mention of agnipariksha. After the incident involving Lava and Kusha, Rama asks Sita to undergo an agnipariksha. Despite emerging unscathed from the fire, Sita refuses to stay with Rama and instead takes Jain initiation.

In the Kathasaritasagara Ramayana too, there is no mention of agnipariksha. In the Krittivasa Ramayana, after Ravana's death, Mandodari curses Sita that her happiness will soon turn to sorrow. Sita is also cursed by Tara and other widows of the men slain by Rama. All this karmaphala acts on Sita and denies her happiness. In the story of Seri Rama, which is reminiscent of Malayalam folk-tales, Hanuman prepares a fire. When she enters the fire, it goes out, and Hanuman saves her from the embers. Many folk-tales talk about other tests that Sita had to undergo like her drying up the Ganga river with the power of her chastity or putting out the sun and so on.

43

Sita of the Adbhuta Ramayana

The Adbhuta Ramayana is a version of the Ramayana that became popular from the twelfth century onwards in India's eastern parts. In Orissa, Bengal, the Northeast and in rural Tamil Nadu, this tale became popular among Shakta devotees (those who consider Devi or Kali as the supreme goddess). They form the third major group in the Bhakti tradition, the first two being the Vaishnavites and the Shaivites. The Vaishnavites worship Vishnu as the supreme manifestation of Parabrahman, whereas the Shaivites believe Shiva is the ultimate manifestation. In the Shakta tradition, which has many tantric rituals attached to it, Kali or Parvati is the supreme goddess.

In the Adbhuta Ramayana, on their way back from Lanka, Rama, Sita and Lakshmana are attacked by Ravana's brother, Sahasra Mukha Ravana (so called because he has a thousand heads and two thousand arms). He is the supreme villain of the Adbhuta Ramayana. The authorship of the Adbhuta Ramayana has also been ascribed to Valmiki. The Shakta tradition says that Valmiki's Ramayana, as we know it now, is but a small part of a grand text—the Adbhuta Ramayana, in which Sita is Mandodari's daughter. There are two versions of the stories. In the folk-tales of Kerala, Sita is Ravana and Mandodari's daughter. Ravana always wanted a daughter.

In the matrilineal tradition of the Asuras, a daughter has more significance than a son. However, Ravana is promiscuous and takes many women. Mandodari is angered by Ravana's infidelities. So, when she becomes pregnant and knows it will be a girl, she goes on a pilgrimage to the Himalayas and Kurukshetra. Ravana does not accompany her, as he and Indrajit are busy fighting the Devas.

Mandodari stays with her father, Mayan, the architect of the Asuras, for some days, and when she suspects her father knows about her pregnancy she leaves without telling him. She roams around the Gangetic plains, visiting various sacred places, offering prayers in the temples of Kashi, Rishikesh and other holy theerthas. When she reaches Mithila, she knows the baby is due at any moment. As an act of revenge towards Ravana, Mandodari decides to abandon the child. She murders the servants who have accompanied her, so that her secret remains safe before delivering her baby. Mandodari abandons the girl child with a heavy heart and returns to Lanka. Janaka finds Sita in a paddy field and names the child Janaki or Sita since she was found in a furrow.

In another variation of the tale, astrologers tell Mandodari that Ravana's daughter will cause his ruin. Mandodari conspires with Ravana's ministers to save Lanka and abandons the child when she is born. As Ravana is being held captive by Karthi Veerarjuna at this time, he is unaware of what has befallen his daughter.

In Valmiki's Ramayana, when Hanuman first sees Mandodari he thinks she looks like Sita. However, he is sure Sita would never share Ravana's bed and concludes it is a different woman. When Hanuman does meet Sita later, he is reminded of Mandodari, giving credence to this folk-tale.

In another version of the Adbhuta Ramayana popular in eastern India, Sita is Mandodari's daughter but has no biological relationship with Ravana. As part of a tantric ritual to have a daughter like Goddess Lakshmi, Ravana had collected milk from a woman who lost her baby at birth. During his war campaigns in the Dandaka forest, Ravana had also gathered the blood of sages for tantric rituals that would make him super-powerful. He had stored both in a secret place in Lanka, waiting for the auspicious time for conducting his black magic.

Mandodari, in a fit of jealousy and depression over Ravana's infidelities, decides to commit suicide. She consumes a mixture of this milk and the blood of sages. Instead of dying, she becomes pregnant and is terrified that Ravana will accuse her of being unfaithful. He had been away from her for more than two years. To avoid Ravana, Mandodari goes off on a pilgrimage to the Ganga. When she thinks she is sufficiently far away from Lanka, she aborts the embryo and buries it in the ground. This is near Mithila, Janaka's land, and the king finds a newborn girl in the furrow while ploughing.

Janaka brings her up as his daughter. Since he had found her in a furrow, she is called Sita. As Janaka is king of Videha, Sita is also known as Vaidehi. Thus, Sita—in the eastern rendition of the Adbhuta Ramayana ascribed to Valmiki—is Mandodari's daughter. She is also Lakshmi and Shakti. The tantric tradition says she is Vaishnava Shakti, distinguishing her from Maheswari Shakti or the Shakti of Shiva.

In this way, the tantric tradition fuses three major devotional traditions—the Vaishnavite, Shaivite and Shakteya. The curse that Ravana's daughter will bring destruction to the Asuras plays an important part here too. In the Adbhuta Ramayana, the evil one is Sahasramukha Ravana, or the thousand-faced Ravana, and not

Dasamukha, or the ten-faced Ravana of Valmiki's Ramayana. When confronted with the mighty thousand-faced Ravana, Rama and Lakshmana faint.

Continuing in the Shakteya tradition, where Brahman's supreme manifestation is Parashakti or Kali, Sita assumes Vaishnava Shakti's form and strikes down Sahasramukha Ravana. The agnipariksha is explained away as a form of a tantric ritual invoking the Vaishnava Shakti. This tradition of giving supreme importance to the feminine form or goddess is unique to the Shakteya tradition.

The folk traditions of the Adbhuta Ramayana emphasize the importance of both destiny and action. This is a combination of karma and the theory of destiny or fate. In this version, Ravana is destined to die because of his offspring. Whichever way he or his people try to avoid it, his fate will come to haunt him. When his wife and ministers remove Sita as soon as she is born and bury her, they don't know that destiny will act irrespective of their choice. However, the folk tradition also emphasizes that the act of Ravana kidnapping Sita and not releasing her brings about his downfall. Thus, Ravana pays for his actions too. This is in line with folk wisdom that human life is a combination of both the choices we make and how the wheel of fortune spins.

Mandodari, in the version where she is afraid of Ravana questioning her fidelity, tries to hide her mistake by ruthlessly burying her baby. However, when the Vanaras, under Angada's leadership, molest her during the war, Ravana accepts her back without subjecting her to any sort of chastity test. The folk tradition emphasizes this fact and says that often we fear things without any basis. Mandodari had assumed Ravana would suspect her, yet when a crisis does arise, he stands by her. Mandodari's action of burying the infant Sita thus proves unnecessary and fatal. Often in life, we commit mistakes fearing the unknown instead of confronting that fear.

The Adbhuta Ramayana's emphasis on the Sahasramukha Ravana is described as how life often unfolds. With Ravana's death, the story should have ended. Instead, after solving one major problem, a more significant problem arises, and Rama and Lakshmana are incapable of solving it. They have fought Ravana for Sita's sake. But in the Adbhuta Ramayana, it is Sita who can kill Sahasramukha Ravana. Thus, Sita, who was supposed to have been saved by Rama, ends up saving him.

44

Pattabhisheka: Rama's Coronation

Rama reaches Ayodhya with Sita, Lakshmana and Hanuman. A massive army of Vanaras and Asuras also accompanies them. They have come to witness Rama's accession to the throne of Ayodhya. As per traditional belief, Rama killed Ravana on Vijayadashami day and he arrived in Ayodhya on Deepavali.

As Rama approaches the city, he sees a group of people living outside the city, on the banks of the Sarayu. He is surprised to find them there. They had accompanied him when he first set forth on his fourteen-year exile. He asks them why they have not returned to the city. They say that Rama had commanded all men and women of Ayodhya to go back but had forgotten to mention those who were neither male nor female. Hence they stayed back.

This folk version talks about inclusivity in our society. Rama is burdened by guilt for having forgotten a group of people in his kingdom. He asks them to march in front of the procession and tells them that their blessing will be equivalent to his, on all auspicious occasions. This continued belief, particularly in India's Gangetic plains, has helped the transgender community gain acceptance in traditional Indian society.

In Ayodhya, Bharata had been ruling on behalf of Rama. He had never sat on the throne of Ayodhya, placing Rama's padukas (wooden slippers) on the throne instead. He had reigned in Rama's name, defeating his mother Kaikeyi's plan to give her son the kingdom. Bharata now invites Rama to sit on the throne. This act is in great contrast to the acts of the other sets of brothers we find in the Ramayana—Bali and Sugriva, or Ravana and Vibhishana. The four brothers of Ayodhya are an example of ideal sibling relationships.

The sages assemble under Vasishta's leadership to crown Rama, and all of Ayodhya celebrates. The image of Rama sitting on the throne, with Sita on his left and Lakshmana and Hanuman standing beside them, or in more recent depictions, Hanuman kneeling at Rama's feet, is considered the most auspicious image in Hindu idolatry. Recently, this icon of Rama's pattabhisheka or coronation has been unfortunately replaced by the inauspicious image of an angry Rama pointing his arrow at a raging sea. Rama's divinity is complete only when all four are present. This is illustrated in the Uttara Ramayana as the story progresses.

Rama gives generous gifts to all those who helped him win the war. All the Vanaras are given fabulous awards, as are the Asuras who accompanied Vibhishana. Rama gives alms and offerings to the Brahmins and sages. But there is one devotee who, anxiously waiting for his gift, finds that he has been ignored. Slowly, rage starts forming in his mind. As the day passes and even the most common Vanara has been gifted something, this person remains overlooked. Finally, when everyone leaves, Hanuman stands with his lips trembling and his eyes fill with tears. Rama has offered him nothing.

Sita notices Hanuman's tear-filled eyes and nudges Rama, who says he does not intend to give Hanuman anything. Hanuman stands with his head bowed as fiery tears of humiliation flow down his cheeks. Sita calls Hanuman and gifts him a necklace of pearls.

Hanuman looks at this inexpensive gift and is angered. He cannot be ignored like this. In a fit of rage, he breaks the string, and the pearls scatter everywhere.

The pearls start whispering something. Hanuman is not able to hear it at first. In the uncomfortable silence, Hanuman stands drenched in anger. But he is not able to ignore the small murmurs coming from the scattered pearls. He puts his ear to one of them and hears the pearl whispering Rama's name. He had thrown away the most extraordinary gift Sita could give him. Feeling guilty, he tries to grab the pearls, but they roll away from Hanuman. The more he tries to grasp them, the faster they spin away. Hanuman pleads with Sita that he has committed a great mistake and had not understood her gift's worth.

Sita tells him that Rama did not gift him anything because he thinks there is no difference between them. 'You are one and the same,' she says. 'You didn't notice that he did not gift me anything either. Nor did he give anything to Lakshmana. You don't understand how dear you are to him, perhaps more precious than Lakshmana or me.'

Rama smiles at Sita's words, and Hanuman falls at Rama's feet to beg for forgiveness. Rama says, 'When we feel ignored, we get angry. However, we rarely look at the reason why a beloved one has ignored us. It is not because we are not dear to them, but because we are beyond any gift. If you do something for those who love you and expect a gift in return, that love has no meaning. You are exchanging your love for a gift. I have never considered you as different from me. I believe, Hanuman, that you have done everything for me because it is your dharma. If so, the one who should be giving the gift is the great God Time. Who am I to dilute the gift or fruit that your karma will bring?'

Hanuman understands his mistake and begs for forgiveness. This folk-tale that talks about the great devotion of Hanuman, and the love and respect Rama and Sita have for their devotee, emphasizes once again the importance of karma and karmaphala. It is not different from the essence of the Bhagavad Gita. By his action, Rama teaches Hanuman the importance of nishkama karma or doing one's duty without expecting anything in return.

Rama begins his rule in Ayodhya and is considered an ideal ruler. To this day, Ramarajya (the rule of Rama) is the phrase used to denote a just and egalitarian system. Rama sends spies amongst his people to understand what they are talking about and how they judge his rule. He needs to know what is in the minds of his subjects. He believes that he is a king because he is the servant of his people. A servant must understand what his masters think.

Sita becomes pregnant, and Rama and Sita are ecstatic. A scion for the dynasty of Ikshvaku is to be born. In one of the most moving passages in Bhavabhuti's Uttara Ramayana, Rama tells Sita tenderly that not a single wish of hers will go unfulfilled. The poet uses a great tool to foreshadow what is going to happen in the future. Sita expresses her wish to see the forest they roamed in for thirteen years. She says she wants to go to the dark woods of Dandaka and see Panchavati again. Rama says he cannot deny any wish of his beloved wife.

The next morning, when Rama's spies arrive, he asks them what the subjects are talking about. Most of them give glowing accounts of how happy the people are. However, after all the others have left, one spy remains, not speaking a word. In Valmiki's Ramayana, his name is Bhadra. Rama senses something is wrong and asks him to speak. Bhadra talks about how happy the subjects of Ayodhya are, but Rama cuts him off mid-sentence and asks him to tell the truth. Thus prodded, Bhadra relates that on the banks of the Sarayu, lives a dhobi, a washerman (in folk Ramayanas, the dhobi's name is Bhadra, and not the spy's).

The spy says that in a drunken brawl, the washerman accused his wife of infidelity. She said he was wrong. At this, the dhobi beats her up and said that he was not an immoral person like Rama, who accepted his wife even though she had lived for a year in another man's abode.

Shocked by this allegation, Rama dismisses the spy but is now disturbed. He knows that Sita is pure but, as the king's wife must be blameless, since it is the king's moral conduct that sets an example for his subjects, Rama concludes his raja dharma is to abandon his beloved wife.

He knows that if he sees Sita's face once again, his resolve might dissolve, so he calls Lakshmana and gives him the order to take Sita to a place called Janasthana. This place lies in the forest, south of Ayodhya. Lakshmana does not understand why Rama is asking him to do this. Rama tells him that Sita has expressed a desire to roam around the woods and Lakshmana asks Rama whether he will be accompanying them. Then Rama tells Lakshmana the truth about why he is forced to abandon Sita. Lakshmana is shocked. He tries to argue with his brother, but Rama stops Lakshmana by saying that this is an order from his king and not his brother.

When Lakshmana comes to tell Sita that the king has ordered him to take her to Janasthana, she does not know that she will never return to Ayodhya again. At first, she thinks that her husband is honouring her wish to see the forest and innocently asks Lakshmana when Rama will join her. Lakshmana has no answer and breaks down. Sita then realizes that something is seriously wrong. As the chariot speeds towards Janasthana and reaches the banks of the Sarayu, Lakshmana tells her the truth.

Guha, Rama's friend, once again takes Lakshmana and Sita across the river. He scolds Lakshmana and tells him that what Rama has done is not right and Lakshmana should have stood up for what is right. Sita is in a state of shock. Across the river is Valmiki's ashram. Lakshmana leaves Sita there, falling at her feet and begging to be forgiven. Then, without another word, he returns to Ayodhya.

Sita, nine months pregnant, finds herself all alone in the world.

The banishment of Sita has troubled sages, bards and auditors alike for many centuries. Even ardent devotee-poets have criticized Rama for this act. Jabali, Rama's atheist minister, once asked Rama whether he would do what was popular or what was right. When Rama left Ayodhya for his exile, Jabali tried to dissuade him saying that the people wanted him to stay. At that time Rama had argued that it was his dharma to follow his father's orders and not go by popular sentiment. Hence Jabali now asks Rama why he is acting on a popular rumour instead of doing the right thing.

In Bhavabhuti's Uttara Ramacharita, Sita tells Lakshmana that even Ravana stood by his wife when misfortune visited her in the form of marauding monkeys. So why was Rama sending her away on the mere words of a washerman? Did her words, or even the agnipariksha she had undergone, mean nothing to Rama?

In the Telugu folk version, the same incident plays out differently as an act of karma and its karmaphala. When Surpanakha was mutilated, Sita did not raise her voice in protest. It was Sita's dharma to question her husband and her brother-in-law when Surpanakha was disfigured. Instead of raising her voice for the dignity of another woman, Sita remained silent.

Surpanakha, in this folk-tale, comes to Sita disguised as a maid. She sees Sita drawing beautiful paintings of the places she has visited with Rama during the exile. She asks Sita whether she remembers how Ravana looked. Sita says she never saw Ravana's face, only his shadow. Surpanakha asks her whether she can draw his face, imagining it from the shadow. Sita is a gifted artist, and she draws an exact replica of Ravana. Surpanakha rushes to Rama. She tells him that Sita has sketched an excellent picture.

Rama reaches his inner chambers and sees the portrait Sita has drawn. It is an exact replica of Ravana. Sita is standing near her painting, beaming with pride. A cloud passes over Rama's face. Surpanakha knows that the seed of jealousy Rama has always carried in his mind has now sprouted. She is effusive in her praise of how perfect the portrait is. Rama storms out and Surpanakha follows him, commenting that only someone who knew Ravana intimately could have created such a perfect painting.

This incident forms the basis of Rama's insecurity, and when the rumour of the dhobi slandering his queen comes to his ears, Rama remembers the painting. Thus, in the circle of karma, Sita too eats the fruits of her inaction. Like action, inaction is a choice.

Thus, the folk version brings out the circularity of life and delivers some justice to Surpanakha.

In other folk versions, Surpanakha sees Sita being taken away by Lakshmana and gives her courage, saying that women are destined to be suppressed, abandoned, fought over and exploited by men. She tells Sita her own story: she loved a man called Vidyutjihva, who used her to attain power and a part of the kingdom from her brother, Ravana. When Ravana discovered that Vidyutjihva was growing ever more powerful, he had him killed. Thus, her brother was the cause of her husband's death.

When Surpanakha complained about the unfairness of it (her becoming the victim of political rivalry between Ravana and her husband), Ravana told her that she could choose any man and he would ensure that she married him. Surpanakha saw Lakshmana and was attracted to him. As per Asura tradition, it was not wrong for a woman to propose marriage to a man and she did so, thinking it to be her dharma. But she was punished by Lakshmana, mutilated and humiliated. When she went to Ravana, instead of keeping his promise, he went after Sita.

Sita is calmed by Surpanakha's words and says that whatever destiny may throw at a woman, she must react with dignity. Sita vows to bring up her child (not knowing she was carrying twins) without Rama's help, and to make her offspring worthy.

Unlike the two folk-tales narrated above, in Bhavabhuti's Uttara Ramacharita, a different plot is used. In this version, Sita, unable to bear her separation from Rama and the way she has been cast away, jumps into the Ganga to commit suicide. The Ganga accepts her and makes her invisible. Sita does not die, but she cannot be seen except by the two lady friends Ganga gifts her, one being the river Tamasa in the form of a woman.

Sita lives in Valmiki's ashram, and the sage helps her raise her twin boys, Lava and Kusha. Meanwhile, Rama sinks into depression after he has abandoned his wife. He laments his fate. He seeks the counsel of Sage Vasishta, who reminds him that his astrological chart indicated that he would lead a glorious but unhappy life. Vasishta also subtly mentions Rama's acts of adharma—when he condoned the mutilation of Surpanakha, and his killing of Bali from behind a tree. Rama remembers Sita's words, that they had committed a grave error by mutilating Surpanakha and would never be happy again. Rama accepts this as the fruit of his action.

Rama's act of abandoning Sita is one of the most criticized actions in the Ramayana. In the Indian tradition, even the gods are under trial.

Nothing escapes the power of karmaphala and destiny. Over many centuries, those who have written various versions of the Ramayana all arrive at a moment of pause here, uncomfortable with this event, their own unease reflected in Rama's joyless existence, as in the Uttara Ramayana. Various methods have been deployed to criticize this action of Rama's.

45

Valmiki's Ashram: Lava and Kusha

In Valmiki's Ramayana, the moment Sita comes to Valmiki's ashram, the Ramayana becomes the 'Sitayana'. Valmiki, who has thus far hailed Rama as the model hero, shifts his allegiance to Sita. He says he is now with Sita, daughter of the earth. She gives birth to twin boys, Lava and Kusha.

In some folk versions, Lava is an only son. The story regarding Kusha's arrival goes like this: one day, when Valmiki is at his prayers, Lava toddles into the forest. When Valmiki finishes and looks around, he finds Lava missing. In a panic, he creates a baby with Kusha grass. After some time, Sita comes in, carrying Lava on her hip. She is surprised to find Lava's look-alike. Valmiki explains that he created the baby Kusha, fearing Lava had gone missing. Sita accepts Kusha as her son and brings him up with Lava.

In Bhavabhuti's Uttara Ramacharita, Sita disappears into the Ganga after delivering Lava and Kusha. Valmiki finds the twin babies and brings them up. The spirit of Sita hovers around Valmiki's ashram, looking after her sons. Valmiki trains Lava and Kusha in the martial arts and teaches them the Vedas and Upanishads. Bhavabhuti uses Rama's son Kusha to unleash scathing criticism against Rama's banishment of Sita. In another work by Bhavabhuti, the Mahavira Charita, various characters criticize not only Rama's act of abandoning Sita but also other inexplicable acts such as Rama's killing of Bali, his support of Surpanakha's mutilation and Tadaka's killing.

In Valmiki's Ramayana, Sita is ever present in the ashram, and she trains her sons under the guidance of Valmiki. The divine weapons of the Ikshvaku dynasty magically appear before Lava and Kusha when they are old enough to be trained in their use. The weapon called the Trayambaka, the heritage of the Ikshvakus, manifests before Lava and Kusha when they attain the age of twelve, thus authenticating Lava and Kusha as scions of the Ikshvaku dynasty and as Rama's sons. Lava and Kusha grow up to be exemplary warriors, and Valmiki teaches them Rama's story—the Ramayana.

> In the Pauma Chariyam, a young Sita traps two parrots in a cage. The parrots know the Ramayana written by Valmiki and sing it for her. Valmiki had only written up to the portion where Rama is coming to Mithila, and so the birds only know that much. Sita is curious to know the future. She tells the parrots that she won't let them free until Rama arrives. The female parrot is pregnant, and the birds plead with Sita to set them free so that they can find a nest before the rainy season. But Sita doesn't relent. Finally, she sends away the male parrot to find out the rest of the story. The female bird dies in the cage, cursing Sita that she too will be abandoned by Rama when she is pregnant. The male parrot returns to find his mate dead. The male parrot curses that he will be born again in Ayodhya and cause Sita's separation from Rama. The male parrot commits suicide by drowning in the Ganga and is reborn as the dhobi whose slander causes Sita's abandonment.

> In the Tattvasamgraha Ramayana, Valmiki prays to become Sita's father. He is granted the boon of being Sita's foster father and Rama's foster grandfather.
>
> In the Northern Recension of the Valmiki Ramayana, the curses by Tara and Mandodari are also considered as reasons for Sita being abandoned.
>
> In the Bhavavartha Ramayana, Sita's karmaphala of suspecting and abusing Lakshmana in Panchavati is the reason for Rama suspecting and abandoning her.

Meanwhile, in Ayodhya, Rama is alone and leads an unhappy life. He misses Sita every moment but continues to rule the country according to raja dharma (the dharma a ruler must follow). He believes Sita to be dead, but refuses to marry again as he had promised Sita that she would be his only wife. Rama is one of the rare gods who has only one wife and is hailed as one who keeps his vow to love only one woman—eka patni vratha.

Bereft of Sita, it is said Rama begins to act without compassion, following only the strict tenets of what he believes to be dharma. This is highlighted in the following tale (thought to be a later addition to the Ramayana).

The Brahmin and the Shudra

One day, a Brahmin appears before Rama, carrying the dead body of his young son. The Brahmin laments that a great adharma is taking place in Rama's kingdom and blames his son's death on Rama's misrule. In an ideal state, death does not visit children, and people die of old age, says the Brahmin. He argues that there has been some violation of dharma in Rama's kingdom, which has caused his young son's death.

Rama sends his spies to find out where the adharma is taking place. The spies return with the news that a low-caste Shudra is doing penance. Rama consults Guru Vasishta, who says that Shudras do not have the right to do tapasya (meditation, austerities) and his tapasya is creating waves of adharma, affecting innocent citizens. Enraged, Rama sets off himself in search of this Shudra ascetic and finally finds him in Janasthana, south of Ayodhya, hanging upside down from a tree, doing penance.

Rama asks him his varna (caste) and the aim of his penance. The man answers that he is Shambuka, a low-caste Shudra, and that he is doing tapasya to go to heaven without leaving his body. Rama cuts off Shambuka's head to punish him for transgressing the varna dharma and the Brahmin boy comes back to life; everyone hails Rama and the justice of Rama Rajya.

This story appears to be a later addition when the caste system had become rigid. Rama, who never had any hesitation in befriending Guha the boatman, or partaking of food offered by Sabari, a tribal woman, suddenly appears as the defender of the caste system in this story.

The punishment meted out to Shambuka for the crime of doing penance is in conjunction with the laws laid down in the infamous Manusmriti, written many centuries after Ramayana. Just as Rama criticizing Buddha was inserted into the Valmiki Ramayana, caste apologists could also have added the incident of Shambuka. This, along with the killing of Bali, the mutilation of Surpanakha, the killing of Tadaka and Sita's trial by fire are the incidents in Rama's life that have garnered the most criticism in later eras.

One explanation folk artists give is that Rama loses his sense of dharma once Sita has gone. He commits these acts when Sita is not with him, whether it is the killing of Tadaka (before he met Sita), or Bali or Shambuka (whom he met after he married Sita). At Surpanakha's mutilation, Sita was a silent witness to the barbarity. Folk-tales explain this away by inventing the story of Surpanakha coming back to take revenge and causing the banishment of Sita, thus completing the cycle of karma and karmaphala of Sita.

In Bhavabhuti's Uttara Ramacharita, the poet is clearly uneasy about the incident. He invents a new tale to justify the action. Though he does not omit the Shambuka killing, he says that Shambuka attains moksha because he was killed by Rama. After his death, Shambuka appears to Rama as a divine presence and tells him that he has achieved his aim and seeks Rama's blessing. Thus, Bhavabhuti softens the harshness of Rama's act by his innovative storytelling.

In latter-day Ramayanas, many Bhakti-era poets were uneasy about Rama's act in killing Shambuka. In many plays, it is not Vasishta but Narada who advises Rama to kill Shambuka. Several poets omit the Shambuka killing episode. In later eras, oral storytellers in temples that did not allow admission to avarnas or lower castes emphasized the killing of Shambuka to strengthen caste beliefs—Rama, the perfect man who carried out his dharma perfectly, with fairness to all, had shown how those who transgressed caste dharma must be dealt with. When politically feasible, they shouted such justifications from upper-caste temples. Today, of course, such tales are often omitted from the rendition of the Ramayana in temples. In fact, such additions in the Uttara Ramayana and the inferior quality of poetry and language have made many scholars conclude it was not written by Valmiki.

In the Ananda Ramayana, Rama goes in search of the Shudra who is practising tapasya, which caused the untimely death of the Brahmin's child. He instructs that no corpse should be cremated before he comes back. Many deaths occur during the time Rama is searching for the Shudra. By the time Rama finds Shambuka, another Brahmin, a Kshatriya, a Vaishya, an oil presser, an iron smith's wife and a cobbler's daughter have also died. Finding that Shambuka is learned, Rama offers him moksha and a place in Vaikunta. But Shambuka asks, 'What about my brothers? How can other Shudras get moksha? They are not educated.'

Rama says that they need to chant only Rama's name and they will attain moksha. Shambuka laughs and says, 'Then in the Kali Yuga, my people, the Shudras, will remain ignorant fools. They will know only some chanting. Where will they get time to chant and sing, when they have to work in the fields of others?'

Rama then says, in that case, they should greet each other by saying 'Rama, Rama' and that will be enough for them. 'You will also obtain moksha and a place in Vaikunta by dying at my hands.' Saying this, Rama beheads Shambuka. As a result, all the dead people from every community, who died just because a learned Shudra was practising tapasya, are resurrected.

Medieval poets effectively utilized such stories featuring Rama to propagate caste discrimination in society. In the classical poetry of the twentieth century, the Jnanpith Award-winning Kannada poet Kuvempu gives a totally different spin to this story. Writing at the height of the freedom struggle and reform movements in Hinduism, the Ramayana undergoes a change yet again in Kuvempu's skilful hands.

> In this tale, Shambuka is an ascetic, and a Brahmin and his son come to visit the saint. The Brahmin finds that Shambuka was a Shudra in his purvashrama (before he became a saint). The Brahmin prevents his five-year-old son from bowing to the Shambuka sanyasi, saying he is a Shudra Muni. The boy dies of a snakebite a little later as a result of this karma. The Brahmin goes to Rama, complaining that he has lost his son because Shambuka, a Shudra, became a mendicant. He requests Rama to kill Shambuka. Rama shoots the Brahmastra at Shambuka, but it doesn't harm him. Rama realizes that a person's caste doesn't determine their worthiness. He instructs the Brahmin to bow before Shambuka, and the Brahmin obeys. As a result, the Brahmin's child is revived.
>
> This is an example of how a story in the Ramayana that was written by medieval priests to reiterate caste differences is turned on its head and used against caste discrimination. Every era produces its own Ramayana based on the needs of the society and stories keep evolving.

Coming back to the story of the Brahmin and the Shudra, after the killing of Shambuka, Rama returns to Ayodhya, but has no peace of mind. Every moment he thinks about the wife he has banished. In Valmiki's Ramayana, Shatrughna knows of Sita's existence and has seen her two sons. However, he does not mention this to Rama, as Rama has banned everyone in Ayodhya from mentioning Sita. The sages advise Rama to conduct the Aswamedha sacrifice for glory and for peace of mind. In this sacrifice, a horse is set free and wherever the horse goes, that land belongs to the king performing the sacrifice. Anyone who dares to stop the horse and claim the land has to defeat the king's army.

To conduct the Aswamedha sacrifice, a necessary requirement is that the one performing it must have his wife by his side doing the rituals. The sages advise Rama to marry again, but he refuses. Instead, he has a statue of Sita made in gold, referred to as Kanchana Sita or the Golden Sita, and he places it beside him when he performs the rituals. The sacrificial horse is set free and reaches Valmiki's ashram. The Valmiki Ramayana is silent on the episodes that follow and directly jumps to Rama and Sita's reunion.

However, many Bhakti-era Ramayanas and Sanskrit plays of the medieval era narrate the exploits of Rama's sons, Lava and Kusha, when they spot the sacrificial horse. They tie it up and challenge the Ayodhya army, led by Chitrakethu, Lakshmana's son. A fight ensues and Sita's sons, who are trained by her, defeat Rama's army. In north Indian folk versions, Lava and Kusha rout Hanuman too. Some versions go to the extent of saying that Lava and Kusha defeat Rama and drag him to their mother. In other renderings, it is Hanuman whom Lava and Kusha drag to Sita. Rama meets Sita, and they have a tearful reunion. Bhavabhuti ends his Ramayana here, without referring to the tragic incidents that follow.

However, in the Uttara Kanda section in Valmiki's Ramayana, the story unfolds differently. Rama conducts the Aswamedha yagna in Naimisha Forest where Valmiki's ashram is situated and gives alms to the many Brahmins who come to attend. He earns their wholesome praise. Amid all this charity, Valmiki arrives with two of his disciples and tells them to sing the Ramayana for everyone to hear.

Lava and Kusha, Sita's sons, sing about the exploits of their father in front of Rama. The courtiers who see Lava and Kusha murmur that they look like Rama. Once they finish singing about Rama's exploits and the killing of Ravana, Rama tells Lakshmana to give the two young men 18,000 gold coins. Lava and Kusha decline to accept, saying they belong to the hermitage and are not enticed by gold, plus they have not completed their rendering of the Ramayana and cannot accept any gift until it is finished.

As they continue, Rama understands that Sita is still alive and is living in Valmiki's ashram. He understands Lava and Kusha are his sons. Rama sends messengers to Valmiki to say that if Sita is found to be pure, she may come to the yagna. 'Let her take an oath in this yagna shala that she is untainted and that Lava and Kusha are indeed my sons,' reads the message.

When Valmiki reads the message, he tells Sita that it is her choice to accept Rama or not. When the messengers insist, Valmiki sends them back saying that as far as he knows, Rama is Sita's god, and she will come to the sacrifice venue the next day and swear her oath there.

The next day, Valmiki arrives with Sita. A hush falls on the assembly. Valmiki then speaks these harsh words to Rama: 'Rama, you abandoned this Sita, who is purity itself. You were afraid of what the world would think of her. You doubted her purity. Even now, in your heart, the poison of doubt remains. You are asking her to come here and swear an oath with Agni (the God of Fire) as her witness. I am Pracheta's tenth son, and I have no memory of having told a lie. I vow that these two are your sons. I have done tapasya for thousands of years, and if what I say now is a lie, may all my punya (merit) be taken away from me. If Janaka's daughter Maithili has sinned, let my very soul perish within me. But let Sita speak for herself.'

Rama sits as still as stone throughout Valmiki's angry outburst. Staring straight through Sita without looking into her eyes, he says, 'I have never doubted Sita's purity. Valmiki Maharishi, please do not accuse me of a sin I have never committed and add to the sins that I have. I sinned in banishing my queen for fear of slander. But I am a king first and her husband later. My dharma to my people is greater than my dharma to my wife. I want her purity to be tested again to silence the tongues that wag against the queen of the land. She must perform the agnipariksha or take a vow of truth with Agni as witness that she has remained pure in heart and body to me. She must vouch that these two young men are indeed my sons.'

Unable to bear Rama's harsh words, Sita does not raise her face in the presence of all the kings and sages but speaks softly, her voice strong and firm. 'If I have worshipped my husband Rama as my god in my heart, in my words, and my deeds; if my love towards my husband is true; if I am unsullied in thought and deed, let my mother Bhumidevi, the earth, who brought me into this world, take me back into herself. I have nothing to live for now. I have done my duty as a wife when I accompanied Rama to the forest for fourteen years. I have done my duty as a mother. I have brought up my sons to be great warriors who can defeat Rama and the army that once defeated Ravana. This is the extent of my love for Rama. My parting gift to him is the sons I have brought up.'

A perfect silence falls, and no one stirs. The ground at Sita's feet parts and Rama watches in shock as Sita vanishes into the womb of the earth before his eyes. He rushes to catch her. Sita is swallowed by the earth, and Rama is left grasping a few strands of her hair.

Rama furiously challenges the earth, saying, 'Give back my Sita or I will level your mountains and dry up your seas! Your forests shall burn, and all your creatures shall perish!' He then invokes the Brahmastra to destroy the earth that has swallowed Sita. To pacify Rama, Brahma appears, saying that everything must end one day. The great God Time has taken Sita as her time on earth is done.

> In the Adhyatma Ramayana, Sita had to leave earth first because she had to prepare for Vishnu's arrival in Vaikunta, as the Rama avatar was about to end.

In the Buddhist Anamakam Jatakam and in Gunadhya's *Brihatkatha*, Rama and Sita unite and live happily ever after. In Gunabhadra's Uttara Purana, there is a mention of the abandonment of Sita, but instead of entering the earth, she becomes a Jain nun. Rama becomes a Jain monk later. In the Pauma Chariyam also, Sita also becomes a Jain nun.

In Bhavabhuti's *Uttararamacharita*, Kshemendra's *Brihatkathamanjari*, Kundamala, Ananda Ramayana's Janaki Kanda, Kathasaritsagara, Jaiminiya Ashvamedha, Padma Purana Patala Kanda, Ramacharitam, Ramalinga Amrita, Rama Jataka, Brahmacharita, Sinhala Ramayana, and many south Indian folktales, Sita and Rama have a happy ending, and Sita never goes inside the earth.

Rama must live on, which he does harbouring guilt for what he has done to Sita.

In later-day Ramayanas, this second abandonment of Sita by Rama created as much criticism as the first. There have been many explanations for the act, and the Bhakti tradition says that since Sita was the avatar of Lakshmi, the wife of Vishnu, she returned to Vaikunta to prepare for Vishnu's own return. In typical medieval fashion, when a woman's chastity and devotion to her husband are exemplified, it is said to be the duty of Lakshmi to return and ready the home for the arrival of her master. Hence Sita returns to Vaikunta, leaving Rama alone.

Some poets and dramatists like Bhavabhuti don't go down this route. In his Uttara Ramacharita, there is no second testing of Sita's chastity. Instead, there is a happy reunion between Sita and Rama. After the defeat of Rama's army at the hands of Kusha, Rama ensures that Kusha and Chitrakethu, Lakshmana's son who heads Rama's army, become friends.

> Rama learns from Valmiki that Lava and Kusha are his sons. At this moment, Sita assumes her mortal form, shedding her cloak of invisibility. The couple has a happy reunion, and the story ends here, fulfilling one of the conditions of Sanskrit drama—that there be a happy ending.

To complete the story as we know it, following Sita being swallowed up by the earth, Rama lives on like an ascetic. He keeps the golden idol of Sita beside him and talks to it as if it is a living person. Rama believes Sita is always present in spirit and refuses to marry again. He divides his kingdom between his kin.

Rama's time, too, is completing its cycle. The great God Time, Kaala, also known as Yama, the God of Death, takes the form of a Brahmin and visits Rama. When he reaches Rama's palace gates, he is unable to enter as Hanuman is standing guard. Yama sends Sage Narada to somehow move Hanuman from the gates of Ayodhya.

Narada plays a trick on Hanuman. When the sages come to visit Rama, Narada advises Hanuman not to bow before Sage Vishwamitra as he was a Kshatriya in his previous life and is not as exalted as the other sages. So, when the sages enter the palace, Hanuman does not bow to Vishwamitra. Narada tells Vishwamitra that Hanuman has insulted him. Vishwamitra complains to Rama that one of his subjects has insulted him and demands death for the culprit. Without knowing who has offended Vishwamitra, Rama gives his word to kill the person. Later, when he realizes he must kill Hanuman, Rama is shocked, yet he must keep his word.

Hanuman is devastated that Rama is going to kill him despite his great love for him. Dharma is more important than anything else for Rama. Hanuman, instead of fighting Rama, sits on the floor and starts chanting Rama's name. Rama shoots arrows at Hanuman and even invokes the Brahmastra, but all his efforts are in vain. The arrows change to garlands and fall on Hanuman's neck. None of Rama's arrows can touch Hanuman.

Surprised, Rama asks the gods for an explanation. Lord Shiva appears and says it is Hanuman's belief in Rama that is more powerful than Rama himself. Rama as the avatar of Vishnu is formidable no doubt, but it is the belief in him (or the staunch belief in anything) that is more powerful than Rama himself. God per se is powerless, but faith in God is what gives one power. Even God cannot withstand the belief of a true devotee.

There are other variations of this folk-tale. In another variation, it is not Hanuman who insults Vishwamitra but the king of Kashi, who takes asylum at Hanuman's feet, saying that a powerful man is going to kill him. When Hanuman discovers that the person coming to kill the king of Kashi is none other than Rama, he is shocked. How can he fight his beloved Rama? But he refuses to abandon the one who has taken asylum at his feet. He argues with Rama that just as Rama's dharma is to kill the king of Kashi, who has insulted Vishwamitra, his dharma is to protect the one who has asked for protection.

This conflict between Rama and Hanuman takes a different turn. It becomes a conflict between two definitions of dharma. Rama's dharma is to kill the person, and Hanuman's dharma is to protect the person. In this folk-tale, instead of emphasizing true devotion, the emphasis is on the difference between different dharmas. Hanuman's dharma to protect and save a life is greater than that of Rama's dharma of punishing a man who has committed a mistake. Hence the dharma of Hanuman wins over the dharma of Rama.

The gods find that even Narada's trickery has not served to remove Hanuman from his position at the gates. As long as Hanuman stands guard, the God of Death cannot touch Rama. Yama sends a messenger to Rama, explaining his dilemma. Rama says he will provide a solution. He summons Hanuman to his chambers and says that he has dropped his ring into a crack in the floor and cannot reach it. Can Hanuman retrieve the ring? Hanuman assumes the form of a bee and enters the gap in the floor. He travels on and on in search of the ring until he reaches the netherworld, Patala Loka. He assumes his own form and faces the king of Patala, Mahabali. Hanuman explains that he has come in search of Rama's ring. Mahabali gives him a knowing smile and points to his right. Hanuman's eyes expand in surprise. There is a hill of rings.

Mahabali explains, 'All these are Rama's rings. There have been countless Ramas from time immemorial. Every time a Hanuman has come searching for a ring, I have given the same explanation. You can take any ring, for all the rings are the same, though they belong to different aeons and belong to different Ramas. There have been infinite Ramayanas, and there will be countless Ramayanas.'

Hanuman takes one of the rings and flies back.

Meanwhile, with Hanuman gone, the God of Death enters Rama's abode. He explains to Rama that his time has come. Rama says he cannot leave Lakshmana, his beloved brother. The God of Death submits that everything will be sorted out as it ought to be, for that is the dharma of Time.

With Hanuman gone in search of the ring, Lakshmana stands guard in front of Rama's palace. Rama promises Yama that none will disturb them, and anyone entering the chamber and seeing them in conversation will be punished with death. To prevent anyone from accidentally entering the room, Rama instructs Lakshmana to stand guard, without mentioning that he is meeting the God of Death.

Sage Durvasa, notorious for his short temper and hasty curses, comes to visit Rama at this time. Lakshmana stops him. Durvasa threatens Lakshmana, saying that unless he is allowed to enter and meet Rama, he will curse the entire Ikshvaku dynasty. Lakshmana knows that if he allows Durvasa in, the sage will die. But if he does not allow Durvasa to enter, the sage will curse the entire dynasty. Lakshmana disobeys Rama's orders and enters his chamber. There, he comes face to face with the God of Time, who tells Rama that his problem has been solved—he did not wish to leave Lakshmana, now Lakshmana himself has presented himself and seen him. Now Rama must sentence his brother to death.

Rama knows he has been trapped. His time has come. Lakshmana understands his beloved brother's dilemma and says, 'Kill me for the sake of the Ikshvaku dynasty. You cannot go back on your word. You even banished Sita for a king's dharma. Greater dharma is to keep your word. Kill me. When I entered this chamber, I knew I would die for disobeying your orders. Throughout my life, I have always followed your orders without question, for that was my dharma. Now I have a greater dharma, to protect Ayodhya and its people. Had I not come in, Sage Durvasa would have cursed Ayodhya. Hence I choose the greater dharma.'

Rama does not have the heart to kill Lakshmana, who has always stood by him. He says that abandoning one's brother is equivalent to killing him, so he instead declares, 'I abandon you, Lakshmana, and exile you from my kingdom. Never show your face to me again.'

Rama thinks that with this punishment he can escape the will of the Lord of Death, who does not comment but leaves smiling smugly at the thought that even the omnipotent Vishnu must bow before him as he is the God of Time.

Abandoned by Rama and exiled from Ayodhya, Lakshmana loses his will to live. He walks into the Sarayu River and disappears into its dark waters. Hearing of Lakshmana's end, Rama decides the time has come to depart this life. He, too, walks into the waters of the Sarayu. The entire population of Ayodhya follows him. Hearing the news, Sugriva and various other Vanaras rush to the spot, as does

Vibhishana. They insist that they too will follow Rama into the waters of the Sarayu.

However, Rama advises Vibhishana to remain king of the Asuras so that they may continue to be led by a devotee of Vishnu. He tells Hanuman that he must not accompany him into the waters for he has to remain immortal. Ever the obedient devotee of his Lord, Hanuman watches as Rama and the other Vanaras disappear into the waters of the Sarayu. And for as long as the Ramayana is told, Hanuman will remain alive.

Rama's tale ends here.

> In Ayodhya, there is a small temple on a hillock near the famed Hanuman Garhi temple. Here, there is an idol of Hanuman who has an angry scowl. The belief is that Hanuman was standing guard at the entrance of the Ayodhya fort at this point when Rama walked away into the Sarayu. Hanuman is angry as he could not prevent death from snatching his swami and therefore has a perpetual angry expression. This is Ugra Hanuman, and priests say that only by chanting Siya Ram can one keep him cool.

The Ramayana, however, has no end. Rama, Sita and Ravana's tale has been told in innumerable ways, evolving according to the time and cultural settings in which it is narrated. I have attempted here to give you a glimpse of the various Ramayana traditions that I have been fortunate to encounter. They have taught me a great deal about life. Whenever I've faced a dilemma in life, I have gone to the Ramayana and its companion epic, the Mahabharata.

Though on one level, I can understand the concepts of karma and karmaphala that form the foundation of these epics, I also know that karma cannot give a logical explanation for everything that happens in life. Like any theory that tries to measure a complex phenomenon, this, too, is incomplete. The Ajivika argument that 'everything is predetermined' may provide as much consolation as thinking that whatever happens is due to our karma. Sometimes, the Charvaka belief—that everything happens through chance, influenced by randomness and without any cause, though difficult to accept (as it makes us puppets in the hands of fate)—appears more logical.

The greatness of Indian thought is the sheer scope and depth it provides. There is no one answer for anything. Every solution gives birth to a thousand questions. I once heard a folk singer put it succinctly, that life has deep meaning but the moment we discover what it is, it loses its meaning. The quest for meaning is what makes life and its idiosyncrasies so beautiful.

No one book can answer all our questions. Hence, Ramayanas will be written again and again. I have just touched upon the vast ocean of Ramayanas in this book. If it prompts someone to wade into this beautiful ocean, I will consider my humble attempt to have been worthwhile. I claim no scriptural authority, and this is just a small tribute to the mesmerizing storytelling tradition of our motherland. If I have inadvertently hurt any believer, I offer my apologies and trust that reading the Ramayana will have made them generous enough to forgive the errors of a humble chronicler.

Om Swasthi Swasthi Swasthi

[Om Peace Peace Peace]

Afterword

How Many Ramayanas?

THE LIST OF VARIOUS RAMAYANAS ARE EXHAUSTIVE AND A.K. RAMANUJAN, IN his scholarly article, places the number as 300. Though I am no scholar, I suspect this is a gross underestimate. Perhaps A.K. Ramanujan is referring to complete Ramayanas where the tales that make up that Ramayana are narrated from the beginning to the end in a structured pattern. Many partial Ramayanas and countless local or 'sthala' Puranas are associated with temples and pilgrimage places. If we take these numbers, there could be thousands or even lakhs of Ramayanas.

From my limited experience as a Ramayana enthusiast, I encounter different versions daily. Every trip to rural India has given me another Ramayana tale or Mahabharata tale. I strongly believe that not even 10 per cent of the oral Ramayanas have been written down. This book is my humble attempt as a storyteller to compile a few tales I have heard. Reading every Ramayana ever written is my dream, but I have not even scratched the surface. I wish some scholars trained in academic research would take equal enthusiasm in folk versions as much as they do in written versions.

The oral storytelling tradition is dying in India due to the onslaught of visual media and social media. Traditional bards are a vanishing breed. These stories will vanish before our eyes, to be replaced by stale television and Internet versions that do not respect the diversity and depth of these tales. There will be no space for nuanced telling and retelling. I hope I have inspired at least a few of my readers to keep a ear out for this vanishing treasure trove of lore and legends related to the Ramayana and Mahabharata.

I cannot claim I have read all the books in the list below. At best, I have referred to a few chapters of some of the books here and there to cross-reference what I am writing. I have used more folk-tales to write this book. However, a list of Ramayanas in various languages is provided below for the enthusiastic reader. If you are inspired to read some of them, my heartfelt respect and gratitude to you. It might not be possible in a lifetime to read all these works that carry the civilizational weight of five thousand years.

This list is compiled using references (listed in the Bibliography) from my personal library of eighteen Puranas (Malayalam translation by DC Books), *Srimad Valmiki Ramayana* by Gita Press, *Ramacharitmanas* by Gita Press, *Adhyatma Ramayana* by Mathrubhumi Press, M.N. Dutta's *Mahabharata*, Fr Dr Camille Bulcke's *The Rama Story: Origins and Growth*, Vettam Mani's *Puranic Encyclopaedia*, A.K. Manavalan's *Ramayana: A Comparative Study of Ramakathas*, M.R. Yardi's *The Ramayana: Its Origin and Growth* and other books. I acknowledge the contribution of all these scholars whose seminal works on the Ramayana have helped me in my pursuit.

Ramayana and Related Works in Sanskrit

Ramayana in the Mahabharata

The Mahabharata contains narratives from the Ramayana four times.

1. The Ramopakhyana of the Mahabharata's Vana Parva is the most detailed, and the story of Dasaratha's eldest child, his daughter Shanta, is narrated in this.
2. The Aranyaka Parva's Rama story, where Hanuman tells the Rama story to Bhima.
3. A story about Rama is found in the Mahabharata's Drona Parva, where Vyasa tells Rama's story to Yudhishthira after Abhimanyu's death to console him.
4. The Mahabharata's Shanti Parva mentions the glory of Rama.

Ramayana in Various Puranas

1. Skanda Purana: Various incidents from the Ramayana are scattered in various Kandas (sections):
   (i) Kedara Kanda: Depicts Ravana's biography, the Rama avatar and Ravana's death.
   (ii) Maheswara Kanda: Narrates Ahalya's story.
   (iii) Vaishnava Kanda: Mention's Dasaratha's previous life; narrates the story of Valmiki's birth; mentions Rama's departure to Vaikunta by walking into the Sarayu River.
   (iv) Brahma Kanda: Summarizes the Ramayana, including the building of the Rama Setu bridge, Sita's ordeal by fire, and the establishment of Rameswaram among other details.
   (v) Dharmaranya Kanda: Provides another retelling of the Ramayana with some variations.
   (vi) Avantika Kanda: Mentions Hanuman's magical deeds and his fetching the Shiva Linga; another version of Valmiki's birth and of the story of Ahalya; and Ravana obtaining boons from Shiva.
   (vii) Nagara Kanda: Narrates a story of Lakshmana's disloyalty and his lusting over Sita. It also mentions Dasaratha's four sons and his daughter (Shanta, the eldest child), another variation of Valmiki's story, another variation of Ahalya's story.

(viii) Prabhasa Kanda: Mentions the Rameswaram story in detail. It also narrates the Ravaneswara story, and the Dasaratheswara story—all major Shiva temples now. Another variation of Valmiki's previous life is also mentioned.

2. Padma Purana: The dhobi's (washerman's) story—where he dubs Sita as a woman who has lived in another man's house and is not fit to be taken back as a wife—is explained in detail. The birth of Kusha and Lava and their battle as young boys with Rama's army is detailed. The Padma Purana gives a happy ending by uniting Rama and Sita after Kusha-Lava's battle with Rama's army. Sita's allegation of Lakshmana's disloyalty, but without the mention of his lust for her, is found in the Padma Purana too. The tale of the killing of Shambuka is detailed. Another variation of the tale of Ahalya is present too.

3. Brahma Vaivartana Purana: The concept of Maya-Sita is explored in detail. Lord Vishnu's dwarapalakas (doorkeepers) Jaya and Vijaya, being born as Ravana and Kumbhakarna, is stressed in this version. Hanuman is Shiva's avatar in this Purana.

4. Vishnudharmottara Purana: This Purana narrates Ravana's tales before the war.

5. Narasimha Purana: Almost the same as Valmiki Ramayana, but Rama is Vishnu himself and not just in human form. The divinity of Rama is stressed as Vishnu himself in this Purana. The concept of Maya-Sita, Ravana never having touched Sita during the abduction and so on, are stressed here. Sita is never abandoned in this version.

6. Shiva Mahapurana: Narrates a tale of Narada; Rama being tested by Shiva and Sati (also used in *Ramacharitmanas*); incidents from the Yuddha Kanda of the Ramayana in detail; Hanuman's birth details; a summary of the Ramayana and so on can all be found here.

7. Devi Bhagavata Purana: Narrates Rama's story with Rama praying to Devi before his war with Ravana.

8. Other Puranas: Apart from the above, the Ramayana can be found in full or partial forms in the Brahaddharma Purana, Saura Purana, Kalika Purana, Adi Purana, Kalki Purana and others with some variations.

Some Other Ramayanas

1. *Yogavashista*
2. *Adhyatma Ramayana*
3. *Adbhuta Ramayana*
4. *Ananda Ramayana*
5. *Tattvasangraha Ramayana*
6. *Kalanirnaya Ramayana*
7. *Bhusundi Ramayana/Adi Ramayana*
8. *Satyopakhyanam*
9. *Dharmakanda*
10. *Hanumat Samhita*
11. *Brahat Kosala Ramayana*
12. *Maha Ramayana*
13. *Samvrata Ramayana*
14. *Lomasa Ramayana*
15. *Agastya Ramayana*
16. *Manjula Ramayana*
17. *Saupadma Ramayana*
18. *Ramayana Mahamala*
19. *Sauharda Ramayana*
20. *Ramayana Maniratna*
21. *Saurayya Ramayana*
22. *Chanra Ramayana*
23. *Mainda Ramayana*
24. *Svayambuva Ramayana*
25. *Subrahama Ramayana*
26. *Suvarchas Ramayana*

27. *Deva Ramayana*
28. *Sravana Ramayana*
29. *Duranta Ramayana*
30. *Champu Ramayana*
31. E.H. Johnston's Northwestern *Valmiki Ramayana*
32. *Gaudiya Valmiki Ramayana*
33. South-Indian *Valmiki Ramayana*
34. Kalidasa's *Raghuvamsa*
35. *Ravanavaha*
36. *Bhattikavya Ravanavadha*
37. *Janakiharana*
38. *Ramacharita* of Abhinanda
39. Kshemendra's *Ramayanamanjari*
40. *Dasavatara Charitam*
41. Sakalya Malla's *Udararaghava*
42. *Raghunatha Charitha*
43. *Raghaviya*
44. *Ramavijaya Mahakavya*
45. *Sreemad Raghuviracharitam*
46. *Janaki Parinaya*
47. *Ramalingamrita*
48. Bhasa's *Pratima Nataka*
49. Bhasa's *Abhisheka Nataka*
50. Bhavabhuti's *Mahavira Charita*
51. Bhavabhuti's *Uttara Ramacharita*
52. Myuraja's *Uddattaraghava*
53. *Kundamala*
54. *Anargharaghava*
55. Rajasekhara's *Balaramayana*
56. Hanumat's *Mahanataka*
57. Shaktibhadra's *Ascharya Chudamani*
58. *Prassana Raghava*

59. *Ullagharaghava Nataka*
60. Hastimalla's *Maithilikavya*
61. Hastimalla's *Anjana Pavananjaya*
62. *Duttangada*
63. *Unmattaraghava*
64. *Ramabhyudaya*
65. *Ramacharitam*
66. *Raghapandaviyam* (punning poetry—Ramayana and Mahabharata)
67. *Raghavanaisadhiyam* (punning poetry with Rama and Nala stories mingled)
68. Chidambara's *Raghavapandaviyam* (Ramayana, Mahabharata, Bhagavat Purana narrated simultaneously using wordplay)
69. Gangadhara Mahadakara's *Sankatanasana Stotram*
70. *Sanniti Ramayana*
71. *Rama-Krishna-viloma-kavyam* (Ramayana in natural order, Krishna's story when read in reverse order of right to left)
72. Venkatadhvarin's *Yadavaraghaviyam or Raghavayadaviyam* (Ramayana in natural order, Krishna's story when read in reverse order of right to left)
73. *Chitrabandha Ramayana* (Illustrated)
74. *Ramalilamrita* (Illustrated)
75. *Hamsasandesha* (Rama sends love letters to Sita in Ashoka Vatika through a swan)
76. *Bhramaraduta* (Rama sends love letters to Sita in Ashoka Vatika through a bumblebee)
77. *Kapiduta* (Rama sends love letters to Sita in Ashoka Vatika via Hanuman)
78. *Kokilasandesha* (Rama sends love letters to Sita in Ashoka Vatika through a cuckoo)
79. *Chandraduta* (Rama sends love letters to Sita in Ashoka Vatika through the moon)

80. *Vataduta* (Sita sends love letters to Rama from Asoka Vatika through the breeze)
81. *Ramagitagovinda* (An imitation of Jayadeva's *Gita Govinda*, but here Rama is the hero and not Krishna)
82. *Janaki Gita*
83. *Sangita Raghunandana*
84. *Ramagitam*
85. *Ramasataka* (In which Ahalya becomes a stone. Thirteenth century CE. Before this, Ahalya is always shown as invisible.)
86. *Raghava Vilasa*
87. *Arya Ramayana*
88. Rama's story in Gunadhya's *Brihat Katha*
89. *Vasudevahindi* (Jain work, where Sita is Ravana's daughter and born in Lanka)
90. Rama's story in Somadeva's *Kathasaritsagara*
91. Rama's story in Kshemendra's *Brihatkathamanjari*
92. Gunabhadra's *Uttara Purana*
93. *Amogharaghava Champu*
94. *Uttararamacharita Champu*
95. Ananta Bhatta's *Ramakalpadruma*
96. Swami Desikan's *Raghuveeragadyam*

Buddhist Ramayanas

1. *Dasaratha Jataka*
2. *Dasratha Kathanam*
3. *Anamakam Jatakam*

Jain Ramayanas

In Prakrit

1. *Pauma Chariyam* by Vimalasuri
2. *Ramalakkanachariyam*

3. *Ramayanam* in *Kahavali* by Bhadresvara
   4. *Siyachariyam* and *Ramalakkanachariyam* by Bhuvanatunga Suri
   5. *Vasudevahindi*
   6. *Uttara Purana*
   7. Puspadanta's *Maha-Puranas*
   8. *Mahapurana* of Puspadanta

In Sanskrit

   1. *Padma Charita* by Ravi Sena
   2. The Ramayana story in *Trishashti Salaka Purusha Charita* by Hemachandra
   3. *Sitaravanakahanakam* by Hemachandra in Yogashastra commentary
   4. *Ramadevapurana* by Jinadasa
   5. *Ramacharita* by Padmadeva Vijayagani
   6. *Ramacharita* by Somasena
   7. *Laghu Trishashti Shalakapurusha Charita* by Somaprabha
   8. *Laghu Trishahsti Salaka Purushacharita*
   9. Gunabhadra's *Uttara Purana*
   10. Kavi Krishnadasa's *Punnaya Chandrodaya Purana*
   11. *Ramavijayacharita Ramayana* by Kumudendu

In Apabhramsa

   1. *Ramayana Purana* by Svayambhudeva
   2. *Balabhadrapurana* by Riyadh

Jain Kannada Literature

   1. *Pampa Ramayana* by Nagachandra
   2. *Kumadendu Ramayana*
   3. Devappa's *Ramavijacharita*
   4. Chandrasagara Varni's *Jaina Ramayana*
   5. Chamundaraya's *Trishashti Shalaka Purusha Purana*
   6. Banduvarma's *Jivasambhodhana*

7. Nagaraja's *Punyasrava-Kathasara*
8. *Anjanapavananjaya* by Jivanasambodhana
9. *Punyasravakathakosha*

Ramayana and Related Works in Some Indian Languages Other Than Sanskrit

Many of the Sanskrit works of Ramayana were produced in the medieval era in the areas that are modern-day Tamil Nadu, Kerala, Karnataka, Andhra Pradesh, Telangana, Orissa, Maharashtra and Bengal. However, an equal number of works were produced in classical languages like Tamil, Telugu, Malayalam, Kannada and Odiya. Here is a partial list of such major Ramayanas.

Tamil

1. *Kamba Ramayana*
2. Ottakuthar's *Ramayanam*
3. *Thakkai Ramayanam*

Telugu

1. Gona Budha Reddy's *Ranganatha Ramayanamu,* also known as the *Dvipada Ramayana*
2. Tikkanna's *Nirvachanottara Ramayana*
3. Kankanti Paparaju's *Uttara Ramayanamu*
4. *Bhaskara Ramayanamu*
5. Ramabhadra's *Ramabhyudayam*
6. *Molla Ramayanamu*
7. Rudrakavi Kandukuri's *Sugriva Vijayamu*
8. Katta Varadaraju's *Dvipada Ramayana*
9. *Gopinatha Ramayana Champu*
10. *Ekoji Ramayana*
11. *Acca Telugu Ramayanamu* by Timmakavi

Malayalam

1. *Iramacharitam* by Rama
2. Cheraman's *Ramacharitam Yuddha Kanda*
3. Ayyipilla Asan's *Ramakathappattu*
4. *Kannassa Ramayanam* by Kannas Panicker
5. Punam Nampoothiri's *Ramayana Champu*
6. Thunjath Ezhuthachan's *Adhyatma Ramayana*
7. *Kerala Varma Ramayana*

Kannada

1. Narahari's *Torvey Ramayana*
2. Narahari's *Mairavana Kalaga*
3. *Jaimini Bharata* by Lakshmisha

Assamese

1. Madhava Kandali's Ramayana
2. Sankaradeva's *Uttara Kanda* and *Rama Vijay*, a play in medieval Maithili spoken in Assam at the time
3. Madhavadeva's *Balakanda* and *Ramabhavana*
4. Harihara Vipra's *Lavakusar Yuddha*
5. Durgavara's *Giti Ramayana*
6. Ananta Kandali's *Jivastuti Ramayana*, *Mahiravana Vadha*, *Patalakhanda Ramayana* and *Sitar Patala Pravesa*
7. Ananta Thakur Ata's *Sriramakirtana*
8. Dhananjaya *Ganakcharita*
9. Gangaramadasa's *Sita Vanavas*
10. Srichandra Bharat's *Mahiravana Vadha*
11. Raghunatha Mahanta's *Katha Ramayana* and *Adbhut Ramayana*

Bengali

1. *Bangla Krittivasa Ramayana* or *Srirramapanchali*
2. Badu Nityananda Acharya's *Ascharya Ramayana*

3. Rameswara Dutta's *Adbhut Ramayana*
4. Chandravati's *Ramayana Gatha* [Available in English translation: *Chandrabati's Ramayana* (2020)]
5. Jagataramaraya's *Adbhut Ramayana*
6. Kamalalochana Dutta's *Ramabhaktisamrta*
7. Samkara Chakravarti Kavichandra's *Adhyatma Ramayana Panchali*
8. Fakir Ramakavibhusna's *Angad Rayabar*
9. Ramachandra's *Vibhisaner Rayabar*
10. Kasrirama's *Kalanemir Rayabar*
11. Dvija Tilsi's *Angad Rayabar*
12. Haridhana Dasa's *Angad Rayabar*
13. Raghunandana Goswami's *Ramarasayana*
14. Jagat Mohan Rama's *Ramayana*

Odiya

1. *Saraladasa Ramayana* (Saraladasa is also known as *Siddhesvara Parida*). This can be found only as an outline in *Saraladasa Mahabharata* and the original is yet to be found.
2. *Vilanka Ramayana* by Siddhesvara Dasa (Some scholars think this is *Saraladasa Ramayana*, but many others differ)
3. *Balaramadasa Jagamohana Ramayana*, also known as *Dandi Ramayana* (Balaramadasa is also known as Utkala Valmiki or Valmiki of Odisha)
4. Nilambara Dasa's *Thika Ramayana*
5. Arjuna Dasa's *Ramavibha*
6. Dhananjaya's *Raghunatha Vilas*
7. Shankara Dasa's *Barahamasa Koili*
8. Mahesvara Dasa's *Tika Ramayana*
9. Kanhu Dasa's *Ramarasamritasindha*
10. Haladhara Dasa's *Odiya Adhyatma Ramayana*

Hindi

1. Tulsidas's *Ramacharitmanas*
2. Vishnudasa's *Bhasa Valmiki Ramayana*
3. Surdas's *Surasagara* (tells part of the Ramayana)
4. *Ramachandrika*
5. Sodhi Meherban's *Adriramayana* (Punjabi/Hindi)
6. Hrudyarama's *Hannumannataka*
7. Laladasa's *Avadha Vilasa*
8. Samyaasundar's *Sita Rama Chaupai*
9. Naraharidasa's *Avataracharita* (Rama avatar portions)
10. Ramaprasada Niranjani's *Bhasa Yogavasishta*
11. Sadala Misra's *Ramacharita*
12. *Govinda Ramayana* by Sikh Guru Gobind Singh

Marathi

1. Ekanatha's *Bhavartha Ramayana*
2. Jani Janardhana's *Sita Swayamvara*
3. Krishnadasa Mudgala's *Yuddhakanda*
4. Muktesvara's *Sanksepa Ramayana* and *Ahi Mahiravana Vadha*
5. Samartha Ramadasa's *Laghu Ramayana, Sundarkanda, Yuddhakanda*
6. Venabhai's *Ramayana*
7. Sridhara's *Ramavijaya*

Gujarati

In Gujarati, we find lots of devotional Rama poetry and songs and translations of Valmiki and Tulsidas. Some famous songs/ poems:

1. Bhalana's *Ramavivaha*
2. Mantri Karmana's *Sitaharana*
3. Bhima's *Ramlila na Pada*
4. Mamdana Bandhaso's *Ramayana*
5. Lavanyasamaya's *Ravana Mandodari Smavada*

6. Uddhava's *Sita Hanuman Samvada*
7. Pramananda's *Ranayajna*
8. Haridasa's *Sita Viraha*

Urdu

1. Munshi Jagannatha Khushtar's Ramayana
2. Munshi Shankar Dayal Farhat's Ramayana
3. Bankebihari Lal's *Ramayan-e-Bahar*
4. Suraj Narayan Mehr's *Ramayana Mehr*

Kashmiri

1. Sinhalese Ramayana story in the rites of Yakuma, an exorcism ritual and masked dance.
2. Kashmiri Ramayana: *Ramavataracharit*
3. Prakasha Ramayana

Persian Ramayanas

Emperor Akbar had commanded his court poets to translate the Ramayana and Mahabharata into Persian, the court language of the Mughals.

1. Al Badayuni's Persian Ramayana
2. Giridhar Das's Persian Ramayana (during Jehangir's reign)
3. Ramayana Masihi (This has Christian influence too. The author was probably a Christian as there are mentions of Jesus and Mary in this as per Fr Dr Camille Bulcke).
4. *Ramayana Faizi*
5. Gopala's *Tarjuma-i Ramayana*
6. Chandarbhana Bedil's Persian Ramayana
7. Lala Amar Singh's *Ramayana Amar Prakash*

Apart from the above major Ramayanas, there are countless devotional poems and compositions, folk narratives and performing arts based on the Ramayana in these areas. The tribal Ramayanas have not been documented for the most part.

Tribal Ramayanas

Many of the tribal Ramayanas are partial, sometimes as anecdotes and mostly as songs. They are passed on orally, and it is doubtful that they can even be counted in their entirety. A few of them are given below.

1. Mappilla Ramayana or Muslim Ramayana, popular among Mapilla Muslims of Malabar and Lakshadweep in Arabi Malayalam language.
2. Bondo Ramayana
3. Oraon Ramayana
4. Santhal Ramayana
5. Munda Ramayana
6. Bihor Ramayana
7. Asur Ramayana (Chota Nagpur Tribes)
8. Pardhan Ramayana (Narmada valley tribes)
9. Wayanad Ramayanas (Many songs among the tribals of Wayanad district in Kerala)
10. Bhaiga Bumila tribal songs
11. Bhilodi Ramayana
12. Many tales among Northeastern tribes
13. Tamil Villupattukal
14. Malayalam Villupattukal

Non-Indian Ramayanas

Sri Lankan

1. Sinhalese Ramayana story in the rites Yakima

Chinese

1. *Anamakam Jatakam* Chinese translation
2. *Dasaratha Kathanam* Chinese translation

Tibetan

The Tibetan Ramayana is mainly based on Gunabhadra's *Uttara Ramayana*, and the *Anamakam Jatakam*.

Khotani Ramayana

Eastern Turkistan's Rama story is similar to the Tibetan Ramayana and has Buddhist roots.

Indonesia

1. *Ramayana Kakawin* (influenced by Bhatti Kavya as per Fr Dr Camille Bulcke) and *Charita Ramayana* of Bali (influenced by Bhatti Kavya as per Fr Dr Camille Bulcke)
2. *Serat Rama* of Java
3. *Serat Khanda* and Ramakeling (Java theatre version)

Malaya

1. *Hikaya Seri Rama*
2. *Hikayat Maharaja Ravana*
3. *Rama Keling*
4. *Serat Khanda*

Vietnam

The Vietnamese Ramayana follows the Valmiki Ramayana (Southern Recension) more or less, such as the one written by Ramakerti, and forms part of Khmer literature.

Thailand

Ramakien

Lao

1. *Rama Jataka* in Lao language states Rama and Ravana are cousins and Ravana abducts Shanta, Rama's sister, before he abducts Sita. Hanuman here is the son of Rama in this as Rama marries Anjana. He is also Angada's father as he marries Tara. Vibhishana marries Shanta after Ravana's death. Rama is also Buddha in this version.

2. Palaka-Palama of Syama, a version of Ramayana, in which Brahma becomes Ravana and Rama is Bodhisattva.
3. *Tualaphi Lankaniya*
4. *Pommacaka*

Myanmar

Rama Yagan

Western Ramayanas (sixteenth century onwards)

European contact with India after the arrival of Vasco de Gama produced many Ramayanas in Portuguese, French, Latin and English. A few of them are listed below. These were written at a time when many of the Indian devotional Ramayanas like the *Ramacharitmanas* were being in written in Indian languages.

1. *Livra Da Saita* by J. Fenico in 1601
2. *De open-deure tot het Verborgen Heydendom* [The Open Door to Hidden Paganism] (1649), in Dutch, by A. Rogerius.
3. *Afgoderye Der Oost-Indische Heydenen* [The Elephant-Headed God] (1672) in Dutch, by P. Baldaue. https://digitalcollections.nypl.org/items/65f34f84-8055-c507-e040-e00a180615fb.
4. *Asia*, in Dutch, by O. Dapper and J. van Meurs
5. *Asia Portuguesa*, in Spanish, by Manuel de Faria e Sousa
6. Ralasiyon Des Eryar's French Ramayana of 1644
7. Portuguese narrative of 1774
8. J.B. Tavernier's French Ramayana
9. M. Sonnerat's *Voyage Aux Indes Orientales et a la Chine* has its own Ramayana story in its travelogue in French.
10. De Polier's French work has a detailed Ramayana in *Mythlogie des Hindous*.
11. Abbe J.A. Dubois's 1817 book, *Description du people Indien* [Description of People of India] has an abridged Ramayana story.

12. *De la Boullaye-Le Gouz* (Portugese Ramayana story)
13. Padre F. Vincenze Maria de S. Caterina de Siena's 1678 *Il Viaggio All Indie Orientali* (Italian)
14. Ziegenbalg's German Ramayana
15. Diago Gonçalves in 1615 had written *Historia do Malavar* in Kerala and in it the Ramayana story, prevalent in Kerala in that period, has been translated. It has uncanny similarities to the *Seri Rama*, *Ramakerti* and *Ramakein* narratives of eastern Asia, indicating the way the Ramayana would have travelled east before Ezhuthachan's *Adhyatma Ramayana Killipattu* made the Malayalam Ramayana more in alignment with the rest of the Indian Ramayanas.

All of the above forms a minuscule percentage of the total number of Ramayana stories and their variations available across the world.

Apart from this, many versions of the Ramayana have been written in various Indian languages, including English, in the last hundred years. Most of the Jnanpith Award-winners have written stories based on the Ramayana or Mahabharata and have given the epics their own spin. The television, film and Internet Ramayanas are continuously adding to this repository.

Acknowledgements

This book is the product of decades of my passion for the Ramayana, Mahabharata and Indian oral storytelling tradition. A book results from years of hard work, not just by the author but by a vast number of people. This may be my sixteenth published book and second non-fiction work, but each time, I wonder how I could have brought it without the selfless and tireless efforts, encouragement and love of so many people.

As the dedication shows, my parents, Chellamal and Neelakantan, who are no longer in this world, were my first influences as storytellers. My writing owes a lot to the cultural milieu of my hometown, Tripunithura in Kerala. I am inspired by Indian folk storytellers, temple arts like Kathakali, and the Indian puranas. Thank you, Amma and Appa.

I would never become a writer without my Aparna, who is the second listener of all my stories. My first listener and adoring critic—who never utters a dissenting word—is my pet, Jackie the blacky. My daughter, Ananya, and son, Abhinav, often wonder how I manage to churn out so many stories across different mediums like books, films and television. How can I make them understand that they taught me how to tell stories? As kids, they made me narrate countless stories, most of which they found boring or terrible. They trained me to become a passable storyteller and helped me continue our family's storytelling tradition.

I learned most of my stories from my parents, and I am trying to pass them on to my children, though it is a tougher task now with so many distractions. The world I grew up in has vanished, replaced by a blinking, flashing world of instant stories and constant simulation. Yet my children have been patient listeners to my never-ending stories, and no amount of thanks can truly express my gratitude for their level of tolerance.

My extended family has always stood by me, even when I wrote books that challenged their beliefs and convictions. They have been my source of inspiration since childhood. My siblings, Lokanathan, Rajendran and Chandrika; my in-laws, Parameswaran, Meenakshi and Radhika; my niece and nephews, Divya, Dileep and Rakhi; and my grandniece, Mitra, have always made our family get-togethers lively with many debates about the Ramayana and the Mahabharata.

This is to my friends, some of whom are avid readers and my critics, while others never care to read any book, let alone mine, but have stood solid behind my creative pursuits. My heartfelt thanks to Santhosh Prabhu, Rajesh Rajan, Cina K.S, Anjali Nair, Reena Saju, Habeebullah Khan, Brinda Lovely, Prasant Menon, Sanju Puliyankalath, Sumit Balan, Biju C., Nisar Ummini, Sujith Krishnan and Premjith P. I hope this spares me the expense of a party!

My since gratitude and thanks to the team at HarperCollins India who have made this book so beautiful. Poulomi Chatterjee, my publisher, and Ridhima Kumar, my editor, a huge shoutout to both of you for your inspiration and encouragement. I owe so much to the editorial team including Sashi Ayer, Nimmy Chacko and Suzanne Hughe. Each of you has put your soul into making this lovely book.

Acknowledgements

Thank you! The graceful illustrations on the cover by Onkar Fondekar and those within the pages by Subu Chowara have added so much value and elegance to this book. Thank you!

I am grateful to the production team of Amit Sharma, Amit Pathak, Naksh Jain, Sahil Ghai and Priti Devi. You gave shape to this dream. The sales team of Rahul Dixit, Vikas Sharma and Gokul Kumar and the marketing and social media team led by Akriti Tyagi, Shabnam Srivastava, Nandini Tripathi and Ameya Desai—thank you for taking my dream to the hands of readers. People like you make the world spin around and keep reading and authors alive. Thank you Arcopol Choudhary, from the Rights team and Anita Sharma of Contracts, for being so helpful and understanding.

I am also grateful to the Audible team that released the audio version of this book four years ago, and to the narrators, Manish Dongardive for the English version and Babla Kochhar for the Hindi version. A big thank you to the scholar Dr Madhavi Narsalay, who vetted the authenticity of this book and translated an extract from Bhavabhuti's Uttraramancarita for this book. My first editor, Chandralekha Maitra, who introduced me to the world of writing and edited the first draft of this book, deserves much praise and gratitude. Thank you so much!

The Hindi audio version of this book was first read and corrected by my neighbour and friend, Manish Kumar. You deserve special thanks.

My special thanks to all the readers of my books. Your words of criticism, praise and suggestions have been my inspiration and the reason I continue to write.

Above all, my heartfelt gratitude goes to the countless bards and oral storytellers, writers, scholars, saints, poets, artists, sculptors, musicians and dancers who have spread, preserved and enhanced the Ramayana tradition around the world.

Notes

1. Bulcke, Camille. (1950). *The Rama Story: Origins and Growth*. Sahitya Akademi.
2. Yardi, M.R. (1994). *The Ramayana: Its Origin and Growth, a Statistical Study*. Bhandarkar Oriental Research Institute.
3. Mani, Vettam. *Puranic Encyclopaedia: A Comprehensive Work with Special Reference to the Epic and Puranic Literature*. Motilal Banarsidass Publishers.
4. Manavalan, A.A. *Ramayana: A Comparative Study of Ramakathas*. Vitasta Publishing Private Limited.
5. Neelakantan, Anand. (2012). *Asura: Tale of the Vanquished*. Leadstart Publishing Pvt. Ltd.
6. Neelakantan, Anand. (2018). *Vanara: The Legend of Bali, Sugreeva and Tara*. Penguin Random House India Pvt. Ltd.
7. Neelakantan, Anand. (2021). *Valmiki's Women*. Westland.
8. Dutta, Madhusudan. (2022). *Meghanada Badha Kavya Ekei Ki Bole Sovvota Buro Saliker Ghare Ro*. New Latika Prakashini. (First published in 1861.)
9. By India, I mean schools of thought that originated and developed in the Indian Subcontinent. Some may be called Hindu now, some may be called Buddhist and some Jain in modern Indian languages including Indian English. Some followers of philosophies like the Vachana of

Basava claim they are not Hindus by religion but a separate religion as such. But all these concepts are applicable to them. Theoretically, there is no scriptural definition of who is a Hindu or Buddhist or Jain. Even as per the Indian Constitution, there is no definition and all who are not Christians or Muslims come under the Hindu umbrella. It is only in neo-liberal left circles that the tendency to differentiate between Hindu and Buddhist, etc., are prevalent. None of these concepts can be boxed narrowly into any religion as there is nothing called religion in India. Religion is a very Abrahamic concept and English as a language has limitations in expressing what are essentially Darshanas (way of looking at life) as religions.

10 Many experts believe that the scriptures mention many Valmikis and the stories have merged over time. Camille Bulcke, in his iconic book *Ramkatha: Utpatti Aur Vikas* (1950), lists many sources, as does Vettam Mani in his Malayalam classic encyclopaedia, *Laghu Purana Nighandu*. In the Uttara Kanda of the Valmiki Ramayana, Valmiki himself claims that he is Brahmin Pracheta's tenth son. Lakshmana also refers to Maharishi Valmiki as a Mahabrahmin and advises Sita to take shelter in his ashram when he abandons her in the jungle as per Rama's command. The first mention of Valmiki's earlier life as a dacoit comes as an oblique reference in the Mahabharata. In the Anushasana Parva, Valmiki says to Yudhishthira that some ascetics called him Brahmancide and that he took refuge in Shiva. After praying to Shiva for thousands of years, he was finally freed from the sin, and Shiva blessed him with eternal fame. In the Skanda Purana, four different stories of Valmiki are told in different kandas (chapters). In the Vaishnava Kanda of the Skanda Purana, the story of a nameless hunter who chants Rama's name and gets a boon to be born in the lineage of Valmiki is given. In this version, Valmiki, the author of the Ramayana, was this hunter who was born to another Valmiki, whose original name was Krnu. In another chapter of the Skanda Purana, a different version of Valmiki is given. There was a Brahmin named Agni Sharma who became a dacoit. He met seven Rishis who convinced him of his wrong ways. But there is no mention of the 'ma-ra, ma-ra' story in it, unlike the first one. In the Nagara Kanda chapter

of the Skanda Purana, the Brahmin's name is given as Lohajangha. The rest of the tale is similar. In another chapter, Prabhasa Kanda of the same Purana, the name of Valmiki in his dacoit life is given as Vaisakha, son of Samimukha. The rest of the story is the same. The Adhyatma Ramayana Ayodhya faithfully copies these stories from the Skanda Purana and adds the event of Valmiki chanting 'Rama, Rama' for years before obtaining enlightenment. But the Adhyatma Ramayana has also been ascribed to Valmiki. *The Ramcharitmanas* of Tulsidas mentions the aforesaid story many times in the *Bala Kanda* (couplet 19), *Ayodhya Kanda* (couplet 194) and *Uttara Kanda* (couplet 130). The story has been repeated with minor variations, especially with respect to the original name of Valmiki, in other Ramayanas like the Tattvasangraha Ramayana, Ananda Ramayana and Torave Ramayana. It was the Krittivasa Ramayana that gave the original name of Valmiki as Ratnakara. This fifteenth-century Bengali Ramayana might have inspired many folk-tales and even Rabindranath Tagore to write his famous drama on Ratnakara. It is in the Krittivasa Ramayana that Ratnakara meets Narada instead of seven saints, and the version I have told here is similar to that of the Krittivasa Ramayana except for some minor details. The tale I've told is from the Malayalam folk version and Valmiki's story changes from place to place. For example, in the Punjabi version, it is not Narada or the seven saints but Guru Nanak who meets Ratnakara, the dacoit, and advises him to come out of his life of sin. There are countless such versions and no one can say which is authentic and which isn't. One of the folk versions prevalent in Punjab and Uttar Pradesh is that Brahma assigned Valmiki, an avatar of Vishnu, the job of sweeping and cleaning. This could be an allegorical reference to how Valmiki, using Ramayana's broom, cleans the readers' souls. Many communities whose traditional profession was cleaning the streets consider Valmiki as their Bhagwan, as their work is as pure and divine as the one Valmiki did.

11 Dasaratha is a king from the Ikshvaku dynasty, but different Puranas have different lineages described for this dynasty. In most Puranic literature, Rama is the sixty-third king in the dynasty, while in the Ramayana, he is the thirty-sixth king. A curious tale can be found in East Asian Ramayanas. In Siam's (Thailand's) Rama Jataka, Dasaratha is Ravana's

uncle. In Malayan Seri Rama, Dasaratha is a descendant of Prophet Adam. In this Ramayana, Ravana abducts Shanta instead of Sita, and Rama and Lakshmana travel to Lanka and fight him. Later, they make a truce with Ravana, and Ravana marries Shanta. On his way back from Lanka, Rama marries Sita. This is the preface to the common Ramayana tales.

12 In the Ananda Ramayana, a Brahmin predicts to Ravana that Dasaratha and Kausalya's son will kill him. Ravana travels to Kosala, sinks Dasaratha's marriage boat on Sarayu and abducts Kausalya. He puts Kausalya in a box and gives it to a whale named Timingila. Dasaratha and his minister Sumantra escape from the shipwreck and go in search of Kausalya. They reach the island where the whale is hiding Kausalya. Dasaratha and Sumantra sneak on to the island, open the box and find Kausalya inside. Dasaratha and Kausalya have a Gandharva Vivaha (love union) on the island. Meanwhile, Ravana boasts to Brahma that he has prevented the marriage, but Brahma informs Ravana about the Gandharva Vivaha. Ravana is livid and wants to kill them all, but Brahma prevents him from doing so. Dasaratha, Kausalya and Sumantra escape from the island by giving slip to the whale. On their way back, Dasaratha marries Sumitra, Kaikeyi and seven hundred other women.

13 In Pauma Chariyam, during Kaikeyi's swayamvara, a war brews between Dasaratha and other kings and Kaikeyi saves Dasaratha's chariot from crashing by putting her small finger in the axle of the wheel. Dasaratha ask Kaikeyi to request one boon, and she says she will ask for it when the time comes.

14 In the southern version of the Valmiki Ramayana, Sumitra's name is not mentioned. In the Krittivasa Ramayana, she is a Sinhala princess. In Buddhist and Jain Ramayanas, Dasaratha had four wives—Aparajita (Kausalya), Sumitra, Kaikeyi and Suprabha (Shatrughna's mother). In the Padma Purana, in the Patala Kanda chapter, Bharata's mother is Surupa and Shatrughna's mother is Suvesa. In the Valmiki Ramayana, Rama takes leave of his 350 mothers. In the Ananda Ramayana, Dasaratha had 700 wives. In the Dasaratha Jataka, Dasaratha has 16,000 wives. In many folk-tales, Rama has seven mothers. In some versions of south Indian Ramayanas, Dasaratha has 60,000 wives.

15 There is no direct mention of Shanta by her name in any of the recensions of the Valmiki Ramayana. In the Gaudiya recension, Shanta is mentioned without her name, but the story is told. In south Indian versions of the Valmiki Ramayana, there is an indirect mention of Shanta being Dasaratha's daughter. Sumantra, while suggesting to Dasaratha to begin his Putrakameshti yagna, asks him to call his jamata (son-in-law), Rishyashringa. In the Gaudiya Valmiki Ramayana and north western Valmiki Ramayana, there are clear hints that Shanta was Dasaratha's daughter. However, many Ramayana renditions also mention that Shanta is Romapada's biological daughter. The Harivamsa Purana, Matsya Purana, Vayu Purana and Brahma Purana also consider Shanta as the biological daughter of Dasaratha's friend Romapada (Lomapada in Eastern Indian versions). The Harivamsa adds to the confusion by stating that Anga Raja Lomapada was also named Dasaratha and Chitraratha. In the Balarama Dasa Ramayana, Shanta is Kausalya's daughter. In the Bhavartha Ramayana, Indra advises Dasaratha to give his daughter Shanta in marriage to Rishyashringa. The Krittivasa Ramayana says Dasaratha had promised to give his first child to Lomapada and thus gave his firstborn to his friend for adoption. But the Krittivasa says this daughter was named Hemalata and not Shanta. In folk versions, Dasaratha's firstborn is called Kukua, Kuckoo, Kikavi, and so on. In Thailand's Rama Jataka and Palak Palam, Shanta is married to Ravana. Like any other character in the Ramayana, Shanta also has multiple names and tales in various versions.

16 Both these words have their roots in the word 'time'. Death is nothing but a function of time, as is life.

17 The Mahabharata says that Sita is Janaka's own daughter. There are four Ramayanas in the Mahabharata, and in all these Ramayana stories, there is no mention of Sita being found in a furrow. Even the Harivamsa doesn't mention Sita's non-womb origin. The Kathasaritsagara Ramayana and the Kurma Purana mention Sita. In the Jain Ramayana, Pauma Chariyam, Sita is born as a twin to Janaka. Bhamandala is her twin brother and was given away by Janaka to another king, thus inverting the Shanta story and showing Janaka's preference for a girl child. The Brahmanda Purana and the Vishnu Purana mention Bhanumana as Sita's twin brother. In some

folk versions of Bengal that I encountered and also in the Kalika Purana, there is a mention of two brothers for Sita who came out of the sacrificial fire. The ritual tilling of Janaka was for getting a son as per the Vishnu Purana, but Janaka accepted Sita and stopped the ritual. In the Bengali (Gaudiya) Ramayana, Menaka, an Apsara, is Sita's mother, while the Krittivasa Ramayana says that the Apsara Urvashi is her mother. In the Valmiki Ramayana, in the Uttara Kanda, Vedavati, molested by Ravana, gives up her life in a sacrificial fire after vowing to be born again as Sita and to destroy Lanka and Ravana. In the Devi Bhagwata, Vedavati is the daughter of Janaka's brother Kushadhwaja and Malavati, and gives up her life using yogic powers and is born as Sita.

18 In the Krittivasa Ramayana, this tale is elaborated. While Kushadhwaja was reciting the Vedas, a daughter jumps out of his mouth and starts reciting the Vedas. Therefore, Kushadhwaja names her Vedavati. A Rakshasa called Shumba kills Kushadhwaja. To take revenge, Vedavati does tapasya. She wants to marry Vishnu. Ravana sees her and tries to molest her. She curses Ravana, saying that she will be reborn through the Ayonija (non-womb) method and will cause the destruction of Ravana's clan and Lanka. She summons yogic powers and immolates herself. However, her body refuses to burn. Ravana waits for many days for the body to be consumed by fire, but Vedavati's body remains pure. Ravana loads Vedavati's body into the Pushpaka Vimana and takes it to Lanka. He asks Mandodari to cook Vedavati so that he can eat her. But Mandodari cooks some other meat and throws Vedavati's corpse into the sea. Varuna takes the corpse to Jambu Dwipa and deposits it at the shores of the Ganga. The body turns into Sita to fulfil its curse. Janaka finds her and names her Sita. There are hundreds of versions of Sita's birth, and these are a few of them.

19 Many stories mention Sita as Ravana's daughter. Here are a few that I encountered apart from the ones mentioned above. The Tibetan, Turkic, Indonesian and Thai Ramayanas explicitly state that Sita is Ravana's daughter. The earliest mention of Sita as Ravana's daughter comes in the Vasudevahindi. In this, Maya, Mandodari's father, finds out that the firstborn of Ravana and Mandodari could be the reason for the fall of the Asuras. He conspires with his ministers, and when Sita is born, they

kidnap the baby, put her in a casket with some gems and diamonds, and bury it in Janaka's fields. Janaka finds her and brings her up. Another version of this story is found in Gunabhadra's Uttarapurana, where Vedavati (Manimati), when harassed by Ravana, commits suicide by proclaiming that she will be reborn as Ravana's daughter and will cause his downfall. Soon, a daughter is born to Ravana and Mandodari, and fearing it to be Vedavati's rebirth, Ravana gives the baby to Mareecha to bury her. Mareecha buries her in Janaka's field and Sita is found by Janaka later.

In the Kashmiri Ramayana, Sita is an illegitimate daughter of Mandodari, born in the absence of Ravana. Fearing her husband, Mandodari buries the girl in a casket, and Janaka finds her. In the Tibetan and Turkic Ramayanas, Ravana abandons his firstborn due to her horoscope and Janaka finds her. In the Javan Ramayana, Ravana's queen becomes jealous of her own daughter's beauty as soon as she is born. She fears her husband will love his daughter more than her, so she shuts up the girl in a box and throws it into the sea. The box reaches Mithila. Meanwhile, to replace the baby, the queen takes the help of Civisana (Vibhishana), who plucks a child from the cloud, Meghanada, and tells Ravana that Meghanada is his firstborn.

In Thailand's Ramakien, Mandodari gives birth to Sita, but fearing the future gives her to Vibhishana to throw away. Vibhishana knows Sita is Lakshmi's avatar so he puts her in a pot and throws it into the river. The pot floats on the petals of a lotus as Sita is Lakshmi. Janaka finds her and takes her with him. But since he is going for tapasya, he buries the pot along with the baby. After sixteen years, he comes back and ploughs the place to find the baby intact. He understands this baby is special, names her Sita and brings her up.

In the Thai Rama Jataka, Ravana assumes the form of Indra and seduces Indra's wife. To take revenge, Indrani is born in Mandodari's womb and she returns as Sita to destroy Lanka. In the Adbhuta Ramayana, Sita is born from the blood of that Ravana kills. Another version is that Ravana collects blood as tax from rishis and Mandodari drinks this blood accidentally. A child is born to her, and she buries the foetus in Kurukshetra. Janaka ploughs Kurukshetra and finds Sita. The Sinhalese Ramayana has a similar version. There are also versions like the Harivamsa that state Sita is born out of fire like Draupadi. South Indian folk versions talk about Sita being born from a tree as a fruit. The fruit is called Sita Phala (custard apple).

20 There are many versions of the confrontation between Parasurama and Rama. In the Valmiki Ramayana, Parasurama appears only after the marriage is over, when the wedding party, including the grooms and brides, is returning to Ayodhya. In Tulsidas's and other popular versions, this confrontation takes place before the marriage, at the Janaka Sabha itself.

21 In the north Indian version, Guha and Kevat are two different people. Guha is not mentioned in the Ramopakhyana. But his character undergoes a change as more Ramayanas are written. In many Ramayanas, the boatman Kevat incident happens immediately after the Ahalya incident when Rama is going towards Mithila. But in later Ramayanas, the Kevat incident happens when Rama is crossing to Chitrakoot.

22 Bhagwatham 10th Skanda, Chapter 22, 17th shloka to 19th shloka.

Bibliography

18 Puranangal (2014). Malayalam translation by a group of scholars of Kaladi Adi Shankaracharya University, of eighteen Puranas. Volumes 1–26. DC Books.

Adbhuta Ramayana (2022). Sanskrit text with transliteration, English commentary with explanation by Ajay Kumar Chhawchharia. Varanasi: Chaukhamba Surabharati Prakashan.

Adhyatma Ramayana (2010). With an English translation by Swami Tapasyananda. Chennai: Ramakrishna Math.

Ananda Ramayana: Attributed to the Great Sage Valmiki (2020). Two volumes. Translated into English by Shantilal Nagar. New Delhi: Parimal Publications Pvt. Ltd.

Asan, Ayyipilla (2002). *Ramakathappattu* (Malayalam). Volumes 1–2. Thrissur: Kerala Sahitya Akademi.

Balcerowicz, Piotr, Ed. (2003). *Essays in Jaina Philosophy and Religion*. Volume 20, Lala S.L. Jain Research Series. Delhi: Motilal Banarasidass Publishers.

Bangla Kritivas Ramayan Sampurn (Hindi Anuvaad Sahit) (2014). Translated by Yogeshwar Tripathi, Prabodh Kumar Majumdar and Navarun Varma. Lucknow: Bhuvan Vani Trust.

Barhat Narharidas dwara Praneet Avtar Charitra (2018). New Delhi: Sahitya Akademi.

Bhatta, Ananta. 'Rama Kalpa Druma'. Veda and Vaidika Paper RORIJ_2766.6.27666. Jodhpur: Rajasthan Oriental Research Institute.

Bhatti, Shri (1898). *Bhattikavya or Ravanavadha.* Volume 1 (Cantos 1–9), Volume 2 (Cantos 10–22). Edited, with the commentary of Mallinatha and with critical and explanatory notes by Kamalasankara, Pranasankara Tripathi. Mumbai: Government Central Book Depot. [Also see section 'Websites' below]

Bhavabhuti (8 CE). *Maha-Vira-Charita.* Translated by John Pickford and originally published in 1871 by Trübner & Co, London.

Bhavabhuti (8 CE) (1903). *Uttara-Ramacharita with the Commentary of Viraraghava.* Edited by T.R. Ratnam Aiyar and Kashinath Pandurang Parar. Bombay (Mumbai): Tukaram Jiwaji.

Bhusundi Ramayana (Adi Ramayana) (Sanskrit Original Path ka Gadyanuvad) (2015). In Hindi. Lucknow: Bhuvan Vani Trust.

Bulcke, Fr Dr Camille (2022). *The Rama Story, Origins and Growth.* Delhi: Sahitya Akademi.

Bulcke, Fr Dr Camille (2010). *Ramakatha and Other Essays.* New Delhi: Vani Prakashan.

Cambridge Library Collections–Linguistics (2009). *A Sanskrit English Dictionary: Based upon the St Petersburg Lexicons.* Cambridge, MA: Cambridge University Press.

Champu Ramayana of King Bhoja (1-5 Kandas) and Lakshmana Suri (6th Kanda). (1898). With commentary by Ramachandra Budhendra. Edited by Kashinath Pandurang Parar. Bombay (Mumbai): Tukaram Javaji.

Chandrabati's Ramayana (2020). Translated from Bengali to English by Nabaneeta Dev Sen. New Delhi: Zubaan.

Chari, S.M. Srinivasa (2009). *Philosophy and Theistic Mysticism of the Alvars.* Delhi: Motilal Banarasidass Publishers.

Chari, S.M. Srinivasa (2010). *Advaita and Visistadvaita: A Study Based on Vedanta Desika's Satadusani.* Delhi: Motilal Banarasidass Publishers.

Chari, S.M. Srinivasa (2018). *Vaishanavism: Its Philosophy, Theology and Religious Discipline.* Delhi: Motilal Banarasidass Publishers.

Collins, Brian (2020). *The Other Rama: Matricide and Genocide in the Mythology of Parasurama.* SUNY Series in Hindu Studies. Albany, NYC: State of New York University (SUNY) Press.

Dasgupta, Surendranath (2018). *A History of Indian Philosophy in Three Volumes*. New Delhi: Rupa Publications.

Devadhar, C.R. (2011). *Works of Kalidasa*. Delhi: Motilal Banarasidass Publishers.

Easwaran, Eknath (2010). *The Upanishad*. Delhi: Jaico Books.

Eknath Maharaj, Sant (2019). *Shri Bhavarth Ramayan: Khand 1 va 2* (Marathi). Edited by Dr Dnyaneshwar Tandale. Mumbai: Dharmik Prakashan Sanstha.

Ezhuthachan, Thunjath Ramanujan (2023). *Adhyatma Ramayana Killipattu*. Kozhikode: Mathrubhumi Books.

Farhat, Munshi Shankar Dayaal (1938). *Ramayan-e-Farhat*. Lucknow: Munshi Nawal Kishor.

Ghate, B.G. et al. (1982). *Bhavartha Ramayana*. Mumbai: Government of Maharashtra.

Gopal, Kavi Raj Shiri Jay. *Valmiki Ramayan Ba Tasveer* (Urdu). Delhi: Dehati Pustak Bhandar.

Hanumat (2007). *Maha-Nataka: A Dramatic History of King Rama*. Translated into English by Maharaja K. Bahadur. Rare legacy reprint. Whitefish, MT: Kessinger Publishing.

Hawley, John Stratton and Wolff, Donna Marie (1995). *The Divine Consort, Radha and the Goddesses of India*. Delhi: Motilal Banarasidass Publishers.

Henry, Jules W. (2022). *Ravana's Kingdom and Sri Lankan History from Below*. New York: Oxford Academic, online edition: https://doi.org/10.1093/oso/9780197636305.001.0001.

Hikayat Seri Rama: The Malay Ramayana (2020). Translated into English by Harry Aveling. Published by WritersWorkshopIndia.com.

Janakiharana of Kumaradasa (1977). A study, critical text and English translation of Cantos XVI–XX by Dr C.R. Swaminathan, and edited by Dr V. Raghavan. Delhi: Motilal Banarasidass Publishers.

Johnson, William J. (1995). *Harmless Souls: Karmic Bondage and Religious Change in Early Jainism*. Volume 9, Lala S.L. Jain Research Series. Delhi: Motilal Banarasidass Publishers.

Johnston, E.H. (1933). 'The Ramayana of Valmiki: Balakanda (North-Western Recension). Critically edited from original MSS by Bhagwad Datta. Lahore: The Research Department, D.A.V. College 1931. *Journal of the Asiatic Society of Great Britain & Ireland*, 65(1): 181-83. doi: 10.1017/S0035869X00072920.

Kale, M.R. (2022). *The Raghuvamsa of Kalidasa*. Delhi: Motilal Banarasidass Publishers.

Khushtar, Munshii Jagan Nath (1920). *Ramayan Nazm Tulsi Krit*. Lucknow: Munshi Nawal Kishor.

Lakshmisha (2011). *Lakshmisha Jaimini Bharata* (Kannada). Edited by B.S. Sannaiah and Dr Ramegowda. Mysore (Mysuru): University of Mysore.

Lal, Banke Bihari (1886). *Ramayan-e-Bahar*. Lucknow: Munshi Nawal Kishor.

Lavakushar Yuddha (14th century) (1954). Edited by Maheshwar Neog. Shillong: State Central Library.

Kaushik, Vivek Sri and Sharma, M.M. (2022). *Sri Hanumad Mahapuranv (Rudravatar Puran): inclusive of 31 Sopan* (Hindi). Delhi: Puja Prakashan.

Kshemendra's Ramayana Manjari (1985). Edited by Bhavadatta Shastry and Kashinath Pandurang Prab. Varanasi: Chaukhamba Sanskrit Pratishthan.

Mahabharata (2022). Sanskrit text with English translation by M.N. Dutta. Volumes 1–9. New Delhi: Parimal Publications, sixth reprint.

Mali, Madhavan Nair V (2003). *Puranakadhamalika* (Malayalam). Kottayam: DC Books.

Manavalan, A.A. (2021). *Ramayana: A Comparative Study of Ramakathas*. Translated into English by C.T. Indra and Prema Jagannathan. Delhi: Vitasta Publishing.

Mani, Vettam (2021). *Puranic Encyclopedia: A Comprehensive Work with Special Reference to the Epic and Puranic Literature*. Delhi: Motilal Banarasidass Publishers, eleventh reprint.

Menon, Varavur Shamu and Unni, Dr N.P. (2018). *Srimad Devi Bhagawatham* (Malayalam). Thiruvananthapuram: Prashanti Publications.

Moily, Dr M. Veerappa (2010). *Sri Ramayana Mahanveshanam*. Volumes 1 and 2. New Delhi: Rupa Publications.

Mayuraja (2008). *Uddattaraghava*. Discovered and critically edited by Dr V. Raghavan. Chennai: Dr V. Raghavan Centre for Performing Arts (Regd).

Nagachandra (2022). *Pampa Ramayana Ramachandra Charita Purana in Prose and Verse*. Bengaluru: Kuvempu Bhasha Bharathi Praadhikara.

Nampoothiri, Punam (1967). *Bhasha Ramayanam Champu* (Malayalam). Thrissur: Kerala Sahitya Akademi.

Narasimha Purana (2018). Translated from Sanskrit into English by Bindya Trivedi. New Delhi: Parimal Publications.

Overbeck, H. (1933). 'Hikayat Maharaja Ravana'. *Journal of the Malayan Branch of the Royal Asiatic Society* 11, no. 2 (117): 111–32. http://www.jstor.org/stable/41559797.

Pampa Bharatham (2009) (Malayalam). Kozhikode: Mathrubhumi Books.

Pandeya, Pundit Ramteja (2003). *Ananda Ramayanam*. Delhi: Chaukhamba Sanskrit Prathistan, reprint.

Panicker, Nirannathu Rama (2019). *Kannassa Ramayana*. Thiruvananthapuram: State Institute of Languages (Kerala Bhasha Institute).

Panoli, Vidyavachaspati V. (1999). *Adi Sankara's Vision of Reality*. Thiruvananthapuram: Mathrubhumi Books.

Prakasam, Vidwan K. (2008). *Vyasa Mahabharatham* (Malayalam). Volumes 1–6. Kottayam: DC Books.

Radhakrishna, Dr K.S. (2022). *Ramayanam, Manushyakathaanugaanam* (Malayalam). Kozhikode: Mathrubhumi Books.

Radhakrishnan, Dr Sarvepalli (2020). *The Principal Upanishads*. Gurugram: HarperCollins India Ltd.

Raghavanaisadhiya of Haradatta Suri (1896). Edited by Pt Sivadatta and Kashinatha Panduranga Parab. *Kavyamālā*, vol. 57. Mumbai: Nirnaya Sagara Press. [Reference sourced from Bronner, Yigal (2010). Extreme Poetry: The South Asian Movement of Simultaneous Narration. New York City: Columbia University Press.]

Raghaviya of Ramapanivada (1942). Edited by L.A. Ravi Varma. Trivandrum (Thiruvananthapuram): Government Press. [Also see Websites section]

Rajasekhara (2011). *Balaramayana*. Edited with translation from Sanskrit into Hindi by Dr Ganga Sagar Rai. Varanasi: Chaukhamba Subharati Prakashan.

Rāma-kṛṣṇa-viloma-kāvyam (1972). Translated from Sanskrit to Hindi, with explanations, by Dr Shri Kameshwar Nath Mishra (M.A. Ph.D. Sahityacharya). Varanasi: Chaukhamba Sanskrit Series Office.

Ramacarita of Abhinanda (1930). Critically edited and with an Introduction by K.S. Ramaswami Sastri Siromani. Baroda (Vadodara): Oriental Institute.

Reamker (Ramakerti): The Cambodian Version of the Ramayana (2007). Translated into English by Judith M. Jacob, with the assistance of Kuoch Haksrea. Royal Asiatic Society Books. London and New York: Routledge.

Reddy, Gona Buddha (2015). *Ranganatha Ramayanamu* (Telugu). Tirupathi: Tirupathi Thirumala Devasthanam.

Rosen, Steven J. (1999). *Vaisnavi: Women and the Worship of Krishna*. Delhi: Motilal Banarasidass Publishers.

Rudrakavi, Kandukuri. *Sugreeva Vijayam* (Telugu). Hyderabad: Tagore Publishing House.

Sahai, Sachidananda (2004). *Lao Ramayana: Gvay Dvorahbi—Rendering into English from Lav Language, a Comparative Study*. B.R. Publishing Corporation.

Sakalya Malla's Udararaghava, with the Commentaries: Sisubodhini, Pradyotini and Samjivani (Sanskrit) (1990). Edited by T. Venkatacharya. Chennai: The Adayar Library and Research Centre.

Sankuni, Kottarathil (2021). *Aithihyamaala: The Great Legends of Kerala*. Translated into English by Sreekumari Ramachandran in two volumes. Kozhikode: Mathrubhumi Publications.

Sarala Dasa Bilanka Ramayana. Bhubaneswar: Binapani Store. https://www.odishanticstore.com/product/sarala-das-bilanka-ramayan.

Sastri, V.S. Srinivasa (2022). *Lectures on The Ramayana*. Madras (Chennai): Madras Samskrit Academy. Reprint brought out by Ganesh and Co. Originally published in 1949.

Shaktibhadra, Mahakavi (1933). *Ascharya Chudamani*. Edited with the 'Rama' and 'Malati' Commentaries in Sanskrit and Hindi by Pt Ramakant Jha. Varanasi: Chaukhamba Vidyabhawan.

Shastri, Satyavrat (2020). *Ramayana in Southeast Asia Volume II: Laos and Cambodian Ramayana* (English). New Delhi: Sahitya Akademi.

Singh, Rai Bahadur Amar (1877). *Ramayan Amar Prakash*. Lucknow: Munshi Nawal Kishor.

Somadeva (2014). *Kathasaritsagara*. Translated by C.H. Tawney as *The Ocean of Story* (Ten Volumes). Delhi: Motilal Banarasidass.

Sonnerat, Pierre (1782). *Voyage Aux Indes Orientales et a la Chine* (French). Paris: L'auteur.

Srimad Valmiki Ramayana (2021). Volumes 1 and 2. Sanskrit text with English translations by Achleshwar. Gorakhpur: Gita Press.

Srimanta Sankaradeva's Uttarakanda Ramayan (2019) (Assamese). Edited by Aradhana Patangia Goswami. Dibrugarh: Banalata.

Surdas (2021). *Sur Sagar* (Hindi). Pankaj Prakashan.

Tattvasaṅgraharāmāyaṇa of Rāmabrahmānanda Sarasvati (2005). In Sanskrit and English. Edited by V. Venkataramana Reddy. Sri Venkateswara University Oriental Series (32). Tirupati: Tirupati Oriental Research Institution, Sri Venkateswara University.

Tejomayananda, Swami (2023). *Discourses on Sri Ramacharitamanas*. Volumes 1 and 2. Mumbai: Central Chinmaya Mission Trust.

Thampi, M.N. Ramakrishna (2001). *Ramayanakathamrutham* (Malayalam) Gokulam Books.

The Bhagavata Purana (2018). Volumes 1–3. Translated from Sanskrit into English by Bibek Debroy. New Delhi: Penguin Random House LLC.

The Kamba Ramayana (2002). Translated from Tamil into English by P.S. Sundarama, and abridged and edited by N.S. Jagannathan. London: Penguin Books UK.

Thirteen plays of Bhasa: Pratijnayaugandharayana, Svapavasavadatta, Carudatta, Pancaratra, Madhyamavyayoga, Pratima-nataka, Dutvakya, Dutaghtotkaca, Karnabhara, Balacarita, Abhiseka (2015). Translated into English by A.C. Woolner and Lakshman Sarup. Delhi: Motilal Banarasidass.

Tiwari, Kedar Nath (2017). *Classical Indian Ethical Thought: A Philosophical Study of Hindu, Jaina and Bauddha Morals*. Delhi: Motilal Banarasidass, second edition.

Tripathi, Satyavrat, Ed. (1992). *Sri Chitrabandha Ramayanam*. Prayagraj: Ganganath Jha Central Sanskrit University.

Tohru, Ohno (2000). *Burmese Ramayana: with an English translation of the original palm-leaf manuscript in Burmese language in 1233 Year of the Burmese Era (1871 ad)*. B.R. Corporation.

Torvey Ramayan by Torvey Narahari (Kumara Valmiki): A Work of 15th Century AD. (2004). Translated by Shanti Lal Nagar. B.R. Publishing Corporation.

Tulsidas, Goswami (2023). *Sri Ramacaritamanasa*. Hindi text with English translation. Gorakhpur: Gita Press.

Unmattaraghava of Bhaskara Bhatta (1973). Sanskrit text with Hindi translation by Acharya Shri Ram Pal Shastri. Varanasi: Chaukhamba Sanskrit Series Office.

Venkatachalam, V. (2017). *Bhasa*. New Delhi: Sahitya Akademi.

Yardi, M.R. (1994). *The Ramayana, Its Origin and Growth: A Statistical Study*. Pune: Bhandarkar Oriental Research Institute.

Countless folk tales, performing arts and oral storytellers.

Websites

Afgoderye Der Oost-Indische Heydenen [The Elephant-headed God] (1672). (Dutch). Available at: https://digitalcollections.nypl.org/items/65f34f84-8055-c507-e040-e00a180615fb

Agastya Ramayana. A link on Scribd to a Malayalam version: https://www.scribd.com/document/368100044/agasthya-ramayanam

Anargharaghava. Available at Internet Archive: https://archive.org/details/in.ernet.dli.2015.281220

Asia (1672) (Dutch). Available at Internet Archive: https://archive.org/details/asiaofnaukeurige00dapp

Asia Portuguesa (1666) (Spanish). Available at Internet Archive: https://archive.org/details/bub_gb_SIofK4nmELEC

Balaramadasa Jagamohana Ramayana, also known as *Dandi Ramayana* in Odiya. Available at Internet Archive: https://archive.org/details/in.ernet.dli.2015.325867

Bhaskara Ramayanamu (Telugu). Available at Intenet Archive: https://archive.org/details/Telugu_TEL_B_0599__R_2204

Bhattikavya or Ravanavadha: Available at Internet Archive:

Vol. 1: https://archive.org/details/in.ernet.dli.2015.326012/page/n1/mode/1up

Vol. 2: https://archive.org/details/in.gov.ignca.23822

Brihatkathamanjari by Kshemendra (Sanskrit). Available at Internet Archive: https://archive.org/details/Brihatkathamanjari/page/n5/mode/2up

Dasaratha Jataka (Pali with English Translation). Available at Internet Archive: https://archive.org/details/dasarathajatakab00fausuoft/page/n3/mode/2up

Dashavatra Charitam (Sanskrit). Available at Internet Archive: https://archive.org/details/in.ernet.dli.2015.322350/page/n4/mode/1up

De open-deure tot het Verborgen Heydendom [The Open Door to Hidden Paganism] (1649) (Dutch). Available at Internet Archive: https://archive.org/details/deopendeuretothe00rogeuoft/page/n45/mode/1up

'Description of People of India' (translated from French to English). Available at Internet Archive: https://archive.org/stream/DescriptionOfPeopleOfIndiaAbbeDuboisJ.A.1817/Description%20of%20People%20of%20India%20Abbe%20Dubois%20J.A.%201817_djvu.txt

Dharmakanda (Sanskrit): https://www.exoticindiaart.com/book/details/dharmakosa-varnasrama-dharma-kanda-set-of-7-volumes-nzc703/

Ekoji Ramayana (Telugu). Available at Intenet Archive:
(Vol. 1): https://archive.org/details/in.ernet.dli.2015.370379
(Vol. 2): https://archive.org/details/EkojiRamayanamuVol2

Hanumat Samhita: https://archive.org/details/HhfO_research-thesis-tantragama-no.-13-hanumat-samhita-hanumat-janma-rahasya-kathana-

Historia Do Malavar (Portuguese with an introductory section in German). Available at Internet Archive: https://archive.org/details/dli.ernet.447851/page/n2/mode/1up

Hrudyarama's *Hannumannataka* (Hindi). Available at Internet Archive. The introduction is in English, the remaining text in Gurmukhi. https://archive.org/details/hanuman-natak-new/page/120/mode/2up

Il Viaggio All Indie Orientali (Italian). Available at Internet Archive: https://archive.org/details/b28765989/page/36/mode/1up

Janaki Parinaya. Available at: https://epustakalay.com/book/261916-janaki-parinaya-by-cakrakavi/

Kannassa Ramayanam (Malayalam). Available at Internet Archive: https://archive.org/details/kannassa-ramayanam

Kankanti Paparaju Uttara Ramayanamu (Telugu). Available at Internet Archive: https://archive.org/details/UttaraRamayanamu_201512/page/n3/mode/1up

Ramavataracharit (in Kashmiri using the English script). Available at Internet Archive: https://archive.org/details/in.ernet.dli.2015.48970/page/n105/mode/1up

Kashur Ramayana by Gamee Prakash Ram (in Kashmiri using Arabic script). Available at Internet Archive: https://archive.org/details/dli.ernet.510163/page/n36/mode/1up

Kumadendu Ramayana. Available at Internet Archive: https://archive.org/details/pvn.kumudenduramayan0000hamp

Kundamala (Sanskrit). Available at Internet Archive: https://archive.org/details/in.gov.ignca.3074/page/n3/mode/2up

Laghu Trishasti Shalaka Purush Charita by Meghavijay Ganivar (Gujarati). Available at Internet Archive: https://archive.org/details/in.ernet.dli.2015.325066

Laladasa's *Avadha Vilasa* (Hindi). Available at Internet Archive: https://archive.org/details/5990010046485AwadhVilas/page/n1/mode/2up

Madhava Kandali's *Ramayana* (Assamese). Available at: https://archive.org/details/in.ernet.dli.2015.452310/page/n2/mode/1up

Maha Ramayana (English translation). Available at: https://yogavasishta.org/

Molla Ramayanamu (Telugu). Available at Intenet Archive: https://archive.org/details/MollaRamayanamu

Pauma Chariyam by Vimala Suri (English translation). Available at: https://ia904706.us.archive.org/4/items/in.ernet.dli.2015.406831/2015.406831.Pauma-Chariyam.pdf

Puspadanta's Maha-Puranas. Available at Internet Archive: https://archive.org/details/in.ernet.dli.2015.539665

Raghaviya of Ramapanivada: Available at Internet Archive: https://archive.org/details/in.ernet.dli.2015.284103/mode/2up

Raghunatha Mahanta's Adhbhut Ramayana: *Asomiya Adbhoot Ramayan*, Ed. 4th. Available at Internet Archive: https://archive.org/details/in.ernet.dli.2015.452255

Ramabhadra's *Ramabhyudayam* (Telugu). Available at Internet Archive: https://archive.org/details/in.ernet.dli.2015.390430

Ramachandrika (Hindi). Available at Internet Archive: https://ia801408.us.archive.org/15/items/in.ernet.dli.2015.483899/2015.483899.RAM-CHANDRIKA.pdf

Rama Jakaka (Lao). Available at: https://thesiamsociety.org/wp-content/uploads/1946/03/JSS_036_1c_PrinceDhani_RamaJatakaLaoVersion.pdf

Ramavijay Mahakavyam (Sanskrit): Available at Internet Archive: https://archive.org/details/in.ernet.dli.2015.281096

Ramayan Kakawin (Indonesian verses with English translations). Volumes 1–3 available at Internet Archive:

Vol. 1: https://archive.org/details/RamayanaKakawinVol.1/page/n17/mode/1up]

Vol 2: https://archive.org/details/RamayanaKakawinVol.2

Vol 3: https://archive.org/details/kakawin-ramayana-03

Ramayan Masihi (Urdu) Volumes 1 & 2 available at Internet Archive:
https://archive.org/details/Ramayan-iMasihiPart1
https://archive.org/details/BadshahnamahOfLahoriVolume2BibliothecaIndicaEdition

Sankardeva's play 'Rama Vijay' (in medieval Maithili spoken in Assam). Available at Internet Archive

Satyopakhyanam. Available at the Internet Archive: https://archive.org/details/UcQH_satyopakhyan-by-dr-shailaja-pandey-no.-56-ganganath-campus

Sreemad Raghuveeram Charitham (Malayalam). Available at the Internet Archive: https://archive.org/details/SreemadRaghuveeraCharitham

Thakkai Ramayanam. Available at: https://www.scribd.com/document/360993077/Thakkai-Ramayanam-Thogudi-1-Part-001

Tikkanna's *Nirvachanottara Ramayana* (Telugu). Available at Internet Archive: https://archive.org/details/in.ernet.dli.2015.372019

Trishashti Salaka Purusha Charita by Hemachandra. Available at: https://www.holybooks.com/trishashti-shalaka-purusha-caritra-vol-1-6/

Ullagharaghava Nataka (Sanskrit). Available at Internet Archive: https://archive.org/details/in.ernet.dli.2015.408425/mode/2up

Uttara Purana by Gunabhadra. Available at Internet Archive: https://archive.org/details/in.ernet.dli.2015.326695/page/n3/mode/2up

Vasudevahindi. Only Part 1 available at Internet Archive: https://archive.org/details/in.ernet.dli.2015.283966/mode/2up

Yogavashista: Available at: https://yogavasishta.org/

About the Author

Photo: Rohit Murarka

Anand Neelakantan is an author, screenwriter, columnist and television personality. He is famous for his counter-telling and unique interpretations of the Indian Puranas. Anand was born in a quaint little village called Thripoonithura in Kerala, on India's tropical southwestern coast. Situated across the beautiful Vembanad Lake, it was noted as the Cochin royal family's seat, as also for its many temples and the classical musicians that the local music school produced. However, with the passage of time and the advent of Gulf wealth, it too, like many other villages, has morphed into yet another of the unremarkable suburban townships that dot the once verdant landscape. Growing up in a village of temples, Anand was introduced very early to the world of myth and legend, Asuras and Devas, heroes and villains, the sacred and the divine.

As the years passed, Anand completed his education, graduated as an engineer, joined the Indian Oil Corporation and moved to a big city—Bengaluru. There, he met and married his life partner, Aparna. They have two children, Ananya and Abhinav.

But the storyteller in Anand would not allow him to remain in his placid groove. The unheard voices of Indian epics and the anti-heroes of legends kept whispering their stories in his ear, urging him to tell their tales. Working late into the night after work, Anand wrote his first novel over seven years—*Asura* (2012). It burst upon the Indian publishing scene like a tornado, sweeping aside preconceived notions of divinity and villainy, right and wrong. It has remained on the national bestseller list ever since and continues to be translated into numerous languages.

Anand was soon swept up by the whirlwind he had created. Writing and storytelling took over his life. Leaving behind his old existence, he relocated to Mumbai and became a widely acclaimed full-time writer for print and screen, and now audio. The chorus of silent characters had finally found their voice.

While *Asura* portrayed Ravana's Ramayana, *Ajaya* related Duryodhana's Mahabharata. *Vanara* told the story of Bali and Sugriva. *Siya Ke Ram* and *Mahabali Hanuman*, both written for television, portrayed Sita and Hanuman's perspectives respectively. Anand is also the author of the *Bahubali* trilogy, prequel to the blockbuster *Bahubali* movies. His other works include short stories, historical fiction and children's books.

www.anandneelakantan.com
Instagram, Facebook, Twitter : @itsanandneel
mail@asura.co.in

List of Anand Neelakantan's works:

Books
Ramayana-based
- (2012). *Asura: Tale of the Vanquished.* Mumbai: Leadstart Publications
- (2017). *Bhoomija: Sita.* Chennai: Westland Publications
- (2017). *Shanta: The Story of Rama's Sister.* Chennai: Westland Publications
- (2018). *Ravana's Sister: Meenakshi.* Chennai: Westland Publications
- (2018). *Vanara: The Legend of Baali, Sugreeva and Tara.* Mumbai: Penguin Books
- (2019). *Pennramayanam* (Malayalam). Kozhikode: Mathrubhumi Books
- (2021). *Valmiki's Women.* Chennai: Westland Publications

Mahabharata-based
- (2013). *Ajaya: Roll of the Dice.* Mumbai: Leadstart Publications
- (2015). *Ajaya: Rise of Kali.* Mumbai: Leadstart Publications
- (2023). *Nala Damyanti: An Eternal Tale from the Mahabharata.* Mumbai: Penguin Books.

The Bahubali trilogy
- (2017). *The Rise of Sivagami.* Chennai: Westland Publications
- (2020). *Chaturanga.* Chennai: Westland Publications
- (2020). *Queen of Mahishmathi.* Chennai: Westland Publications

Children's books
- (2020). *The Very Extremely Most Naughty Asura Tales for Kids.* New Delhi: Puffin Books
- (2023). *The Tale of the Naughty Flying Mountains.* New Delhi: Puffin Books
- (2023). *Mahi: The Elephant Who Flew Over the Blue Mountains.* New Delhi: HarperCollins India
- (2024). *The Tale of the Naughty Prank.* New Delhi: Puffin Books

Non-fiction
- (2024). *The Asura Way, The Contrarian Path to Success.* Mumbai: Jaico Books

Audiobooks
- (2021). *Many Ramayanas, Many Lessons.* Audible.com
- (2021). *Nala's Damayanti.* Storytel.com
- (2024). *Amba.* Storytel.com

Television
- *Chakravartin Ashoka Samrat* (Colors TV), Broadstory, Screenplay, Script
- *Siya Ke Ram* (Star Plus), Broadstory, Episodic Story
- *Sankatmochan Mahabali Hanuman* (Sony TV), Broadstory, Screenplay, Script
- *Adaalat–2* (Sony TV), Story and Screenplay
- *Sarfarosh: Battle of Saragarhi* (Netflix), Broadstory, Story, Screenplay
- *Swaraaj* (DD National), Broadstory, Screenplay
- *Taj: Divided by Blood* (Zee 5), Broadstory
- *Shrimad Ramayan* (Sony TV), January 2024, Broadstory, Script and Screenplay

HarperCollins *Publishers* India

At HarperCollins India, we believe in telling the best stories and finding the widest readership for our books in every format possible. We started publishing in 1992; a great deal has changed since then, but what has remained constant is the passion with which our authors write their books, the love with which readers receive them, and the sheer joy and excitement that we as publishers feel in being a part of the publishing process.

Over the years, we've had the pleasure of publishing some of the finest writing from the subcontinent and around the world, including several award-winning titles and some of the biggest bestsellers in India's publishing history. But nothing has meant more to us than the fact that millions of people have read the books we published, and that somewhere, a book of ours might have made a difference.

As we look to the future, we go back to that one word—a word which has been a driving force for us all these years.

Read.